MIDNIGHT THIEF

MIDNIGHT THIEF

LIVIA BLACKBURNE

HYPERION
LOS ANGELES   NEW YORK

First Edition
10 9 8 7 6 5 4 3 2
G475-5664-5-14253
Printed in the United States of America

Library of Congress Cataloging-in-Publication Data
Blackburne, Livia.
　　Midnight thief / Livia Blackburne.—First edition.
　　　　pages cm
　　Summary: "Kyra, a highly skilled seventeen-year-old thief, joins a guild of assassins with questionable motives. Tristam, a young knight, fights against the vicious Demon Riders that are ravaging the city"—Provided by publisher.
　　ISBN-13: 978-1-4231-7638-1
　　ISBN-10: 1-4231-7638-3
[1. Robbers and outlaws—Fiction.　2. Assassins—Fiction.　3. Knights and knighthood—Fiction.　4. Fantasy.]　I. Title.
　　PZ7.B532235Mid 2014
　　[Fic]—dc23　　　　　　　　　　　2013021230

Reinforced binding

Visit www.hyperionteens.com

SUSTAINABLE FORESTRY INITIATIVE　Certified Sourcing
www.sfiprogram.org
SFI-00993

THIS LABEL APPLIES TO TEXT STOCK

For Mom and Dad

ONE

This job could kill her.

Kyra peered off the ledge, squinting at the cobblestone four stories below. A false step in the darkness would be deadly, and even if she survived the fall, Red Shields would finish her off. She stared a few moments more before forcing her gaze back up. The time for second thoughts had passed. Now she just needed to keep moving.

The jump ahead was two body lengths long, so Kyra backed away from the ledge. Ten steps, then she drew a breath and sprinted forward. She pushed off just before the drop, clearing a gap of three strides before softening her body for the landing. There was a slap of soft leather on stone as she hit the next ledge. The impact sent a wave of vibrations through the balls of her feet, and Kyra touched a hand to the wall for balance.

Too hard, and too loud.

Silently cursing her clumsiness, Kyra scanned the grounds, looking for anyone who might have heard her. If she squinted, she could make out faint outlines of buildings around her—some as high as her ledge, some even taller. The pathways below were lined with torches that flickered, casting shadows that played tricks with her vision. Since she couldn't trust her eyes, she listened. Other than the wind blowing across her ears, the night was silent, and Kyra relaxed. Tucking away a stray lock of hair, she set off, dashing deeper into the compound.

Two days ago, a man had come to The Drunken Dog, introducing himself as James and asking for Kyra by name. He'd moved with a deliberate confidence, and his gaze had swept over the room, evaluating and dismissing each of its occupants. When Kyra had finally approached him, James laid out an unusual offer. There was a ruby in the Palace compound. He wanted her to fetch it for him, and he was willing to pay.

"The Palace is guarded tight," Kyra had told him. "If you want jewels, you'll better get them elsewhere."

"This ruby's got sentimental value," he'd replied. Kyra didn't consider herself the most astute judge of character. But she also wasn't an idiot, and she'd swallow her grappling hook before she'd believe that this man would do *anything* for sentimental reasons. The pay he offered was good though, and the job an intriguing challenge. The Palace was a far cry from the rich man's houses Kyra usually raided, with their handful of sentries guarding two or three floors. The Palace's massive buildings were patrolled by so many guards it was impossible to walk the grounds undetected. Rumor had it that even the rooftops were closely watched.

Which was why Kyra was neither on the ground nor on the rooftops. Instead, she balanced on a ledge outside a fourth-floor window, darting from shadow to shadow. The moon had not yet risen, and darkness concealed her from the Red Shields below. Unfortunately, it also hid the ledges from her own sight; the boundary between stone and air was easy to miss. From time to time, she slid a foot out to check her position, tracing her toe along the edge to fix the border in her mind.

Yes, she could die tonight. But as Kyra crept through the darkness, her doubts faded against the excitement of a challenging job. Those who knew her understood her skills. They knew she had no fear of heights and never lost her balance. But not even Flick, the closest thing to an older brother she had, understood the sheer joy that came over her every time she raced through the night. There was something about the way the darkness forced her to rely on her other senses, the way her body rose to the challenge. Her limbs silently promised her she would not fall, and by now she knew she could trust them.

The buildings across the path gave way to a courtyard with three trees, and Kyra slowed her pace, counting windows as she passed. The seventh from the southwest corner, James had said. These outer palaces were guest rooms for country noblemen visiting the Council. They were built securely but emphasized comfort more heavily than the fortresslike inner compound. And thus, they had glass windows instead of shutters, making it easy to see that the bedroom inside was dark. A minute fiddling with the latch, and the pane swung open on greased hinges. There was a shape on the bed, snoring in the loud and punctuated way of men who had indulged too much in rich food and drink. Kyra wondered for a moment what it would be like to get fat, to eat so much and work so little. No matter. Tonight, the nobleman would share some of his bounty.

She started with a dresser next to the bed, coaxing open the top drawer. Silk caught the dry skin of her fingertips. Apparently, the nobleman had a penchant for embroidered silk handkerchiefs. Not the jewelry box she sought, but Kyra took one and slipped it into her belt pouch. After checking the rest of the dresser, she moved to the desk. The latch gave easily to her pick, but there was nothing inside but documents and seals.

The sleeping nobleman shifted, and Kyra dropped to the floor. He rolled over, snorting loudly before his breathing once again settled. Kyra counted ten breaths, then went to the chest, taking care with the hefty cover. The top layer was fabric. Soon, she was up to her elbows in velvet night-robes, but still no ruby. If there was a jewelry box, it almost certainly would have been in the dresser or the chest. James had assured her that the nobleman wasn't the type to hide his jewelry. Could he have been mistaken?

She combed the room again, feeling along the floors and walls for trapdoors, even running her hands over the bed's thin mattress. Still nothing. Kyra bit her lip. The moon was rising, a thin crescent above the horizon that announced the coming dawn. She'd already stayed too long. Taking one last glance around the room, she crept back out the window.

Getting out was harder than coming in. Her limbs were slow from a night without sleep, and her nerves were frayed from being so long on her guard. By the time Kyra reached the meeting spot two blocks outside the Palace, the sky was visibly lighter, and she was in a considerably worse mood.

Two men awaited her at the street corner. They hadn't seen her yet, and she took a moment to study them. The first was solidly built, with a stubborn jaw and brown hair curled close to his head—Flick. When Kyra had first told him about the job, he'd listed all the reasons she should refuse, from the dangers within the Palace to his suspicions about James. Her friend's arguments had been more reasonable than Kyra cared to admit, but by then she'd already decided. Since Flick couldn't dissuade her from going, he'd insisted on escorting James. The two men had watched her cross the wall a few hours earlier, and now they awaited her return. Kyra felt a twinge of guilt when she saw the tense set of Flick's shoulders. He'd been worried.

Behind Flick, Kyra recognized James. He was slimmer but taller, with pale coloring and a wiry, athletic build. He exuded confidence, studying everything around him with languid readiness. His expression was impossible to read.

Both men's eyes flickered to her hands as she came closer, then to her belt.

"It in't there," she said, answering their unspoken question. Perhaps her voice was sharper than it should have been, but she was tired.

There was a brief silence as the two men digested her news. Finally, James spoke. "What do you mean?"

"I flipped the whole room—the dresser, desk, the chest at the foot of the bed. No jewelry box."

"You searched the entire room?" James raised an eyebrow.

Kyra spat on the ground. "Look, unless he sleeps with the rock in his smallclothes, it wasn't there."

"Maybe you went to the wrong place."

There was a hint of derision in his voice, and it galled Kyra. Trying hard to control a flush of anger, she reached into her belt pouch for the handkerchief she'd taken from the noble's dresser. She flicked it at James, who snatched it out of the air with surprising quickness.

"This handkerchief's got the fatpurse's initials embroidered on it. See if it matches your mark."

Kyra made no effort to hide her frustration as James inspected the embroidery. Payment for the job depended on handing over the jewel, so she'd taken a long and dangerous night's work for nothing. She felt a hand on her shoulder. Flick, knowing her temper, was silently warning her not to push anything too far. Kyra gritted her teeth. James studied the handkerchief, after a while not even looking at it, but through it. Finally, he looked up, and his demeanor abruptly changed.

"Very well," he said, voice now smooth and agreeable. "Mayhap he didn't bring the stone to the Palace." James untied a pouch from his belt and tossed it at Kyra, who almost didn't react quickly enough to catch it. "That's the agreed-upon price, plus some extra. I believe this will cover your effort."

Without another word, he turned and walked away.

TWO

The Drunken Dog was an establishment that awoke at night and slept during the day. Every evening, the small tavern brightened with the clink of flagons, loud talk, and the occasional song (often led by a slightly inebriated Flick). But come sunrise, the place dimmed. Pale sunlight shone through the small windows but couldn't match the warmth of the Dog's evening revelry. By the time Kyra and Flick walked into the main dining room an hour after dawn, only a few stragglers remained.

Brendel, the new talesinger, was packing up his lute. He raised his hand in greeting. "Ho, Flick, will you be here tonight? I'll be playing 'Lady Evelyne and the Felbeast.'" Brendel was a journeyman, and for his masterpiece—the work that he hoped would promote him to a master—he was putting the popular legend to song.

Flick grinned. "Let me sing the felbeast, and I'll grace you with my presence."

A man in a corner booth raised his flagon in Flick's direction. "Felbeast? With them long lashes and pretty eyes, Master Flick should be singing Lady Evelyne."

As the men roared in laughter. Kyra slipped past Flick and sat down at an empty table. After the noise died down, a woman's voice called from the kitchen. "Kyra! Flick! Have you eaten yet?"

Despite her exhaustion, Kyra smiled. It didn't matter when or in what condition she walked into the dining room. That was always the first question Bella asked.

"No, Bella." Flick's voice carried a tragic air that rivaled Brendel's best performances. "We haven't eaten in weeks. What's left?"

There was a pause as Bella took inventory. "I have some leftover lamb stew and a few rolls. It should be enough if Flick reins in that greedy maw of his."

Flick pantomimed a knife to his chest and sank into a chair. A plump woman, brown hair streaked with gray, carried out a tray with a basket of bread and two bowls of hot stew.

"What mischief have you two been stirring up?" Bella placed the food in front of them and wiped her hands on her apron. Kyra slouched into her chair, hoping Bella wouldn't notice her unkempt hair and dirty clothes, but Bella grabbed a rag from a nearby table and brushed the dust off Kyra's back. "I see this girl's been working."

Flick broke off a piece of bread and dipped it in his stew. "Kyra had an adventure last night," he announced, ignoring Kyra's warning look. Bella's forehead creased with concern, but a whistle sounded from the kitchen. As Bella rushed to tend the kettle, Flick dug through his bowl and started picking out turnip pieces.

"I don't understand," Kyra muttered, half to herself.

"You're wondering why he gave you the coin?" said Flick. He'd made a pile of turnips on his bread plate and absentmindedly pushed them toward Kyra, who dumped the pieces into her own bowl.

"He was only supposed to pay me if I brought the stone," Kyra said.

"The ruby didn't exist."

Kyra started at the certainty in Flick's declaration. Flick chuckled.

"Ah, Kyra, fearless thief. Able to outclimb a squirrel on any tree and outrun a mountain lion in total darkness." He tugged her ponytail. "Take your eyes off the ledges once in a while. You might actually see something."

Flick was insufferable when he decided to play smug older brother, but today she was curious enough to humor him. Kyra crossed her arms. "By all means, Grandfather. Share your wisdom with me."

He flashed a quick grin before hunkering down over the table. "Kyra, think about it. Say you pull in a thief to nip some fatpurse's trinket. You offer her decent coin, but still, you're paying less than what the trinket's worth. The thief comes back empty-handed, swearing she couldn't find anything. What's your first thought?"

"You think he'd suspect I kept the ruby? That's silly. If I could find someone to buy jewels, I'd be living in them fancy houses, not cracking them."

"You know that, and I know that. And maybe even James knows it's near impossible to find buyers these days. But there was a lot of coin at stake, and James wasn't suspicious at *all*.

I know. I was waiting with him at the meeting place. When you didn't show up on time—"

"I know. I'm sorry."

He shot her a stern look. "As well you should be. But when you didn't show up on time, he didn't get suspicious. Didn't react at all. He just...waited. And you saw how he was when he was asking you questions. Any idiot could tell he didn't really care." Flick's expression turned serious. "Looking back, I'm an idiot myself. I was so sure you'd break your neck in the Palace that I plain overlooked the other ways things could have gone wrong. You were lucky, Kyra, no thanks to me."

"I can take care of myself," Kyra said automatically.

Flick laughed. "Better than I would have imagined a lass of seventeen ever could."

"So I'm seventeen now?"

He made a big show of looking her up and down. "By height alone, I'd wager you were twelve, but wasn't seventeen Bella's last guess? Something about you gaining the poise of a young woman? You really should just pick a birthday—let Bella bake you a cake once a year."

Kyra rolled her eyes. The real version of events was less poetic. She'd started her womanly bleeding three years ago, and she'd been the same height for the past year. Based on these signs, Bella recently declared that Kyra was seventeen. Kyra decided to let Flick keep his version of the story.

"So what do you think James wanted?" she asked.

"It's a puzzle, but I've got a feeling you'll see him again."

Flick stopped as Bella dropped off some warmer rolls.

10

"Wait, Bella." Kyra fished into the pouch James had given her and pushed a handful of coins into Bella's hand. "You've fed us too much lately."

The older woman looked at the money dubiously.

"I didn't steal anything," Kyra promised. "Right, Flick?" Technically, she'd nipped a handkerchief, but she decided to let that slide.

Flick folded his hands behind his head, amused. "For once, she's right. Better take it, Bella. You never know how long it will be before Kyra earns another honest coin." He jumped back in his chair to avoid Kyra's slap.

Bella dropped the money into her apron, and Kyra sighed inwardly with relief. Bella paid her employer out of her own pocket for meals she gave away, and though the cook would never admit it, Kyra knew she was struggling to make ends meet. News of barbarian raids in the outer villages was becoming commonplace these days, and as supply lines into the city slowed, all of Forge's inhabitants tightened their belts. She worried that softhearted Bella was too generous for her own good.

"What did that strange fellow want with you?" Bella asked.

Kyra hesitated, not wanting to hide anything from Bella, but uneager to face her reaction. "He wanted me to nip something from the Palace compound."

The dish Bella was clearing froze in midair. "The Palace?"

Kyra sheepishly related the rest of the story, and the older woman shook her head. She turned an accusing eye on Flick. "And you let her do that?"

"Bella, you know as well as I do that Kyra does what she wants."

Bella shook her head. "Are you determined to rush to an early death, Kyra? It's all romance and adventures until you realize you're not immortal." She picked up Flick's empty stew bowl and returned to the kitchen.

Kyra stared after Bella, momentarily cowed. Bella's only son had been lost at sea years before she started working at The Drunken Dog. Word was that he had wanted to see the Far Lands for himself.

"Mayhap she's right," Flick mused. "Me and the other lads—we do a few raids here and there to make ends meet, but this is all you do. And you keep taking more risks. It's really not good for a lass. Just one mistake at the wrong time—"

"You're right, Flick. I'll change my ways. Why don't you find me a young man who'll marry a lass who spent her childhood begging on the streets?"

Flick threw up his arms. "Just think about it."

"I already have. I can't get odd jobs around the city like you. I can't make enough as a serving lass to cover my lodging, and I have no intention of marrying right now. And you know I need more coin for the gutter rats."

As Kyra scooped up the last of her stew, Bella returned from the kitchen. "Speaking of gutter mice, Idalee was here looking for you."

"Idalee?" Kyra asked. "She doesn't often come this far in."

"I sent her back with some stew. She didn't say where she'd be, but I assume you can find her?"

Flick glanced at Kyra. "You fixing to look for her?"

Kyra suppressed a yawn. "She's probably wandering the city right now. I'll catch a nap and find her this evening."

Kyra dreamed she was climbing. But instead of the Palace walls, she scaled a rock face in a hot, sandy landscape. The sun beat down on her hands and face, and though her arms grew weak, she never quite reached the top. It was late afternoon when Kyra finally woke. The cliff face lingered in her mind, but Kyra had long given up on making sense of her dreams. Instead, she dressed to go into the city. Idalee was probably done with her rounds for the day, and if Kyra left now, she would have a good chance of finding her.

As Kyra stepped out the front door of The Drunken Dog, a sharp voice called to her.

"You, girl. In the trousers." Kyra turned out of habit, then regretted it when she saw the speaker was scarcely older than a girl herself, dressed in a gown that cost more than a year's takings for Kyra. Her fingers were adorned with jewels, and her wrists and neck were ringed with trader charms—basilisk scales, love stones—the type of fanciful trinkets that honest folk ignored and the wealthy squandered their money on. The girl and her two shieldmen were clearly out of place in the dusty streets outside The Drunken Dog. She probably found it romantic to be exploring such a neighborhood. If the girl's carelessness got her in trouble here, it would be the folk who lived here who paid for it.

The girl gestured imperiously to Kyra. "Carry my bags for me."

Kyra hesitated. She had no respect for a spoiled nobleman's

daughter, but her shieldmen looked mean. People skirted around them, clearly glad the girl had focused on Kyra instead of them.

"Well, hurry up," said the girl.

Kyra could hear Flick's voice in her head, telling her not to do anything stupid. "Mayhap milady could have her soldiers carry her bags for her."

The girl rolled her eyes. "I'll pay you. Don't pretend you don't need the money."

Kyra stiffened. When she finally replied, her voice was low and steady. "I'm sorry, milady. I in't your packhorse." The girl's eyes widened, and Kyra ran for an alleyway. Once around the corner, she shinnied up a pole and pulled herself onto the rooftop. She peeked over the edge to see the nobleman's daughter still staring in the direction of the alleyway. Not one to push her luck, Kyra backed up and hurried on her way.

The city of Forge took the form of several concentric rings. At its center was the Palace compound, with the Fastkeep at its heart and the outer compound surrounding it. The wealthy, or "wallhuggers" as some called them, formed the first ring outside the compound walls, taking advantage of the security the Palace provided. Outside that ring, craftsmen and merchants set up their shops, relying on the wealthy to keep them in business. The Drunken Dog, where Kyra rented a small room, was slightly outside the merchant ring—far enough from the Palace to avoid the authorities' notice, but close enough to the markets to cultivate its diverse mix of patrons.

Kyra skirted along rooftops, heading away from the merchant district until she reached the outermost ring of the city. This area also had houses and shops, but the buildings were less clean and the streets less orderly. Gradually, the carpentry of the houses became more run-down; the piles of trash in the street grew larger and more numerous.

She climbed down and continued at a brisk pace, pausing periodically to drop a coin into an outstretched hand. Kyra felt her nerves tingle, her awareness sharpening out of habit. Every landmark had a memory attached. At one street, the baker's wife passed out scraps after sunset. One road over, behind a wooden fence, there was a space where a small child could huddle while others ran past.

It was on these streets that Flick had found her a decade ago. She'd been suspicious of him at first. The boy's clean face and untorn clothes immediately marked him as an outsider. Though, at fourteen, he hadn't yet reached his full height, he was still nearly twice her size. Kyra had scowled and slipped into one of her hiding places, but he returned the next day.

"Your hands look small. Can you reach between the slats of a fence?" he asked her.

Kyra checked to make sure the other children were in view before moving closer. Flick told her that a lady had dropped her purse behind a locked fence. It was just out of his reach, but if Kyra would help him get it, he promised her half the pickings. It was simple enough, and surprisingly, the boy was true to his word. After that, he kept coming back with more ideas. He learned about Kyra's penchant for climbing into high places, and she learned that he roamed the streets because his mother was becoming too ill to care for him. In time, Flick started bringing Kyra food even when there were no jobs.

They became business partners of sorts, and eventually

friends. It was Flick who took Kyra to The Drunken Dog and introduced her to Bella, Flick who told Kyra that she could stop living on the streets if she made enough money. Somehow, Bella convinced the owner of The Drunken Dog to rent a room to Kyra, and in hindsight, it was a good thing she had. Most of the children from Kyra's younger days were gone. Kyra had no idea where they were or whether they were still alive.

"Griffin feathers, milady? Bring you good luck." A small boy with stringy hair thrust a tattered bunch of feathers at her.

Kyra almost walked past him, then sighed and turned around. Everything about the boy betrayed him as new to the streets, from the way he failed to blend in, to his carelessness in addressing strangers. She took the boy's trinket and rolled it between her fingers. "You new at this?"

Confusion flashed across the boy's face. "Just a quarter copper each, milady."

Kyra handed it back to him. "You can't take chicken feathers and say they're from griffins. People in't that dull."

The boy jerked his hand back. "You in't never seen a griffin before."

"No, but I've seen a chicken. Look, the traders can say anything they want about their goods, and folk won't argue with them. But nobody'll believe you went across the Aerin Mountains. You'll end up with your money taken if you're lucky, or flogged and pilloried if you're not."

Real fear flashed through his eyes, and Kyra's annoyance gave way to pity. She shook her head and handed the boy a coin. "It's clever, I'll give you that. You out here alone?"

The boy hesitated, then gave an unconvincing shake of his head.

"Come with me. I'll take you to some others."

She continued on her way. If he'd refused to follow, she would have let him go, but she heard the boy fall into step behind her. As the streets grew narrower, the buildings crowded together so the upper stories hung over the pathways, blocking much of the already waning sunlight. As a child, Kyra had never noticed the smell of garbage and sweat, but now she wrinkled her nose and walked faster.

Eventually, Kyra heard children shouting in the distance. She followed the sound until the alley opened into a secluded courtyard. Fifteen pairs of bare feet pounded the hard-packed dirt. The children had dust on their faces and tears in their clothing. Their game tonight was a new one, with rules Kyra didn't recognize. But like the other games, it involved a lot of running. Running was the easiest way to stay warm.

Kyra edged closer, and several children broke away from the game, shouting her name. She smiled and squeezed a few shoulders as they gathered around. "I've got someone new for you," she said, finally turning to acknowledge the griffin boy. "Show him how things work."

"We've seen him around," said a girl with knobby arms and tangled black hair. "He didn't want to talk to us."

"Now he will." Kyra gave him a push toward the others before turning back to the black-haired girl. "You come looking for me, Idalee?"

"Where were you last night?"

"Working." She paused for a moment, reminded of James's mysterious behavior. "Why'd you come to The Drunken Dog?" In many ways, the area around The Drunken Dog was safer than Idalee's usual haunts, but Kyra worried about her wandering away from her friends.

"Lettie's sick again."

Kyra frowned. Idalee's younger sister was constantly ill. "Take me to her?"

As the girl pulled her down a side street, Kyra couldn't help noticing how Idalee had matured since their first meeting. Two years ago, Kyra had been in the neighborhood when she heard shouting. She ran up just in time to see a skinny girl charge an older boy headfirst, knocking him down and pounding at him with remarkable ferocity. The other children were in an uproar, and Kyra picked up more than a few bruises pulling the two apart. It took some work to sort things out, but eventually she pieced together that one of the older boys had tried to take Lettie's supper. Despite the tongue-lashing that Kyra delivered to all involved, she couldn't help but admire Idalee's spirit, and tiny Lettie reminded Kyra of her own childhood in the streets. While Kyra would never admit to having favorites, she found herself spending more and more time helping these two.

Idalee led her to a dead end, where several boards had been placed in a crude lean-to. It was too small for both Idalee and Kyra to fit comfortably, so Kyra pushed aside the cloth covering its opening and peered inside. Someone shivered underneath a pile of blankets. "Lettie?"

The form shifted and a small, round face turned toward

her. The child's normally large eyes were half closed, and Kyra could tell from Lettie's raspy breathing that something wasn't right. Every time the child took a breath, she winced. Kyra put her hand on Lettie's forehead. It was warm to the touch.

"Can she walk?" Kyra asked Idalee.

"A bit, but you've got to go slow, and she coughs if you walk too fast."

"Well, I can't carry her all the way," Kyra muttered. She thought for a moment. "Why don't I take Lettie back with me? I'll bring her to a healer tomorrow."

Though Kyra's landlord might not like that plan. Last year, Kyra had let Idalee and Lettie stay with her during a blizzard. When Laman discovered them, he'd pulled Kyra aside and made it clear that he had no intentions of turning The Drunken Dog into an orphanage. Well, Laman didn't need to know, and Bella wouldn't say anything.

Idalee nodded. "Come on, Lettie, you're going home with Kyra." She coaxed her sister out of the blankets and tied a small gray cloak around her neck. Lettie coughed but didn't complain. The little girl whispered a question as she took Kyra's hand.

"What?" Kyra asked. Lettie always spoke in a barely audible tone. Kyra leaned closer and laughed.

"Well, I don't know if there's any more stew, but I'm sure Bella will have something equally tasty tonight."

As Idalee had predicted, Kyra and Lettie's walk back to The Drunken Dog took quite a while. The tavern was already filling with a lively after-dinner crowd when they returned. Brendel had set up in his favorite corner and was tuning his lute in front of a brightly colored painting of dragons and dryads. Kyra remembered that he was going to sing "Lady Evelyne" tonight.

"Lettie, do you want to hear the talesinger?"

Kyra guided Lettie to a table, then ducked into the kitchen to fetch some food. Lettie's eyes opened wide at the chicken pie Kyra brought out.

"Don't burn your tongue," Kyra said. Lettie gripped her spoon with an eagerness that made Kyra suspect her warning was useless. As they both dug in, Brendel strummed a few chords and cleared his throat.

"Good evening, good gentlemen and ladies." There were some good-natured heckles from the audience, which the young talesinger acknowledged with a charming grin. "I've always loved the tale of noble Lady Evelyne, and I know many of you do as well. Tonight, I am honored to play for you the first act, which I just finished penning"—he made a show of counting on his fingers—"seven hours ago."

As the laughter died down, Brendel launched straight into the opening chords. He sang of the felbeast—the giant bear-creature that ravaged the countryside long ago. Kyra glanced nervously at Lettie during one of Brendel's more convincing growls, but the child, fascinated by Brendel's quick-moving fingers, seemed unfazed. Then the talesinger switched to a softer melody. In a high falsetto, he sang the part of Lady Evelyne. She wept for her people and wondered if the carnage could be stopped. The noble lady gathered her courage, bid good-bye to her family and betrothed, and entered the forest to confront the felbeast.

"That's how we know the ballad in't true," said a familiar voice at Kyra's shoulder. "A real fatpurse would have sacrificed a servant girl instead."

Kyra turned her head.

Behind her, James inclined his head in greeting. "Good to see you again. Join me for a flagon?"

Brendel's song washed over Kyra as she scrambled to gather her wits. "Right now?" she asked.

He gave her a mocking smile. "Unless you're eager to hear the ballad."

Kyra jerked her head toward Lettie, who was so engrossed in Brendel's performance she hadn't yet noticed James. "I can't leave her alone."

"She'll be fine. Keep her in view while we talk."

Kyra scanned the room, hoping to see Flick in the crowd, but he wasn't there. For a moment, Kyra considered telling James that she really did want to hear the rest of the ballad. But then, what was she afraid of? The only thing James had done so far was overpay her. Kyra schooled her features and nodded. Lettie barely acknowledged Kyra when she tapped her on the shoulder and told her where she was going.

James led her to a nearby table. As Kyra slid onto the bench across from him, he beckoned to a serving girl and ordered two mugs of ale.

"I trust you got some rest this morning?" he asked.

"I trust you got some rest this morning?" he asked.

"Aye."

The ensuing silence was interrupted by the serving girl returning with the ale. James pushed one mug toward Kyra. She wet her lips but didn't drink.

"How long have you been in your current trade, Kyra?"

"About eight years." Kyra wrapped both hands around the mug. The chill seeped into her palms and made her shiver.

"Is it a good living?"

She hesitated. "Why are you asking?"

"Of course, I apologize for my rudeness," he said smoothly. "You're right to be suspicious. I'm asking because we were impressed with your work last night."

"Who's 'we'?"

"We're looking for someone with your skills. Your agility, how you can move without being seen. You searched the compound for longer than you'd planned without getting caught, and you kept your head when you couldn't find the loot. I see your skills have served you well in your current way of life."

"I'm a thief," she said curtly.

"A thief," he echoed. "How much coin do you make, as a thief?"

"Enough." She didn't quite succeed in removing the defensiveness from her voice.

James scanned the dining room. "Enough to feed yourself and pay for decent lodging." His tone made the sentence seem more a question than a statement. Kyra felt an uneasy stirring in her stomach. Did he know she was short on coin? She wasn't in danger of being evicted, but recently it had become much harder to pay her lodging. The entire city was suffering from the attacks in the outskirts.

James continued. "Why does someone with your talents have to scramble for rent?"

So he did know. What else did he know about her? "We've got to be careful," she said. "Wallhuggers get suspicious if there's too much going on."

"Then why not move to less-guarded homes?"

"If someone can buy guards to watch his trinkets, he's got more than his fair share. I in't fixing to steal someone's bread money. And even with the wallhuggers, we need to be careful what we take. I won't risk my neck for a jewelry collection when nobody in the city buys stones anymore. Folk are scared, 'cause of the raids." Kyra paused and shifted her eyes to his face. "Actually, I'm wondering who you'd lined up to take that ruby."

"Ah, the ruby." James met Kyra's gaze, the corners of his mouth lifting as if sharing a private joke. "Pity you couldn't find it." He might as well have admitted flat out that the ruby had never existed. "We deal mostly with the wallhuggers," James continued before Kyra had a chance to think further. "If you worked with us, you wouldn't have to worry about taking someone's dinner. You wouldn't have to worry about coin at all. We take good care of our own."

"How good is that?"

"How'd you like to own a house in the city?"

"A house?"

Just the thought made her mouth go dry. Only the nobles

and merchants owned property. What he was offering was impossible. Though with the way he'd paid her this morning...

"You still haven't told me who you are," she said.

"We're a group who takes opportunities as we see them." He chose his words carefully, picking his way through his sentence like a jeweler selecting stones. "Sometimes we cooperate with others; sometimes we pursue our own plans."

"And your plans don't always agree with the Palace," Kyra finished.

"The Palace serves money and privilege. They uphold the laws because the laws suit them. The rest of us have to fight to control our fates."

Several factors suddenly came together. James's words and appearance—his quickness and the aura of quiet lethality that surrounded him—brought some old stories into Kyra's mind.

"The Assassins Guild," she blurted.

His lips curled into a smile. "There are some in the city who call us that."

Images flitted through Kyra's mind. A secret band of men who exercised power in Forge's underworld. Deadly assassins who killed with impunity. "The whispers are real, then? The Guild is back?"

"It depends on which stories you've heard. We're not murderers for hire. We just do what's needed to reach our goals."

"And what are those?"

"As I was saying, the city favors those who are born into power. But not all in power use it well, and not all with money deserve it. We act as a... balancing force. To make sure that those born outside the Palace walls don't get trampled by those born within."

She snorted. "Are you trying to tell me that the Guild is some kind of talesinger's hero? The stories can't all be false."

His smile was quick and tight. "In case you haven't noticed, the Palace's got armies at its beck and call. They need more convincing than mere words and a handshake."

Kyra shook her head. "Your goals are too high-thinking for me. I just do what I need to get by."

"You say that, but your actions say otherwise. Didn't you just tell me that you only steal from the rich? But you don't have to share our goals to help us. The benefits for you would be more immediate."

Kyra noticed she had begun to lean away from him. Perhaps he noticed as well, because he continued. "We don't need you as an assassin. You're too small. I'm guessing you're useless in a fight, despite your speed."

Though she recoiled at the thought of killing for hire, she bristled at his dismissive tone. "Then what do you want me for?"

"The strengths you've built over the last eight years. We need someone who can get in the Palace without being noticed."

"If you want me to get something for you, just hire me."

"It can't be job by job. You're good, but we'll need to train you further. You'll need to gather information from the Palace without raising suspicions."

"What was wrong with the way I cracked the Palace last night?"

Now he looked amused. "I apologize again. I was unclear. We know you can crack the outer Palace compound. What we need is someone who can do the same thing, but in the Fastkeep."

Kyra let her breath out with a hiss. "That's dangerous."

"You don't strike me as someone who'd worry about that. You'll be well compensated, of course."

"What's the point if I'm dead?"

"Are you refusing my offer, then?"

Kyra opened her mouth to say yes, but no sound came out. Despite the insanity of what he was proposing, she was intrigued. There was no reason to completely refuse him now. "I'll think about it," she said.

"Very well," he answered. "See Rand over there?" He gestured toward a redheaded man drinking at one of the other tables. She nodded.

"If you change your mind, tell him. He knows where to find me."

"The Assassins Guild?" asked Flick. "I'd think assassins would be too busy killing people to be secretly running the city."

Flick bounced Lettie higher in his arms as he and Kyra weaved between horses, people, and wagons. Lettie was weaker today, barely moving as she snuggled into Flick's shoulder.

"He says they're not assassins for hire," Kyra explained again.

"What do they do, then, bake sweet buns and feed orphans?"

She'd had the same doubts, but somehow it was annoying to hear them from Flick. Kyra scowled. "You're not a plum citizen yourself."

He ignored her jab. "What exactly is it that James wants from you?"

"Same things I've been doing—raiding and fetching. He didn't go into specifics." She took a deep breath. "I could use the coin."

Flick was silent for a moment. "How far behind are you?"

"I'm paid up on my lodging now with what James gave me. But I'm still going from job to job. I don't like that."

He frowned and shifted Lettie's weight to his other hip. "Mayhap I could help."

"No, you can't. You've got your own money troubles. Why are you arguing so much, anyway? You're usually the first to hatch something against the wallhuggers."

He didn't argue her point, but after another pause, he spoke again. "Maybe we can figure something else out. I don't trust him."

They stopped in front of a cottage. "This is Miranda's house," Flick said, freeing one arm to knock on the door.

"How do you know her?"

"She hired me and a friend once to patch up her wall."

A small woman with silver hair and wizened hands answered.

"Flick!" Miranda beamed and reached up to give him a hug. Kyra rolled her eyes when they weren't looking. This was typical for Flick. Gets hired to do one odd job, and on their next meeting, the woman greets him like a long-lost son. Flick was always trying to get Kyra to meet new people, and some introductions took better than others.

"This is my friend Kyra," Flick said, lightly pushing her forward. "And this"—he patted Lettie on the head—"is our patient." Lettie smiled shyly and clung to his chest.

The odor of dried herbs hit Kyra as she entered. She looked for the source and spotted shelves of jars along the walls, carefully labeled in precise handwriting. Some of the jars—mint, dandelion root, willow—Kyra recognized. Others looked to be from across the Aerins, which was intriguing. Not many healers could boast such rare herbs. One empty jar read SEAWEED— NYMPH GROWN. Another, labeled GRIFFIN TAIL, had a few tattered feathers at the bottom. Kyra noticed that they didn't look anything at all like the chicken feathers the boy in the street had been selling. Meanwhile, Miranda was listening to Lettie's breathing, looking at her tongue, and occasionally asking Kyra questions.

"Her lungs are weak," the healer finally said. "I can give her herbs, but the best thing would just be to keep her warm." Miranda mixed some herbs with water and started it boiling on the stove. "It will cost more than usual, I'm afraid. Medicines are scarce since the Demon Riders started raiding the countryside."

"Demon Riders?" Flick asked. Kyra leaned in to hear better. News of the barbarians was becoming too common for comfort.

"I've not seen them," said Miranda, "but I *have* gone out there to help the injured. The survivors talk of folk who ride on the backs of giant beasts."

"How bad are the raids?" asked Flick.

"They come quickly, they leave quickly. They go mostly for livestock, but they're brutal to those who resist them. It's a horrible sight to see." Miranda sighed. "I help those I can, but many are beyond help by the time I get there. The caravans don't travel as often since the raids started, and they've raised their prices for all their goods. Rare ingredients are all but impossible to come by. I could have saved some from infection if I'd had dryad hair, but the Far Ranger caravans no longer come here. They come too far, traveling over the Aerin Mountains, to risk losing it to barbarians."

"Dryad hair?" asked Flick. Like Kyra, he was skeptical of the fantastical stories from across the mountains.

"One of the best remedies I know," said Miranda. "Nothing on this side—herbs, roots, animals—comes even close. But the supply has just trickled off." Miranda removed the boiling pot and poured its contents through a cloth, straining out the leaves. "But enough of this. We'll scare the child. Just be careful if you leave the city." She transferred the potion into a leather flask and handed it to Kyra. "Have her breathe the fumes whenever she has trouble."

"Come here, Lettie." Kyra opened the flask and stuck it under the girl's nose. The child obediently took several deep breaths. "Feel any different?" Kyra asked.

Lettie nodded. "It hurts less."

Kyra scrutinized the girl, surprised that the herbs would work so quickly. But there did seem to be a difference. The tension was gone from Lettie's face, and she no longer winced with each breath.

"This potion should be good for a week," Miranda said. "Would you like some herbs for more batches? It would be four coppers per measure."

"How much would we need?" Kyra asked.

"We could try three weeks' worth and see if she improves."

Three weeks' worth would be twelve coppers. Kyra did some calculations in her head. If she bought the medicine, would her money last until she found another job? It would be tight, but she could probably do it. She pulled out her coin purse and paid the healer, thanking her again as they left.

"Why don't you go back," Kyra told Flick as they stood outside Miranda's house. "I'll take Lettie straight to Idalee. I don't want to keep them apart too long."

"You know your way from here?"

"Well enough."

Flick straightened, a sly grin on his face. "Well then, I might stop by the wool district on my way back."

Kyra raised an eyebrow. "You still courting that merchant's daughter? She's a mite above your station, don't you think?"

"Above my station? I'll remind you that I am the son of a nobleman."

"*Bastard* son."

Flick raised his arms in an exaggerated stretch as he walked away. "I'm still closer to the wall than you."

Kyra watched him go, buoyed slightly by his good spirits. Flick hadn't seen his father since his mother died. She'd been a merchant's daughter as well, but was thrown out by her family when they found out about her affair with Flick's father. She managed to get by for a while as his mistress—until she became ill and the nobleman lost interest. Any mention of his father used to send Flick into low spirits, but it seemed that even deep wounds healed with time.

Kyra tied the medicine to her belt. "Want to try walking?" she asked Lettie.

Their progress was slow, but they weren't rushed for time, and it was interesting to explore a new part of the city. These streets were quieter than the ones around The Drunken Dog, the houses more spread out. As they walked, Kyra thought over James's offer. Flick was right. There was something unsettling about James. But still, the thought of interesting work and regular coin was tempting.

Ahead of them, the road narrowed into a footbridge. Two Red Shields stood at the bottom of the steps, and Kyra suppressed her usual instinct to run. It was unlikely that they were after her, and backing away would just draw attention to herself. One of the Red Shields, an ugly fellow with a rust-colored beard, stopped her as she and Lettie came closer. "Bridge toll. One copper."

"Toll?" asked Kyra.

"One copper. Is it your ears or your head that's slow?"

She knew better than to respond to his insult. "I in't heard of any bridge tolls," she said.

The other Red Shield, a stocky man with a wide nose, came closer. "New orders from the Palace. This past week," he said with a smirk.

It was a farce. The Red Shields were lining their own pockets, and they didn't care if Kyra knew. If she was wise, she'd pay the toll and be on her way. But she was low on coin already after buying the girl's medicine.

Kyra took Lettie's hand. "We'll go around the other way."

She'd taken two steps when a hand closed around her arm. "That's against the rules, girl," said Rust Beard. "Pay up."

Kyra froze, forcing herself not to flinch at his grip. If she were alone, she might have been able to run for it, but not with Lettie. She fished around in her purse for a coin, trying to keep the resentment from her face as she handed it over. Rust Beard grinned as he pocketed it. His friend wandered away, seemingly satisfied, but Rust Beard scrutinized her. "Toll's gone up," he said. "There's an extra charge for them that try to evade the first payment."

He reached for her coin purse, clearly expecting no resistance, but she stepped back, jerking her purse out of his reach with one hand while she pushed Lettie behind her with the other. "Hands off, pig."

She regretted her words as soon as she spoke. The Red Shield's eyes narrowed, and Kyra barely had time to yell at Lettie to run before the Red Shield lunged toward Kyra, grabbing for her arm. He wasn't as fast as he could have been, and Kyra stepped sideways, avoiding his grasp. As he stumbled, she pivoted away, scanning the streets for Lettie and feeling a rush of relief as she saw the girl disappearing into an alleyway. Before Kyra could follow, the Red Shield seized her elbow and pulled her backward. He caught her around the waist, pinning her arms. Kyra yelled and stamped down on his foot. His grip loosened, and she thrust back with her elbow. The man doubled over, and she squirmed out of his arms.

As she broke free, his friend closed in from the front and aimed a fist toward her head. Pain exploded on one side of her face and she fell hard onto the dirt. She gasped for breath, stunned and blinded. She felt a weight as one of them straddled her chest and pinned her left arm to the ground. Desperate, she jabbed at his eyes with her free hand. He swore and lifted his arm to deliver another blow. She raised her hand over her face and turned away.

There was a thud, a yell of surprise, and then the Red Shield on top of her pitched forward. Someone pulled him off her, and Kyra dragged herself onto her elbow, breath coming in painful gasps. Both her attackers lay on the ground, unconscious. Above them stood a man who looked vaguely familiar.

"Filthy Palace scum." Her rescuer spat on the ground. He was of average height, heavyset, and wore the coarse wool tunic of a commoner. Carrot-colored hair topped a freckled face marred by a scar over one eyebrow. He turned toward her. "James told me to keep an eye on you."

Now she remembered. This was Rand, the man James had pointed out to her at The Drunken Dog. Had he been following her? Given the circumstances, she couldn't bring herself to be angry.

Rand walked from one Red Shield to the other, checking their pulse. "They'll live," he said. He offered her a hand and she took it, wincing at her new bruises as he pulled her to her feet. The side of her leg felt moist, and she looked down. As the smell of herbs reached her nostrils, her heart sank. Lettie's potion had spilled in the fight. She grabbed for the bag of herbs at her waist. It was ripped, and there were dry leaves scattered over the ground.

"The herbs," she breathed.

Rand was unsympathetic. "Them's the least of your worries right now. We've got to go."

Kyra knew he was right, but she couldn't stop thinking about the herbs. They had been so expensive.

Suddenly, she remembered that Lettie was still hiding. She ran in the direction the girl had gone, shouting her name, and sighed with relief when a shape detached itself from the shadows. As Kyra ran closer, she saw Lettie shrink away in fear. Kyra raised a hand to her face. Her cheek was sticky with blood, and she realized how frightening she looked.

"It's all right, Lettie, I'm all right," she said, stretching her arms out. Kyra took Lettie's hands and turned to Rand. "I've got to take her to her sister."

He glanced at the child and gave a curt nod.

They proceeded in silence toward Lettie's neighborhood. When children's voices sounded ahead, Kyra stopped. "Lettie, can you go the rest of the way by yourself?" She didn't want Idalee to see her in this condition. "Tell Idalee to keep you warm. I'll come by with more herbs for you."

Lettie nodded.

"Good. Off with you." She pushed Lettie toward the courtyard. When she was convinced that the girl had safely rejoined the other children, Kyra sighed and allowed herself to sag.

"If you're fixing to go around baiting Red Shields, you should carry a dagger at least," Rand said.

"I don't usually do this."

"That's a pity."

She didn't bother to answer.

With just the two of them walking, the silence was more noticeable, but she was in no mood for conversation. Only when they were almost at the tavern did Rand speak again.

"It's James's job to convince you to join us," he said. "So I won't waste my breath talking at you. But you don't have to let the wallhuggers trample you like this. We'd teach you to fight, to take care of yourself." They stopped at the back door of the tavern. Rand didn't follow her to the doorstep. "Just think about it," he said before walking away.

Kyra watched him leave, then turned back to the tavern. She put her hand on the doorknob and started to turn. It was still early in the evening. Even from out here, she could see the crowd through the window, hear the drone of conversation. People would see her come in. Word would get to Bella.

Kyra's bruises started to throb, as if her body wanted to give a detailed report of everything that required fixing. She was suddenly angry—at the Red Shields for attacking her, at herself for letting her guard down, and at the city and everyone in it for making everything so hard. Kyra let her hand go limp, and the doorknob rebounded with a click. She stumbled back a few steps. Then she turned and ran for the street.

"Rand," she called. He was halfway down the street already, but he stopped and turned around. Ignoring her aching muscles, Kyra jogged to catch up with him.

Kyra opened her mouth and hesitated. Flick would not like this, nor would Bella, but she pushed that thought out of her mind. "Take me to James," she blurted before she could change her mind.

"Follow me," Rand replied. And turning around, he led her back into the city.

FOUR

She followed him into a quiet neighborhood, with few taverns and even fewer people on the darkened streets. Rand made no allowance for her injuries, and Kyra hurried to keep up with him. Her head ached, and several times she startled at a man's voice behind her, only to realize the speaker wasn't even looking at her. Rand led her off the road and across an empty plot of land, finally stopping in front of an enormous wooden building. It looked like a storehouse used by trade caravans—boxlike and functional, two stories high and made of cheap wood.

"This is it?" she asked. She had expected something more clandestine. An underground hideout perhaps, or a chamber behind a false wall.

Rand pushed through the door, and Kyra found herself in an equally nondescript hallway. To her left, an entryway opened into a giant room stacked with boxes. A few men loitered inside, the rough type that Kyra usually avoided. Their eyes lingered on her, and Kyra hastened after Rand.

He knocked on a door at the end of the corridor.

"Come in," said James.

His voice sent a chill down her spine. Kyra briefly wondered if she was making a mistake, but Rand motioned her in with a jerk of his head. The study they entered was sparsely furnished and immaculately clean. James sat at a wide desk facing the door. He looked at Rand and then Kyra, gaze sweeping her from head to toe. Kyra lowered her eyes, suddenly ashamed of her battered state. If James had ever found her impressive, he would be hard-pressed to keep that opinion now.

"What's this?" James asked.

"Red Shields," said Rand.

James scrutinized Kyra again, as if he were making a mental catalog of every bruise and scratch. "You were supposed to keep an eye on her," he said to Rand.

"She's alive, in't she?"

They looked at each other, exchanging some wordless communication, before James turned back to Kyra. "Wash off in the basin out back. Rand will show you."

It took Kyra a moment for her to recognize his words as a dismissal. She choked out an acknowledgment before following Rand out the back door. It opened into a dirt courtyard. In the center was a barrel of water that looked clean enough. Kyra submerged her scratched forearms and carefully rubbed off the dirt. When she finished, Rand handed her a stack of rags and went back inside. Relieved to be alone, Kyra wet a rag and splashed water on her head, letting out a long breath as streams ran down the swollen side of her face. Her panic from the attack had worn away, and in its place was an emotion she couldn't quite name. It was as if the ground were unsteady, or the buildings around her might collapse without any warning. Nothing felt safe.

"Rand says you don't carry a knife."

Kyra jumped at the voice. She turned to see James leaning against the door frame.

"I don't need to. I can usually get away," she said. "But this time I had a little one with me."

"Two Red Shields tried to take your coin?"

Kyra nodded. Her hair was damp against her forehead, and she nudged it aside.

"So what will you do?" James asked. "Go to the magistrate? Complain to him about misbehaving soldiers?"

There was no overt sarcasm in his voice, but it wasn't really a question. The Palace would be more likely to arrest her than help her, and James knew it. Kyra looked at him, then at her scratched forearms, and weighed her options.

"If I join you, what jobs will I do?"

"Watch the Palace. I would know the layout of the Fast-keep. Your first job would be to map it, starting from the perimeter, and once you're ready, moving toward the center."

"Drawing maps? That's all?"

"That's the first step. I've got a bigger job in mind for you afterward."

"And what's that?"

"I'll tell you in a few months, when you're ready. You can't know all our secrets at once. If you do that last job, it'll earn you a house. But either way, we'll pay you well."

Flick's voice echoed in her head, words of caution she

couldn't quite ignore. "If I get caught by the Palace, and folk know I run with you, it wouldn't be good."

James chuckled. "Of all possible objections, I didn't expect that one. If the Palace captures you *now*, you'd be in bad straits whether you were with us or not, I promise you. If you join us, you'll be better paid, better trained, and safer. You've seen what Rand can do. He in't even our best. But there's only so much you can see from the outside."

"You'll train me?"

"We'll teach you to handle a knife and hold your own. You're fast and skilled. There's no reason tonight had to end like this."

There was something about the way he carried himself and security in his words—a promise she couldn't bring herself to turn down. Kyra twisted the rag in her hand. Flick and Bella would come around. They always had before.

"I'll try," she said.

James nodded, mouth curving into a slight smile. "Glad to hear it. Welcome to the Guild."

FIVE

There was no warning. No sound, no shout of alarm. Tristam had been riding with Jack on an outskirts patrol and had fallen slightly behind as they rounded a corner. By the time he caught up, Jack was facedown on the path, covered in dirt and grimacing in pain. Tristam stared a moment before his training kicked in. He drew his sword and whipped up his shield, barely breathing as he scanned the road for enemies.

But there was nothing—only open fields of livestock and the boulder they'd just ridden around. Birds chirped in the background, oblivious to any disaster.

"What happened?"

Jack coughed. "Stupid horse," he rasped. "Don't know what got into him."

Tristam looked at Jack, then at his gelding grazing peacefully nearby, as Jack's words slowly sank in. "Your horse threw you? On a routine patrol?" He made a halfhearted attempt to stifle the first chuckle, then gave up and doubled over laughing. Jack was a talented horse talker and possessed an uncanny

41

rapport with any steed he rode. Tristam had never seen him have trouble with a horse, let alone fall off one.

Jack scowled. "Once you're done laughing, can you help me up?"

Tristam dismounted and crouched next to him. "What happened?"

"Gray spooked right after I rounded that curve. I don't know what it was."

"Anything broken?"

"No, but I hit my head."

Tristam offered Jack an arm. His friend pushed off the ground, wobbled, then slowly straightened. Once up, Jack tried to walk, but his balance was off. He pitched first to one side, then the other, stumbling until he caught himself on a nearby tree trunk.

"How do you feel?"

"Dizzy."

Tristam felt a slight twinge of guilt for laughing. "Perhaps you should rest this round and join me on the next one."

Jack nodded, brows furrowed. "I'll just sit by that boulder for a while." He staggered toward it, again stumbling wildly from side to side. And suddenly, Tristam understood.

"Here, let me help you." He took Jack's arm over his shoulder, sinking a little under his weight as they made their way toward the boulder. After five steps, he placed his hand on Jack's back and pushed, at the same time hooking Jack's leg out from under him.

Jack yelped and fell forward, rolling over his shoulder and springing back to his feet with surprising agility for someone

42

with a head wound. He laughed as he dusted himself off. "Is that how you treat your injured comrades?"

Tristam put on his sternest expression. "You deserved it. I should turn you in for shirking duty."

"Shirking duty?" Jack's face fell into a well-practiced mask of innocence. "Why would I do such an irresponsible thing?"

"I'm guessing that brunette up the road making calf's eyes at you has something to do with it. What'd you do? Round the corner, jump off the horse, and throw dirt all over yourself?"

Jack threw a mock punch at Tristam, who shrugged out of the way, but not quickly enough to avoid the headlong charge that followed. Tristam caught Jack in a bear hug as he went down, but they were both laughing too hard to do any real damage.

"You never miss anything, do you?" said Jack as he rubbed his shoulder—a real bruise this time, courtesy of Tristam.

Tristam dusted off his tunic. "You may best me at riding, my friend, but subterfuge is not your strong point. Come, we're wasting time."

"What gave me away?"

"People with vertigo don't lurch like that. They center their weight between both legs. Take a closer look next time you walk into a tavern. Your show of reeling back and forth required more balance than most people have when they're sober."

Jack whistled as they kicked their horses into a trot. "Someday I'll fool you, Tristam."

Tristam just chuckled. They followed the road past the farm and into a patch of forest. The air smelled of fresh leaves and sunshine, and Tristam let himself relax, enjoying the light breeze through his tunic. Most of their training took place on the Palace grounds in the city proper, and these monthly patrols of the surrounding farmland were a rare treat.

It hadn't yet sunk in that this was one of the last times he'd ride this circle with Jack. They'd entered the Palace together as pages and trained side by side for the last ten years, sneaking out at dawn for extra fencing practice and sitting long hours over strategy lessons. But once they were knighted, they'd most likely go to separate units.

"These outskirt patrols are always dull," said Jack.

Tristam glanced in his direction. "I like them. They remind me of home."

"You *would* feel that way, country boy."

Tristam raised an eyebrow. "If you really want to talk to her, I'll cover for you. One circle only though."

Jack slapped his thigh. "Do I believe my ears? Tristam the model squire, allowing me to shirk my duty?" He let out a martyr's sigh. "No, no. I suppose I should conduct myself like a proper knight-to-be. I'm afraid you're rubbing off on me. Though she was pretty..."

"A farm girl. Your mother wouldn't be pleased."

"My mother needn't know."

Tristam decided that didn't need a reply.

After a moment, Jack spoke again. "Have you decided what you'll do next month?"

"After we're knighted? I'll be applying to the road patrols."

"Following the Brancel family tradition? The Master Strategist will be disappointed."

"He'll have his pick of worthy applicants."

"But not his star pupil." Jack lowered his voice in imitation of the old knight. "That young Tristam. Best mind for strategy I've seen in ten years."

Tristam shrugged self-consciously, not thrilled about the conversation he'd eventually have to have with his favorite instructor. "It's just that I'll go crazy if I have to stay in Forge any longer. Too many lords to impress, rules to follow."

"And now he's complaining about rules. Who are you, shape-shifting demon? What have you done with my friend? Though, on the other hand…" Jack stroked his unbearded chin. "I'm not sure I want him back…"

Tristam rolled his eyes. "You know what I mean. I'll do a knight's duty if it's patrols or actual work. But the politics, the court dinners, all the ways a knight is supposed to behave…"

"What is it about you Brancel men? All this talk of duty and honor, but you insist on performing your service at the edge of civilization. Why so eager to run for the trees?"

"Visit our manor and see for yourself."

"Think I'll like it?"

Tristam thought about his family's land, remembering the quiet trails, the sunrise coming over the mountain. When he went home, he took off for days into the forest, sometimes not seeing another person the entire time. And even at the manor, he wasn't saddled with the obligations of court life. His family's staff was small and had known him all his life. He was free to be himself, rather than a courtier in training.

"You'd hate it," Tristam said.

Jack laughed. "It's not that I dislike scenery. It's just that if I have to choose between forests and pretty girls . . ." Suddenly, Jack sat up straight. "Do you hear that?"

A bell rang faintly in the distance.

"It's an alarm bell at the farm up ahead," Jack said. "Come on." He kicked Gray into a gallop.

An alarm bell? Tristam couldn't remember the last time something went wrong in the outskirts. He urged his horse after Jack.

Any hopes for a false alarm disappeared as he rode in. Panicked screams sounded all around, mixed with the lower-pitched bleating of frightened livestock. The farm was a mass of confusion, with villagers running away from a threat he couldn't see. Tristam cast around, trying to make sense of the chaos. Out of the corner of his eye, he saw dead or wounded villagers and livestock scattered around the grounds. A frightened woman darted across his path, and Tristam's mare swerved just in time to avoid trampling her.

Ahead of him, Jack disappeared around a corner. Tristam pushed to close the distance between them while avoiding panicking residents. Then he rounded the corner and stopped, pulling so hard on his mare's reins that she threatened to rear.

Jack was still riding full speed toward a sheep pen behind the barn. Inside the pen, a giant wildcat fed on a sheep's carcass, powerful muscles moving under sleek black fur as it tore into its meal. Next to the beast stood a woman. She wore simple clothing made of animal hide, and her unruly blond hair hung freely down her back. She had an intimidating grace as she laid one hand on the cat's flank, calmly watching its progress.

Tristam realized with a start that she wasn't the only one in there. A farmhand cowered in the corner, trying to make himself as invisible as he could. The man looked too terrified to flee.

Jack didn't slow as he neared the enclosure, but urged his horse on, either not hearing Tristam's shouts to wait or just ignoring them. Gray sailed over the fence into the pen. As dirt flew and sheep scattered, the farmhand jumped the fence and ran. Tristam reined in his horse and gritted his teeth in frustration. There wasn't enough room in the enclosure for both of them.

Jack drew his sword. "I command you to surrender."

Despite his growing fear, Tristam found himself mesmerized by the wildcat. It was a beautiful creature, or would have been if it hadn't been tearing into the sheep with deadly sharp claws. Its head, when lifted, came as high as a man's, and its sleek fur gleamed in the sunlight. As he watched, the creature licked its lips and raised its head, circling around to Jack's left, away from his sword arm....

Too late, Tristam shouted a warning. The cat moved with impossible speed—Jack didn't have a chance. The creature's claws dug a gash from Jack's shoulder to the bottom of his horse's flank. The gelding whinnied and fell heavily on its side, pinning Jack beneath him. Immediately, the cat lunged for the horse's throat, sinking its teeth in and holding on as the animal shuddered.

Tristam screamed, a ragged sound that he hardly recognized as his own voice. In an instant, he was off his horse and running toward the pen. The cat raised its head and focused its amber-slitted eyes on him, and Tristam froze, suddenly realizing his mistake. After one last glance at the motionless Jack, the creature jumped lightly over the fence. Crouching low, it advanced slowly, gaze never deviating. Cursing his moment of madness, Tristam drew his sword, every muscle tight with fear. He had seen how quickly the cat could move.

The animal sprang for Tristam's throat. Tristam's reflexes took over, and he dropped to the ground, blindly slashing with his sword. He felt the blade hit the cat's underside, but the sword edge glanced off its stiff black fur. The cat landed behind him and coiled around. It seemed more focused now, even eager. Tristam hastily raised himself to a crouch, keeping his shield and weapon between himself and the cat. At the cat's next charge, he threw his shield up as he thrust his sword at its neck. The impact jarred his arms, and the cat's claws sent splinters flying off his shield. The beast screamed. When they broke apart, there was a shallow slash across the creature's shoulder. Tristam gritted his teeth and braced himself for the next attack.

The charge never came. It took Tristam a few moments to realize that the woman had spoken. Now both the cat and the woman looked into the distance. Hoofbeats sounded behind him, but Tristam didn't dare turn to look. The cat exhaled through its nostrils and loped back to the livestock pen, crouching down as the woman vaulted over the fence onto its back. She dug her hands into the hair of its neck, and the two sped off across the field and into the forest.

Tristam stood there, petrified, breath coming in painful gasps as he stared after his attackers. Finally, he regained the presence of mind to wonder who was coming. Far up the road, soldiers dressed in Forge's red livery galloped toward the farm. Tristam waved his arms, and a few riders branched off toward him.

Jack.

Tristam jumped into the livestock pen, dread squeezing his chest. His friend was pinned beneath his horse and barely conscious. Blood flowed from the gash in his side, and his breathing was shallow. The part of Tristam's mind that knew about battle wounds whispered that this was mortal, but Tristam ignored it. Jack was going to be all right. He had to be. Tristam removed his shirt and knelt down, pressing the fabric to Jack's side with clumsy hands. The cloth didn't even cover half the gash, but he was *not* giving up.

He needed more bandages. Tristam prepared to take off his inner tunic, but then Jack's eyes flew open. The grimace of pain on his face was real this time. Tristam cradled Jack's head in his arms, looking for a way to distract him.

"This is the second time today a pretty girl has knocked you off your horse," was all he could think to say.

The corners of Jack's eyes crinkled. Perhaps he was trying to smile. It was hard to tell. Then his eyes lost their focus, and his head fell to one side. By the time the soldiers arrived, Jack was dead.

SIX

The veteran knights called it battle guilt. They spoke of it as they took Jack's body away, and as they sat with Tristam in his grief. *When you lose a friend in battle,* they said, *it's natural to feel like you're to blame. But don't let those thoughts consume you. War is fickle. Just fight your best and let the ghosts of every battle rest in peace.*

Tristam had heard the lectures before, had even agreed with them and thought them wise. But he hadn't known how meaningless they would be when confronted with a grave-stone, how they crumbled like ashes against the unrelent-ing accusations in his head. He should have ridden faster. He should have tried harder to get Jack to leave the pen.

The only injury Tristam had sustained was a bruised hip. With every step of his horse, the ache radiated up his back and toward his shoulder. Perversely, he welcomed the pain, even shifted to make it worse. It somehow helped ease the guilt as he traveled the same country road, passing by the curve where Jack had pretended to fall off his horse the day before. The order had come in this morning. The Minister of Defense was investigating the attack and required Tristam's presence.

The farm was somber after yesterday's tragedy. The few workers around walked quickly and didn't acknowledge his presence. Most obvious signs of the attack had been removed; the dead had been buried and the wounded taken to the healers. But it wasn't possible to erase an attack like that in one day. A gate still hung off its hinges, and the dirt was uneven in places, trampled and churned by panicked crowds. And of course, it took more than one night for blood to wash away. Tristam hesitated at the road before forcing himself onward in disgust. What kind of knight was he, if he couldn't even return to the scene of a battle?

His mare was skittish about being tied by the road. As Tristam soothed her, a knight in full armor approached. Tristam raised his hand in greeting. "I am Tristam of Brancel."

The knight nodded. "Malikel wants to speak with you."

Tristam started. "Sir Malikel? Of the Council?"

"I know of no other Malikel in Forge. Councilman Willem is here as well."

The names were enough to snap him out of his self-pity. Though he had only seen them from afar, Tristam recognized them right away. Head Councilman Willem was a formidable man, with a lordly manner and penetrating eyes. He'd been appointed to the Council at the age of thirty-five, a decade younger than any other councilman, and had risen to his current post in ten years. Next to him stood Sir Malikel, unmistakable with his dark brown skin and close-cropped hair and beard. Malikel was the only foreigner in the Council, and rumor had it that he had started his career as a common mercenary in Minadel. His appointment as Minister of Defense had been unheard of at the time, and was a testament to Malikel's unparalleled brilliance as a strategist. Though his enemies at court made snide comments about his background, even they did not question his decisions on the battlefield. Under any other circumstance, Tristam would have been thrilled to meet him.

"Councilmen," said the knight accompanying Tristam, "Tristam of Brancel is here."

Willem acknowledged Tristam's bow with a nod. "The Council thanks your family for your long record of service to the city. From what your instructors say of you, I'm expecting great deeds from you as well."

Malikel extended his hand. "My deepest condolences. I understand Jack was a good friend of yours." It was a simple statement, but somehow Tristam got the impression that Malikel meant it. "We wouldn't usually ask a squire to return so quickly after a battle," said Malikel, "but the enemy is a new one, and you were the closest witness."

"It's my privilege to serve the city." Tristam hoped he sounded more sincere than he felt.

"I need to get the full account from you while it's still fresh in your memory. Can you take us to where it happened and walk us through what you remember?"

The other knights fell away as Tristam led Malikel and Willem around the back of the building. Where to begin? Tristam started with the alarm bell and Jack riding to the farm. He described the chaos and his first sight of the strange woman with her wildcat. The farmhand trapped in the pen. It was by no means a smooth account, with both men watching him so intently. Tristam found himself directing his words to Malikel, who had a way of listening that made it easier to get the words out.

"This woman," Willem asked after Tristam finished, "was she with any others?"

"I didn't see any—"

Tristam stopped short as they came to the livestock pens. He'd known that the sight would trigger memories, but he still wasn't prepared for their intensity. He closed his eyes against the rush of images—the screaming crowd, the cat's sharp claws. After a few moments, the flashbacks subsided and Tristam let out a ragged breath.

"This is where it happened."

The Councilmen entered the pen, but Tristam hung back. It was empty now. The workers must have moved the sheep—or perhaps the barbarian woman had opened the gate. The dirt was stained with blood where Jack and his horse had lain.

"You say the cat was inside here?" said Malikel.

"Yes. Jack rode his horse in as well. I was on the other side, outside the fence." *Doing nothing.*

Willem cleared his throat. "This is a small pen. Young Jack shouldn't have come so close to the enemy without reinforcements."

Tristam stiffened at Willem's words. "With all due respect, sir, Jack rode in to help a trapped man."

Willem raised his eyebrows. "And traded his life for a

farmer's. I admire your friend's bravery, but he didn't do you or the farm any favors by getting himself killed."

"Perhaps we should focus on the matter at hand, Willem," said Malikel. The words brought Tristam back to his senses, and he swallowed the retort on his tongue.

"You're right, of course," said Willem. "My apologies, Tristam. It was not my desire to make this any more unpleasant for you."

"No offense taken, Your Grace," Tristam replied woodenly. But Willem's words haunted him. Had Jack's attempt to save the man actually been a foolish mistake?

Willem dusted off his hands. "Regardless, I think I've seen all I needed to see. I will leave the rest in your capable hands, Malikel." He swept his eyes across the farm. "The barbarians choose a bad time for this. Our treasury is already stretched thin."

"Indeed," said Malikel with a wry smile as Willem walked off. "We are all concerned about how the attacks will affect the treasury."

Tristam deemed it unwise to reply. Finally, Malikel turned his attention back to Tristam. "These are definitely the Demon Riders we've heard about from traders and farms farther out. There have been reports for the last few months, but they've never come within a day's ride of the city before."

"Has anyone spoken to them?" asked Tristam.

Malikel shook his head. "The Demon Riders don't seem interested in negotiating. They take what they want, and they're vicious enough to get it." He surveyed the farm. "We'll have to increase patrols in the area."

It seemed such a paltry effort. Were they just going to wait around for the barbarians to attack again? Tristam once again saw Jack's face in his mind, eyes glassy from blood loss. "May I ask a question, sir?"

"Of course."

"Why haven't we pursued the riders and tracked them down, rather than waiting for them to come to us?"

Malikel paused, and Tristam wondered if he had spoken too presumptuously. But the official didn't seem annoyed when he responded.

"It's a fair question. We will do that, but the forest is large, and their attacks are spread out. None of the merchants or other travelers have ever seen evidence of where they're settled. I'll send out search parties, but I expect it could be a while before they find anything."

Tristam's next thought rushed into his head, accompanied by a quickening of his pulse and a fierce determination to see the idea through. "Sir, I have another request."

"Yes?"

He wiped his palms on his tunic, steeling himself. "I would like to submit my request to work under you, for the Ministry of Defense."

For the first time in their conversation, Malikel looked surprised. "I was under the impression that you are not yet a knight."

"I will be in a month, sir."

"Your commander informed me you were planning on joining the road patrols. Why make this request of me now?"

The question gave him pause. If he went through with this,

he would stay in the city. He felt a tightening in his chest at the thought of abandoning his plans. But then, could he really join the road patrols with a clear conscience? Ride off into the forest and let others deal with Jack's murderers? "My commanders will testify to my character and performance. I'm at the top of my cohort in combat and in strategy—"

"I am perfectly capable of assessing your qualifications myself, Tristam," said Malikel. "That wasn't my question. What I want to know from you is why you're requesting this."

Malikel's response startled him, and Tristam suddenly found himself tongue-tied. "Jack was a good friend of mine," he said, stumbling over the words. "I can't sit idle while those who attacked him are still attacking our city. Sir, I've seen these cats up close. I've fought them. I would be useful to the search."

"True," conceded Malikel. He fell silent, again studying Tristam. "Your commanders do speak highly of you."

"I promise you I will work hard, sir."

Malikel nodded. "It's an unusual request, but I will consider it."

SEVEN

The walls of the inner compound were three stories high, constructed of smooth granite and topped with a walkway wide enough for three men to walk abreast. The sides of the wall were vertical except for the very bottom, when they bent outward to form a wider base. Kyra found that if she sat where the sides angled off, she could lay a parchment across her bent knees as she sketched.

Unlike the outer portion of the Palace, the Fastkeep was older and built for security. The buildings here were squat granite structures with thick walls. Occasionally, Kyra saw a courtyard, but these grassy spaces lacked the trees and fountains that graced the outer Palace.

She shivered. Although the top of the wall shielded her from the wind, the granite's chill seeped through her trousers and the back of her tunic. It would have been warmer inside the buildings, but she had strict orders not to go indoors. She'd found the nights difficult at first without the benefit of movement to keep warm, but weeks of sitting out at night had acclimated her to the cold.

Kyra put the finishing touches on her map and tucked away her charcoal. Carefully, she rolled up the parchment and slid it down the back of her tunic before turning around to grip the wall. She listened for footsteps. Satisfied that no one was nearby, Kyra threw her grappling hook over. The clink of its landing rang through the darkness.

The sound was too loud for comfort, and she wasted no time in pulling herself up. Once away from the wall, Kyra allowed herself a quick stop by the kennels. As she came close, several noses pushed between the slats of the fence. A few dogs whined loudly, and Kyra shushed them with a whisper. She'd always been a good dog talker. Even the fiercest guard dogs whimpered and rolled over, baring their bellies to her in fear. Flick teased her about it, saying that dogs were the best judge of character, but he couldn't deny that her gift was useful in that line of work.

Once safely out in the city, Kyra jogged to the Guild. Two shadows detached themselves from the side of the building as she approached. The larger shadow planted itself squarely in front of her.

"Let me through, Bacchus," she said, her shoulders tensing. "I've got something for James."

Bacchus snorted. "The fine lady." He didn't move.

Kyra moved to step around him. Bacchus started to block her again, but the other shadow spoke. "Let her through, or you'll hear from James."

Bacchus glared and stepped aside, muttering loudly about a good-for-nothing wench. Kyra skirted past him to the door and entered without knocking.

She glanced into the storeroom as she passed. One man she didn't recognize was polishing weapons at the back. Rand was also there, talking to a man whom she thought was called Alex. Rand saw her and beckoned her over. Alex gave her an amused look and sauntered to the window without speaking.

"I'm bringing a map to James," she said.

"He's busy," said Rand. "We can get a round in."

Kyra's bones ached at his words. Practice fights with Rand were more like beating sessions. She was learning, but still hit the ground nine times out of ten. She suspected that was why Rand enjoyed them so much. "I'm tired, Rand," she said.

"What else are you fixing to do while you wait? Pick flowers?"

Kyra scowled, pulled the map out the back of her tunic, and laid it safely against the wall.

"Bare-handed," he said, motioning her toward some straw mats. "Hit me." He raised his fists.

Fistfights were a lost cause, since Rand was so much stronger. He easily blocked her punches while overpowering any of her own attempts to defend herself.

"What's the point?" she asked, raising her hands.

"You won't always be armed."

She humored him with a test jab to his nose. He brushed it out of the way and she skipped back before he could return the blow.

"Faster," he said.

She lunged again. He blocked. Her other hand was raised in front of her face, and he knocked it back into her nose.

"You get hit enough by other people," he said. "No need to

start doing it yourself." In the corner of her eye, Alex chuckled. She stepped back, exasperated.

"That's enough. I'm bringing this map to James and then I'm going to sleep." As if on cue, she heard a door open and close in the hallway. Kyra grabbed her map and headed for James's study.

"Come in."

James didn't look up as Kyra laid the map on his desk. She waited without speaking. Finally, he set aside the papers he'd been studying and stood, unrolling the parchment and holding it open against the table.

"The east wall," Kyra said.

James didn't respond. Kyra watched his eyes as he scanned the pathways and buildings she'd drawn. James lifted a hand from the parchment's edge and traced his finger along a line.

"This walkway here, is it bare or lined with trees?"

"That part's got young trees." She took out her charcoal and reached to mark the detail. James shifted slightly to accommodate her but remained squarely over the table.

"And these rooms over here," he pointed. "Did you look inside them?"

"I saw a bit from the window. They look like rooms for official records. Lots of cabinets."

He studied the map a while longer. Finally pushing it aside, he looked up at her. "Has Rand been teaching you to fight?"

"We've been practicing." Kyra wrinkled her nose. It still tingled from Rand's blow.

"Are you learning?"

She shrugged. "Ask Rand."

He glared at her. "I didn't hire you to skip around drawing maps forever. I need you inside the buildings, and I need you to be able to handle the occasional guard."

They'd been over this before. Kyra took a deep breath, trying to gather some patience. "Why's fighting so important for going indoors? It's the same guards, and nobody's seen me yet."

"It's closer quarters inside," said James.

"And there's more places to hide. I've been doing this for a long time," she said.

"That's enough." There was an edge to his voice. "For what I pay you, I expect you to learn quickly and do what you're told."

Kyra bit her tongue.

He sat back down at his desk and turned his attention back to his papers. "I'll talk to Rand. I expect you to be ready in a few weeks. Is that clear?"

She pressed her lips together. "Aye."

"Good."

Flick found Kyra tossing pebbles down the second-floor hallway of The Drunken Dog. She was crouched on one knee beside a pile of rocks, her back to the staircase, weighing stones in her hand before throwing them one by one with a twist of her wrist. A few bounced off the wall at the end and came to a stop, while others ricocheted at an angle and clattered around the corner. Flick came up behind her and swiped two rocks from the back of the pile. Kyra ignored him for a few more tosses, then pulled both her knees to her chest and looked up at him.

"I heard you take them," she said.

"Of course you did, master thief."

A door halfway down the hall opened, and a disgruntled man looked out. "Quit the racket. I'm trying to sleep."

Flick kicked Kyra before she had a chance to retort that it was well past noon. He gave the man a cheerful smile. "Sorry, Byron. We didn't think anyone was still here. Though I'll wager you had a late night because luck favored your dice last night?"

Byron grinned. "My purse is a mite heavier this morning."

"Keep that up, and you've got to buy us all drinks," said Flick.

"Mayhap I will, if luck smiles again."

Flick gave Kyra a stern look as Byron returned to his room. Kyra rolled her eyes before he could start lecturing her about her rudeness. Flick shrugged in resignation.

"So what now? Is the Guild teaching you to kill people with gravel?"

Kyra snuck a glance at Flick's face, but he seemed relaxed enough. They'd had a rough couple of weeks after she'd joined the Guild. He'd yelled at her, hurt that Kyra had made such a big decision without confiding in him, and worried about her safety. They didn't speak much for a while, but eventually it became too exhausting to be angry at each other, and things slowly drifted back to normal.

"The rocks are a blind," she said. "If I throw these on a stone floor, they might make enough noise to busy the guards while I slip by. I just need practice getting them where I want."

"You know, if you stayed out of the compound, you wouldn't have to worry about guards at all."

Kyra twirled a stone between her fingers. "James is demanding I learn to fight—keeps on saying he wants me to handle the occasional guard."

Flick guffawed. "You? Against a shieldman? He'd just toss you over his shoulder while he calls his friends."

Kyra dug her knuckles into Flick's shin and watched without pity as he yelped and jerked his leg away. She understood his point though. A thief's main protection lay in avoiding detection, and fighting a guard would be admitting to failure. It only took a second to sound the alarm, and even if she escaped, the resulting lockdowns would make it impossible for her to return. Concepts like this seemed obvious to Kyra and Flick, but they somehow evaded James.

Flick squatted next to her.

"So what do they have you doing now?"

"You know I can't tell you the details."

He snorted. "Pardon me for sniffing after Guild secrets. Tell me generally what you do, then."

"I've not turned into a hardened killer if that's what you're wondering. I in't even stealing these days."

"And they don't mind?"

"Most of them."

"Most?"

Kyra kicked herself and affected her most nonchalant shrug. "It's nothing. Just some of the men don't think I can carry my weight."

"Really?" Flick looked genuinely surprised. "After they've seen what you can do?"

She thought for a moment. "I guess they've not seen me work. I go to the Palace alone."

"The lads around here were skeptical when you first started joining me on jobs. But they shut up after a few times out with you."

"I'd forgotten that." Kyra gathered the stones. "I need to go. I'm supposed to meet Rand."

She waved good-bye and slipped down the stairs, relieved that he hadn't pressed her further. As understanding as he'd been today, she still didn't want to give him any new reason to object.

Brendel was sitting alone in the dining room, humming and scribbling on a parchment with one hand while tapping the table with the other.

Kyra sidled up to him. "How goes your masterpiece, good talesinger?"

"The meter's wrong," muttered Brendel.

Kyra looked over his shoulder. "The part with the bees?"

Brendel nodded, still scribbling. "Don't ever be a talesinger, Kyra. You'll end up as crazy as I."

"I've seen worse," said Kyra. "How much of your tales are true, Brendel? Have you been to the Far Lands yourself?"

"Of course they're true. Would I lie to such a pretty face?" He punctuated his question with a wink.

Kyra rolled her eyes. Brendel put his pen down and looked at her, his expression turning serious. "I really don't know," he said. "I've traveled many places and heard many tales. Some of them sound pretty far-fetched. But then..."

"Then what?"

"I've never been across the Aerins, but I talk to people. And you start noticing differences between the folk who believe the tales and those who don't. Those who don't, they're folk like you'd meet every day, living their lives around Forge. The ones who believe the tales though, they're the ones who've traveled farther. I've met a few Far Rangers myself, and they've told me some pretty spectacular things."

"Think they're stretching?" Kyra asked.

"Could be. Or maybe there's really something out there, beyond the mountains. What do you think, Kyra?"

Kyra shrugged. "If a griffin landed in front of me, I'd pay attention. But I've enough to think about than to go chasing after them. Though I wish a hive of bees would solve my problems."

Brendel laughed. "Don't we all?" The talesinger waved her on her way.

According to legend, Lady Evelyne won over the felbeast by bringing him fresh honey. The monster was so touched at her kindness that he didn't kill her, instead taking her into the forest to live with him. Kyra amused herself for a while by imagining what the assassins would do if she showed up with a honeycomb. Somehow, she doubted it would be enough to win Bacchus's friendship.

In many ways, life had improved since she joined the Guild. She no longer worried about money; her lodging was paid off for the next few months, and she still had some extra. (In fact, Kyra was playing with the idea of renting an extra room at the Dog for Idalee and Lettie, since Lettie was still getting sick.) Also, Kyra was picking up useful skills. Though her fighting lessons

65

with Rand were humiliating, Kyra had to admit that they would come in useful if anyone tried to push her around again.

But joining the Assassins Guild had its disadvantages. As a thief working by herself, she had known the details of every job she undertook. Working with James, however, was like exploring a dark building with a single candle flame. Kyra didn't know why she was drawing maps, or even what she would be doing the following week, much less what big job James eventually had for her.

Then there were the other assassins. They were all men, hardened by their years in the Guild, and even the ones who weren't overtly hostile looked down on her. As long as James made her work alone, Kyra didn't see any way to earn their respect.

Kyra wiped any sign of worry from her face as she arrived at the Guildhouse. As always, a few men were standing around the storeroom. Kyra walked by Bacchus, who was applying liquid from a vial to one of his daggers. Kyra shuddered when she realized it was probably poison.

Rand had already set up some straw mats and was leaning against a stack of boxes, tossing a dagger in the air.

"Am I late?" she asked, watching the light reflect off the spinning blade.

Rand shook his head and motioned her closer. He handed her a sack heavy with coins.

Kyra weighed the sack in her hand, puzzled. "Is this for next month?"

"It in't for you. This is for any folk who need it. Tell them it's from the Guild."

"Really, anyone?" Was James trying to win favor within the city?

"Can't be your friends and can't be yourself."

"Who exactly are my friends?"

Rand grinned. "That's for James to decide. I'd play it safe though." He jerked his head toward a man in the corner. "Ho, Jason. Show the lass your arm." Jason scowled, but pulled up his sleeve. Even from a distance, Kyra could see the angry burn scars across his arm. "That's what happens if James catches you dipping into the handouts. Understand?"

Kyra nodded. She would certainly have no trouble finding folk who needed the coin.

Seemingly satisfied, Rand gestured toward the mat. Kyra put down her things and stepped on, feeling the rough strands through the bottom of her shoes. The mats were better than the stone floor, but they still weren't a welcoming surface to fall on. As they stood facing each other, Rand grabbed a sheath from his belt and covered his dagger, tying it well with a leather thong so it wouldn't slip off during the fight.

"You got yours?"

"Aye," she said. At least with knives, they weren't quite so unevenly matched. She reached for her ankle and released her knife from its bindings, slipping it out the leg of her trousers. It had a plain handle and a blade the length of her hand. By now, she was getting a sense for its reach in a fight.

Rand attacked as soon as she stood up, coming at her with a downward thrust. She stepped sideways, backing lightly out of his reach. She was starting to get the hang of it. The secret was to stay away from him and keep moving. At close range, anyone in the Guild could overpower her with brute strength. But she was faster than most, and if she stayed alert, then she had a chance.

"What are you, a dancer?" Rand said. "Pretty moves won't do any good here."

Rand belonged to the "insult well and often" school of practice fighting. At first, it had made Kyra nervous, but it did make things more interesting. She smiled. "If I'm just a pretty dancer, come get me."

He rushed her again, this time with a more controlled attack. As Rand passed, she dropped to the ground and hooked her ankle around his knee. She didn't move away in time, and he fell on top of her, pinning her knife arm with his side. For a moment she was stunned, but as he shifted to bring his own knife around, Kyra realized her legs were free. She kicked up and wrapped both ankles around his head and under his chin. The unexpected move snapped his head back and he loosened the pin on her arm. Twisting her wrist, she grabbed her dagger and passed the sheathed blade across his throat.

A fair kill. Kyra whooped in triumph and flopped back down, grinning at the high ceiling as she caught her breath. It was clumsy, but she'd take it. Her elbow was raw from pressing against the mat, and she waited for Rand to get off her so she could inspect it.

"What you think, Rand? Not bad for a thief girl."

"Pure luck. When you do that one out of every two times, *then* you can say something." But there was amusement in his voice.

"Most times you won't have the luxury of rooting after a fight."

At first she thought it was Rand speaking, but then her opponent climbed to his feet to reveal James watching from the side. This was the first time he'd seen her practice. Kyra jumped up, all cockiness draining away as she turned to face him.

James locked gazes with Rand until the redhead cleared his throat and looked away. As Rand stepped off the mat, James removed his outer tunic, tossed it on a nearby box, and took his place. He reached a pale but well-muscled arm toward Rand, who tossed over his dagger. James caught it and beckoned Kyra toward him. She stood, frozen in place, wondering what he wanted and why he was there. James motioned again, more curtly. This time she obeyed.

"Let's see what you've learned," he said, settling into an all-too-comfortable fighting stance. It wasn't a request.

Kyra tried to ignore the prickling up her spine as she raised her blade and they started to circle each other. She had never seen James fight before. He moved deliberately with no wasted motion, graceful yet dangerous, and his eyes never deviated from her face. There was no taunting or boasting. James just circled her with cold, unswerving focus. He said nothing, and his face gave no indication of his thoughts.

A long time passed with no attack. Out of the corner of her eye, she noticed that activity around the warehouse had stopped. People were watching.

James continued to circle her. Kyra wiped her sweaty hand on her trousers. Was he expecting her to make the first move?

She felt slightly light-headed. Her breathing became quick and shallow, and she struggled to slow it down.

Finally, she lunged at him, thrusting her blade toward his torso. He moved aside just enough to avoid the sheathed tip. She felt a stunning blow on the side of her face at the same time her legs swept out from under her. The ground came up hard. She lay there for a few moments, eyes closed, not wanting to see who was watching.

"Keep mapping for now," she heard James say. Painfully, she rolled onto her side, keeping her eyes on the ground as he walked away. A loud laugh sounded from the corner of the warehouse, and Kyra felt her face flush with shame. To her horror, she felt tears prickle behind her eyes. She forced them back by sheer will and looked toward the source of the laughter. It was Bacchus, slapping his thigh in amusement before following James out.

EIGHT

The sting of that fight stayed with her. It was days before she could look another Guild member in the eye, and more than a week before she could think about James without flushing in shame. To work off her frustration, Kyra trained harder than ever, practicing in every free moment and grabbing Rand for lessons whenever he was around.

And it started to pay off. She became faster with a knife; the movements started feeling more natural. But she was also constantly sore and covered with bruises. Her olive skin camouflaged them to some extent, but she still had to dress strategically to hide her latest bumps. Kyra was doing her best to pull her sleeve over a blue spot on her wrist one afternoon as she helped Bella in the kitchen.

In Bella's world, knife work implied something completely different from Kyra's lessons at the Guild. James and Rand might be formidable opponents, but no one could possibly match Bella's skill with a cleaver. Kyra watched in fascination as the cook quartered and trimmed five newly slaughtered chickens with efficient speed, deftly transforming them into ingredients for the night's stew.

Bella glanced at Kyra as she dropped the last chicken quarter into the pot.

"I appreciate your efforts to remove every last bit of peel, dear, but if you keep this up, we'll have no turnips left."

Kyra shook her head in mock resignation. "I really think Idalee's got more of a knack for this than I do."

They both looked at Idalee, who sat at the opposite side of the long kitchen table, very seriously chopping potatoes. Next to her, Lettie played with a lump of bread dough.

"Mayhap you're right," mused Bella.

Kyra pushed her stool back and lowered her voice. "You really think she'll be helpful, Bella? I don't want them making trouble."

"They won't. Idalee's smart and determined to work hard. Laman doesn't mind hiring her as long as she does the work and Lettie stays quiet. Are *you* sure about covering the rest of her lodging?"

"I'll be fine." She checked again to make sure Idalee wasn't listening. "James pays me plenty."

"Here, let me do the rest." Bella took the knife and rolled the remaining turnips away from Kyra. "You've taken a liking to them two, haven't you? I don't see you renting rooms for any of the other gutter mice."

Kyra shrugged, self-consciously tracing the grains on the table surface. "I don't know," she said. "Lettie's so small. I was that small once."

"I really don't know how you survived out there by yourself. Lettie had Idalee, at least."

"Don't remember much. Just really wanted to survive, I guess."

"From what I could gather, you had a tough time. You were a suspicious little mouse when we met. The first few times I fed you, you watched Flick eat half the bowl before you dared swallow anything."

"Really?" Kyra couldn't decide which was more amusing—that she'd suspected Bella of poisoning her food, or that she'd been willing to sacrifice Flick as her taster.

"And then there were the nightmares," said Bella.

Those, she did remember. The nightmares had followed her off the streets into her early years at The Drunken Dog. Flashes of bright heat. A woman's dark eyes. Teeth. She remembered Bella coming into her room when she woke up screaming, holding her and stroking her hair until she stopped. That gesture, more than anything, was what had finally broken through Kyra's walls.

"I don't have them as often anymore," said Kyra. And she was better at suppressing her screams when she woke. Kyra supposed she was too old these days to run to Bella, but a selfish part of her still missed Bella's touch.

"I'm glad to hear it. And you've done well for yourself. You rented your first room with your own earnings," said Bella.

"I stumbled on a flush trade." Kyra gave the cook a wry smile. "I could train Idalee. . . ."

"Please don't. I've given up on straightening you out, but I still hold out hope for these girls."

"I'm surprised you're at The Drunken Dog, Bella." Bella didn't speak much of her past, but Kyra knew that she and Flick's mother had been merchants' daughters. Not nobility by any means, but not the type to be spending time with thieves and gutter rats.

Bella spun a turnip against her carving knife, peeling off the skin in a long spiral. Kyra grabbed the longer shreddings from the table as they fell. "About fifteen years now, sixteen since my husband passed. And if you'd told me seventeen years ago that I'd end up at the Dog, I would never have believed it." She put the knife down. "It was hard. You're old enough to understand now. My husband was gone. Who knows what had befallen my son in his eagerness to chase griffins and mermaids? Not many places would take a woman in, and I was lucky that Laman knew and respected my husband. I needed work and a place to stay. I couldn't afford to be choosy."

Kyra had a sudden vision of a younger Bella, clutching her bags at the door of the tavern, jaw clenched in determination as she looked over the tavern's rougher patrons. "I suppose it took some getting used to."

"It did." Bella was looking off into the distance now.

"Did it get better?"

She looked thoughtfully at Kyra. "I got used to it. But what really made it better was finding Flick again. And meeting you."

"Really?"

"Well, I'd given up on ever finding my sister. When she sent for me, and I found out she was dying..." Bella trailed off for a moment. "I see her in Flick sometimes. And the two of you gave me hope. Most of the patrons here are hard, jaded. The

74

two of you still had some innocence about you, despite what you'd gone through."

Kyra gave Bella a crooked smile. "Innocence? Do you still think that?"

"You two are more innocent than you think, and less innocent than I'd like."

It occurred to Kyra that with Bella's son dead, she'd have no one to care for her when she grew old. The responsibility would fall to her and Flick. Kyra found that she liked the idea.

"Well, Bella, if it makes you feel better, you don't have to worry about Idalee following my footsteps. She doesn't have the knack for it."

"Just as you don't have the knack for preparing vegetables." Bella eyed the pile of shreddings. "How did I do?"

Kyra held up the longest shredding, about the length of her forearm. "Not bad, but not your best." She fetched the scrap bucket and held it as Bella swept in the turnip peels.

"Are you leaving?" said Bella. "I have some leftover roast from lunch."

Kyra obediently served herself some roast before excusing herself.

She thought about Idalee and Lettie as she left the tavern. What was it that made them different from the others? If Kyra was honest with herself, it was Lettie who really tugged at her heart. While the other children evoked memories of Kyra's adventures with Flick, tiny Lettie tapped at more painful times—the earliest years before Kyra was old enough to fit in with the other children. Those were a blur of cold nights and days without food, scavenging like an animal in Forge's alleyways. She'd been different from the others. Younger, smaller, and darker, strange in the way she moved and hid in the shadows. The other children had given her a wide berth. They'd feared her, even though she was too small to pose a danger to anyone. Though things got better, Kyra never got rid of the nagging feeling that she had barely survived, that she owed her existence to a few strokes of luck. Did she help Lettie out of compassion or out of some selfish desire to rewrite those memories?

The Guildhouse was more crowded than usual, with about a dozen people gathered in the storeroom. James stood at the back, speaking with Bacchus and a few others. The rest of the men were scattered amongst the wares. Some were stacking boxes against a wall, while others were just standing and talking.

"Rand," she called. "Why's everyone here?"

He looked surprised to see her but sauntered over. "Job tonight. James needs the extra hands to raid an armory."

"An armory?"

Rand shrugged. "That's all he's told us." He joined a cluster of men as they erupted into laughter at some joke she couldn't hear.

Kyra had never seen the Guild mobilize such a large group before, but she doubted James would explain his plans to satisfy her curiosity. She glanced around the room one more time, looking for someone else she could ask, but aside from Rand, there wasn't anyone she knew well enough to talk to. She moved on to James.

"Why are you here?" he asked brusquely. His expression

clearly signaled that she needed to say something or get out of his way.

"Am I to keep mapping this week?"

"Aye."

"I've gone over everything twice."

"Go over it again."

A clear dismissal. James directed his attention back to the man he was talking to. Frustrated, Kyra turned toward the door.

Someone plowed into her from behind, and she stumbled into the wall.

"Sorry, miss," Bacchus called with a grin. A few of the men looked in her direction and chuckled as Bacchus entered their circle.

She usually ignored Bacchus's jabs, but this time something snapped. Maybe because it was the first time Bacchus had physically touched her, or perhaps Kyra had just kept things bottled up for too long. She earned her keep in the Guild just as Bacchus did. If she ever left, it would be on her terms. She strode toward the group, furious, but stopped when she saw Bacchus's face. He looked smug, delighted even, that she was reacting. She stopped. What was she going to do, yell at him? Attack him with James watching? She couldn't fall into his trap. But she also couldn't let this continue, not if she was going to stay in the Guild. She took a shaky breath, glanced once more at Bacchus, then spun around, heading straight back to James.

"Take me tonight."

James stopped midsentence and stared at her.

"Take me with you tonight, on the job."

She expected him to be angry at her interruption, but he gave her his full attention.

"Why?"

"If you're cracking an armory, you can use me. I'm a thief, remember?"

"You're supposed to be mapping."

"I'll make it up later this week."

"I won't pay you extra for this."

Kyra fought to keep her voice steady. "That in't a problem."

James studied her face, then gave a curt nod. She might have imagined it, but he even looked slightly pleased. "Fine. You can come, but don't get in the way."

Kyra merged with the rest of the group as they followed James out the door. They moved as a silent unit through the chilly streets, and Kyra focused on the sound of their boots against the gravel. As the cold night air worked itself into her tunic, she found herself wondering what exactly she had volunteered for.

A tall stone building became visible in the distance, and they stopped. A nervous man waited at a street corner. His eyes flitted briefly over the group of assassins as James approached him.

"I tried the key," said the man. "It didn't work; they must have changed the locks."

There was a tense moment of silence. James's mouth tightened. "The key doesn't work?"

The man reached into his pocket and took one out. "I tried it last week, and it was fine. I'm sure it was fine." His voice was shaking. "There were rumors . . . a raid at the Palace . . . the new Minister of Defense cracking down. . . ."

Ignoring the man's ramblings, James handed the key to Bacchus, who took it and disappeared down the street. A few minutes later, he came back, spat on the ground, and shook his head.

"Tell me again," James asked the man. "The key worked last week, but somehow it doesn't work now?"

"I swear I tried it," said the man. "I can get the new one. It should only take a fortnight."

"We don't have a fortnight," said James. He turned away from the man in disgust as two assassins grabbed and held him.

James pointed at Bacchus and two others. "Come with me." As he turned, his gaze fell on Kyra. "You too."

Bacchus led the way, dashing from house to house. Kyra followed his trail, unsure whether to be pleased or terrified that James had included her. They stopped in the shadows across the street from the armory's door. It was an old building, and judging from its architecture, had been repurposed from some more elegant function. Both the massive door and the walls were decorated with intricate carvings, and the building's bell tower rose high above the surrounding houses.

James turned to Kyra. "Pick the lock. Watch for guards—there's two of them making rounds."

Kyra nodded, her heartbeat quickening as she scanned the road. No sign of the guards. She reached for her lock pick as she sprinted to the main door. Ears tuned for approaching footsteps, she inserted her lock pick and twisted the lock, but stopped. Something didn't feel right. Her stomach clenched as she probed the tumblers. She'd heard of these locks before. The tumblers pointed in different directions. They couldn't be picked. Kyra squeezed her eyes shut. This was not the time to fail.

She retreated back to the group. "The lock can't be picked," she said.

"You can't pick the lock?" asked James.

"Nobody can."

He had already turned away from her, a move that cut deeper than anything he could have said. "Get the guards." The other assassins dashed toward the building and separated, melting into the shadows at different points. Then, silence. Long minutes passed until finally Kyra heard footsteps. A guard rounded the corner, scanning the road.

It happened quickly. Suddenly, the guard was clutching at his throat, falling backward into Bacchus. The assassin kneed the small of his back, and the guard stopped struggling. As Bacchus dragged him back to James, Kyra saw that the man was still conscious, face twisted in pain. The guard's eyes fell on Kyra and their eyes met. She stood, petrified by the pain and pleading in his eyes. Why was he looking at her? She was powerless here. He had to see that.

Another assassin came back, dragging a second guard.

"Search them," said James. The assassins stripped the men of their clothing, inspecting pockets and lining.

"Nothing," said Bacchus.

James jerked his head. Another assassin grabbed one of the guards and pinned his arms behind him. Bacchus walked to face him and looked to James for a cue. James nodded and Bacchus struck him across the face. His blow connected with a sickening thud. Kyra's stomach churned and she looked away.

"Where's the key?" James's voice was quiet.

"We don't have it." Another blow, and a muffled groan. The guard sputtered. "Beat me all you want. We don't have the key," he said.

Bacchus looked happy to oblige. Kyra shuddered and once again averted her gaze. She forced herself to look at the building, concentrating on the intricate carvings, following it up the side of the archway to a high window....

"I can get us in," she blurted.

Her voice sounded loud in the darkness and she felt everyone look at her.

"What?" said James.

"The window. I can get to it and unlock the door from the inside."

"The windows are all shuttered and locked."

"Not the second-story windows. The high one, in the bell tower." She heard a few incredulous murmurs, but as she looked closer at the building, she became more sure of herself. The window was actually a set of three tall and narrow slots that looked wide enough to squeeze through. She didn't see any bars or shutters, and the decorative stonework leading up to it gave plenty of footholds.

"You sure?"

"Give me a quarter hour."

All eyes shifted to James. "Do it," he said.

Kyra wiped her hands on her trousers as the others cleared away from her. The stonework didn't begin at ground level, but there was a ledge above the first floor. Using a nearby barrel as a step, she jumped and caught the ledge, pulling herself over.

She stood for a moment, belly to the wall, probing it with her fingers. The rock would support her weight. She took a breath and dug her fingers into two of the deeper carvings. One foot went up next, and then she pushed herself up as she reached for a higher handhold. Soon, she had worked out a rhythm and climbed steadily up the side of the building.

Her spirits lifted as she climbed. This was what she could do, and do well. Kyra was aware of her audience and, after the day's frustrations, couldn't resist showing off a little. Her swings were higher than usual, and her final jump from the stonework to the window perhaps more dramatic than it needed to be. Finally, she hung from the window, her hands clinging to neighboring slots. With another breath, she pulled herself up and slipped an arm in. From there, it was a quick scramble to squeeze her head and torso through, and the rest of her body followed.

The bell tower was strangely peaceful. There was a platform where the bell was supposed to be, and everything was covered with a thick layer of dust. From there it was easy to find the stairs back down, and it was indeed about a quarter hour after she started when Kyra turned the bolt and opened the front door. She caught different expressions as the men passed by. Some regarded her with appreciation. Rand stared at her as if seeing her for the first time. More than one looked at her with fear in their eyes, and she caught Alex making a sign to ward off evil spirits. Bacchus's gaze still wasn't friendly, but it didn't hold his usual sneer.

James was the last to enter. After he passed, Kyra let the

door close. When she turned around, all the men except James had gathered below the atrium's high archways. The head assassin stood next to her.

He caught her eye. "You did well."

It was the first time since she joined the Guild that he'd praised her, and she found it surprisingly hard to hold his gaze. She looked away, taken aback at the flush rising in her cheeks and glad that the darkness kept it hidden. She was a professional, not some giddy farm girl.

"It's what I do."

They walked in silence to rejoin the group. Right before they reached the rest, Kyra remembered. "The guards. What happened to them?"

"They're being held outside. We'll release them once we're done."

She searched his eyes for as long as she dared. James looked back at her, gaze calm and steady.

"Come see me tomorrow before you go into the Palace," he said. "We can discuss your next step."

NINE

The beagle loped through the sparse underbrush, stirring up dust with her nose and ears as she zigzagged along an invisible trail. She'd tracked without fail this morning, but now her focus was wavering. Any rustle in the bushes became an excuse to slow down, any birdcall an invitation to look around.

"Let's take a break," Tristam said. The dog talker, a young shieldman named Martin, whistled sharply. The hound made a tight turn and sat down, tongue lolling. Tristam leaned against a tree as the five shieldmen with him settled nearby.

Martin poured some water for the beagle and scratched it behind the ears. "She's bored with the scent," he said. "And her left paw is sore. I don't think we'll get more work out of her today."

"How do you see all that?" Tristam asked.

Martin shrugged. "Practice helps. But I've always been able to read them, and they've always been friendly to me." As if to illustrate his point, the beagle pressed up to him and started licking his face. Martin fended off her efforts halfheartedly, turning his head so he could talk without getting kissed full on. "Even when I was knee high, the neighborhood dogs would come wagging their tails. My da too. Runs in the family, I guess."

"I had a friend who was like that, only with horses," said Tristam. "They loved him—always coming to beg for treats or get rubbed down. He could pick up on their moods, and they always did what he asked."

"Sounds like a handy trick for a knight to have," said Martin.

"It served him well," said Tristam. Though he wondered now if Jack's gift had hurt him in the end. If Gray had not been so obedient, would the horse have taken Jack into the pen with the demon cat?

"Here's another set of tracks." Another shieldman crouched near a cluster of trees and pointed at the dirt.

It had been tracks and droppings the entire trip and nothing else. No sign of human habitation, no campsites. They'd followed the trail through the forest for two days, but the dogs just led them in circles.

Tristam brushed a layer of dust from his forehead. "I don't think we're going to find anything. Let's go back to Forge."

Relief washed across his companions' faces, and Tristam couldn't blame them. He walked ahead of the group, brooding as they began the long hike back. Malikel was a fair commander, but all the same, Tristam didn't look forward to delivering news of yet another failed expedition.

Working under Malikel had brought a blur of changes and new responsibilities. Most of Tristam's days were spent in the Palace reviewing reports and poring over maps. And after Tristam was knighted, Malikel started sending him on scouting missions in the forest. He welcomed those chances to get out of the city, but it wasn't easy leading a team of guards into the wilderness, especially since many were older than he was. Time after time they found nothing.

You could be out on the road patrols right now, with nothing to worry about except where to set camp, said a spiteful voice in his head.

"Is everything all right, Sir Tristam?" Tristam cleared the frustration from his face as Martin came up next to him. It was still new, this need to set an example and keep morale high. The days of riding with Jack, rolling their eyes and making cracks behind the commander's back, were over.

"Just call me Tristam. You know Malikel doesn't place much stock in titles or ceremony."

Martin grinned. "I thought about that, Sir Tristam. The problem is, everybody else still does. If I get used to dropping the 'sirs,' I might forget with someone else. Then things would get unpleasant."

Tristam smiled despite himself. He liked Martin. The cheerful shieldman would have made a fine squire had he been higher-born. While the other Red Shields stayed aloof from their commander, Martin often spoke to Tristam. Either the young Red Shield was too young to have learned to keep a respectful distance from his superiors, or he was just too gregarious to help himself. Selfishly, Tristam couldn't bring himself to discourage him.

They picked their way through the forest, ducking under the occasional branch. "Do you believe the whispers, sir?" asked Martin.

86

"What whispers?"

"The villagers say the Demon Riders raise their cats like their own children, nursing them at their own breasts. They say that's how the cats grow so big, and why the cats are so obedient to their masters."

"That sounds painful," said Tristam with a grimace.

Martin fought to keep a straight face. "Does indeed, sir."

"Well, they can keep that secret to themselves," said Tristam. "I'd be happy just to find them."

"It's like they disappear into thin air, in't it?" said Martin.

Tristam let out a breath, no longer bothering to hide his frustration. "This is our third trip out. We should have found something by now."

Week after week, new reports came in from traumatized farmers. Livestock slaughtered, villagers injured or killed. Adding more patrols hadn't helped much. Oftentimes, soldiers only arrived after the barbarians had fled.

"It doesn't make sense," said Tristam. "The tracks are here, and they're fresh. But why don't we ever find anything else? If only these trees could talk." Tristam paused. "Martin, when are we reporting to Sir Malikel tomorrow?"

"Midmorning."

He conjured the map of the forest in his mind, trying to determine how far they were from the city. "Lead the group back for me. I'll stay a little longer."

Martin looked at him suspiciously. "You're not planning to do anything unwise, are you?"

"No, nothing foolhardy. I just have a hunch."

"If I may speak freely, Sir Tristam, you should at least tell us what you're planning. Sir Malikel won't be pleased with us if something happens."

"Fair enough. Maybe we're going about it the wrong way, looking for them when we clearly know they come here often. We should stay here and wait for them to come to us."

Martin frowned. "May I have permission to accompany you, sir?"

"I can't ask you to do that, not without more thought. It's too—"

"Too dangerous? You're starting to contradict yourself, sir."

Tristam chuckled. "It *would* be nice to have some help, but I can't command it of you. This isn't a Palace order; it's just my crazy idea."

"It's just a few more hours out here. How much trouble could we get in?"

It seemed unlucky to respond. But the decision was made, and Tristam informed the others.

His mood improved as he and Martin split up to find hiding places. The plan might not be a stroke of genius, but it felt good to be doing something different. A fallen log beside a boulder provided adequate cover, and Tristam settled behind it after brushing away his footprints. Despite the log's musty smell, it was a comfortable hiding spot.

Eventually, the birds and insects started calling again. Intermittently, Tristam whistled and heard Martin's whistle in response. As it grew darker, the air became cooler. Thankfully, it was warm for early summer, and his cloak kept him comfortable. The moon was just beginning to rise when a twig snapped close by.

Curious, Tristam peered around the log. Several shadows passed a few paces from his hiding place. Large shadows. Tristam jumped to attention. He waited until the footsteps grew fainter, then slipped out of his hiding place. Ahead, he could see something moving. Broad shapes, with four legs and a feline grace. A thrill of excitement ran through him and he followed, ignoring his doubts about the wisdom of trailing several enormous beasts.

The shadows moved at a quick pace, weaving between the trees, when suddenly, they merged with the rest of the forest. Tristam blinked. The forest was still.

"You're far from the city, knight." A lightly accented voice spoke from behind him.

Tristam spun around and inhaled sharply.

It was her. The dark blond hair, leather clothing, the haughty tilt of her chin. After weeks of nightmares, there was no way he'd fail to recognize that face. Tristam's hand went to his sword.

"Keep that in its sheath unless you wish your throat torn open."

Tristam saw the cat then, advancing on his left with hungry eyes. For a moment, Tristam struggled against the compulsion to lunge for the woman anyway, avenge Jack before the cat reached him. Then, something moved in his periphery, and Tristam snapped his head around to see another beast approaching from the other side. Slowly, Tristam let go of his sword.

"What are you doing here?" asked the woman.

"I could ask the same thing of you, barbarian." He should have been terrified, but his fear was fading away, replaced by weeks of suppressed rage. All he wanted to do was hurt her. Make her pay for what she'd done, whether he survived or not.

The Demon Rider tilted her head, looking at him curiously. "We've met before."

"We have."

"Your friend," she said slowly. "He was careless."

"He was doing his duty."

"And now you wish to avenge him. That is unwise."

"I *will* avenge him."

The woman gave an almost imperceptible shake of her head. "No, you won't." She made a sharp gesture with her fingers. The cats lowered their heads and growled. Again, Tristam reached for his blade. He'd go for the woman first. Run her through before the cats fell on him.

"Call off your pets." Martin's voice sounded clearly through the trees. Tristam turned to see him with an arrow nocked and aimed at the Demon Rider.

Her eyes narrowed. As if responding to some unseen signal, the still-growling cats stepped back. For a moment, Tristam stared dumbfounded. Then he scrambled into action, drawing his dagger and moving behind the Demon Rider, careful never to step between her and Martin's bow.

"Martin's an excellent shot." He forced the woman's arms behind her and pressed the dagger into her back. He had never seen Martin at the archery range, but confidence, real or feigned, was the only way they'd get out of there alive. "Don't test him. You're coming with us." He turned to Martin. "You have a rope?"

Martin slowly lowered his bow and untied a rope from

his belt. Tristam watched the cats nervously as he bound the woman's hands. She didn't resist him, but there wasn't a hint of fear in her muscles. Though—he snuck another glance at the demon cats—why would she be afraid? She wasn't the one holding two gigantic beasts at bay with a dagger.

One of the wildcats hissed.

"If your cats come any closer, you're dead," Tristam said, pulling the rope tight. "You better make sure they behave themselves."

"The cats will kill you if you try to take me."

"I believe you," said Tristam. "But you're still going to escort us safely to the road. We'll let you go when we get there."

The woman's eyes passed over the two of them, calculating, and Tristam started her moving before she had a chance to call their bluff. To Tristam's relief, the cats stayed back. He hardly breathed as they dragged their prisoner toward the horses. The cats followed them from a distance, never getting too close, but always poised to spring. There was an unsettling intelligence in their eyes. Tristam somehow got the sense that they knew exactly what was going on.

"Martin, keep an eye on those . . . creatures." Last thing he needed was for one to ignore his master's command and come to her rescue.

The next half hour was lifted straight out of his nightmares. Marching through the forest, demon cats trailing a stone's throw away. Holding Jack's murderer at the tip of his dagger, yet knowing that he'd have to release her. Tristam's tunic dampened with sweat and his arms began to ache from keeping such a tight hold on the woman. He didn't know how far he could push this, but they needed to be on their horses with a good head start if they wanted any chance of outrunning the demon cats.

Agitated hoof steps sounded ahead. Through the trees, he glimpsed Lady tossing her mane, pulling her bridle at the demon cats' scent.

The Demon Rider spoke again. "If I get on that horse, the cats will attack."

"We'll let you go once we're astride." Tristam nodded to Martin, who mounted his horse and aimed his bow to stand watch as Tristam jumped into his own saddle. "Send your cats to that far boulder."

The woman narrowed her eyes, but inclined her head. The cats backed away, though not as far as Tristam had requested. "They'll go no farther," she said.

That would have to do. "All right, Martin, ready to ride?" Tristam muttered.

"Aye, sir."

He took one last look at the Demon Rider, then gave his horse a sharp kick. Lady jumped into a full gallop. Tristam crouched down as the forest blurred past, urging Lady to go even faster. Behind him, he heard Martin fast on his heels. He rode without looking back until he finally saw farmland in the distance. He couldn't lead the beasts into the farms.

Tristam risked a look over his shoulder. Martin rode madly on his heels, but beyond that, the road was empty. Cautiously, Tristam brought Lady to a halt. The two of them scanned the distance behind them.

"You all right?" Tristam asked between breaths.

"Tired, but kicking."

"I suppose you're going to tell me what an idiot I was for wanting to stay out there by myself."

Martin grinned. "No, Sir Tristam, I would never dream of such impertinence."

"One Demon Rider and two cats?" asked Malikel.

"Yes, sir."

Tristam rubbed his eyes against the sunlight streaming through the window. It had been impossible to sleep after he got back, and he was now paying for it. His head throbbed, and there was a foul taste in his mouth that he couldn't rinse out. Next to him, Martin stared at a pile of books on Malikel's desk, blinking to bring them into focus.

"You're sure this was the same woman?" asked Malikel.

"She recognized me," said Tristam. He shivered as he recalled her voice, her odd way of speaking. Over the past two months, he'd imagined confronting her more than a hundred times. He'd envisioned yelling, threats, a fight to the death. But not the precarious standoff that had occurred last night.

Malikel pushed two mugs toward them. "Drink up. You're both paler than these parchments."

The tea was strong, with the mix of spices common to Malikel's homeland of Minadel, a couple of weeks' journey south of Forge. Too many flavors in one vessel for Tristam's taste, but it did help clear his mind. Martin took a sip, hid a grimace behind his mug, and put the drink back down.

"Did she say anything about who they were, where they came from?" asked Malikel.

Tristam shook his head. "Nothing. She's a strong beast speaker though. Her cats obeyed her completely."

Malikel was silent for a moment. "We'll have to think about this further. But at least we have some confirmation that they're out in the forest."

There was a knock on the door. By the time Tristam registered the sound, Malikel was already halfway to the door. Tristam and Martin scrambled to their feet, but Malikel waved them back down, and they reluctantly sat, exchanging uneasy glances at letting their superior do such a menial task.

Malikel opened the door to reveal a shieldman and signaled for Tristam to wait while he and the shieldman walked into the corridor. Through the doorway, Tristam saw the older man's face darken as the man spoke.

Malikel motioned for Tristam to join them.

"There's been a raid," Malikel said curtly. "Come with me, Tristam; you have an eye for detail."

"A raid?"

"One of the Palace armories was broken into last night. I have my suspicions about who was involved, but I need someone with fresh eyes."

Malikel questioned the guard as they followed him into the city. "I thought we had the locks changed in all the armories and storehouses."

"We did, sir, and only two copies of the key were made."

"And the armory guards?"

"There were two of them, and neither of them had a key. Both guards are missing."

"This is what I was trying to avoid." Although Malikel kept his voice level, Tristam could see the anger in his brow.

A group of men in Palace uniforms were already at the armory when they arrived, some examining the building's outer grounds while others rushed in and out with parchments. He made quick note of the armory's thick walls and solid door as a tired-looking official came out to meet them.

"Sir Malikel."

"Nels, what's missing?" Malikel asked.

Nels sighed, raising a hand to rub his temple. "Fifty to seventy-five sets of studded-leather armor. They didn't touch the heavier ones."

"How did they get in?" Malikel asked.

"There's no sign of damage to the doors, and the locksmith insists these locks cannot be picked. The Palace armor steward and I have the only two keys."

"Could someone have copied the key?" asked Tristam.

"It's possible. Anything's possible."

Nels led them inside, past the atrium, and into the back rooms, where the armor was kept. Their first stop was a large chamber, a quarter of which was stacked with boxes. The room had stone walls with no windows and only one door.

"This is where the leather armor was kept," said Nels. "They took most of it."

The more Tristam thought about the robbery, the stranger it seemed. Fifty to seventy-five sets were enough to outfit two or three units. It was too many for a band of brigands to use themselves, which meant that whoever stole this probably intended to sell it to someone with a sizable force of armed guards. Within Forge, only the Palace employed so many soldiers. There were the neighboring cities of Parna and Edlan, but why would they go to the trouble of stealing something as simple as leather armor?

"What do you make of this, Tristam?" asked Malikel.

Tristam shared his confusion, and Malikel nodded, seemingly satisfied with Tristam's reasoning. "I agree. It's unlikely that Parna or Edlan is behind this. And none of the noble houses of Forge employ this many soldiers. So what does that leave us?"

"I don't know. Is someone building a secret army at Forge's expense? It seems far-fetched."

"It does. And yet..." Malikel led Tristam to the back of the room, away from Nels's hearing. "There's unrest in the city. Whispers amongst the common-born against the Palace. My men have been picking up on it for years. Nothing concrete, but enough that I ordered all the locks changed in our important storehouses. Apparently, that was not enough."

"But who could possibly..."

"Are you familiar with the stories of the Assassins Guild, Tristam?"

"The only Guild I know of is the one from the history books."

The older knight nodded. "About a hundred years ago, they were a threat in the city, dealing in illegal trade and eventually becoming powerful enough to influence the government. The Palace was able to capture their leaders, and the Guild dissolved. But in the past decade, there have been rumors that it never completely disappeared. And since becoming Minister of Defense, I've encountered hints that they, or some organization like them, are returning to power. Reports of strangers asking our low-level servants for information, for example."

"So someone is recruiting spies," said Tristam. Espionage was by no means new to Forge, and all squires learned the basic history. Edlan and Parna were always trying to gain an upper hand, but they usually infiltrated the nobility to learn the goings-on at court. "Perhaps it's not too bad, if they've only been able to get to the servants."

"Don't underestimate your servants, Tristam. They're capable of more than you think. My predecessors as Defense Minister were too busy waving their swords at Parna and Edlan to notice the threats right around them. If they hadn't been so quick to discount the abilities of the poor, they might have acted against the Guild before they grew strong enough to breach our walls." They circled back to Nels. "Show us the rest of the building," said Malikel.

They visited the other storerooms, but none had been touched. Tristam began to see why Malikel would be worried. The raid had been accomplished with unnerving precision. The burglars had known exactly what they were looking for. And even more disturbing was the fact that they'd left no signs of how they had broken in. That, combined with Malikel's suspicions about the Guild . . . Tristam had to fight the urge to look over his shoulder.

After they covered the ground floor, Nels led them to the

unused upper floors. A few smears in one hallway's dust pattern caught Tristam's eye—not quite footprints, but the dust wasn't as smooth as in the other corridors.

"Sir Malikel," Tristam called. He picked his way down the edge of the hallway, careful not to disturb the dust. It led to a small room, meant to be a lookout point perhaps, with three narrow windows opening high above the street. Holding his breath at the musty smell, Tristam crossed to the windows and peered out. The drop was dizzying. He spent a few moments watching the tiny people below before returning his gaze to the windowsill. They were dusty, but one slot was much cleaner than the others.

"Someone was up here." Tristam moved aside to let his commander take a look.

"It looks like it, but how did he get up here? It's too high for a grappling hook, and there are no buildings nearby."

Tristam looked through the window again. The buildings across the road were much too low to offer a way up, and there were no obvious rooftops to either side. An arrow trailing a rope, perhaps? But the armory's façade was solid stone, with no place for an arrow to lodge.

"I don't know," Tristam said. "But if someone had indeed climbed through this window, he could have opened the front door for the others."

"Perhaps," said Malikel. "Stay up here, Tristam, and take a closer look at this room. Let me know if you find anything else."

TEN

Kyra pressed her back against the wall, palms flat on the cold stone of the alcove, ears trained toward the footsteps down the hall. This section was tricky. The door she needed was in the middle of an open hallway. Once she was out there, she'd have no cover while she picked the lock.

She waited until the footsteps faded and glanced into the corridor. Empty. Kyra took her chance and ran down the hallway. The candles cast flickering shadows that settled somewhat as she stopped outside the door.

The knob didn't turn. Kyra hadn't expected it to, but she never knew when someone would forget and save her some work. She looked around again—still safe. Kyra inserted a thin piece of metal into the bottom of the keyhole, twisting it and maintaining pressure as she reached for her lock pick. Some thieves favored sets of picks in different shapes and sizes, but Kyra preferred to carry just one. It required more practice, but one was lighter, simpler, and quieter to carry. Kyra kept twisting the lock as she inserted the lock pick into the top of the keyhole, delicately pushing up tumblers one by one. She knew this lock well by now. The first tumbler to give was about two-thirds of the way in. Then it was the innermost tumbler.

She stayed alert for sounds as she worked. If a guard passed, she'd have to run and start over. Tonight, however, she teased up the last tumbler without incident. The lock clicked open. Tucking her tools back into her belt, Kyra slid into the empty room and locked the door behind her.

The room was lined with cabinets, with a few desks in the middle. By now, she knew that older records were kept in the cabinets while newer ones were usually on the desks. She took a pile of records from the nearest desk, making note of their position and order, and took them to the window, shuffling through in the dim light until she found the one she wanted. Kyra then replaced the rest, fished out a pen and parchment from her belt, and grabbed an ink bottle from the table.

She copied the record line by line. Bella had taken it upon herself to teach Kyra how to read and write a few years ago, and Kyra was glad she had. James's surprised look when she'd told him had been worth it. It took a good half hour to copy the whole thing, but finally she capped the ink bottle and returned the original to its place. She blew on her parchment, then crept back toward the door and pressed her ear against the wood. It was quiet outside.

Kyra made it down a few corridors before she heard footsteps again. She only had time to duck into a side hallway, press against the wall, and hope nobody looked back. The smell of roasted ham teased her nose, followed by three kitchen servants. One carried a half-eaten ham. Another had a platter of cheeses, and the last carried a plate of leftover fruit. The servants would take them back to the kitchen, where they would eat what they wanted and throw the rest out. It was painful to see all this waste, but Kyra couldn't risk following them. The footsteps faded, and Kyra almost started out when she heard someone else. She held her breath as a Red Shield walked past. His scarlet tunic made her flinch. The guards at the armory had worn the same red uniforms. Several times now she'd woken up in terror and lain awake in bed as the beatings replayed in her mind. James had promised her she wouldn't have to kill, that he'd set those guards free. But still... She pushed those thoughts aside and focused on getting out of the Palace.

James was in his study when she arrived at the Guildhouse. She dropped her parchment on his desk. "Trade route schedules for this month."

"Good."

She watched his eyes as he scanned the paper, trying to figure out what he used this information for. "I saw some other records tonight that might be useful. Recent payments for locksmiths."

James looked at her in surprise. "From the Minister's command to change storehouse locks?"

She nodded, pleased at his rare display of interest. "A list of buildings and locks. I can copy it tomorrow."

"Well done. This new Defense Minister is getting to be a headache."

Kyra took her leave. A few blocks from the Guild, a crowd clogged the road, and Kyra slowed to take in the scene. The people were gathered opposite a store, muttering discontentedly but softly. Apparently, they were afraid to anger the shield-men who marched in and out, loading parcels onto a wagon. A middle-aged shopkeeper stood by the door. Anger and frustration were clearly etched in his face, but he made no move to stop them.

Kyra worked her way into the crowd, ears open for gossip. She nudged a woman next to her. "What's going on?"

The woman glanced at her. "The herbalist couldn't make his rent because the trade caravans lost their cargo last week. Caravans finally came this week, so the landlord's taking his rent out of his wares."

"It in't his fault the caravans were raided. How's he supposed to meet his next month's rent with nothing to sell?"

The woman snorted. "Why don't you explain that to Sir Knight?" She gestured toward a young knight who stood by the wagon overseeing the operation. The knight had dark hair, a high-bridged nose, and an aristocratic bearing. He was also surprisingly young, not much older than Kyra, and he said little as the soldiers carried out their duties. Kyra noticed that he avoided looking at the storekeeper. The coward nobleman couldn't even face up to what he was doing. He'd go home tonight to the Palace and enjoy a hot meal while the storekeeper and his family scrounged their remaining coppers.

Kyra was working her way closer when someone grabbed her elbow and she fell against a well-muscled chest. Kyra looked back, opening her mouth to protest, when she found herself face-to-face with James. She snapped her mouth shut, tongue suddenly dry. James's expression clearly said to be quiet, and his eyes flickered meaningfully toward the soldiers. She turned back to the store, pretending that nothing had happened.

"Don't draw attention to yourself." James's voice was a breath on her ear, so soft even she could hardly hear it. "Wait, then follow."

The crowd shifted behind her, and out of the corner of her eye she saw James disappear into a nearby tavern. Kyra couldn't guess his intentions, but following him seemed wiser than continuing to gawk at the spectacle. She counted a few more breaths before going after him.

He was waiting in the entryway and acknowledged her with a quick nod, though he offered no response to her inquisitive glance. A large man, unsteady on his feet, laughed as they walked past. "Tastes running younger these days, James?" The look James shot him was pure ice. The drunk straightened and walked away. James took a seat facing the window and signaled for some ale.

"You're too timid," he said.

"What do you mean?"

He jerked his head in the direction of the drunkard. "The way you react to fools like him. Like you're fading into the wall."

Had he taken her here just to insult her? "I in't rolling over and showing my belly. I know the type. It's less trouble to ignore them."

"That's the problem. You're avoiding trouble from them, but they should be the ones afraid of *you*."

"Right. I'm sure Rand quaked in his boots when he bruised my shoulder last week."

"You're getting better."

"How do you know?"

"I've been watching."

The simplicity of his words—and the way he looked straight into her eyes as he answered—made her fall silent. The serving girl arrived with the ale. James flipped her a coin and looked out the window toward the crowd.

"Why are we here?" asked Kyra.

"It's quieter here," he said simply. Kyra drummed her fingers on her ale mug until he finally spoke again. "I see you've been watching the rent collection."

Kyra shook her head, indignation rising in her chest. "It's not his fault the caravan didn't make it in. Is his landlord so strapped for coin he can't wait a few months?"

"What will you do about it?"

Kyra stopped and stared. "What?"

"Will you let the landlord keep his rent, or return it to the shopkeeper?"

"Why are you asking me?"

"Because you're one of few folk who can do anything about it." When she continued to stare at him in confusion, James laid two fingers on her jaw and guided her gaze back toward the herbal shop. "Who's emptying the shop?"

She pulled back from his fingers. "Shieldmen."

"Just any shieldmen? What are they wearing? Who's commanding them?"

"They're Red Shields. There's a knight leading them."

"And what kind of nobleman can request the service of the Palace guards?"

"He'd be high ranking. In with the Palace somehow."

"Not just that," said James. "He'd have to *live* in the Palace. And where do you think they're taking his wares?"

Kyra's mouth dropped open as she understood his meaning. She laid her palms on the table, staring at its surface as her mind raced. "There's several storehouses in the outer compound. They're too big and cluttered for me to flip through myself. I'd have to know which ones hold the herbs."

She paused, stymied for a moment. James watched patiently.

"But there'd be records," Kyra blurted, answering her own question. She suddenly remembered that there were others in the room and hastily lowered her voice. "They keep the inventory list somewhere. I could easily fetch it."

"Very good."

Kyra closed her eyes, mentally tallying the rooms she needed to search. James was right. She could do something about this, and the rush of power was exhilarating.

"But once I find the herbs, I'll need help raiding the storehouse. I can't do it alone."

"We can help. Just find out where they are, and we'll make it happen."

ELEVEN

Over the next few days, Kyra worked harder than she'd ever worked before. She entered the Palace early and stayed dangerously late, going from chamber to chamber, digging through piles of records. The warehouse inventory wasn't kept with the trade schedules, so Kyra broke into neighboring rooms. She was determined, and it paid off. One week later, Kyra dropped a stack of parchments on James's desk.

"The herbs are all kept together, in a building on the eastern side of the outer compound. It looks like the landlord in't even using them."

James scanned the list. "There's too many here for us to carry out without a wagon. We'll have to decide which ones are the most valuable."

Kyra grinned. "Our landlord was also curious about the coin it'd fetch. He had the Palace herbalist price them, and I nipped that list too. Looks like he has a good stash of Far Ranger goods—the strange ones that the wallhuggers can't get enough of. The dryad-raised flowers by themselves are worth a good quarter of all that was taken."

She stood back, arms folded, not bothering to hide how pleased she was with herself.

"You're enjoying this. Taking things back from the fat-purses," said James.

Kyra gave a quick nod, which James acknowledged with a slight smile.

"I suspected you would," said James. "You've got the skill, and you've got the drive. You could go far if you wanted. It doesn't take long to rise in the Guild. I was fifteen when I joined."

James had never spoken about his past before, and Kyra wondered how old he was. His face had no trace of boyish roundness, and his skin was smooth except for a slight crease at the corners of his eyes. He was older than she was, and probably older than Flick. But he was still in his prime. His quickness testified to that, the taut readiness obvious even as he sat at his desk. She thought back to their fight, remembering his intense gaze and fluid movements. How had he risen to power at such a young age? What did he have to do?

"Why did you join?" she asked him.

"Same reasons as most others. I wasn't an orphan, but I might as well have been. Outside, you're limited by your lineage, your family. In the Guild, if you do things right, you'll go far. Use what you have to your advantage—your abilities, your speed. Some look down on you because they think a lass is too fragile to do what it takes. But even they won't be able to deny your skill."

"Do *you* look down on me because I'm a lass?" she asked.

"No." He studied her a moment, his blue eyes pensive. "Not at all." The last phrase was soft, as if he were talking to himself.

Silence hung for a moment. And then James gestured toward the parchment. "Let me look at these, and we can plan the raid in a few days."

Rand was in the hallway as she left James's study. He leaned against the wall, thumbs hooked in his belt.

"Thought he'd given up on women after Thalia," Rand said.

Kyra only half heard him. "Hmmm?"

Rand snorted and rounded the doorway into the storeroom.

"Wait, Rand, what'd you say?"

He let her follow him across the room before he finally turned around. "Curious, aren't we?"

She scowled. "I didn't hear you. Who's Thalia?"

"Dancing lass at the Scorned Maiden. Red hair, hot and cold at the same time. She was something to see." Rand winked, which annoyed Kyra even more. She never did understand the obsession with dancing girls. "She hated the wall-huggers something fierce too. Never seen a lass with that much fire in her."

"And she and James . . ."

"Been six years, and he in't returned to the Scorned Maiden."

Kyra stopped short, intrigued despite herself at the thought of James having a lover. He was usually so distant—at least he had been until recently. "What happened?"

"His rival got to her, when they were fighting over the Guild." Rand spat on the ground. "A coward and a rich man's lapdog, that one. But it was hard to tell friends from enemies, with all the double-talk and secrets. James tried to wait it out—didn't want to invite trouble—but they surprised us. We lost

Thalia and barely escaped ourselves. That was the last time James ever gave anyone a chance to strike him first." Rand looked at Kyra, a smile playing at the corners of his lips. "Not the tale you expected? There are safer men to pine over."

"I in't pining over—"

But Rand had already walked away, chuckling as he went. Kyra stared after him, tempted to follow, but decided against it. People always talked. The regulars at The Drunken Dog had speculated for years about Kyra and Flick, and now it looked like the Guild was talking about her with James. There was no point in letting it bother her. James was interesting as an assassin and a leader, and Kyra was curious about his past, but that was all. Though she could see why women might find him attractive. Had Thalia known that her life was in danger? Kyra wouldn't be surprised if she had. There was something about James—his intensity of purpose and strength of personality—that could inspire a woman's loyalty despite the cost. Kyra took one last glance toward his study before stepping outside.

The city at midday was a welcome distraction, with markets bustling. Cooks wearing the uniforms of noble houses perused rare mushrooms and spices, while mothers with barefoot children haggled for eggs and flour. A young woman walked past Kyra with a basket of bread. The fresh smell made Kyra's mouth water, and she turned her head to find the woman's stall, thinking to bring a few loaves back for Bella and the girls. It still felt strange to be able to buy things without worrying about money. Strange, but good.

Just then, a woman screamed in the distance. The terror in

the sound cut straight to Kyra's bones, and she snapped her head toward its source. For a moment, no one in the marketplace moved or spoke. Then a man's voice carried over the crowd.

"It's a barbarian attack. Alert the Palace!"

TWELVE

Summers in Forge were hot and dusty. Roads and stonework absorbed and reflected the sun, and passing crowds kicked up dirt, which in turn stuck to Tristam's drenched tunic. Of course, the Council would decide that this was the perfect day to extend an aqueduct. So here he was, with his contingent of shieldmen, passing rocks in the midday heat.

"Bet you wish you weren't working under Sir Malikel just now," said Martin as he hefted yet another cut stone to Tristam.

"Why's that?"

"Because if you were working under anyone else, you'd be supervising."

Tristam grunted and passed the rock to the next man in line. Martin was probably right, but in Malikel's unit, knights and shieldmen worked side by side. "Nonsense." Tristam mustered a grin that felt more like a grimace. "What greater honor can there be than to be roasted to a crisp and worked to the ground so that Forge's noble citizens can have fresh water?"

"I'd forgo that honor for a bath and a nap in the shade, myself."

"No more mention of shade, or I won't last the afternoon."

Tristam wiped the sweat from his brow and surveyed the progress. Despite his complaining, he was actually grateful to be on such a simple assignment. There was something to be said about physical labor, when the task was straightforward and the reasons were clear. The same was not true of his other jobs. One in particular still lingered in his mind. Malikel had recently assigned him to the city's northwest quadrant, and Tristam's contingent had been called in for a rent collection. The herbalist had admitted to failing his rent when Tristam asked, and Tristam understood that Forge's laws needed to be upheld. But days later, he still couldn't forget the despair in the shopkeeper's face as the Red Shields emptied his store, nor could he dismiss the simmering anger in the crowd that had gathered to watch.

Martin's voice intruded on his thoughts. "How goes the search for the barbarians?"

Tristam gave Martin a sideways glance. "You're just full of cheerful conversation today, aren't you?"

"That bad?"

"We've not skirmished with them in three weeks."

Martin's expression brightened. "So they've pulled back."

Tristam's laugh must have been sharper than intended, because a few Red Shields looked at him in alarm. "If only. There have been the same number of attacks. They're just getting better at avoiding patrols. They've changed their pattern of attack. It used to be mostly farms and the occasional caravan. Now it's the other way around."

"That's strange. What do you make of it?"

He shook his head. "One week would be a coincidence. We have a large area to patrol, and relatively few soldiers. But three weeks in a row . . . there's something going on."

"Kind of makes you wish we were out there instead of building an aqueduct, doesn't it?"

Tristam didn't trust himself to respond. It had been one thing to give up the road patrols when he thought he'd be making a difference. But after all this time patrolling the forest, talking to villagers, and poring over attack reports, the Demon Riders were slipping even further away. It was maddening.

Shouts sounded from down the road, and a messenger rode up yelling for someone from the Palace. A crowd of people surrounded him. Tristam heard something about a barbarian attack.

"Make way." He pushed through the crowd. The messenger's eyes were wild with fear. "What's this talk of an attack?"

"In the city, sir."

"The city?" Was the man mistaken?

The messenger forced the words out between gulps of air. "The northern perimeter. I rode at the first sign of them."

It sank in that this was really happening. Tristam grabbed the messenger by the shoulders. "Carry your news to the Palace and muster reinforcements. Make sure they're in mail or plate armor, and outfitted with as many spears as possible. Those wielding swords should use the point rather than the edge. You can't slice through a cat's fur, but you can part it." He turned his gaze to the other soldiers. "Return to the Palace, outfit yourselves, and go immediately to the northern perimeter. Does anyone have a spear?" Tristam asked. One of his shieldmen volunteered his weapon. Tristam grabbed it, dismissed the crew, and ran for his horse. He didn't have armor, but there was no time. The barbarians were getting bold if they were attacking the city perimeter. He needed to get a better look at them.

He rode as quickly as he could down Forge's crowded streets. The messenger hadn't given him an exact location, but as Tristam reached the northern perimeter, he navigated simply by going against the current of people.

As he rode closer, shapes resolved themselves out of the chaos. Tristam slowed, steeling himself against the nauseatingly familiar scene. People ran into each other in their panic. The injured already lay scattered in dirt—the lucky ones pulled to the gutters, the unlucky ones trampled. Three demon cats prowled the road in front of him. Two dug through a market stall, pawing their way through chunks of ham and fish. The third, and largest, was crouched over an unconscious Red Shield.

Tristam leveled his spear and kicked Lady into a charge. The cat didn't look up until it was too late. His spear pierced its chest with a crunch of bone. The impact traveled all the way up his shoulder. The beast screamed, and battle heat rushed through Tristam's veins, only to turn to dread when his spear broke off with a loud crack. The demon cat staggered back with Tristam's weapon embedded in its flesh as Tristam threw his broken spear shaft aside.

Roars filled the air—the other two demon cats had noticed the fight. The largest one clamped its jaws around the injured beast to drag it away, while the other, a sleek tawny-yellow creature, advanced on Tristam. The young knight pulled on his reins, guiding Lady back and desperately hoping that reinforcements would come soon.

The beast sprang. Tristam threw himself sideways to avoid its claws as Lady screamed and bucked. He hit the ground hard, first bruising his shoulder and then cracking his head on the cobblestones. Spots swam in front of his eyes, and he scrambled out of range of Lady's hooves. The cat sidestepped his steed and bared its teeth.

Tristam heard a shout from behind the demon cat. A rock glanced off the beast's shoulder, and the creature turned to see its new attacker. Tristam put his hand to his head, wincing at the pain as he tried to see around the beast. A slender girl, olive-skinned and dressed in trousers and a tunic, was yelling and waving her arms. Was she crazy? He opened his mouth to command her off the street, but his voice came out as a croak. Before he could draw another breath, the girl had run around the corner with the demon cat in pursuit. Tristam staggered to his feet, trying to ignore the hammers pounding at his brain. He grabbed the rock the girl had thrown and limped after them.

There was no sign of either the girl or the cat. Had they turned down another street? He gathered himself to follow, when a man shouted in a language Tristam didn't know. Another cat came into sight, this one pure white, with a rider on its back. The Demon Rider was a man this time, with muscular arms and long black hair that hung to his waist. There was something inhuman about the way the barbarian watched him. Was that anger in his eyes? Disdain? Tristam met his eyes, fury in his own gaze as they stared each other down. The white cat growled deep in its throat, but the Demon Rider shook his head and spoke a command. Both cat and rider turned away, and Tristam slumped against the wall. Then he looked closer at their retreating figures, and his breath hissed out in disbelief.

⊠ ⊠ ⊠

The rock bounced harmlessly off the demon cat's flank. The beast turned away from the injured knight and watched the stone roll away. Then it locked its eyes on her.

Kyra spun on her heel and ran.

She stumbled as she turned the corner, stubbing her toe on something hard, but Kyra forced herself to keep going. Behind her, the cat's growls grew louder. What had possessed her to help that knight?

A windowsill caught her eye, and she scrambled for improvised hand- and footholds to climb as quickly as she could. With every step, Kyra expected to feel claws on her shins, tearing into her flesh. When she cleared the first story, she finally chanced a look down. The cat wasn't there, and Kyra kept climbing. Only when she'd pulled herself onto the roof did she catch a glimpse of movement in her peripheral vision. She scrambled back as the demon cat launched itself off a tree, landing softly on padded feet right where Kyra had been standing.

She should have remembered that cats could climb trees.

It came at her now, like a kitten pursuing a bird, only so much bigger. Kyra desperately looked around. She couldn't get back down, not with the cat right there. Her only choice was to run.

Kyra sprinted across the rooftop, jumping over steps and

praying that she wouldn't step on any weak shingles. She could feel the massive cat chasing, could sense its heavy paw pads as it bounded after her. Kyra reached a gap in the rooftops and leaped. As her feet touched the next roof, a weight pushed her forward. There was a slashing pain as something sharp cut her shoulder blade. She landed hard on her forearms, curling herself into a ball as claws raked her shin and slid off.

She lay there, stunned, but nothing happened. Finally, she twisted her head to see. The cat stood a pace away, delicately sniffing at her injured leg. It made a guttural sound and slowly licked her shin with a rough tongue.

The wet touch shook Kyra out of her stupor and she pushed herself to standing, stumbling onward only to collapse again at the pain from her injured leg. She sat back up, facing the cat and doing her best to scoot away. The demon cat stormed toward her and knocked her down, bending its head down to hers. Kyra closed her eyes and turned her head. She felt the animal's hot breath on her face and resigned herself to the worst. Then the breaths receded, and the pressure on her chest released. Kyra opened her eyes to see the demon cat several strides away, looking at her intently through amber-slitted eyes. Then it turned and bounded off.

THIRTEEN

Kyra winced as the cold cloth touched her shoulder.

"Hold still," Rand growled. "It's just a scratch."

She tried her best not to move, but it stung. "Any others hurt?" she asked as he rinsed his washcloth.

"None from the Guild. Everyone else was smart enough to stay out of the way. You're lucky the Red Shields arrived before that beast did you any true harm."

Kyra wondered what Rand's reaction would be if he knew that she'd put herself in harm's way in order to help a nobleman. And not just any nobleman—the knight who'd overseen the herbalist's rent collection. Kyra wasn't sure herself why she'd done it, though it gave her some perverse satisfaction to think that the wallhugger owed her his life. For all his expensive weapons and training, he'd be dead if it weren't for a city girl with a rock. And soon she'd take back those herbs he'd wrested from the storekeeper.

"Any news from the southwest district?" she asked.

"Alex was down there. Said the barbarians didn't make it that far. Your friends at the Dog are likely fine."

Could be, but she was eager to get back and see for herself. "How is she?"

Kyra looked up to see James, arms crossed as he appraised her condition. She had wound a sheet around herself for modesty as Rand tended her back, and she pulled it more tightly around herself.

"I'm fine," she said.

"Will she be able to climb?" James asked Rand.

"She'll heal up well enough. The scratches aren't deep."

James bent over her, pushing her lightly forward to look at her back.

"I'll take over," he said, waving Rand away. Rand raised his eyebrows but gathered his things and left.

Kyra leaned forward and studied the floor, oddly aware of James's movements as he stepped behind her. There was a rustle of clothing as he sat down, and the sound of the washcloth being wrung. James didn't use any less pressure than Rand, but his touch was quicker, more precise, and less painful.

"You should have been more careful," he said after a while.

"I know." Kyra shook her head. "Just panicked, I guess." She drew a sharp breath as James touched a particularly sore spot.

"Easy." He laid his hand at the base of her neck and squeezed gently. Kyra slowly let her breath out, and James continued cleaning.

"Just stay out of the way. You should know how to do that." He dabbed the area dry. "Hold your arm out." James took her wrist between his fingers and guided her arm to the side, pressing a bandage to her shoulder and expertly wrapping it with a long cloth. "We'll have to move back the raid a week or two.

Keep your shoulder clean. Change the bandages every day, and come back when you can move normally again." He stood up to leave.

"James—" Kyra called before he moved out of earshot. He stopped.

She drew a breath and spoke before she lost her nerve. "The armor we took from the armory raid . . . I was trying to remember what style it was."

"We took several different kinds." His face gave nothing away.

"But most of it was leather, wasn't it? With metal studs."

James gave a noncommittal shrug. "It's a common type of armor. Why do you ask?"

Kyra blinked rapidly, once again seeing the Demon Rider in the marketplace, clad in his oddly familiar leather armor. "No reason," she said. "I just like to remember what I take."

"We took many sets of armor that night. I'd have to check the records to get the specifics. Any other questions?"

She flushed red, unsure as to whether she imagined his mocking tone. "No, that's it."

"Good. Come back when you're ready."

☒ ☒ ☒

"They had armor this time. Leather-studded armor." Tristam leaned over Malikel's desk, emphasizing his assertion with a firmly planted palm.

"You're sure it's from the armory raid?" asked Malikel.

"I spoke to Nels. It matches his description of what went

missing. It's just too much of a coincidence. They must be getting help from the Assassins Guild."

"And now you're thinking..."

"Maybe they had help avoiding the patrols."

Malikel nodded his agreement. "Go check. I'll join you in a couple of hours."

Tristam rubbed the bruise on the back of his head as he walked to the archive room. The Palace healer had lectured Tristam about facing enemies without reinforcements, and as much as he hated to admit it, she was probably right. Tristam owed his life to that girl who'd thrown the stone at the demon cat. He'd combed the streets after the attack, hoping to thank her, or at least find out if she'd survived. But there had been no sign of her.

The archive room was empty, and Tristam went straight for the far cabinet, pulling out the parchment on which he'd recorded the barbarian raids since the first farm attack. He had a feeling he was close to the answers he needed about the Demon Riders. He just needed to look in the right place.

He slid his fingers down the left side of the paper, scanning the dates, looking for any clue, any hint of a connection. The attacks were spaced out unevenly but had averaged about one or two per week for the past four months. The barbarians' first engagement with Palace troops had been in May, when he and Jack had stumbled across that fateful farm raid. Over time, encounters had trickled off, and in the past three weeks, they had evaded troops completely.

In addition to the attack logs, there were patrol schedules, some of which he had helped draw out. They were set only a few days in advance and purposely changed from week to week.

Tristam laid the patrol schedules on the table next to the attack logs. At first glance, there didn't seem to be any pattern between patrols and attacks. But then... He stopped and checked the last four attacks. They all occurred in regions for which there had been no patrol assigned that day.

Tristam jumped as the door opened and Malikel walked in. "Did you find anything?" the older man asked.

He related his findings. "The pattern only holds for the past four attacks, so I can't be sure. But it's suspicious."

Malikel lowered himself into a chair, face grim. "You realize what this would mean, if what you say is true?"

Tristam nodded, fighting a rising dread. Patrol schedules were a closely guarded secret, set a few days beforehand and known only to a select few. This was far more serious than a low-level servant informing on daily activities. If the barbarians had known the patrol schedules, then the Assassins Guild's reach was much, much, deeper. "It could still be a coincidence," he said, though his voice lacked conviction.

Malikel shook his head. "It isn't. Think about the way the attacks have changed recently. How their targets have changed."

"The trade caravans." The realization killed any remaining hope he had of being wrong. "The barbarians are focusing on trade caravans because they now have their schedules." Schedules that were again known only to select Palace officials.

"We need to know everyone who is privy to this information," said Malikel.

Tristam nodded. "I will compile a list of all knights and officials who are informed of the patrol schedules. We can start questioning people tomorrow."

FOURTEEN

"Kyra, Flick, look!" Idalee stood with a bowl in her right hand. Behind it, she had stacked two plates along the length of her arm. Now the girl was taking careful steps around the kitchen, hovering her other hand over the dishes to keep them from falling.

Flick applauded. "You'll be helping out in the dining room in no time." Idalee beamed and continued her slow circle.

Kyra forced a short smile and tried not to think about paying for broken dishes. She turned back to the kettle where Lettie's herbs were boiling. "I think this is the last batch she'll need," she said to Flick. "She's hardly had trouble lately."

"Moving here has been good for her." He reached for an empty bowl and held it steady as Kyra poured water into it.

"Idalee, you're going to break them!" Kyra snapped. The girl, who had been adding yet another plate to her load, jumped and very nearly proved Kyra right. Luckily, she held on long enough to dump the dishes onto a table. The plates clattered but stayed intact.

"Whoa, Kyra!" warned Flick. Kyra turned back and lifted the kettle spout just as boiling water overflowed the bowl.

"Sorry," she muttered, reaching for a rag. From the corner of her eye, she saw Idalee give her a puzzled look and leave the kitchen.

Flick looked askance at Kyra. "You all right? You've not been yourself since the attack."

"I know." She avoided his eyes. "I'm just having a hard time forgetting the demon cats."

"You sure that's the only thing?"

Kyra glanced around the kitchen. There was no one else there, and the sound of stew boiling muffled the voices in the next room. She hated admitting she was wrong, but...

"How do you decide what's too much?" Kyra asked.

"Too much?"

Kyra started to elaborate but stopped, wondering how much she could reveal.

"What are they having you do, Kyra?" Now Flick sounded worried.

"Nothing," she said quickly. "I mean... I've not done anything myself."

"But you're bothered by what they do."

"I suppose. They're... I don't know. Some things... right now they scare me, but I worry I'll get used to seeing it."

"Worried you'll turn into them?"

Kyra nodded uncertainly.

To Flick's credit, he let the moment pass without reminding her that he'd warned her of that very possibility. Instead, he was silent as he stirred the bowl. "I *have* seen folk change over time. Some of the lads spent too much time around the wrong people. They got used to it too, and either got in trouble or turned into someone they didn't want to be."

"And it's not just that," said Kyra. "What if the jobs are helping them do something I don't want to help with?" She wondered if that made any sense, but Flick nodded.

"They don't tell you the reason for your jobs."

"No." She shook her head. "I can't figure James out. What if I'm actually helping them bring down the city or something?"

Flick laughed. "That would be impressive indeed." Kyra kept her mouth shut about the demon cats and the armor.

"Look, Kyra, you know how I feel about them. If something doesn't feel right, you should get out." Kyra held a flask steady as Flick filled it.

"It's not that easy. Some of the jobs are worth it. I feel like I'm making things better." She wanted to say more—how good it felt to live without money worries, how nice it was to be taking care of people rather than leaning on Bella and Flick, but she couldn't find the right words. And were those her only reasons? An image of James flashed through her mind, and she ignored the sudden tightness in her stomach.

"And I don't know anything for sure," she finished lamely.

Flick sighed. "I in't really the one to go to for moral dilemmas, Kyra. Bella's better at that."

"Bella didn't even like it when I was just stealing."

"Bella's a good woman, and surprisingly understanding."

Kyra twisted the cap onto the flask, closing it tight. "I'll figure it out."

Flick looked up. "You're not reporting to the Guild this week, are you?"

"No, James told me to rest."

"Me and the lads are raiding a house in the northeast quadrant tonight. We could use a good cracker."

"One of the big houses?" She perked up despite herself. It had been a long time since she'd run anything with Flick, and she missed those trips.

"You in?"

Kyra straightened, an enthusiastic reply on her tongue, when her motion pulled at the scabs on her back. "Oh," she said, "my shoulder."

"That's all right, you won't have to climb. It's an easy job. It'd just be fun to have you in the crew."

True, if she didn't climb, her shoulder would probably be fine. "But if something happened, and I reopen the wound..."

"Nothing will happen. It's an easy crack. One guard, no dogs."

He was probably right. But on the off chance that he was wrong...James had delayed the raid once already because of her shoulder. She bit her lip.

A muscle tightened on Flick's jaw, and his smile disappeared. "Forget I asked."

Kyra jumped, startled at how his tone had changed. "No, it's all right. I can—"

"It's fine, Kyra. Really," Flick's voice was tight, his words clipped. "We have enough men. No need to risk your shoulder."

He stood up. "I should go check my ropes." He left the room before Kyra could say anything more.

When Kyra returned to her room that night, she heard whimpering from Lettie and Idalee's quarters. She knocked lightly on the door, then peeked inside when the whimpering didn't stop. Through the darkness, Kyra could see Lettie turning and kicking on the bed.

"Lettie?" Kyra whispered, and moved closer. The girl continued to flail about, but was obviously sound asleep.

Kyra glanced to the other side of the bed, surprised that the older girl wasn't comforting her sister, only to see that no one was there. She sat down and stroked Lettie's hair, whispering comforting words much as Bella used to. The child opened a sleepy eye and closed it again. Her breathing steadied, and she relaxed.

Kyra tucked the blankets around Lettie and took care not to jostle the mattress when she stood. Was Idalee gone because Kyra had snapped at her earlier? She doubted it. It wasn't like Idalee to run out like that. Kyra searched the hallways of the upper floor, then the lower floors. She was beginning to worry when, finally, she found Idalee sitting outside the back door with a blanket wound tight around her shoulders. The girl gave a self-conscious smile as Kyra approached.

"It's late," said Kyra gently.

"I know. I should go back in."

Kyra sat down beside her. "Any reason you're out here? Was it because I snapped at you today?"

For a moment, Idalee looked confused. Then she shook her head. "Oh no, not that."

"I'm sorry, by the way," said Kyra.

Idalee shrugged her scrawny shoulders. The girl seemed preoccupied with other thoughts.

"So why aren't you in bed?"

Again, that self-conscious smile. "It's silly," Idalee said.

Kyra nudged Idalee with her hip. "Well, I already know you're silly, so you don't have to be embarrassed."

There was a long pause. "I just like to sleep out here sometimes," Idalee said.

"Why?"

Idalee scrunched up her face, still hesitating, until she finally let out a breath. "I don't want to get used to sleeping in a bed. In case I have to go back out there."

Kyra knew the fear deeply, the worry that getting off the streets had been a fluke, that she would somehow lose everything and end up back where she started. She'd grown better at suppressing it over the years, but it had never completely disappeared.

"We won't let that happen."

The words felt empty, weightless even as they left Kyra's lips. Kyra could tell from Idalee's expression that the girl didn't believe her. Idalee had seen too much of life to be comforted by a trite remark.

Kyra sighed. "Sorry. I'm not sure why I said that. I know you're not a child anymore."

Idalee tucked her bare feet farther under her blanket. Bella had given her shoes, but the child never wore them. "No, I understand," she said. "Sometimes it's better to pretend we can control things."

Kyra put an arm around Idalee and pulled her close. "When I first started living here," she said, "I squirreled away a roll from every meal. I always kept at least six rolls in my room. Fruits and meat pies too, sometimes. For a while, Laman couldn't figure out why there were so many rats around."

Idalee smiled. "He forbade me and Lettie from keeping food in my room when I moved in." She paused, and her voice became more hesitant. "Lettie's a lot happier than she used to be. She's got so much more meat on her bones now than when it was just me trying to feed us."

"You've always taken good care of Lettie. Even when it was just the two of you."

Idalee wiped a furtive hand across her eyes, and Kyra pretended not to notice. It was then that she remembered. "I'd forgotten. James gave me some extra coin to share with anyone who needed it. I can't give it to my friends, but I'm sure we could pass it to the other gutter rats. Do you want to visit them tomorrow?"

"Coin?" Idalee looked confused. "Just to give out?"

"That's what Rand said."

Idalee's eyes brightened and she gave a quick nod. "They'd really like that."

Kyra smiled. "Great. We'll find them tomorrow evening."

It would be good for Idalee. For both of them.

She reported back to the Guildhouse a few days later. James was surveying the storeroom.

"How's your shoulder?" he asked.

"Like new."

"Really? I'd expected it to take a few more days."

She swung her arm experimentally. There was a lingering bit of stiffness, but it wasn't bad at all. "Mayhap it wasn't as bad as it looked." As proof, she pulled her tunic down over her shoulder. The skin was new but whole, and there were hardly any scars. James traced the pattern of what had been a claw mark. The light touch made her shiver.

"You're right," he said.

A voice in her head pointed out that with her quick recovery, Kyra could probably have run that job with Flick, no problem. She pushed it aside. They'd done fine without her—come back with several bags of flour and dried meat. She'd offered to help him carry his spoils into the back room. He'd declined.

James led her to his study, where he took out a map and rolled it open on the table. It was one of her earliest drawings of the outer compound.

He pointed at a building midway between the outer and inner walls. "This is the storehouse, right?"

Kyra nodded.

"Ideally, I'd send four men in, plus you. That's enough to carry out the herbs of most value without being weighed down. The question is whether we can get four men in this far."

Kyra looked closely at the storehouse, considering several possible routes. "I don't think we can. There's guards doing half-hour rounds in this region. We'd likely run into several, and a crew that big is hard to hide."

James traced a path with his finger. "What about this way, through the kennels?"

"The kennels?" Sometimes James had the strangest ideas.

"There are less guards, but that's because they don't need to patrol an area housing several dozen guard dogs. We'd never get through without raising the alarm."

"Do they bark at you?"

"No, but I'm a dog talker. They'll stay quiet for me, but I in't good enough to get four strangers through."

"We can drug the dogs. I've something that will put them to sleep long enough to get us by. They'll be groggy in the morning, but not enough to alarm the handlers."

Kyra cocked her head. "Put a kennel full of dogs to sleep? How strong is this medicine?"

"It'll do the job, if you can get it into their water bowls."

She wondered for a moment how much easier life as a thief would have been if she'd been able to get dogs to nap for Flick and the other boys. Kyra looked at the map with new eyes, intrigued by the possibilities. "How long does it take to put them out?"

"You'll want to wait at least three hours to make sure all the dogs have taken some. Even then, you'll need to be on the lookout for any that didn't get enough. Not all of them will drink it right away."

"I can do that." She could probably encourage them to drink too.

"When the dogs are ready," he continued, "you can meet us outside the east wall."

She nodded, forgetting her doubts about the Guild as the excitement of planning took over. "I can lead you in from the perimeter. Between the wall and kennels, there's one guard we'll have to dodge. We'll be safe enough passing through the kennels if the dogs are asleep. On the other end, there's one other Red Shield, but he only passes once every thirty minutes. Once we're inside the storeroom, we'll be fine if we close the door and keep the noise down. They hardly ever check inside."

"Good." James looked down at the map. "Then the question is who to bring. I'll need my best."

"Bacchus?" asked Kyra. He seemed to be one of James's favorites.

"No. Whoever goes in will have to take orders from you, and I don't trust him to do that." The corners of his mouth crept up when he saw Kyra's expression. "Aye, I do notice what goes on in the Guild. Bacchus *is* one of my best. He's loyal. He'll take a knife for me without question, and he's gotten us out of trouble more times than I can count, even when it was my mistake that put us there. But he can be . . . stubborn, about some things. He'll come around with time."

"All right," said Kyra. "No Bacchus, then." She had to admit it was a relief. Bacchus had not been openly hostile since the armory raid, but they weren't exactly the best of friends.

James squinted at the wall, lost in thought. "Alex is solid all around. We'll take him. Rand's fast, but he loses his head under pressure. Shea can keep him in line if we keep them together. Will you be the only one scouting ahead?"

"Should be. I don't see why we'd need other scouts."

"This will do, then. Shea can't fend off multiple guards, but if we stay together, it shouldn't be a problem."

"You know your men well," said Kyra.

"Your job is to crack the Palace. This is mine."

She wondered if James had a similarly clear picture of her

own strengths and weaknesses. She snuck a glance at his face as he studied the map. There really was something about him, and Kyra no longer found it hard to believe that he'd risen to power at such a young age.

After the broad strokes were planned out, they went back through for the specifics. James asked about the area in minute detail—the guard schedules and shelter available on each segment of their path. With each additional point they discussed, Kyra's respect for James grew. He had a remarkable memory, referring to details she had given him weeks ago, and an impressive ability to map out multiple possibilities and contingency plans at each step. Kyra couldn't remember the last time she'd had such an engrossing discussion. They spoke the same language, instinctively agreeing on the important issues and working off each other's ideas in quick succession.

"Can you pick the storeroom locks?" James asked.

"Not the outside door. I'll have to climb in one of the windows and pick the inside entrance. Can you four hide that long in the open?"

"You're not the only one who can dodge guards, Kyra."

She looked up, worried she had offended him, but his eyes were friendly, even amused. Suddenly self-conscious, she looked down.

"Of course," she said. "We'll have an hour or so in the storeroom. Will that be enough?"

"If we work quickly."

Kyra noticed how close together they were standing—so close she could feel the heat from his forearm as they both leaned over the desk. She flushed and drew her arm away. James pushed back from the table, studying her again with a thoughtful expression. "I've never met anyone quite like you, Kyra." His voice was soft, lacking its usual edge.

Kyra wondered if she should step back, but her body wouldn't cooperate. Instead, when she sensed James leaning toward her, she lifted her gaze to meet his. She was dimly aware of the rise and fall of his chest as he moved closer. Then he hesitated, lashes flickering as he looked from her eyes down to her lips. Kyra shivered and closed her eyes.

She heard his sharp intake of breath and felt him move away. When she opened her eyes, James was again turned toward the table, face closed.

"It's a good plan," he said, deftly rolling up the map. His voice was cold, businesslike. "I'll tell the others. We'll do this tomorrow night."

Kyra stumbled back. She needed air.

"Is there a problem?" asked James.

"No," she stammered as she backed out the door. "It's fine."

Kyra turned and fled into the hallway, taking in huge breaths as she burst out the door into the summer breeze. Over and over, she replayed Flick's warnings. James was a trained killer. She shouldn't trust James. *Couldn't* trust him. And she needed to pull herself together before tomorrow's raid.

As she walked home, her thoughts gradually cleared. With James a half hour behind her, Kyra felt more herself. But even as her confusion faded, she remembered how it felt to stand next to him. Her forearm was still curiously warm. She touched it and wondered how long it would be before the heat faded.

FIFTEEN

In the meantime, Kyra had a job to prepare for. It was one thing to climb the ledges herself, a wholly different challenge to lead others through the grounds. She had gear to check, maps to review, and schedules to memorize. Kyra buried herself in these tasks, going step-by-step through their route and making note of all the places they could hide. For good measure, she sharpened her dagger and replaced the length of rope she used with her grappling hook. It was good to have something to concentrate on, and if James sometimes intruded on her thoughts, she pushed him aside and planned harder.

The next evening, she entered the Palace early. There was a lavish party in the outer compound, and Kyra had to hide periodically from giddy couples out for a walk. Thankfully, drunken voices carried far, and tipsy lovers were not the most observant of people.

The kennels were open air, surrounded by a tall fence. Peering through the slats, she saw fur-covered bodies and heard the occasional snuffle but didn't see any signs of people. Good, the handlers were gone for the day.

The gate creaked slightly as she pushed it open, and fifty sets of canine ears turned in her direction. There were a few whines. One or two dogs bowed to placate her, and a few of the braver ones sniffed in her direction. Kyra let out a slow breath and closed the gate behind her.

The animals were kept according to type. Closest to the fence were small hounds with floppy ears and friendly dispositions. These were kept in pens of five. The larger attack dogs lived farther back. Each of the bigger dogs was chained to its own doghouse, probably to prevent fights from breaking out.

Kyra made her way around the entire kennel, first hitting all the enclosures. A pinch in each bowl, James had said. The beagles were of two minds. Half cowered in the corner while the other half stayed close, showing her their bellies and whimpering. She mixed the powder into their bowls with no problem. After those, she moved on to the attack dogs. Most whined and backed away. One particularly large wolfhound growled when she came too close, but quieted when she shushed him.

After hitting all the water bowls, Kyra retreated into a corner, hugged her legs, and waited. The dogs remained restless for a while, but gradually returned to their business. Some lay down while others scampered amongst themselves. Gradually, they curled up on the ground, sinking into deep slumber. As more fell asleep, she returned to the ones still awake and commanded them to drink. Finally, the kennel was still except for a few beagles, who blinked sleepily. Kyra was sure they'd soon succumb as well.

"Good night," she whispered as she made her way out.

She used the trek back as a chance to compose herself.

Whatever her thoughts about James, she couldn't afford to be distracted tonight. Still, when Kyra reached the meeting spot, she was glad for the darkness that obscured her face. James, Rand, Alex, and a fourth who must have been Shea waited for her outside the compound. Her heartbeat quickened when James met her eyes.

"The dogs are asleep," she said.

"Good," said James. His manner showed no hint of what had passed between them the day before, and she was grateful. "Let's go."

The four men pulled masks over their heads, and Kyra took the lead climbing back up the wall. Once at the top, she scanned the interior. No movement. She tugged lightly on the rope, and it stretched taut as the next person pulled himself up. She recognized Rand by a lock of red hair that had escaped his mask. Kyra made a mental note of each man's clothing and build so she could identify them from a distance.

One by one, the others climbed over and blended into the shadows on the other side. James came up last, his pale eyes a marked contrast against his black mask. They locked eyes briefly. Kyra was the first to look away. Once he made it over, Kyra followed him down. The group gathered on the other side of the wall, silent specters holding a wordless conference. James motioned at her and pointed down the path. She nodded and set off at a light jog.

The moment they started moving, she knew these men were good. She could barely hear them as they trailed her, following her steadily through the compound's twists and turns. They didn't trace each other's footsteps exactly, but each picked his own path depending on where the others were. Every man made certain to scan in a certain direction, so that the group as a whole had eyes on all sides. They moved as a constantly shifting unit, always aware of one another, no one falling behind.

They approached a crossing where guards often passed. Kyra slowed and, sure enough, heard footsteps in the distance. She raised her hand, and the signal passed back from one assassin to the next until they all took shelter. Kyra ducked behind a bush and waited. A Red Shield marched down the path and continued past. She waited ten breaths after she no longer heard his boots, then waved the others across to the kennel.

No sound came from within as she unlocked the gate this time. A few dogs stirred when it creaked open, but none opened their eyes. The assassins filed in one by one. Kyra locked the fence behind her and led them toward the far gate.

They were three-quarters of the way through when a sharp bark echoed through the kennel. The sound was piercing in the thick silence, and Kyra jumped as the men around her sprang to attention. A guard dog in the back corner pulled at his chain, baring his teeth at the intruders. Had he somehow avoided drinking his water? She advanced on him slowly, holding his eyes, doing her best to project authority. He growled deep in his throat. As she came closer, however, he seemed to notice his pack mates' unnatural silence. The dog backed up until he finally cowered against the doghouse, whining piteously.

Whining, she could deal with. Nobody would hear him from outside. Later, she'd allow herself to sigh in relief, but not now. She turned back, moving quickly now to the other gate.

She paused at the opposite entrance to wait for another guard to pass by. Then they continued to the storehouse.

Kyra hadn't been in this particular storehouse before, but she'd seen others like it. The lower windows were locked, but the upper ones were easily opened. It was simple, even trivial after her time in the heavily guarded inner compound, to shimmy through one of the higher windows, make her way down, and open the door for the others.

James led the way in, striding down the row of wares. Once in a while, he gestured toward some boxes for someone to take. Kyra's job was lookout. She posted herself outside the door and scanned for signs of anyone coming.

There was a crunch of boots on gravel, and Kyra raised her hand. James caught her signal and motioned to the others. All four men melted into the shadows. Kyra pulled the door shut and positioned herself right by the entrance, looking out through the crack where door met hinge.

A manservant stepped into view. Why was he wandering around at this time of night? Kyra raised her hand again in warning as he neared. The others stayed motionless behind her. The manservant stopped in front of the door, taking out a key. Kyra pressed herself flat against the wall. If he looked inside and didn't come in, it was possible he wouldn't see the men in the shadows. The bolt slid back, and the door opened inward. He entered, passed right by Kyra, took a few more steps, and stopped. Kyra held her breath, willing the man to turn back.

Then she heard him gasp.

Kyra was the first to get to him. Reaching up from behind him, she clamped a hand over his mouth as she drew a dagger against his throat. His eyes rolled back as he tried to see her and a cold sweat broke out over his skin, or was it her own? She peered around his shoulder at James for instruction. The head assassin raised a finger and made a slicing motion across his throat.

She froze. No.

Staring back at James, she shook her head. James pressed his lips together and repeated his gesture. Still, Kyra didn't move. James fixed his eyes on Rand, motioning him to Kyra with a jerk of his head. The redheaded man stepped toward them.

At Rand's approach, Kyra's hostage squirmed in her grasp and thrust his elbow back, catching her painfully in the ribs. She tightened her hand reflexively over his jaw. Her knife dug into his throat. Warm liquid washed over her fingers. The man stiffened and gasped for breath—a gasp that turned into a gurgle as he sank to his knees and slid out of Kyra's petrified grasp.

It was like the world around her disappeared. The storehouse turned fuzzy; sounds became muffled. Everything went out of focus except for the manservant's body, crumpled now at her feet. Kyra stared at him, then at her blood-soaked hands. What had she done?

James wasted no time. Ignoring Kyra completely, he signaled Rand. With well-practiced efficiency, Rand disentangled the body from Kyra, threw it over his shoulder, and carried it outside. James gave a few short instructions to Shea and Alex, who picked up some last bundles and scanned the area to clear any signs of their presence. Then he approached Kyra, who was still frozen near the door.

"Clean yourself off and stay out of the way."

Within minutes they were ready to leave. As Shea pulled her out of the storehouse, she looked for the body but didn't see it anywhere. Her mind was thick and cloudy, disconnected from the rest of her. Somewhere in the fog, there might have been thoughts screaming to be heard, but she walked in a haze. At one point, they were in front of the kennel, and James ordered her to unlock the door. Somehow, they made their way out.

James grabbed her arm outside the Guildhouse, so hard that she cried out. But the pain brought her back to her senses, and she looked up to find him staring at her.

"Wash yourself out back," he said.

Kyra fled out the back door, casting about until she got her bearings. She saw the basin and thrust her hands in. This late at night, the water was freezing. She whimpered at the shock, but she kept her hands submerged, rubbing them underwater until she could no longer feel them. When they finally came clean, she inspected her clothing. Her outer tunic was stained and crusted with red-brown splotches. She pulled it off and threw it away in disgust.

She was shaking violently now, chilled by the cold water and wind. She crept, trembling, back into the Guildhouse. The others were still unpacking the bundles, and James stood talking to Alex in a corner. Kyra stepped toward them, then stopped. She couldn't. Even Rand looked dangerous and frightening in the flickering lanterns. Kyra took one last look at James to make sure he wasn't watching and bolted for the front door. Once out on the street, she ran.

Her lungs burned and she gasped for breath as she slipped through the back door of The Drunken Dog. She didn't hear any sounds from the dining room, but there was still light coming from the kitchen. She couldn't face Bella, not now. Kyra dashed up the back stairs, moving as quickly as she could without making noise. Only when she was in her room did she finally stop to breathe, but even as her own movement slowed, the room started spinning, and she collapsed. Her body gave way to racking sobs. She lay there, curled in a ball, hugging her legs through the convulsions.

She didn't realize how loud she was until her door opened. Bella didn't ask any questions, but simply knelt down next to Kyra and cradled her head in her lap. And Kyra let herself be held, as if she were once again the lost child who had just come in off the streets, plagued by nightmares and suspicious of the world. She clung to Bella, and Bella patted her back and stroked her hair until her sobs finally subsided.

Later, after Kyra had quieted, rinsed her face, and accepted a cup of water, Bella finally spoke.

"You're losing yourself, Kyra. Is it worth it?"

Somehow, it didn't really surprise Kyra that Bella guessed the heart of her situation, even if she didn't know the specifics.

"Lettie and Idalee," she objected halfheartedly.

"They got along fine before you started helping them, and they'll be fine now. They're smart girls. Between the two of us and Flick, we'll figure something out."

Kyra didn't argue. She was exhausted, and Bella was right. Her days with the Guild were over.

SIXTEEN

Would the setbacks never end? First, stolen armor. Then, leaked patrol schedules. And now, a successful raid of the Palace itself. When was the last time this had happened? Certainly not in his lifetime. Tristam pushed down his frustration as he and his fellow knights listened to the storehouse keeper's report.

"They didn't take much," the keeper, a plump man named Finley, said to Malikel. "But they knew what was valuable. Rare herbs and medicines, only the best. But even those, they didn't take much of. They seemed to be in a hurry."

Tristam suppressed a bitter chuckle. So even though a group of unknown men had snuck into the supposedly impenetrable compound, past the best-trained guard force in the region, and carried off a fortune in medical supplies, they could at least take comfort in the fact that the thieves had felt the need to hurry while doing so.

A Red Shield rushed in, breathing heavily. "Sirs."

"Yes, soldier?" said Malikel.

"We've found a body."

The Red Shield led them behind the building to a pile of

rocks, recently gathered for some building repairs. The guards had removed the top layer, revealing the victim hidden underneath. The body looked to have been hurriedly disposed of, still in the clothes he'd been murdered in, and clearly showing a neck wound.

"That's my missing man." Finley's voice shook as he turned away. "I'll have to speak to his family."

Tristam didn't envy him that task. "Who will be organizing his funeral? I'd like to contribute to the arrangements."

Finley gave him a strange look. "The Palace doesn't pay for memorial services for servants, sir. Just knights and other nobility."

"Oh," Tristam said. "I was not aware." He needed to stop forgetting that things were done differently in the city. His father had always paid the funeral expenses of those who died while serving Brancel Manor. But apparently, there was no room for these gestures in Forge's busy machinery.

To his relief, Malikel chose that moment to start giving commands. "Search the body and the surrounding area. Look for anything that might tell us more about the intruders."

As everyone scattered to the tasks, Tristam lingered by the rock pile. Like the armory raid before it, this robbery was eerie in its precision. There were no signs of how the robbers had entered the compound or even of how they'd entered the storehouse.

He turned to Finley. "You say the locks to this storehouse can't be picked?"

"Yes, milord, we replaced them according to Sir Malikel's orders."

"What about the windows?"

"They are well locked too."

"All of them?" He knew his voice was harsh, but he couldn't help it.

"All the ones within reach."

Tristam backed up, squinting up at the top of the building. The sun proved too bright for him, and he closed his eyes, only to suddenly open them again. "Can you take me to your top floor?"

"Of course, milord."

The top floor smelled of herbs and dried fruit. As was common with upper floors, it was warmer here. The builders had placed small windows close to the ceiling to let out the warm air in the summer.

Tristam peered over the sill of the closest one. The Palace maids were either shirking their duties or were too short to reach the high windows. The outer edge of the windowsill had a thin layer of dust, as did the next. The dust of the third window, however, had a streak across it, as if a halfhearted housekeeper had taken one pass with a dust cloth.

Tristam stared at this third window as the clues rearranged themselves into a new theory. A mysterious, high-climbing thief, breaking into buildings previously thought impenetrable. Leaked records that had been known only to a few trustworthy people. He'd been looking for informants within the Palace, but if the Guild had this much freedom of movement, they didn't need informants. Why go to the trouble of turning Palace officials, when you could just browse through their notes?

"Thank you, Finley," he said. "I'll need to speak with Sir Malikel."

They would start with the record rooms. Station guards in there at all times, morning and night. And there would be no more writing down of the patrol schedules. All commands would be delivered verbally.

And then, they'd wait and see.

SEVENTEEN

"Where's the key?"

The armory guard would have fallen to the ground if not for the assassins holding him up. When he didn't answer, Bacchus took another swing. The guard grunted and spit out a mouthful of blood.

Kyra grew increasingly impatient as she watched. Bacchus was incompetent and soft. They would be here forever with him in charge. She ran forward and pushed him out of the way.

"Give me your knife," she growled. When Bacchus didn't react, she snatched it from his belt and pressed it against the guard's throat. . . .

Kyra woke to screams from downstairs. She panicked for a moment before realizing that the screeches were mixed with laughter. Just Flick and the girls, playing some game. She cast a hand over her eyes. It had been three days since they raided the Palace. Three straight nights of nightmares, and they weren't getting any better. In her dreams, she was always the aggressor, the violent criminal she feared she was becoming. Every time she closed her eyes, she felt the man's blood running over her hands.

Another chorus of laughter erupted from the kitchen, and Kyra cast off her damp blankets. Sunlight streamed through the window, and her stomach demanded breakfast. She looked around, hoping she had some leftover bread, but her room was depressingly spare. Besides her cot, there was just her equipment chest, a bag of clothes, and a bare table by the door. There was no getting around it—she'd have to go downstairs.

She'd spent the last few days in self-imposed isolation. Bella had approached Kyra several times after her breakdown, wanting to help. A few times, Kyra had almost told her everything, but she couldn't in good conscience endanger Bella or the girls. So instead, Kyra made excuses and kept to herself. Her friends weren't the only ones she avoided. Kyra had not returned to the Guildhouse since the raid. James would have noticed her absence by now, but she couldn't face him. Not yet.

When Kyra stepped into the kitchen, Flick was chasing a squealing Idalee as Lettie cowered in the corner.

"Watch out, Kyra! Flick's a felbeast!" Idalee shrieked as Flick scooped her off the floor and spun her around.

"I see." Kyra forced a smile. "Does Bella know you're playing these games?"

Lettie tugged on Kyra's tunic. "We're not scared. We just hit him on the nose and he turns into a handsome knight. Brendel told us."

That *was* how the legend went, though from the girls' pleased expressions, Kyra suspected that Brendel hadn't told them the rest of the story. The felbeast was indeed part man, and Lady Evelyne fell in love with him in his handsome human form. But as the months went by, Evelyne found that the felbeast still retained his animal nature. Unable to reconcile her love for him as a man and the horrors he committed as a beast, Evelyne flung herself down a ravine. The felbeast, upon finding her broken body, fled deep into the mountains and was never heard from again.

Flick set Idalee down and ran his fingers through his tousled hair. His grin faded somewhat as he met Kyra's eyes, and she suddenly really wanted to apologize. Kyra suppressed the urge. Smoothing things over now would just mean more questions she didn't want to answer.

There was a moment of awkward silence. "Lettie," said Flick. "Don't you have something for Kyra?"

The girl's eyes brightened and she ran off, returning with a lump of dough cupped in her hands. Kyra bent closer and saw that it had been shaped into a small dog.

"Wow." Kyra bent down, honestly impressed. "Did you make this?"

Lettie nodded. "It's for you."

"Thank you." It was impossible to miss the change in Lettie since she'd moved in with them. The child talked more and was remarkably creative with whatever kitchen scraps Bella gave her. Kyra couldn't help but wonder what would happen once she quit the Guild. If they couldn't scrounge enough money to keep the girls here, where would they go?

"Kyra, you all right?" asked Flick. Kyra realized she'd squeezed her eyes shut.

"I'm all right. Just tired."

"Are you sure?"

Flick's concern rattled her more than she could handle.

She took the dog from Lettie and used the opportunity to turn away from Flick.

"Tell you what. Let me go put this somewhere safe."

She retreated back up the stairs, shedding any attempt at hiding her turmoil as she stepped onto the second floor. She couldn't stay with the Guild. She knew that, and Bella had promised they would figure something out for the girls. But it still didn't make her feel better. Kyra was two steps into her room, rubbing her temples, when a voice spoke behind her.

"Where have you been?"

Kyra whipped around, crouching as she grabbed for her dagger. James sat at the table by her door, watching her with narrowed eyes.

"How'd you get in here?" She scanned the room. He seemed to be alone.

"Why haven't you come in the last three days?"

Kyra drew a breath and forced her muscles to relax. She needed to be calm for this conversation. "I'm sorry. I should have come in."

"Will you disappear every time we have a mishap?"

"A mishap?" Kyra almost choked. She clenched her fists to hold off another flashback, and any attempt at staying calm went out the window. "I slit a man's throat like a pig at the slaughterhouse."

"It happens, Kyra. Especially in a trade such as ours." He was so calm, as if he were talking about a spilled bowl of stew.

"I in't in your trade, James. You hired me as a thief, not an assassin."

"I know why I hired you. What happened three nights ago

was unfortunate. It will happen less as you become better at your craft."

Would it really? Or would she just stop caring? Turn into the cold-blooded killer of her nightmares? A few weeks ago she'd been horrified to see the armory guards captured and beaten. Three days ago, she'd slit a man's throat.

"What did you really do to the guards from the armory raid, James?"

He waited just a little too long to answer, and a chill settled over her skin. "I'm out," she whispered, shaking her head. "I can't do this."

His expression hardened. "You're overreacting."

"No, I'm not."

"So you'll just leave? What happens when the next storekeeper gets his goods seized? Will you turn a blind eye?"

"The cost is too great."

"And what will you do for coin? Where will your adopted sisters live?"

"That's none of your business."

James fell silent. Kyra fought the urge to step back. Had she pushed him too far? When he spoke again, his voice was dangerously calm.

"Close the door, Kyra. And have a seat."

"No, I'm going back downstairs."

"We're just going to talk some more, about things better not overheard."

His tone dared her to disobey and, as much as she wanted to leave, James wasn't the type she could ignore without consequences. She pushed her door shut.

"The Palace Council's stepped up its attacks on the Guild," he said. "The new Defense Minster, Malikel, is more competent than his predecessor. He suspects what we're doing in the Palace, and he's taking steps against us."

She knew this. She'd brought him records of Malikel's orders.

"I've considered sending men to take care of him, but it's unwise. Our biggest advantage is the Council's sluggishness. Any attack from us might just spur them against us. It's better to take a finer approach."

He paused and looked her in the eye. "Malikel lives in the Fastkeep. It's hard to get to, but you've mapped it several times. Do you remember where the officials' quarters are?"

She nodded.

"Good, you've been paying attention. I want you to kill him tonight."

Kyra gaped at him.

"He takes tea every morning that he mixes from dried herbs. I want you to sneak into his chambers, find the herbs, and pour clearberry juice over them. A small amount will do the trick. Palace healers will think his heart failed."

Had James lost his mind? "You're crazy." She stared at him, trying to shake the feeling that she was in some incomprehensible dream. James gave no reaction, just regarded her calmly.

"How did your friends fare during the barbarian attack?" he finally asked.

"They're fine."

"There's a lad you spend time with, in't there? Flick? And of course the cook and the two lasses."

She didn't bother to answer. James now looked out the window, his voice taking on a philosophical tone. "They were lucky to get out of harm's way. Not everyone is that lucky."

"I see." Kyra's tongue was dry in her mouth, and she listened on with dread.

"The lasses, especially, have been fortunate considering where they came from. The streets of Forge are by no means safe. There are people, you know"—he trained his eyes back on Kyra—"who do things to children that make a pig in a slaughterhouse seem lucky."

Kyra's hands began to shake as James's meaning sank in. "You said I wouldn't have to kill anyone."

"Plans change."

It was the same tone of voice he'd used when talking of the nonexistent ruby, and Kyra suddenly understood. His insistence on fighting lessons. The way he'd humiliated her when she first joined the Guild. Her resulting determination to prove herself.

And prove herself she had.

"You wanted me as an assassin from the beginning."

"You're very skilled, with abilities I've never seen in anyone before, and you took to your training remarkably fast. Your first kill was clean and quick." No shame crossed his face. Not a hint of guilt as he spoke of molding her into his personal weapon.

"The kill was an accident," she whispered.

James directed the full force of his gaze at her. If there had ever been any warmth in their dealings together, it was gone. "What did you *think* would happen when you held your knife to his throat? What were you hoping for, Kyra? Don't make this harder with delusions of moral superiority. You're not some talesinger's heroine. You're a former gutter rat who steals for a living."

That got her in the gut. Words of denial tangled at the base of her throat, threatening to close off her airways.

James continued. "I thought time in the Guild would grow you a spine, but your maturity lags behind your talents. This is no child's game that we play. We're dealing with the Palace and the Council, the most powerful men in the three cities, and the swords they control. You don't win this war with petty raids on their storehouses. You draw blood. Do you think Malikel or any of his soldiers would think twice about killing you? You're nothing to them. Street scum to be ignored, played with, or abused."

He looked her over, appraising her like a piece of damaged china. "I'll make you a deal," he said. "I'll have one good kill from you for all the resources I've invested in your training. Do this one job, and I'll let you leave. But it needs to be done tonight."

He reached below the table and brought up a parchment and a small leather vial. "One of your maps and a bottle of clearberry juice. I've circled Malikel's chambers, as well as the living quarters of his most trusted men. It should be easy enough to understand. Of course, you don't have to accept, but every choice will have its consequences."

EIGHTEEN

Kyra didn't know how long she stayed in her room after James left, replaying the conversation in her head. She was a fool, many times over—for joining the Guild, for trusting James, for thinking that she could get involved, and that she could leave.

James was wrong. There were steps she wasn't willing to take. The kill had been an accident. She wasn't an assassin, and she wouldn't kill a Council member. She couldn't.

But James was more than capable of carrying out his threats.

The thought brought Kyra to her feet, and she barreled downstairs two steps at a time, images of the girls bound and captive flashing through her mind. Kyra burst into the kitchen to find Idalee grinding peppercorns with Bella.

Bella raised her head. "Kyra?"

"Where's Flick?" Kyra asked. She surreptitiously scanned the room, shrinking under Bella's worried eye. The kitchen looked normal. Stew bubbled on the stove. Everything was in its place. No assassins hidden under the cabinets.

"He went to the wool district," said Bella. "Do you need

him?" The cook put down her pestle and moved toward her. Kyra took a half step back. Maybe it wouldn't hurt to tell Bella what had happened. Maybe it would be all right.

"Just tell him I'm looking for him," Kyra said roughly. She fled into the dining room before her resolve could crumble any further.

The midday crowd hadn't come in yet, and she settled into a booth, hugging her knees. That's when she noticed two slightly familiar men in the corner. Both wore cloaks that hid their faces, but when she looked in their direction, one pulled his hood back and winked at her. The signal jolted through her. Kyra jumped up and headed for the kitchen, only to back up as Idalee came in with a platter of shepherd's pie. Kyra watched with rising dread as the cloaked men thanked Idalee and slipped her a coin. The unsuspecting girl returned to the kitchen, and Kyra settled herself back into the booth. She wasn't going to leave Idalee alone with those two.

The men bent over their meals, for all appearances engrossed in their own conversation. Kyra rubbed her temples and tried to concentrate. She had to get everybody out of the tavern, away from the assassins. Perhaps if they escaped out the back? And she needed to find some way to get word to Flick.

By the time Bella came to set the table for lunch, Kyra had a rudimentary plan. She could get one of Flick's friends to start a fight in the dining room to distract the cloaked men. She'd grab everyone, sneak out the back, and find a hiding place close by until they could get out of the city. As Bella, Idalee, and Lettie joined her at the table, Kyra glanced out the window. Her gaze settled on a familiar face, and she gasped. Across the street, behind the constant stream of people and carts, stood Shea from the Guild.

"What are you looking at, Kyra?" asked Bella.

"Nothing," Kyra said. "I thought I saw someone I knew."

She kept quiet for the rest of the meal, trying not to choke on the food that she shoved mechanically into her mouth. Thankfully, Idalee was in a talkative mood, and Kyra kept quiet. There were too many eyes, and Kyra didn't dare give the assassins any reason to suspect she was trying to warn the others. After lunch, Kyra noticed more Guild members, some outside the tavern and others mixed in with the dining room crowd. With each discovery, her plans for escape unraveled further. She and Flick were no match for multiple assassins, and a simple barroom fight wouldn't be enough to distract them all. Perhaps she could create a stronger diversion? She ran through a list of possibilities. A fire was too dangerous. Multiple fights, perhaps?

As dinnertime approached, Brendel set up in his corner and began to play. He sang, first of Evelyne's passionate love with the felbeast, their brief but beautiful time together. Kyra wanted to throw her spoon across the room and cover her ears. In the real world, beasts didn't turn into men. Instead, it was the other way around.

Flick finally returned after the evening meal. He had a neatly dressed girl on his arm—the wool merchant's daughter.

"Flick!" It was such a relief to see him.

"Kyra." He gestured to the girl, who was looking around the tavern with wide eyes. "This is Gabrielle. You were looking for me?"

Kyra took a quick glance toward her watchers. One of them met her eyes and shook his head. Kyra swallowed hard. "I just had a question," she lied. "I've figured it out."

Flick cocked his head, watching Kyra carefully. "You sure?"

"Aye."

A flash of confusion crossed his face, and he took a step closer. "Look Kyra, I know we—"

"I'm fine," she interrupted. "Headache, that's all."

She grabbed what was left of her dinner and fled upstairs. In the silence of her room, Kyra urged herself to think. Even if she was able to escape with Bella and the girls, where would they go? The Guild had eyes all over Forge. Would they have to run to another city? Live in the woods? Maybe James was right. What had Malikel or anyone in the Palace ever done for her? Why was she risking so much to spare a nobleman who wouldn't give her a second thought?

There was a sharp rap on her door. Kyra drew a breath and wrapped her fingers around the hilt of her dagger, holding it ready at her side as she inched the door open. The hooded man, the one who had winked at her, stood in her doorway. His eyes flickered to her weapon.

"Be across the Palace wall in an hour," he said, and walked away.

Kyra closed the door again and buried her face in her hands, the weight in her chest threatening to choke her. It was no longer safe to stay at the inn. Fingers shaking, she changed into dark clothes. To her belt, she tied the bottle of clearberry juice. After a moment's thought, she grabbed a mask and stuffed it into her pocket. She would feel safer tonight with her face covered.

She left through the dining room, walking by the hooded men and meeting their eyes briefly as she passed. As she opened the door, they gathered their things to follow. The assassins trailed her by half a block on her way to the Palace, though they didn't follow her over the wall. When she was far enough in, Kyra climbed onto a high ledge. She sat down and hugged her knees, digging her nails into her forearms as she willed herself to think out her options.

There were certainly still assassins at the inn, and it was too late to get everyone to safety. What if she turned herself in? Could the Palace offer protection? Kyra felt sick at the prospect of arrest and trial. An association of this magnitude with the Assassins Guild would certainly mean death, especially now that she had innocent blood on her hands. And could she even trust the Palace? Or would they just torture her for information and leave her friends to the Guild's mercy?

Kyra reached to her belt and untied the vial, letting the shape blur before her. No matter what she did, someone would die tonight. Malikel was a knight who'd accepted the risk of death when he pledged his allegiance to the city. Bella and the girls, they were just innocent bystanders, victims of—of what? Kyra's own stupidity. Everyone had warned her against the Guild, but she'd been caught up by the lure of challenge, of security, by her own fascination with James. The clues had been there, but she'd ignored them.

Bella would tell her not to go through with the job, even if by killing Malikel she'd be saving four others. But Bella hadn't seen the assassins' eyes that morning as they followed Idalee around The Drunken Dog. She hadn't heard the chill in

James's voice when he delivered his threat. Kyra retied the vial to her belt. Blanking her mind to the dread and self-loathing that threatened to overwhelm her, she continued farther into the Palace.

The living quarters were deep inside the compound. Several times, Kyra had to double back to avoid guards, but eventually, she was perched outside the topmost windows, ready to enter. The shutters made a high squeaking sound as Kyra pried them open, and she stopped, heart skipping a beat. She peered through the opening. No one was inside. Kyra waited for her pulse to calm and tried again. The shutters didn't make any more noise when she pushed them wider, but there was no way Kyra could risk a noise like that again. She would have to leave them slightly ajar.

Sooner than she expected, Kyra found herself in front of a pair of solid oak doors, reaching for her lock picks. The lock yielded all too quickly to her efforts. It was so easy now, to enter the Palace and do what she wished. James had molded her well.

The room was plain for a wallhugger's. A man breathed lightly on a sturdy four-poster bed. Other than a woven rug on the floor, there was little decoration. Kyra stayed away from the bed, skirting along the edge of the rug. It would be easier to do this if she didn't see Malikel's face. Instead, she focused on the herbs. If she took tea every morning, where would she keep it? The chest at the foot of his bed contained only weapons, but a quick search of his dresser turned up a pouch of dried leaves.

Her hands were clumsy as she untied the pouch. All she

had to do was put a few drops in there and leave. Maybe he wouldn't take a large dose. Perhaps the healers would save him in time. She just needed to convince James that she had tried. Again, she forced her mind blank. Leather thongs gave way to her slow fingers and she laid the open pouch on top of the dresser. She closed her eyes, taking a deep breath before reaching for the vial's cap.

She couldn't do this.

Kyra's hands shook so badly that she'd spill the contents of the vial if she opened it. Spots swam before her eyes. She took a step back, clutching her stomach. But if she couldn't go through with the kill, what could she do?

Malikel shifted in the bed, and Kyra dove to the floor, digging her fingers into the thick rug. Cursing herself for letting her guard down, she crawled through a back doorway, slipping through just as he sat up.

She huddled behind the open door. Perhaps he would go back to sleep. For a moment, there was silence, and then she heard footsteps. A dim light flickered through the doorway, and only then did Kyra realize her mistake.

She had left his herbs on top of the dresser.

Kyra froze as she heard a knock on the double oak doors, barely breathing as Malikel answered. She heard what must have been Malikel's greeting, and a younger man answered. The voices grew louder as they stepped back inside. It would be just a matter of time before they discovered her.

She cast around for an escape route. With the candlelight from the next room, she saw that she was in a sitting room off the main chamber. There was a window here, but to get to it she'd have to run past the open doorway. Peering through the crack of the door, Kyra caught a glimpse of the men as they paced the room. She had to time her escape for a moment they both faced away.

NINETEEN

The shutter on the high window was slightly ajar. It was pitch dark outside, and no light shone through the tiny crevice. But there definitely was a crack, and a feeling of coolness—not quite a breeze—that seeped into the corridor and cut through the hallway's musty air.

Tristam rubbed his eyes. His newest theory about the Assassins Guild was making him paranoid. Not every open window was left by a spy. Most likely the maids had opened the shutter to air out the corridor and forgotten to close it. He shook his head and continued toward his quarters, only to stop a few steps later. How often was it, really, that the maids opened these windows? He circled back.

As Tristam passed by Malikel's room, he saw a faint light under the door. Again, he stopped, unable to shake the feeling that something was off. Had the light been there a few moments ago? Tristam bent his head and listened. He heard some footsteps through the door and knocked quietly. The doorknob turned, and Malikel peered out.

"Tristam." The older man was still wearing his dressing gown and had the disoriented expression of someone who had just woken up. "What brings you by at this late hour?"

Tristam paused, somewhat embarrassed to share his vague suspicions. "I don't really know. Something didn't feel right. Why are you awake?"

Malikel gave a quick, focused nod. "A noise may have awoken me." He motioned Tristam in. "As you said, something didn't feel right."

Tristam entered Malikel's quarters, scanning the area for anything out of place. The fire was out, but that was to be expected at this hour. "One of the high windows was open in the hallway," he told Malikel. "It's a small thing, but—" He stopped short. "Do you usually leave your herbs out like that?"

Malikel picked up the herbs off his dresser. "No," he said, his face drawn. "I keep them in the drawer, and certainly not open like this."

There was a sound from the sitting room, like wood scraping on wood. Tristam reached for the dagger at his belt and fought the urge to swear when he realized he didn't have it.

"Tristam." Malikel took two short swords from a chest and handed one to Tristam. Tristam nodded his thanks and inched toward the door, barely breathing. He could see nothing unusual through the open doorway. Checking to make sure Malikel was behind him, he readied his weapon and stepped in.

The room was empty, but one set of shutters was half open.

Forgetting caution, Tristam crossed the room in three strides and leaned out the window, squinting into the darkness. There was a hint of movement to his left. As soon as he turned his head, the movement stopped. Slowly, his eyes adjusted and the figure of a man resolved itself on the ledge. The stranger was covered from head to toe in black, which made him almost invisible at that height with no torchlight to illuminate him. Sudden elation swept through Tristam, tinged with panic. It was him. The spy he'd been seeking, and he was *not* going to get away.

Tristam drew his head closer to the wall. He didn't like exposing any part of himself to this figure, but he didn't dare let him out of sight.

"You're surrounded by guards," he called. The figure didn't move. "Stay where you are. If you try to escape, you won't make it out alive."

There was a pause, and the intruder slowly turned his head toward Tristam. Despite the darkness, Tristam had the impression that their eyes met. Then the masked figure turned and ran.

Tristam pounded his leg in frustration and shouted out the window for guards. If he'd had any doubt about whether this was the mysterious intruder he'd been seeking, it disappeared as soon as he saw the man run. The figure, seemingly oblivious to the great height, moved with a grace that he wouldn't have thought possible. He ran along a ledge less than a foot wide, ducking under overhangs and barely grazing the surface with his feet. When the intruder reached the edge of one building, he jumped to the next and kept going until an arrow glanced off the wall in front of him. He stopped and surveyed the gathering crowd below, shifting his weight from foot to foot as more guards gathered with bows trained in his direction.

"I want him captured alive," Tristam shouted before racing downstairs and outside.

When he burst through the door, the courtyard was in chaos. The man was gone and Red Shields were rushing into the building. Tristam grabbed the nearest soldier and demanded to know what had happened.

"He went into one of the windows."

Tristam started to follow the guard inside, but stopped himself. There were plenty of people searching the building; one extra person wouldn't help. He needed a better plan. If he were the intruder, where would he go?

The obvious answer was back outside to the ledges. That was where no one could follow him, and where he could best stay hidden. And unless the intruder was prepared to spend days hiding amongst the Palace buildings, he would try to get out of the compound before dawn.

What was the most direct path, if one were traveling from ledge to ledge toward the compound wall? If the spy headed south, the buildings led straight to the perimeter. Perhaps he could head him off there. There were a lot of "ifs" in that line of reasoning, but he couldn't think of a better plan. He detained guards as they ran past.

"We can intercept the intruder at the compound wall," he told them. "I want men stationed along the length to watch for his escape." Tristam dealt out assignments as quickly as he could. Once the guards were on their way, he too ran south.

The intruder was fast, but he'd have to slow down at the wall. It didn't matter how fleet-footed he was—the buildings were too far away for anyone to jump. Once he got there, he'd have to come down to ground level, and he'd have to pause to throw a grappling hook.

Tristam slowed to a stop at the edge of the inner compound. Pathways and grass lined the inside of the wall. The area was usually lit by only a few torches, but guards had come by and added more. With the extra light, it would be hard for anyone to pass undetected. Tristam found a sheltered spot with a wide view and settled down. Only then did he notice how knotted his muscles were, the tight clench of his stomach. This was their first real lead in months. They couldn't let him escape, not now.

In his mind, he saw the masked figure again. What kind of man did it take, to so coolly and methodically slip through the Palace defenses? To betray his own city to bloodthirsty beasts? It was frightening to realize that the assassin had been inside Malikel's room while the official slept. His commander was far from helpless, but still . . . Was this person the secret behind the Assassins Guild's recent rise?

As he waited, his breathing slowed and heat faded from his veins. He rubbed his arms and stomped his legs to stay warm. It would do no good to see the criminal only to trip over limbs cramped from the cold.

A shadow flickered in his peripheral vision. Tristam strained his eyes toward the movement. A masked figure stood close to the wall, huddled against the stone and doing something with his hands. Tristam's breath caught, and he scanned the area for backup. The closest guards wouldn't hear him unless he shouted. It was better to catch the intruder by surprise.

The man stepped back from the wall and swung his rope to cast it over. Tristam started toward him. He didn't make any noticeable sound, but the dark figure froze and looked straight at him. So much for surprise. Tristam yelled for guards, hollering like a madman as he launched himself at his quarry. The intruder hesitated a split second before backing up again, lobbing his grappling hook over the wall with a practiced motion. Tristam quickened his pace.

The assassin tugged on the rope and started climbing, and Tristam felt a moment of panic. If the intruder reached the top and took the rope, he'd escape again, and letting him go unpunished was not an option. Tristam sucked air into his burning lungs, gathering himself for one last burst of speed. He didn't slow as he neared the wall, but jumped instead, grabbing for the man's leg. The unforgiving stone knocked the breath out of him, but his hands closed around an ankle, and they both fell to the ground. The intruder landed on top of him with a yell.

There was something about that voice, but in the ensuing struggle Tristam didn't give it much thought. A knife flickered above him and he jerked his head to the side, bridging his hips up and throwing his opponent over. It was surprisingly easy. The stranger was smaller than he had expected, and in a wrestling match, Tristam had the clear advantage. The force of the throw slammed the intruder's knife hand against the ground, and Tristam took the opportunity to strike his wrist. The knife fell out of the man's limp fingers and Tristam pushed it out of his reach. Tristam pinned his opponent to the ground and held him by sheer weight, ruthlessly crushing his movements as reinforcements arrived. He finally had him. The man who had eluded him all this time. And he would give Tristam answers.

His captive's eyes rolled to the side, taking in the gathering guards. Finally, either from fatigue or acceptance of the odds, he stopped struggling. Once Tristam was no longer fighting for his life, details from the chase and the fight started to fit themselves together. The realization came gradually, settling in as the excitement faded away. It was a crazy notion, but now, with no knife to distract him and being in such close contact with his adversary, there was no denying the evidence. Gingerly lifting one hand, he grabbed the stranger's mask and peeled it off.

A cascade of tangled brown hair fell out as a familiar and unmistakably feminine face stared up at him.

TWENTY

As Kyra's captor stared at her face, the world resolved into details—his eyes, wide with shock and recognition, the insignia on his tunic that marked him as a knight, and the circle of guards that killed any remaining hope of escape. A chill wind blew across her forehead, still damp with sweat. Kyra shivered. When was the last time someone had seen her face on a job? She might as well have been naked.

In her mind's eye, she saw Bella and the girls, eating lunch while the assassins watched. The image fueled her strength and she twisted in the knight's grasp, freeing a leg and thrusting her knee into his abdomen. He grunted and she scrambled out from under him.

Then the guards closed in. Two sets of hands seized her and hauled her to her feet. Pain shot through her shoulder as someone shackled her wrists behind her. She cried out and kicked her heel into the shin of the guard behind her. He swore and loosened his grip, but didn't let go. Then another Red Shield drew a dagger and pressed the point to her throat, daring her to move again. She didn't.

The knight who'd captured her stood and dusted himself off, still breathing hard from the struggle. His jaw was set in anger, but his eyes were uncertain. Kyra stared back at him. Did he recognize that she'd rescued him in the marketplace? Would he be grateful?

He signaled to the guards. "Take her to the interrogation room. Careful, she's vicious."

The world went dark as someone threw a hood over her head. Rough hands patted her down and tore away her belt pouch. Someone shoved her from behind, barking a command to move, and Kyra stumbled forward to keep from falling on her face. The hood was stifling and there wasn't enough air. They marched her down a cobblestone path, then into a building and down a flight of stairs. There they finally pulled the hood from her face and she gulped in a fresh breath.

She had never been inside an interrogation room before. The stone-walled chamber was bare except for a table and four chairs. There were no windows; the only light came from a single flickering oil lamp. Her guards led her past the table and pushed her into a chair. The clank of her shackles echoed through the room as a guard fastened Kyra's chains to a ring on the floor. Then most of the soldiers left, leaving two to watch her.

What were they going to do to her? Every inch of her body ached, and the guards watched her every move. One sneered at her, lips curled in disgust as if she were a rodent. If only they hadn't taken her lock picks . . . She could hear James taunting her: *This is what happens when you help the enemy. Mayhap the knight will give you a dungeon cell with a window, in gratitude for saving him.*

Footsteps and voices filtered in from the corridor, and Kyra sat up straight. Two men came in. One she recognized as the young knight who had captured her—Sir Tristam, the guards had called him. He'd rinsed his face and changed into a fresh tunic, and Kyra was suddenly aware of the layer of dirt covering her from head to toe.

The second man was older and wore official's robes. With a start, she recognized Malikel. Awake now, he had a commanding presence she hadn't seen earlier. She should have killed him when she'd had the chance. A twist of her wrist, a few drops was all it would have taken. *Do you think Malikel or any of his soldiers would think twice about killing you? You're nothing to them. Street scum to be ignored, played with, or abused.*

"Your name?" asked Malikel.

She couldn't have responded if she had wanted to. If she opened her mouth, she would fall apart.

"Your name," he repeated. The guard beside her raised his arm. Kyra flinched and looked away. Out of the corner of her eye, she saw Malikel shake his head.

"This will be a long day if you refuse to answer even that simple question," he said. "If I were you, I'd save my battles for later."

"Kyra." Her voice was dry and cracked.

Tristam leaned over the table. "I recognize you." He spoke softly. "You were in the northwest quadrant the day of the attack. You threw a rock."

"Little good that did me," Kyra whispered. The shackles dug into her wrists. She tried to adjust her arms, and pain shot through her shoulder again. "I should have let you die."

Belatedly, she realized she should have played along, tried

to gain his sympathy. But it was too late. Tristam's face hardened, and he pushed back from the table. "What were you doing in the Palace?" he asked roughly.

"There's coin in the Palace. I need to eat."

"You weren't here for a simple burglary. I needn't explain to you why that's a ridiculous notion."

She forced herself to look him in the eye. "If you know so much, why don't you tell me why I'm here?"

"You work for the Assassins Guild."

Kyra fought to keep her expression neutral as her stomach plummeted.

"I've never heard of a woman involved with them before, so you must be ambitious. Ruthless." He watched her carefully, as if he were trying to see through her eyes and glean the thoughts behind them. "You must have had to work twice as hard to get where you are. How many people did you kill to get them to accept you?"

Ambitious? Ruthless? Had he *ever*, even once, had to worry about his next meal or where he would sleep? Had he ever watched assassins stalk his family? "You have no idea what you're talking about," she hissed. She didn't realize she had stood up until a guard pushed her back down. She sat, trembling, mouth clenched shut.

Malikel put a hand on Tristam's arm, gently pushing the young knight back. "You're right, Kyra. We don't know very much about you," said the older man. "But you're not helping yourself by staying silent. I don't know how strong your ties were to the Guild, but they're outside the walls, and we have you right here. I would think hard about your allegiances."

The perverse irony of the situation struck her. What would her interrogators think if they knew how much she hated James right now? But the assassin's threats were too fresh in her mind, and Kyra wasn't naïve enough to think the Palace would show her any mercy if they knew the truth. Time. She needed time to think.

"We'll give you some time to think things over," said Malikel. Kyra almost jumped. Had she said that last thought out loud? The official turned toward the guards. "Take her to a cell. We'll continue tomorrow."

TWENTY-ONE

The girl squirmed in Bacchus's grasp, her face smeared with tears and dirt. The two stood in a thick mist. Menacing shadows moved in the fog around them.

Bacchus grinned as he took out his knife. "Which finger do we take off first?"

Kyra turned to see James beside her, arms characteristically crossed over his chest as he watched Bacchus with approval.

"She's weak," the head assassin observed. "Not like you, Kyra. Children are entertaining from time to time, and useful. The key is knowing when they need to die."

Kyra found that she agreed. The girl did seem rather pathetic. As if to agree with her, the shapes in the mist moved closer.

"Bacchus," called James. "Let her do it."

Kyra felt her excitement build as she closed in. This would prove once and for all that she belonged with the Guild, with James. From the mists, Kyra heard growls of approval. Teeth flashed in anticipation.

Lettie didn't struggle when Kyra raised the knife for the kill. Instead, she looked up at her with wide, trusting eyes.

She woke to complete darkness and the smell of urine, mold, and moss. Her cell had no windows, and she had no idea what time it was. Kyra lay curled on her side, listening to the sound of her own ragged breathing. The hard stone bruised her hip, but she knew everything would hurt more if she tried to stand.

She couldn't erase the images from her dream. Had it been Lettie the whole time or just at the end? She would never hurt Lettie in real life. Or would she? The scene was too vivid, the bloodlust too strong. Perhaps she was going mad. Or maybe James was right, and the assassin inside her was just waiting to come out.

Footsteps sounded outside her door. She barely had time to sit up before lantern light flooded the cell. Kyra cast a hand over her eyes. The guards surrounded and shackled her in a well-practiced routine, hooding her again before marching her out. Her muscles protested at the abrupt start, but she doubted her escorts would slow at her request.

Tristam waited in the interrogation room, arms crossed, as her guards shackled her into place across from him. This time, she took a closer look at the knight. He was tall, with a broad chest, muscular shoulders. While he didn't have Malikel's commanding presence, there was a sense of focus about him. He really wanted something, and Kyra had a feeling it involved her.

"Are you ready to talk?" His voice was cold, with no trace of the uncertainty from the day before.

Bacchus's voice echoed in Kyra's head, teasing her like the

lamp's dancing flames. *Which finger do we take off first?* Was that what they'd do to Lettie if she said anything?

When she didn't respond, Tristam spoke again. "We don't have time for games. If I get nothing from you today, we'll deliver you to the torture chamber."

Kyra's breath caught despite herself. He was serious about the torture.

"Your compound is secure, but it's got its weaknesses," she said. "I can show you where they are."

Tristam's jaw tightened. "I said no games."

"I in't playing games."

Tristam scrutinized Kyra in the dim light. "You're offering me a small amount of information to avoid telling me what I really want to know."

She had to be careful. The knight might be hostile, but he was not slow. "It's useful information," she countered, feigning a confidence she didn't feel. "Easy to check, and you don't have to lift a finger to get it out of me. If you're not satisfied, I'll be here for more chats."

He eyed her suspiciously. "Fine," he finally said. "What can you tell me?"

Kyra grabbed at the first detail that came to mind. "The windows aren't secure. The glass windows in the outer compound have locks that can be picked. The shutters in the high windows of the inner compound as well."

"We already know that. Do better."

Kyra put a hand to her temple. The chamber's musty air was giving her a headache. "It'd be easier if I had a map of the compound."

The corner of his mouth crept up. "Your memory will have to do."

Did he really think she would benefit from a map? She'd bet a month's wages that she knew the compound better than he. "Give me a blank parchment, then, and a piece of charcoal."

Tristam looked skeptical, but signaled a guard to fetch the supplies. Kyra spread the parchment in front of her, touched the charcoal down, and pulled up her mental map. It made her feel more secure, having something to focus on that she knew well.

"This is the inner compound wall," she said, sketching a rough outline of the buildings on the north side. "The meeting rooms, the dormitories, and these storage sheds are secure. But the library's not."

Out of the corner of her eye, she saw Tristam's fist clench. It bothered him to hear about his precious Palace being compromised. If she were wise, she would tread carefully. But she was angry, and there was some comfort in showing the wall-huggers their failings. Kyra's strokes grew bolder as she traced out the compound's gigantic library. "The north door has a weak lock. You'll want to replace it. Especially 'cause once you get into the library, you can climb out the second-floor window, and it's simple to skirt around the outside to the record rooms."

By the time she finished speaking, Tristam had regained his composure. He summoned a guard. "Have the locksmith look at the north door of the library. Tell me what he says." The knight turned back to Kyra, his expression wavering between annoyance and reluctant acknowledgment that she might be useful. "What more can you tell me?"

She closed her eyes, recalling the different paths that she

took, the gates with broken locks, and the pathways with fewer patrols. Occasionally, Tristam asked for more details, and every so often he sent off some notes for verification. He became less hostile as each of her tips checked out. Lunch was brought to them at midday, and he pushed the tray toward her.

"Eat." He paused. "You've done well," he said grudgingly.

The chicken thigh she dug into was no match for Bella's hearty cooking. "Have I earned myself anything?"

"A morning's reprieve."

The afternoon continued similarly. All her tips came back verified, as she knew they would. But she was running out of things to tell him. She started to slow, to hesitate as she sifted between her most hard-won secrets, and she could tell from the way Tristam watched her that he noticed.

"How did you get through the kennel?" Tristam asked late in the afternoon.

Kyra opened her mouth, then slowly closed it. "What do you mean?"

"How did you get through the kennel when you raided the Palace storehouse? That's the only way you could have gotten a group of men that far in."

"I've no idea what you're talking about." Her expression of stubborn innocence fooled neither of them.

Tristam stared at her for a long moment. Then he looked to the door, and Kyra saw guards waiting, ready to lead her out.

"No need to blindfold her," Tristam told them. "She already knows her way around."

The guards escorted her out the door but turned her away from her cell, instead leading her out of the building. Tristam followed, walking slightly behind her. "Where are we going?" she asked.

"We're transferring you to another location," said Tristam. The ominous announcement was balanced by Kyra's relief at being taken outside. It was late afternoon, and the air and sunlight felt fresh on her face. For someone who so often worked at night, she was surprised at how much she had missed the sun. Ahead, Kyra saw a crowd of people walking toward them.

"Move off the path," Tristam said. "We'll let them go by." Her guards led her a distance off and they waited by a cluster of bushes.

It was a somber crowd, dressed in grays and blacks. Few spoke, and they progressed at a slow, solemn pace.

"A funeral." Tristam's soft voice sounded right beside her. "For a loyal servant of the Palace. He served here fifteen years, up until his death."

A woman led the party. Quite a bit older than Kyra, but her face was still smooth and her hair not yet gray. The woman was not crying, although her face showed the effort it took to maintain control. She kept herself together, Kyra guessed, for the five children walking beside her. They ranged from Lettie's age to almost her own. Unlike their mother, the children wept openly. As Kyra studied their features, a suspicion began to form.

"He was a good man, a devoted father," Tristam continued. Kyra looked at him out of the corner of her eye. There was something odd about his voice. He watched her intently as he continued talking.

"It was a tragedy for all of us when he was killed in the storehouse raid four days ago."

Tristam continued talking, but Kyra didn't hear him. She was fixated now on the pallbearers, and the body that lay upon the platform they carried. The body was covered, but her imagination supplied the details. How could it not? She would never forget his face, the panic in his eyes as she held the knife to his throat, his strangled cry, the way his body slowly went limp.

Tristam's fingers dug into her arm and she winced at the pain. It took her a moment to realize he wasn't attacking her, but holding her up. She took a breath and willed her legs to do their job. His grip loosened as she steadied. Her gaze returned to the widow and five children, and she stared after them as they turned a corner. If they had seen her, they showed no sign of knowing who she was. She hoped they'd never find out.

Kyra slumped as the tail of the procession disappeared. "You're not really moving me to another cell," she said.

"No."

She would have expected Tristam to look more pleased with himself. He had obviously brought her to the courtyard expecting some reaction, and she had given one that implicated her as clearly as if she had written ASSASSIN on her forehead. There was some satisfaction in his eyes, but beyond that, he looked . . . curious.

"What do you want from me?" she asked.

"He's not the first to die at the Guild's hands. And he won't be the last."

Kyra snuck another look at the knight's face. He spoke

softly. The curiosity was still there, but now his words had the probing focus of a hound who'd scented blood.

"Last month, two guards disappeared after an armory raid. We never found their bodies. They had families as well. Wives and children, and ailing parents."

She knew what he was doing now. If she'd been untied, Kyra would have clawed at his face and clamped her hands over his mouth.

"The widow today, she fainted when she heard the news. The littlest one, the daughter," he continued. "She still doesn't understand that he's gone. She keeps asking—"

"Stop," she said.

He waited.

"Grant me one favor." Her fists were clenched, and she shook with the effort of maintaining what was left of her composure.

"What is it?"

Kyra hung her head, all fight drained out of her. The man she killed deserved justice. Kyra had been a fool to think she could escape it. Even if she kept it from the Palace, her crime would haunt her nightmares. "Just outside the southwest merchant district, there's a tavern called The Drunken Dog. The cook is named Bella, and she watches two children. There is also a...frequent patron named Flick. Send someone to find them and put them under guard in the Palace. Once they're safe, I'll tell you what you want to know."

"You want us to protect them?"

"They're under threat."

Tristam hesitated. "We don't house commoners in the Palace."

Would he refuse her? She'd already said too much, and there was no way to take it back. "Please." It cost her to beg, and she couldn't look him in the eye. "I give you my word I'll answer your questions after that."

She kept her eyes on the ground. Tristam said nothing, and Kyra was aware of the guards watching them. Somehow she'd stumbled into a pit she couldn't escape. She just regretted dragging Flick, Bella, Idalee, and Lettie with her.

When the knight finally spoke, he was uncertain, as if surprised at his own words. "Perhaps we can make an exception. I'll speak with Malikel."

TWENTY-TWO

Kyra could smell the fear emanating from the man's pores. She breathed deeply and smiled in pleasure. Her knife was balanced against his throat, and she felt the tension in his muscles as he stood frozen against the wall. Assassins surrounded them, watching.

She was about to make her move when the assassins dissolved into mist. The fog dropped and condensed, taking the shape of huge beasts. Giant demon cats, licking their lips in anticipation, tails snaking back and forth, eyes fixed on her victim.

"What do you want from me?" she asked.

One of the cats spoke. "We're proud of you, daughter. This is your kill. We won't interfere."

If it was blood they wanted, she would give it to them. In one smooth movement, her knife traced a line across her victim's throat. The man rolled his eyes and sank to the ground, and she dismissed his weakness with disdain. Grasping her knife, she raised it high so she could plunge it into him one more time....

Suddenly, she was awake. James and the others faded, but the knife was still there, hovering above her body and aimed at her chest. Reflexively, she brought up her arm as it came down. The weapon cut a painful trail across her forearm and glanced off to the side. She kicked up hard. Her assailant doubled over and stumbled back. Kyra recognized the red-and-white livery of a Red Shield.

She struggled to regain her bearings. The last thing she remembered was falling asleep in her cell after the funeral. And now a guard was trying to kill her.

Why?

As her mind struggled to catch up, her body attempted a more defensive position. Kyra pushed herself to her feet, but standing so quickly made her vision cloud over. She braced against the wall for another attack, resigned for the worst. But instead, she heard the clang of her cell door. Her attacker's footsteps faded. By the time her vision cleared, she was alone.

Her right forearm throbbed painfully, and she pressed the bottom of her tunic against the wound to stop the bleeding. Drawing a ragged breath, she sat down and cradled her injured arm. The building was silent, with no signs of anyone, friendly or unfriendly, passing by.

Her breathing slowed, but the horror stayed in her chest. It wasn't just the attack. Her nightmares were getting worse, the emotions becoming more vivid each time. The violence and bloodlust clung to her, try as she might to erase them.

Kyra lifted a corner of the cloth to inspect her wound. The bleeding had not completely stopped, but it had slowed. Her hand was curled in an unnaturally tight fist. She tried to spread her fingers, but they barely twitched.

Alarmed now, Kyra tried again. Had the knife cut some

tendons? That wouldn't explain the almost painful muscle spasms that now immobilized her entire forearm. Kyra jumped to her feet. The room spun around her and she put her hand to her mouth to keep from vomiting. Spreading paralysis and nausea—she had heard of this at the Guild. No wonder her attacker had left. The poison would do the rest of his work for him.

Fighting down panic, she crossed to the cell door. If she banged on the door, would a passing guard hear? As Kyra drew breath to shout for help, she saw a faint light lining the edge of the door. In his haste to escape, the assassin hadn't closed it properly. She tugged experimentally on the handle. The door didn't budge, but the padlock on the other side was fastened poorly. She might be able to tease it open.

Her eyes fell on her bowl and spoon from dinner. The back of the spoon might work. She slid the handle through the opening. Although her mind was fuzzy, her hand knew what to do. The door swung open and she stumbled out into the hallway, silently thanking Flick for all those times they'd tried to outdo each other with their lock picks.

The corridor was lined with doors leading to similar cells, all closed. It was strangely quiet, and there was no sign of the man who had tried to kill her. Kyra crept up a spiral staircase at the end of the hallway, only to duck back at the red flash of a uniform. But as her heartbeat slowed, she realized that here also, it was overly quiet. There were no footsteps, no movement. She peered around the corner again. A guard lay on the ground, unnaturally still. Kyra gritted her teeth and inched closer, looking only at his belt to avoid triggering her nausea.

Her hands brushed his waist as she took the key ring. His body was still warm.

If she could make her way outside, she could call for help. But did she want to? Kyra had been around the Guild long enough to recognize the effects of lizard-skin venom. It caused disorientation in the victim, but the paralysis was the most dangerous. Once it spread to her vital organs, she'd die. She had an hour at most, and only if she could find a skilled healer who knew poisons.

If a guard found her, he'd drag her back to the cell, and she'd be dead before morning. She needed someone who would recognize the symptoms and know which healer could treat her—which meant her best hope was Tristam or Malikel. It was a bizarre situation. Here she was free of her cell, and not only was she about to walk straight back to her captors, she was also desperately hoping that she would find them. Malikel lived on the fifth floor in the officials' quarters, all the way across the courtyard. Tristam was with the younger officials on the ground floor.

She unlocked the door at the top of the stairwell, only to close it again at the sound of footsteps. When the footsteps faded, she crept through the door and into the courtyard. The cool air made her shiver more than it should have.

As she moved, images from her nightmare flashed through her mind. The smells stuck with her—the man's fear, the overpowering scent of his blood. Or was it her own blood she was smelling? As she reached the other side of the courtyard, she finally succumbed, bending over and retching into the bushes. The noise echoed too loudly off the walls. Finally, with her half-digested dinner pooled in the dirt, her body stopped convulsing. Kyra picked herself up and pried open the door to the officials' quarters, trying to ignore the stiffness that had now spread from her arm to her shoulder.

A rush of warm air hit Kyra's face and she blinked rapidly. Where was Tristam's room? She closed her eyes, trying to see the map James had given her. It had been on there. She was sure of it, but the map's lines turned blurry in her mind. Kyra settled on her best guess. Her first knock was pathetically soft. Her second attempt made her head swim, but at least the sound carried. The door opened, and Tristam peered out, blinking in confusion. His hair was disheveled, and he was bare-chested. Shock swept over his features at seeing Kyra. His body tensed. Then his eyes flicked to her arm, taking in the wound, before settling back on her face.

"I need a healer...poisoned blade." Talking took more breath than she was willing to spare.

He kept the door between them but reached through and placed two fingers under Kyra's chin, tipping her face toward him. She tried to meet his gaze as he examined her eyes, but she couldn't focus. He touched the back of his fingers lightly to her cheek. She flinched away at his icy touch.

"You're right." His voice was soft, but his movements now took on a new urgency. He disappeared into his room. When he reappeared, he had thrown on a loose tunic. Tristam stepped into the hallway with no hint of his prior wariness. "Can you walk?"

She nodded and hoped it was still true.

Tristam half supported and half steered her down the corridor. "Who was it?"

"A Red Shield." She stumbled. Tristam caught her as she pitched forward. Again, he tipped her face up to the candlelight. Kyra wondered just how bad she looked.

"This isn't working," Tristam muttered. "You need a healer now." He reached behind Kyra's knees and lifted her into his arms. Kyra watched dazedly as blood from her forearm left a streak on his white tunic. In other circumstances, she might have objected to being carried like a child, but now she just let herself crumple.

Candles, doors, stones blurred by. "Do you know the poison?" he asked.

"Lizard skin."

"What's the antidote?"

For some reason, it struck Kyra as funny that she didn't know. She started to chuckle but choked instead.

"Kyra?"

"I don't..."

He laid her on a soft surface. She heard Tristam pound on a door and call for a healer. She was having trouble breathing now, her lungs expanding only a finger's width with each breath. Between gasps, she heard a woman asking questions. Cold hands probed her wounded arm, while others raised her head and poured something into her mouth. She choked on the bitter liquid. Soon, the room and voices faded to nothing.

TWENTY-THREE

"Do you think this is a genuine assassination attempt?" She recognized that voice, but couldn't place it.

"Ilona says the poison is almost always lethal," Tristam replied. "Kyra should be dead."

"You acted quickly."

"I'm still impressed that she found me."

Kyra was slowly gaining control of her eyelids. At first, they fluttered uselessly, but with some effort she forced them open, only to snap them shut at the bright daylight. A moment later, she made a second attempt. This time, the light wasn't so blinding. She was in a room, sparsely furnished except for jars of herbs stacked around her.

As the memories rushed back, Kyra took an urgent inventory of her limbs. She flexed her fingers. Stiff, but they responded. She could also curl her toes. Relief flooded through her. If she could move her fingers and toes, hopefully she could move everything in between.

"Ilona, she's awake."

Kyra turned her head to see Tristam and Malikel next to

Kyra turned her head to see Tristam and Malikel next to her bed. The movement made her skull pound, and she closed her eyes again.

"Can you understand me, Kyra?"

A woman was bending over her. Kyra moved her head in her best approximation of a nod.

"You're very lucky to be alive. Are you thirsty?"

Her jaw felt rusted shut. "Aye," she finally managed to say.

The world spun as Ilona helped her sit. The healer waited a few moments before holding a cup to Kyra's mouth. The water washed over her dry lips. Some made it into her mouth, while the rest splashed onto the blankets.

Ilona turned to the two knights. "I suppose you won't wait to speak with her."

"We'd wait if we could," said Malikel.

Silence hung as Ilona gathered her things. When she left, Kyra turned her head to look at the knights. It took some effort to focus on their faces. Her gaze briefly met Tristam's. The suspicion was gone from his eyes, and Kyra realized she no longer feared him.

"Thank you," she said.

"Thank Ilona. She's the one who saved you."

Malikel leaned toward her, speaking slowly so she could follow. "The guards last night were drugged. All of them woke a few hours later and reported in, save one, who has disappeared along with his family. He was also the one to pass around the drugged water to the rest of them. He could have acted alone, but his methods suggest the Assassins Guild."

Tristam shook his head. "He'd been in the guard force for twenty years," he said. "We had no reason to think..."

"Maybe they threatened him," said Kyra.

Both men turned to look at her. "What do you mean?" asked Malikel.

"That's what they did to me." Kyra gasped as she followed that train of thought. "Bella, Flick, did you—"

"They're safe," said Tristam. "We found them after you were attacked, and they're under guard. What do you mean, the Guild threatened you?"

She closed her eyes in relief. As long as they were safe. "I wanted to leave the Guild. James—the head—wouldn't let me. He said he'd kill them if—" She stopped abruptly.

"He wanted you to kill Sir Malikel, didn't he?" Tristam said.

Kyra avoided their eyes. After all the stalling and the games, it was finally out. "I had a flask of poison I was supposed to put in Malikel's herbs. I dumped it when I couldn't carry through."

There was a moment of silence as the men digested this.

"How long have you been with the Guild?" asked Malikel.

"A few months." Kyra's speech was starting to slur. Her eyelids felt heavy.

"Why did you join them?"

"They needed someone who could get into the Palace. I needed coin. They protected me from—" She broke off, sluggishly remembering that the Red Shields who'd attacked her had been from the Palace. It was so hard to know whom to trust, what to say.

Perhaps her garbled speech masked her lapse, because

Malikel didn't acknowledge it. "Tell me one more thing," he said. "Does the Assassins Guild have any dealings with the Demon Riders?"

Kyra's eyes snapped open and she straightened in her bed. Nausea rose dangerously high in her throat. "You think so too? I'd suspected. There was the armor."

Malikel leaned forward in his chair. "Do you know how they got access to trade schedules?"

And just like that, the jolt of energy left her. Trade schedules. She closed her eyes. "He got them from me. I copied the schedules and gave them to him." The Demon Rider attacks, the raids on the trade caravans. They had been her fault.

"I think that's enough for today," said Malikel. "Tristam, we have much to discuss."

Kyra expected them to call the healer back in, but instead Malikel helped her lie back down on the bed. She watched them go, reeling at what she'd learned, the truth about the Guild that she could no longer deny. But right behind that realization, a wave of exhaustion followed as her wounds caught up with her. The two collided and dragged her back into darkness.

She slept for most of the next two days. The rest was good for her body, but as Ilona weaned her off the stronger sleep herbs, Kyra's nightmares returned. Several times a day she woke up in a cold sweat to a reality that wasn't much better. How could she have been so blind to James's plans?

Ilona helped her regain her strength—first helping her stand, and then to walk. When Kyra was alone, she wondered about her future. Now that everything was out in the open, she had no idea what would come next.

On the third day, Tristam and Malikel came to see her again. The councilman's expression was stern, and he entered with a gravity that made Kyra's stomach heavy with dread. Tristam was also more subdued than usual.

"I won't lie to you, Kyra," said Malikel after they'd settled down. "You're guilty of murder and high treason. The penalty is death, and neither Tristam nor I have the authority to change that."

A lump rose in Kyra's throat and she turned her face away. She had known this was the case, but somehow, she had hoped...

"We can't change your sentence," said Malikel, "but we can delay it. If you can help us against the Assassins Guild, the Council will grant a stay of execution."

Kyra waited until she was sure she could speak. "So either I die now, or later."

"You do have one hope. If you help us against the Assassins Guild, we can bring your case again before the Council. They've been known to reduce the sentences of prisoners who served them well. In previous questioning, you've been loyal to the Guild. Now that they've tried to kill you, and you know their connection with the Demon Riders, are you still so eager to defend their secrets?"

She studied their faces, trying to gauge the truth behind Malikel's words. "How do I know I can trust the Council?"

There was a dark humor in Malikel's eyes. "The Council

194

shifts to the tides of politics. If you're looking for security there, you'll not find it. The only thing you can be sure of is what you know of the Assassins Guild, and what they have done," said Malikel.

At least he was being honest. Kyra tried to think, but her mind fell apart. It was a devil's bargain.

"Can I see Flick and Bella?" she asked.

The knights exchanged a glance.

"We'll let you see them, if you want to," said Malikel. "But you may not. They think you're dead."

"They what?" Kyra grabbed her chair to keep from falling off. "What did you tell them?" Tristam reached to steady her, but she jerked away. "What did you tell them?"

"Calm down, Kyra." Malikel's commanding voice cut through her hysteria. "It's for their protection. You, of all people, should know that even being under guard in the Palace doesn't keep you safe from the Guild. If James wants to harm them, he'll find a way. But if you're dead, he has no reason to."

She imagined Flick and Bella hearing the news, Bella's hand over her mouth, Flick pounding his fist against a wall.

"How did they take it?"

Tristam looked down. "Not well, as you'd expect. But at least they're alive."

She shook her head, gripping the edge of her chair like a lifeline. "Flick will do something stupid if he thinks the Guild killed me. He'll get himself killed." Her voice rose as she spoke. "You don't know what you're doing."

And here already, she was falling prey to the noblemen's machinations. Of course they would be making her decisions for her. Dictating how her life should go.

"I don't know him like you do, Kyra," said Tristam quietly. "But I don't think he will. Flick knows that he's all they have now."

"He doesn't *know* that. He *thinks* that because you told him I was dead." She paused. "Who knows I'm alive?"

"Even the guards think you were killed. Only key members of the Council know you survived."

"But we could still tell Flick and Bella. They can be trusted."

"We will if you insist," said Malikel, "but they'll be watched as soon as we take them out of the compound. If they let anything slip, or act in a way that arouses suspicion . . . Remember, you can always tell them later, once the danger has passed. But you can't take it back once they know."

She glared disbelievingly at both of them. "How do I know that you even spoke to them? How do I know you're not lying to me?"

Tristam cleared his throat. "Idalee pulled the sheets and blankets off her bed and slept on the floor because the mattress was too soft. Flick took all the radishes out of the stew before eating it."

Kyra lowered her eyes, not wanting them to see how much Tristam's descriptions had affected her. Neither knight made any further argument, but just sat waiting. Did they have a point? She despised herself already, but she would never forgive herself if her friends came to harm.

"Fine," she said. "Keep it this way. And I'll help you against the Assassins Guild, if only to keep them safe."

Lizard-skin venom worked quickly and left the body slowly. According to Ilona, Kyra had to take doses of antidote for the next twenty days. Only when the poison was completely purged from her body would she be out of danger. Even the tiniest remnant of venom in her blood, left untreated, would gradually accumulate in her vital organs and kill her. One upside to this was that the Council deemed her less of a flight risk. Instead of keeping her in her windowless dungeon cell, she was allowed to stay locked in a room in the healer's wing.

Ilona's morning visits were the only part of the day Kyra looked forward to; the healer's gentle presence somehow made her isolation more bearable. Tristam visited her in the afternoons to speak with her about the Guild. He was no longer hostile. In their conversations, he listened to what she had to say and granted her rest if she felt tired. More than once, she caught him looking at her as if she were a puzzle he couldn't solve. But the knight remained distant. She told him what he needed to know, and their interaction ended at that. Kyra missed Bella's gentle touch, Flick's carefree jokes and contagious smile. She wondered how Idalee and Lettie were coping with news of her death, and how long she'd have to deceive them. Tristam told her that her friends had returned to the city, and Kyra hoped they were able to settle back into their lives.

"Tell me more about your raid of the Palace storehouse," Tristam said to her one afternoon.

"I've recounted everything and mapped out the route for you. What more do you want?" she asked.

"Why did you choose that particular storehouse?"

"Because the landlord didn't need the herbs, and the merchant did."

"What?"

Kyra looked at him. "The landlord. Who took the herbs."

"Kyra, what are you talking about?"

He really didn't know. "The herbs in the storehouse were taken from a shopkeeper who couldn't make his rent. His landlord took payment out of his wares instead."

"How do you know this?"

"I watched the rent collection. You were there." There was a flash of recognition in his eyes, but he still looked doubtful. "Look in your records if you don't believe me."

Tristam gave her one last calculating look. "Maybe I will." He jotted something down in his notes. "Tell me more about James. What's he like?"

Kyra sighed, seeing that this line of inquiry was over. "James is a strong Guildleader," she said. "He knows his men well, and he knows how to get folk to do what he wants. He manipulates people and uses their emotions against them."

"Does he share his power with anyone?"

"There's no clear second-in-command, but he's closer to some of his crew than others. Bacchus is one of his favorites."

"What was your relationship with James?" asked Tristam.

She had been tracing the wood-grain lines on the table and now her fingers turned white with pressure. Her eyes flew to his face.

"What do you mean?"

"Did you speak with him often? Did you know him well?"

From his tone, she realized it was an innocent question. Kyra swallowed.

"No," she said. She avoided his eyes. "I didn't know him well at all."

What *had* her relationship been with James? She felt sick at the way she'd felt and acted, like a giddy farm girl who'd lost all sense at a suitor's first wink. Had he really been attracted to her, or had he just been manipulating her to his ends? Her bitterness at what he'd done sat heavy in her chest, but at the same time, she couldn't believe that it had all been a lie. James's pride at her gradual improvement had felt real, as had the conviction in his voice when he spoke of their city. Kyra thought back to the afternoon they'd spent planning the raid. Something had happened there. She just wasn't sure what.

Tristam had stopped writing and was watching her carefully.

"You're not telling me everything," he said.

"There's nothing to tell," she said too quickly. Kyra wished he'd stop looking at her. She, for her part, looked everywhere but at Tristam.

"You cared for him, didn't you?" Tristam said softly, his eyes opening up with the realization. "He threatened your family to get you to kill Malikel, but that was only after things broke down between the two of you. Did he take you into his bed?"

In hindsight, it was a good thing Tristam had quick reflexes, because things didn't end well for prisoners who hit their captors. As it was, he caught Kyra's wrist just before her palm struck his face. For a moment, they were frozen there, Kyra shaking with fury, Tristam focused and unyielding.

"I may not be one of your noble-born ladies," said Kyra, voice trembling with anger, "but I in't an alehouse whore." She pulled against Tristam's grip, but he held firm. "Nothing happened between me and James."

He didn't let her go, though his gaze softened in a way that bruised her pride. "You're a puzzle, Kyra."

Kyra gathered her strength and twisted her arm out of his grip. "What you think matters nothing to me," she lied. "There's no more to say on this matter."

TWENTY-FOUR

Tristam shuffled through his stack of records, trying his best not to hunch his shoulders protectively over them. Though he had permission to view these documents, there was still a clandestine flavor to his questions today.

He looked over at Martin. "Any luck?" The two of them had taken over the records room, and piles of parchments were stacked all along the table between them.

Martin chewed on his cheek as he sorted through his own pile. "Looks like Kyra's right. The goods taken by the Assassins Guild belonged to Lord Edwin of Perkins. The Palace confiscated the wares from one of his renters on his behalf. The man was late to pay his rent because the trade caravans were attacked. He ran an herbal shop in the northwest quadrant, and a group of soldiers were sent a few weeks..." He trailed off.

"Yes, that was us," said Tristam. So Kyra had been telling the truth. The Guild hadn't been raiding for simple gain. They'd had a very specific goal. "Do the records say anything else?"

Martin's lips moved silently as he read the rest of the report. He wasn't a fast reader, though he was getting better with practice. "There's a note here says the storekeeper appealed to the magistrate for extra time, but he lost his case."

"It does seem hard to turn a profit if you have nothing to sell. Lord Edwin's never struck me as a pleasant man," said Tristam. "I wonder why the magistrate ruled in his favor."

"They didn't tell you when they sent us?" asked Martin. "They keep us Red Shields in the dark, but I thought you'd know the whole story."

Tristam shook his head. "I only knew that he hadn't paid his rent. None of the rest. It's not a soldier's place to question the Council's decisions." That was what his commanders would have said to him, though repeating their words didn't make him feel any less uneasy.

Martin gave a resigned shrug. "They've always favored the landlords. My uncle lost his smithy last year when he broke his arm."

"I'm sorry to hear that."

"I'm sure the magistrate had his reasons." Martin spoke with his usual pleasant tone, but avoided looking Tristam in the eye. It was a sober reminder that even though he and Martin got on well, they were still from different worlds. There were things the shieldman would never be completely open about to Tristam.

"How are the interrogations going?" asked Martin. Tristam couldn't tell if the young shieldman was changing the subject on purpose. "There's all kind of stories flying around about the assassin lass. Can she really kill a man by batting her eyelashes?"

Tristam raised an eyebrow. "Is that really what they're saying now?"

Martin's smile was unrepentant. "There are better stories than that one, though mayhap inappropriate to repeat."

Tristam decided he didn't want to know. The last thing he needed was to have the barrack's bawdy tales in his head when he was actually questioning Kyra. "The interrogations are... interesting."

"What do you mean?"

He hesitated. "She saved my life, you know."

For once, Martin was startled into silence. "What?" he finally said.

"This was before we captured her. The day the Demon Riders attacked the city, I broke my spear, and a cat cornered me. The beast would have killed me, but Kyra threw a rock and lured it away. I looked for her, but I didn't see her again until I captured her."

Martin whistled. "I'll wager she regrets that move now."

Tristam gave a wry chuckle. "She said as much, when I brought that up. I don't know what to make of her. You saw us fighting that night. She would have sliced me in two if I'd let her. Kyra's dangerous, and I can't let myself forget that. But..."

"She in't exactly the vicious criminal we thought we were chasing?"

That wasn't a bad way to put it.

They were interrupted by a servant entering the records room. "Sir Tristam. Councilman Willem requests your presence."

"Willem?" From across the table, Martin opened his eyes wide.

"Yes, sir. In his study."

"Mayhap he wants to give you a promotion," Martin said as Tristam gathered his things.

Somehow, Tristam doubted it.

Willem's study was lavishly decorated. The antechamber was covered wall to wall with intricate tapestries, and the furniture was hard oak, decorated with gold leaf. Willem sat at a large desk in the inner room and motioned for Tristam to have a seat.

"I want to congratulate you on your successful interrogation," Willem said. "It was very clever, holding the funeral where the prisoner could see it. I admit I was skeptical about your age and experience when Malikel put you in charge of the prisoner, but you have proved me wrong."

"Thank you, Your Grace." Tristam was pleased with how the funeral had turned out. Because he'd needed it for the interrogation, the Palace had agreed to pay for the family's expenses. But had the councilman asked to see him simply to congratulate him?

"Malikel has his . . . quirks," said Willem. "But sometimes he proves effective. I hear he's just left for Parna."

"Yes, Your Grace. He's gone for a fortnight."

"A pity he's not here. The Council has a pressing matter that cannot wait for his return. I've been discussing your prisoner with other members of the Council, and we're all struck by how she evaded capture by climbing the walls and ledges. From all reports, she is quite remarkable."

Why did it bother him that the councilman referred to her as his prisoner? By any definition, it was true. Kyra was under lock, and he had put her there. He saw her again, clutching her wounded arm, eyes feverish with poison. She'd crumpled against him when he'd picked her up.

"Her abilities are indeed something to see," he said to Willem. "She can do things that I would not have thought possible."

"It seems a waste to have such a tool and let it stay locked up, especially when we're at war."

He hid his distaste at Willem's words. "Did you have something specific in mind, Your Grace?"

"We do," said Willem. "I understand you made a few attempts to track the Demon Riders in the forest."

"I'm afraid I have not been very successful, sir. The one time I encountered them, they almost killed me."

"We think that the prisoner might have a better chance of spying on them successfully."

Kyra, as their spy? Did the Council trust her? "It's true that she's very quiet, and fast," Tristam said carefully.

"Say we asked her to do this, with the possibility of reducing her sentence if she's successful. To the best of your knowledge, would she be willing?"

Tristam paused, suddenly unsure. "I understand her better than I did before, but still not well enough to predict her decisions. Judging from her past, she's not averse to risk, and she may welcome the chance to go outside. But she's almost regained all her strength. If we let her run free in the forest, the temptation to escape may prove too much."

"We've anticipated that and have instructed the healer Ilona to withhold the last few doses of antidote."

Tristam tensed. "Sir?" he asked.

"The small amount of poison left in her body shouldn't interfere overly much with her health," said Willem. "We believe that the need for her final dose should motivate her to return to the Palace."

"I see." So they were holding the poison over her as a threat. "Did Ilona agree?"

"Ilona knows her place. She will bow to the wishes of the Council."

"Perhaps we should wait for Malikel's return."

"There's no time. The last dose of antidote is to be delivered this week. Either way, the Council has made a decision."

An unpleasant suspicion came to mind. "And if Kyra refuses to do this, will she still get the antidote?"

"Venom antidote is scarce. Without Far Rangers to replenish our stores, we need to ration our supplies wisely. And that includes prioritizing those who are actively serving the Palace. Do I gather that you object, Tristam?"

Tristam fought to keep his voice even. "If I may speak freely, Your Grace, I've been working hard to win her trust, and a move like this may undermine my efforts."

"I understand your concern, but the city is in danger. We don't have time to proceed gradually."

Tristam looked down, reminding himself to speak carefully, that he was addressing the most powerful man in Forge. "I suppose, Your Grace, that these tactics remind me too much of what the Assassins Guild would do."

"How so?"

"It's underhanded, and it's cowardly."

Willem's expression hardened. "Watch your tongue, young knight. You speak above your station."

The rebuke hit him with almost physical force. Tristam took a slow breath. "My apologies, Your Grace. I spoke inappropriately."

"One of my biggest misgivings about putting you in charge of the prisoner was your youth. At your age and experience, I worried that you'd be unduly influenced by a female prisoner so close to your own age. I expressed my doubts to Malikel, but he vouched for your maturity and character. I hope you don't prove him wrong," said Willem. "Remember that we're working toward the same goals. You lost a good friend to the Demon Riders, isn't that right?"

"Yes, sir."

"And you do wish to defeat them, do you not?"

"Yes, sir." And the frustrating thing was, he did. He still wanted it, more than anything. And now that Willem had put the idea in his head, he could see how Kyra could help them if she were willing. But that was the sticking point. She wouldn't be willing with a threat like this hanging over her.

"Remember also, that the prisoner is already under a death sentence. We are offering her a chance to avoid it. Can I be assured of your cooperation, Tristam?"

It wasn't really a question. "Yes, Your Grace."

"Good. Then I will accompany you to speak with her."

"Now?"

"I see no reason to wait."

207

Tristam was surprised at how desperately he wanted to stall, but he couldn't find a way. He was bound to obey the Council, and Willem was its head.

Kyra was sitting at her table when they walked in. Under Ilona's expert care, the color had returned to her cheeks, and her dark eyes were alert. She didn't look like an assassin. She looked like a young girl—a pretty one at that, with her small stature and delicate features. She started to say a greeting but stopped when the head councilman walked in.

"This is the prisoner?" asked Willem.

Kyra looked away. Her expression grew stony.

"Yes, Your Grace."

Willem gave her an evaluating look. "She's small, for all the trouble she's caused."

Kyra didn't respond or remove her eyes from the floor. But Tristam had spent enough time with her to see the slight stiffening of her posture, the way she curled slightly more into herself. He cut in before the councilman could continue.

"Kyra, we came to ask something of you. It's dangerous, but you might appreciate the opportunity to go outside."

She took a cautious glance up at the mention of "outside."

Willem gave Tristam an expectant look, and Tristam cleared his throat. "As you know, I spent some time in the forest tracking down the Demon Riders. I did find them once, but they nearly killed me. The Council thinks you may have better luck than I."

"Better luck tracking them down?" She spoke quietly, her eyes flickering occasionally to Willem.

"I can help you track them down. What we need is someone who can observe them without getting caught. I've seen you move. If anyone could spy on them undetected, it'd be you."

"I see." He could see her trying to figure out if there was more to the story. "Do you have a plan?"

"We'd have to clear the specifics with the Council, but you'd probably spend a few days with me in the forest. We can ride out under cover of night, and we'll find a place where the tracks are thick. Then, we just wait."

"You want me to watch them, not fight them?"

"We want to know where they live and how many there are. What their plans are and if they have any weaknesses."

She pursed her lips and eyed him cautiously. "I can't stay quiet if I'm dragging chains."

And here it went. He took a breath. "You won't be chained."

Her eyebrows flew up at this. "The Council will let me run free in the forest?"

He didn't answer, resentment locking his jaw tight. Willem broke in. "Your last few doses of antidote will be withheld for now. Ilona will give you the rest after you complete this task."

Tristam saw the exact moment when it sank in, when her expression changed from wary consideration to cold understanding. "I see." Her voice took on an edge. "I don't really have a choice."

He felt some contrary satisfaction in seeing her anger. For a moment, Tristam was tempted to sit back and watch things unravel. But then Willem looked at him, a clear warning in his gaze.

"Remember, Kyra," said Tristam, "everything you do in service could be considered by the Council in lightening your sentence."

"I'm just a bloodhound, in't I? And the poison's my leash."

"We're trying to help you." The words tasted false on his tongue.

"Of course. Like the Assassins Guild wanted to help me."

"The Assassins Guild wanted to *kill* you, Kyra."

"And you'll delay my death. *If* I'm useful." The betrayal in her eyes was directed straight at him, and it bothered him more than he cared to admit.

He opened his mouth to reply, but stopped when he saw Willem watching him. He wasn't going to convince Kyra with platitudes that he didn't even believe. As much as he hated this, he was a knight of Forge and duty-bound to serve the Council.

"Councilman," he said, "may I please have a word alone with Kyra?"

"You may have a moment."

As the door closed behind Willem, Kyra turned her gaze back to Tristam, her entire body tense. Tristam closed his eyes and let out a long breath.

"Kyra, I'm sorry about this. It's not my decision. It was handed down by the Council."

"And you're helping."

"I don't have a—" He stopped and gathered himself. "Look, it doesn't have to be like this. I know it's an underhanded tactic, but really, even if the Council weren't holding the poison as a threat, you'd do it anyway."

Kyra regarded him as if he were a snake about to strike. "And why is that?"

"Because you helped bring the Demon Riders to Forge."

His words affected her just as he'd expected. She winced. He'd already used her guilt against her once, when he'd brought her to the manservant's funeral. At the time, he hadn't thought twice about the tactic, but now that they had the beginnings of trust between them, it felt dirty. He reminded himself of the vows he'd taken to Forge and forced himself to continue on.

"I know you're sorry, Kyra, and I know you want to make amends for it. This is your chance. Don't think about the Council or the threats. What matters is that the city won't be safe until we drive out the barbarians."

Tristam watched the emotions flicker across her face— anger, confusion, and regret. She was quiet for a long time, and even as Tristam's skin crawled from the trap he'd woven around her, he realized that he hoped she'd agree. Not only because he wanted to defeat the Demon Riders, but because if he could convince her that she wanted this, she'd hate him less for playing along with the Palace's games.

"Fine," she said. "I'll do it."

He thanked her. She didn't look at him as he left.

As the door closed behind him, their earlier conversation about James drifted back to him. *James is a strong leader,* she'd said. *He manipulates people and uses their emotions against them.* At the time, he'd thought James cunning and ruthless, a dangerous man with no principles. But as Tristam entered Willem's study to deliver the news, he couldn't help but wonder if he'd been too quick to judge.

TWENTY-FIVE

"Watch out!" shouted Tristam.

Kyra jumped back, barely avoiding the mare's flailing hooves. The horse tossed her head and rolled her eyes, and Kyra backed even farther away, trying not to imagine what would have happened if she'd been just a hair slower.

"I told you horses don't like me."

The mare stopped kicking, though she stamped her feet and snorted in Kyra's direction.

"Now I believe you." Tristam inched closer, cautiously reaching out to take the horse's reins.

The young man Tristam had introduced as Martin whispered to the horse and stroked its mane. "If Muse won't take her, I don't know who will. We in't going to find a gentler horse."

It annoyed Kyra to be talked about as if she weren't there. "Forget this," she said. "I'll take my chances with the poison."

Tristam raised his eyebrows and turned back to the mare. And he was right not to believe her. As much as she resented the Council's games, now that she was in the stables, so close to the open air, there was no way she was going back to her locked room.

They fared no better the second time. The third time, Muse's hoof clipped Kyra's shoulder, and she stumbled back against the wall.

"Kyra!" Tristam reached a hand to steady her.

She shot him a furious look.

"That didn't sound good," said Martin.

"May I?" Tristam asked, motioning toward her shoulder.

She almost wished it were broken, just so Tristam could deliver the news to Willem. Tristam peeled her hand away from her shoulder and probed it with his fingertips. She drew a sharp breath when he pressed on the bruise. Though truth be told, he was being very gentle—his brows furrowed in concentration, his eyes going frequently to her face to check if he was hurting her. These days, she didn't know what to think of Tristam. Moments like this tempted her to let down her guard, but then he'd do something—lie to her family about her death, act as Willem's mouthpiece—to lose her trust. Kyra's legs started to cramp, and she realized it was because she was still trying to back away from him into the barn wall. She scowled and forced herself to relax.

"It doesn't feel broken."

She reluctantly raised her arm. "I think I'm all right."

Tristam exhaled in relief. "We're going to have to find some other way. Wait here," he said, motioning to Kyra and Martin. "Stay out of sight."

Kyra retreated into a corner, relieved to escape the homicidal horse. Martin leaned against the wall. She picked straw off the floor and broke each strand into pieces, making no attempt at conversation.

"You were really part of the Assassins Guild?"

Kyra looked up to see Martin looking at her with friendly curiosity.

"I was," she said, slightly taken aback.

Martin grinned. "I'm relieved to find you normal looking. With all the stories flying around, I was half expecting you to be ten feet tall and have three arms."

His smile was infectious, and Kyra found herself reluctantly smiling back. "It'd be hard to climb if I was ten feet tall."

Martin shifted his weight, and Kyra noticed the crimson *F* embroidered on his tunic.

"You're a Red Shield," she said. For some reason she'd assumed he was a stable hand. She tried to suppress her automatic disgust at that emblem.

Martin blinked at the change in her tone. "Aye," he said cautiously. "And my da and brothers as well." When she didn't respond, he continued talking. "It in't a bad life. The coin is decent. I'm lucky, since I'm a dog talker. There's enough commanders who want dogs, so we get to choose."

"You picked Tristam?"

"Sir Malikel, actually. But Sir Tristam is a good sort too. Sir Malikel attracts a friendlier type."

Kyra supposed that Tristam wasn't cruel, but she wouldn't exactly have categorized him as friendly.

They were interrupted by Tristam's voice outside. The two of them came out to see Lady hitched to a horse-drawn cart— the kind used by servants to carry firewood.

"You can't be serious," she said.

"It's this or get your brains kicked out. Trust me, Lady is just as unhappy about this as you are."

He did have a point. Kyra climbed in, and an amused Martin threw a cloth over her.

"Stay out of sight until we reach the forest," said Tristam.

Then they were off. Through the slats of the cart, Kyra caught glimpses of a neighborhood she didn't recognize. Perhaps Tristam thought familiar surroundings would prove too tempting. Nonetheless, even seeing an unfamiliar part of the city was comforting after her days in the compound. Out at night, with the moon reflecting off the rooftops, and the wind blowing over her head, she could almost pretend she was on another job. The clatter of Lady's hooves rang louder across the cobblestones than they would have during the day. A few times, Kyra glimpsed others on the streets, but no one stopped them.

But her comfort gradually disappeared as they traveled farther. The buildings thinned out, separated first by farmland and then forest. By the time the sun came up, the smell of bark and leaves had replaced that of manure and livestock, and she saw nothing through the slats but trees. Finally, the wagon rolled to a stop and Tristam pulled back the cloth. Kyra sat up to see that they were deep in the forest, by a small wooden guardhouse.

"We'll leave the horse and cart here." He put his hand to her waist as she stood, and Kyra jerked away from him. Tristam stepped back. "Force of habit," he said irritably. Was he blushing? "I suppose you don't need my help to get off the—"

"No." Kyra jumped off and ran past him toward the guardhouse. Though she couldn't help wondering . . . what would it be like to be treated like a lady? Out of the corner of her eye, she saw Tristam leading his horse inside. The serving girls at The Drunken Dog would have killed to be escorted around the forest by a young knight. But then, all they knew about knights were from Brendel's ballads. She wondered if they'd still want to be carried in a handsome knight's arms if the deal included an assassin and a poisoned dagger.

After Lady was comfortably stabled, they continued by foot. This was an old forest, with large, thick-trunked trees that grew as high as Kyra could see, and as they continued, Kyra began to feel more and more uneasy. The sunbeams shifting through the leaves and the wind's faint rustle seemed to hide some unknown danger. It didn't make sense. There were certainly just as many dangers in the city, but Kyra couldn't shake her agitation.

"Do you know anything about tracking?" Tristam asked.

"Why would I know anything about tracking?" Kyra asked, teeth clenched as she dodged another branch.

Tristam turned to face her. "Look, Kyra. I know you're not happy with me. But it's going to be an unpleasant trip for both of us if we're at each other's throats the entire time."

She faltered at his rebuke. "I've never been out in the woods before."

"Never?" Tristam's surprise showed in his voice. "I spent my entire childhood in woodland just like this. My family's manor is out in the forest."

"I can tell."

"Tell what?"

"That you're comfortable here." She couldn't put it into words, but he moved differently. Even in the past hour, the tenseness had left his muscles—a tenseness that she hadn't noticed until it was gone. He stood taller, though he'd already been head and shoulders above her. He was more self-assured, and it seemed as if a weight had lifted off him.

Tristam gave a quiet smile. "You should come out here in the fall. The leaves are beautiful when they turn."

Kyra didn't respond. A faint impression was forming in the back of her mind, of walking through a similar forest. Or rather, of being carried, the way Flick carried Lettie. There was something threatening about the memory, and she shook her head to clear it.

They continued in silence as Tristam looked for signs of the Demon Riders, occasionally examining a snapped branch or kneeling to look at footprints.

"The last time I saw the Demon Riders," said Tristam, "it was at night—I think they may travel after dark. I see some fresh tracks, so we can stay here overnight if we can find cover."

The forest was mainly devoid of underbrush, but they found a patch of bushes where a tree had fallen. Tristam showed Kyra the types of leafy flexible branches they needed to make a shelter, and they spread out to gather materials. Moving around the forest was different from walking in the city. It was almost impossible to take a step without landing on a dry leaf or crackling twig. Kyra scowled at the noise and made a game of stepping softly. After a while, she started to get the hang of it—a trick in the way she placed her foot and shifted her weight.

After some hours of work, they had an impressive shelter. Bushes made up three walls, and Tristam had woven branches in the gaps. Beneath the cover of night, it would be easy to miss.

"Did they teach you this in knight training?" Kyra asked.

"No, I used to do this as a boy, before I became a page." Tristam stepped back to examine his handiwork and gave a satisfied nod.

"So you lived near the forest?" she asked. "Is the rest of your family still there?"

"My father, mother, and my younger sister are. My two older brothers are road patrol knights, so they don't spend much time at home. They monitor the forest roads far from the city, mostly trade routes. Perhaps it's because we live where we do, but my family's always been drawn to the road patrols. We like being away from civilization."

It was strange to think that Tristam had a family. Obviously, he hadn't sprung up fully grown just to capture and interrogate her, but still, the idea of him belonging somewhere, of having people he cared about and who cared about him, was intriguing.

"Why are you not there with your family?"

"I thought I would join them. But everything changed when Jack—" He stopped. "There's still some time before sundown. We should get some rest so we can both stay up the night. Why don't I take first watch? It's been a long day, and you're still healing."

Kyra pretended not to notice the abrupt change in topic. "Aren't you worried I'll murder you in your sleep?"

It was just an offhand comment, but he looked at her thoughtfully. "I've seen your reaction to death," he said. "You won't kill me."

"I'm touched." But as Kyra looked for a place to lay her

blanket, she couldn't deny her relief at his vote of confidence, however backhanded it was.

They were running. Or rather, the man carrying her was running and she was looking over his shoulder as leaves and branches flew by. There was growling and snapping of teeth in every direction. The man stumbled. Kyra screamed, but he caught himself—and her—before they tumbled to the ground. He set her down and bent over double, head down, his weatherworn face creased even further with exhaustion. Around them, the growls grew louder, frightening and familiar at the same time.

A crash of branches close by, and the man picked her up again. Sharp twigs scratched her face and hands. He set her down and took out a jar filled with something black and foul-smelling. She cried when he smeared it on her face and hands, then on her arms and the rest of her body.

"Stay still. Don't make any noise."

She choked down her sobs. The man took one last look at her. "Be brave," he said, and left. She was alone, and the growls were coming closer.

Kyra woke up screaming. Branches swayed above her, mixing with the stuff of her dreams and sending her into a greater panic. She was on her feet shaking off her blanket, when she glimpsed Tristam staring at her a few paces away. Slowly, her wits returned and she stood like a cornered deer until her breathing slowed.

"Nightmare?" he asked.

She nodded, not quite trusting herself to speak.

"Sit down. You're shaking." Tristam came toward her slowly, as if afraid she would bolt. He took her blanket and wrapped it around her like a cloak. The weight of his hands on her shoulders was comforting, and she was almost reluctant to pull away, but she grasped the blanket and settled back down.

She'd had the dream before, but never so clearly. "I think I've been in a forest before."

"You dreamed about it?"

"It was very clear."

He sat down on a fallen log, still watching her as if he expected her to panic again. "I gather that Flick and Bella are not your real family."

She shook her head. "In my earliest memories, I'm alone on the streets. Flick and Bella didn't find me until later."

There was a familiar flash of sympathy in his eyes, and she waved it away. "Don't pity me. I was luckier than most of the gutter rats. And Bella and Flick were as good as any family once I found them."

"They do seem to care about you."

Kyra pulled her blanket tighter, as if by doing so she could pull her memories close. "Bella's son died before I met her. I think she needed someone else to mother." Now Kyra was dead too, as far as Bella knew. One more heartache to add to Bella's long list. She pushed the thought aside. "Flick and I also bickered a lot. We still do. But he never took my coin or my food, though many times we needed for both. At least until I learned to earn my own coin."

Kyra stopped when she remembered how she'd earned more money and that she was talking to a Palace knight. She braced herself, waiting for him to call her a lawless thief. She'd had no choice in the matter, she thought fiercely. If he'd been starving, he'd have done the same.

To her surprise, he gave a gentle chuckle. "You think I'm going to say something about you being a thief."

"You didn't mince words about me before."

"I was angry." He paused. "It was unfair of me."

Kyra didn't know what to say to that.

He leaned forward, looking first at his hands in front of him, and then raising his eyes to hers. "Do you ever wish you knew more about your real family?"

She searched him for any sign of mockery, but he seemed sincere. "What gutter rat doesn't? I was jealous of the serving girls. They were always gossiping—this one grousing about having her mother's hips, the other about her father's complexion. I thought they were so lucky just to know how tall they'd be, how they'd turn out." She smiled wistfully. "I would have liked some warning that I would be so small."

Tristam had a way of listening that made her feel like he really took in what she said. She'd resented it in the interrogation room, but out here, it was kind of nice.

"I suppose there *is* some comfort in having a path set out for you," he said. "Some younger sons resent having siblings to live up to, but my brothers were good to me. I respected them and learned a good deal." He caught her eye. "Of course, things are different now that I've decided not to follow in their footsteps."

Kyra remembered what he'd said earlier about joining the road patrols, and how abruptly he'd changed the topic. She bit her lip, gauging his receptiveness. "Who's Jack?"

Tristam's shoulders stiffened, and he made a visible effort to relax again. "I suppose there's no reason to keep it secret," he said. "Jack was a friend. We came to the Palace the same year and trained together almost up until I became a knight."

"Was?"

"He was killed in the first Demon Rider raid. I joined the city's defense to avenge his death. I thought it would be a simple thing, but it grew more and more complicated. The Demon Riders evaded us despite our best efforts. There were people working against us, leaking our secrets to the barbarians. I hated them and vowed to capture those responsible, but even that was not what I expected." Tristam paused. "Sometimes, when you look more closely at your enemies, they start looking less like enemies."

Kyra realized with a jolt that he was talking about her. Tristam was still lost in his own thoughts.

"I've been meaning to ask you something," he said. "Though I'm not quite sure how to say it."

"Tristam, you've been interrogating me for weeks. And now you can't ask a question?"

There was a twinkle of amusement in his eyes before his expression turned serious again. "When you watched the rent collection, you saw me there?"

She nodded. "You stood right by the wagon, commanding the Red Shields."

"And when the Demon Riders attacked Forge, did you recognize me when you saw me on the streets?"

When Kyra nodded again, he fell silent, as if he were

turning words around in his head. "You didn't have to throw that rock," he finally said. "It nearly got you killed."

Again, she worried he was mocking her, but the only thing she saw in his eyes was curiosity and a desire to understand.

"I did hesitate," she said. "But I guess there wasn't much time for thinking."

"I'm grateful," he said, "for what you did."

The night passed without any sign of the Demon Riders. As the sky began to lighten, Kyra refilled their water bottles at a nearby river. The spray was cold in the morning air, and Kyra took a few moments to stretch her stiff limbs. Tristam was rearranging their packs when she came back with two full water skins.

"Here," she said, laying them down behind Tristam.

He jumped at her voice. "How did you do that?"

"Do what?"

"Come up behind me so quietly. I'd be on latrine duty for a month if my commander had seen you sneak up on me like that."

Kyra shrugged. "I've been practicing."

Tristam shook his head. "Do it again. Just walk to that tree over there."

She humored him, strolling to the tree he had pointed out and noting with satisfaction that her footsteps were almost completely quiet, though she could hear the occasional rustle. When she came back, he was shaking his head, staring at her as if she'd grown an extra arm.

"I've never seen anything like it. I spent an entire childhood in the forest and still make more noise than you do after a day of practice."

"Maybe you need to lose some weight." Kyra walked back and tapped gently on his well-muscled stomach. She smiled impudently up at him, and there was a glint of grudging amusement in Tristam's eyes as he took her hand to pull it away. He was just a second slow to let go of her. It was barely noticeable, but long enough for Kyra to go still, and to understand that their conversation last night had cracked the walls between them. It would not take much to bring them down completely.

They stepped away from each other at the same time.

"Should we break camp?" she asked. She touched the spot on her palm where his fingers had been, but let go when his eyes flickered to the movement.

Tristam let out a slow breath. "Let's move to a different place tonight."

They did a respectable job of pretending nothing had happened. The two of them kept a careful distance between them as they traveled, and when they spoke, it was about the trail and their mission. Kyra spent the silent periods between conversations calling herself choice names. She knew better, after James, than to make eyes at any man who held a knife over her. She'd seen enough of life to know how dangerous a nobleman could be to any city girl, much less a prisoner of the Palace.

They spoke little as they hiked, and eventually, Tristam picked a spot for their second shelter. Kyra busied herself with gathering leaves and branches, but when it came time to enter the shelter, she was reluctant to go in. She told herself it was because she was tired of cramped spaces, and not because she felt self-conscious to be in such close quarters with Tristam. She looked around. It was late summer, and the trees were lush with leaves.

"The shelter's too cramped. I'm spending the night up there." She pointed to a particularly dense tree.

She could tell from the look in Tristam's eyes that he knew the real reason she didn't want to stay close. He slowly nodded his acquiescence. "Give it a try."

Climbing always cleared her mind, and this tree was a joy to climb. Smooth bark, well-spaced branches. It might as well have been a ladder created for her benefit. She went up a good distance and settled herself into a fork.

"Can you see me?" she shouted.

"Are you sure you're not spawned from squirrels?"

"So you can't?"

"You'll be fine. Just don't fall down."

From the treetop, the forest looked quite different. There was much more sky and more sun, but it was actually harder to see to the front and sides because leaves blocked her view. Kyra wondered if she'd be able to see Forge if she climbed higher.

Soon the sun waned, and cricket chirps replaced birdsong. Kyra found herself tiring more quickly than she'd expected. It was still early compared with what she was used to, but she was feeling the lingering effects of the poison. Her eyelids grew heavy, and she considered tying herself into the tree.

She was awakened by the brushing of leaves across her face, first one by one, then clumps at a time as she tipped off her branch. Kyra grabbed at leaves as her eyes snapped open, sending a few handfuls to the ground before her hands closed on solid wood. She hung there for a moment, palms raw, and squinted down toward Tristam's shelter. She couldn't see if he had noticed or if he was even awake.

That had been a bit too close. Slowly, Kyra pulled herself back up and added sleeping in trees to the list of things she wouldn't do again. She waited for the crickets to resume their chirping, but they didn't. There was a rustling to her right, perhaps ten trees away, but she couldn't get a clear view.

Kyra climbed down, lowering herself from branch to branch until her feet touched dirt. From behind the bushes, Tristam looked at her questioningly. She caught his eye but didn't try to explain. Better to be quiet. From the ground, she couldn't see as well, but she could still detect the rustling in the distance—a shifting of leaves that went against the wind.

She left Tristam at the base of the tree and ran toward the movement. Somehow, the forest felt safer at night. The cool air invigorated her, and whatever dangers she feared earlier seemed less threatening with the darkness to keep her safe. As she came closer, Kyra slowed and ducked behind some trees, her breathing loud in her ears as shapes resolved in front of her. There was a line of shadows hiking through the trees. They had long hair and were clad in strange wraparound tunics. The Demon Riders walked silently in single file, gracefully stepping over roots and ducking under branches. Kyra couldn't see all of them from where she was, but there must have been at least a hundred.

A crash of foliage above Kyra made her jump. Nearby, a tree bent and swayed under an invisible weight as leaves rustled and rained down. Against the moonlight, Kyra saw a shadow: a long tail, curling and straightening in the branches.

Kyra dove back behind the tree, heart pounding wildly. Had the beast seen her? She kept absolutely still, too terrified to move. But there was no roar or shout. Kyra reminded herself to breathe and risked another look.

Now that she noticed one demon cat, she saw others. Four cats total, leaping from tree to tree in the same direction as their riders. The entire group was traveling somewhere. She trailed them, staying well behind the group and timing her movements so they were masked by the cats' tree landings.

Kyra grew more and more alarmed as she followed them. The Demon Riders were headed toward Forge. She trailed them a little longer, hoping they would turn, but their path didn't waver. If they really were going to the city, she needed to find Tristam. Making one last note of where they were, Kyra retraced her steps. She burst through the trees to find Tristam pacing the ground in front of his hiding place.

"They're on the move," she said without preamble.

"The Demon Riders?"

"They're going to Forge. We have to get back."

She could see his dark eyes moving as he absorbed her words. He gave a curt nod. "Let's go."

She dashed back in the direction from which he'd come, but she soon realized Tristam wasn't used to running in the dark. Several times, Kyra rushed ahead, only to have to wait as Tristam caught up. Even at that pace, he was coming dangerously close to twisting an ankle. Thankfully, the demon cats left so many fallen branches in their wake that even Kyra could follow their trail.

The tracks continued to lead straight toward Forge. After a while, Kyra and Tristam ditched the trails for the main road. Kyra breathed a sigh of relief when they reached the guardhouse and hitched Lady back up to the cart.

Finally, the trees gave way to farmland. In the red glow of dawn, she could see the outlines of Forge. But it was too early for sunrise. Tristam had noticed the glow as well, and he reined Lady in. Kyra hopped out to get a better look.

"No," Tristam whispered.

Kyra's skin prickled as she realized his meaning. "Are you sure?" she asked.

Tristam's eyes remained fixed on the horizon. His hands clenched the reins in a death grip. In the distance, the red flickered and grew as the first plumes of smoke rolled into the sky.

TWENTY-SIX

The city streets were dark. So dark that the flames in the distance didn't make sense. Kyra could almost pretend that it was a mistake, but as they rode farther in, past quiet houses and darkened storefronts, they heard screams and smelled smoke. They began to see people. First a few, and then more and more ran toward them, fleeing the inner city. Soon, the roads were too clogged for the cart, and they continued on foot, working their way upstream. With so many people around, Kyra couldn't see anything beyond what was right in front of her. All she could do was follow blindly in Tristam's wake, dodge the onslaught of people, and hope the tall knight had a better view.

Tristam turned and grabbed Kyra by the shoulders. "The fire's in the southwest district," he shouted.

Kyra stared at him in horror. "The Drunken Dog!"

The smoke grew thicker as they ran, burning Kyra's eyes and coating her throat. She almost crashed into a soot-covered man supporting a hobbling woman. Nearby, a young girl stopped and doubled over, coughing uncontrollably. Palace soldiers appeared in the mix, shouting as they attempted to control a crowd that only half saw them. Kyra desperately scanned faces as she ran but recognized no one.

Kyra heard a roar behind her and spun around. A demon cat backed a terrified woman and child against a wall. The cat crouched low, tail waving in the air. A guard jumped in front of them, spear ready. The cat slashed at the guard, and he jumped aside just in time. Tristam put a hand to his sword. Kyra stopped as well, torn between helping him and finding her family. Tristam looked at her, and she knew that he'd read her thoughts, just as she knew he was trying to decide if he could trust her in the city alone. For a split second, he hesitated.

"Go check on the inn," he said, turning his eyes to the creature. "I'll be there as soon as I can."

He drew his blade and shouted a challenge. The demon cat coiled around to engage him. As Tristam and the guard faced the animal, Kyra forced herself to turn away. With no weapons, she was no help to them, and she needed to get home.

Without Tristam to clear a path for her, the crowds paid Kyra no heed. She fought her way through, collecting bruises and bumps as she jostled her way upstream toward the fire. One man barreled straight into her. He would have knocked her off her feet if she hadn't fallen into another man, who swore at her to watch where she was going. Kyra pushed on, consumed by her need to get home. Maybe it was just a coincidence that The Drunken Dog was at the heart of the fire. Maybe.

Ahead of her, flames leaped from rooftops toward the sky. Buckets lay forgotten on the ground, the guards now desperately fighting off the invaders. In one square, a group of three demon cats and their riders faced off against a handful of soldiers. Kyra kept her head low and skirted past.

As she neared The Drunken Dog, the flames on either side of the street grew, and the smoke became so thick she had to duck low to keep from choking. Even though she stayed in the middle of the road, the heat from the fires on either side pressed down on her head and shoulders. She cast a hand over her face to block falling ashes and kept going. Finally, she passed through the heart of the blaze, and the angry flames gave way to burned-out ruins. A charred sign caught her eye and she skidded to a stop, lungs burning. Half the letters were reduced to charcoal, but the sign unmistakably belonged to the bakery a few stores past The Drunken Dog.

How could she have run right past the inn and not noticed? A voice in her head whispered a reason she didn't want to hear. Kyra retraced her steps, unwilling to believe it, but there was no denying the sight that greeted her. Charred posts marked where the walls of the tavern used to be, surrounding a blackened floor. Fallen timbers and boards, all that was left of the second floor and roof, lay in piles on the ground. It was all destroyed: the dining room, Bella's kitchen, everything.

Kyra clasped her hand to her mouth, silencing the cry that rose up in her throat. She rushed in, ignoring the precariously hanging timbers. Smoke made her eyes water, and splinters, still warm, threatened to puncture the leather soles of her shoes. Still, she dashed from room to room, scouring the ruins. The building was destroyed, but there were no bodies. Kyra stopped. No bodies. They might have escaped.

She ran outside and scanned the street. The Drunken Dog

was so close to the center of the attack. Could anyone possibly have made it out safely? Her eyes fell on the one structure still standing: the stone market building. Shapes were visible through the windows, and they weren't dressed like Demon Riders. Kyra dashed for the door and almost impaled herself on a sword. A Red Shield blocked her way.

"I'm looking for my family," she said.

She must not have looked like a Demon Rider, because he moved aside. "Get in, quickly."

The main hall smelled of sweat and fear. Murmurs and quiet sobbing muted the sounds of battle but didn't quite drown them out. Kyra ran from one stall to the next, searching through faces. People were crowded into every corner. Finally, she glimpsed a familiar figure, his arms draped protectively around two young girls. The girls covered their ears as they huddled on the ground. All three of them had faces blackened with soot, and streaked—even Flick's—with tears.

"Flick!" Kyra forgot about the demon cat invasion, forgot she was supposed to be dead, and barreled toward them, stopping short as they looked up and registered her face. There was a moment of shocked silence. The girls gasped. Flick stared as if he thought he'd gone mad.

"Is it really..." he said.

She nodded. Flick stared for another second before he shouted her name, voice cracking with emotion. He grabbed her shoulders and pulled her to his chest, holding her so tightly she thought he was going to break her ribs. Kyra squeezed her eyes tight against the tears that threatened to spill. It would be all right. She wanted to just stay here, lean against him, and forget everything. He kissed her soot-stained forehead and squeezed her again before holding her back out to look at her.

"They told us you were dead."

"I know. I'm..." She choked on the words. Idalee and Lettie stared wide-eyed, as if unsure if she was really there. Kyra reached out and pulled them close. She shouldn't have worked for the Guild. She should have listened to Flick, to Bella...

"Where's Bella?"

A shadow crossed Flick's face, and Kyra froze. He looked toward a group of women bent over someone on the ground. "She was stuck in the kitchens when the fires started. We were lucky we could get her out—"

She didn't wait for him to finish. The crowd of women parted at her approach, and Kyra trembled as Bella came into view. The cook was pale beneath the soot, eyes closed as she struggled for breath. Forcing back tears, Kyra laid a hand on Bella's arm. Bella turned at the unexpected touch, eyes fluttering open.

"Kyra? Is that you?" Her voice was hoarse and weak.

"I'm really here." Kyra could no longer hold her tears back. "I'm so sorry, Bella."

Bella reached up and brushed Kyra's arm with a shaking hand. "Were those knights just fooling us?" Bella's voice trailed off and she coughed. Kyra laid a hand on her shoulder and waited until the spasms subsided.

"We were trying to protect you. The Guild..." Kyra stopped again. Did it really matter? "I'm so sorry."

Bella smiled. "Don't be. You did your best....I'm proud of you."

Proud? If there was one thing she didn't deserve right now, it was Bella's approval. That had always been Bella's mistake, to see good in Kyra that wasn't there.

"We need to get you a healer," Kyra said. Her voice was sharp with urgency. "We need a healer," she called. Around her, people stared, and she realized her foolishness. If there had been a healer in the room, she would have helped Bella already. Did Kyra expect another one to walk through the door?

Bella coughed and Kyra clutched her hand. The cook's eyes closed again, her breathing shallow and labored. Occasionally, her eyes moved in agitation beneath her eyelids. Kyra stroked Bella's arm and face, as the cook had so often done for Kyra after her childhood nightmares. She felt a familiar pressure on her shoulder and knew without looking that it was Flick, just as she knew that the two shapes that pressed up next to her were Idalee and Lettie.

They stayed there, holding each other for comfort while Bella's breathing grew weaker, fading from low gasps to the barest flutter. Kyra didn't know when it actually ended. Just that at one point, Flick checked Bella's pulse and arranged her arms in the final resting pose. Kyra let it all out then, clutching the girls as she sobbed into Idalee's hair, leaning into Flick as he held on to all of them. Perhaps she needed to be strong for them, but she just didn't have it in her.

Bit by bit, sunlight replaced the fire's red glow. She was dimly aware that the soldiers' shouting became less urgent. Eventually, she stopped hearing demon cat roars, and the market building began to empty. Kyra still didn't move or speak, just stared at Bella's now peaceful face and let her mind go numb.

A hand touched her shoulder. "Kyra."

She turned with a start. It was Tristam. He looked much the worse for wear, with a bruise beneath one eye and blood splattered over his tunic. There was pity in his eyes.

"We need to go back to the Palace."

She didn't want to go back. She didn't want to do anything but stay here, still as stone while the world crumbled around her. How many weeks ago had it been, when she'd sat in Bella's kitchen and made foolish plans to care for her when she grew old? She'd been so naïve.

"Kyra," Tristam tried again. She still didn't respond, and Tristam took her arm, gently pulling her up.

Another hand closed over the knight's wrist. "You're not taking her," said Flick. "Not like this. Not without any explanations."

"Flick, no," Kyra murmured. He was no match for an armed knight.

Tristam's body went rigid as his eyes fell on Flick's hand. There was anger in his face, and for a moment none of them breathed. Then Tristam exhaled, and all his strength seemed to leave him. His voice was thick with exhaustion when he spoke.

"I'm sorry for your loss, Faxon." His use of Flick's real name startled Kyra. "I'm bound by oath as a knight to watch Kyra and keep her under Palace custody. But even if I weren't, it's the safest place for her right now. The Guild has tried to kill her once. They must not know that she's alive."

Kyra snapped out of her stupor. "But what about them?" she asked, gesturing to Flick and the girls. "They're not safe either."

There was a long pause, then Tristam finally spoke. "Very well." He turned to Flick, who was staring blankly at the smoldering ruins. "Come with us. You and the girls will be safer there. We failed once to protect you. I'd like to do better, if you'll let me."

It was a somber walk back, picking their way through the invasion's aftermath. At first, Kyra attempted to shield Idalee and Lettie from the worst of the carnage, but she soon gave up. There was just so much. In bits and pieces, when the girls were out of earshot, she filled Flick in on the events since her capture.

No one challenged them upon entering the Palace. Although the fire had not breached the walls, the injured were already pouring in. A tent had been set up in the main courtyard, and healers picked their way amongst the victims.

As they stepped deeper into the compound, Flick became noticeably tense, gaze moving suspiciously in every direction. Tristam too changed from the young man who'd joked with Kyra in the forest, taking on the weight and authority of a knight of Forge. The easy camaraderie they'd shared just hours before fell away, and she was once again very aware that she was his prisoner. Tristam led Kyra and her friends to a spare room, where Idalee and Lettie collapsed almost immediately, too tired even to be distracted by the fine furniture. Kyra kissed their foreheads, and Flick tucked blankets around them. When they closed the door behind them, Kyra looked questioningly at Tristam. After roaming the city and forest unsupervised, she wasn't sure where she was supposed to go.

"Let's put you back in Ilona's patient room," Tristam said reluctantly. Kyra wondered if he also found the Palace walls stifling. "I have to keep you under guard while you're in the Palace. Flick can stay in one of the rooms here."

"I'd like to speak with Flick," she said.

Tristam thought briefly, then nodded. "You can have a few moments after we get to your room."

There was no conversation as the three of them made their way to Kyra's chamber. They took a back route and Kyra kept her cloak low over her face, but she couldn't help thinking how silly it was to continue hiding when she had been out in the open so long. When they reached the healer's wing, Tristam unlocked the door to Kyra's room. "I'll be out here," he said.

The patient room was strangely tranquil, an oasis of quiet that didn't fit the night's events. It was also too clean for someone as soiled with dirt and ash as she was. Avoiding the furniture, Kyra collapsed on the floor against the wall, and Flick settled down beside her. They were silent for a long time.

"It's all my fault," she finally said.

Flick turned to face her. "You don't know that."

"Of all the places they could have started a fire, they chose that neighborhood."

"If not our section, they would have burned another. The Demon Riders did this, and James. Not you."

"You don't understand. James couldn't have done this without me."

237

There was pause as Flick digested her words. "What?"

Kyra closed her eyes and drew a shaky breath. For a moment, she was tempted to keep that part of the story to herself. But the guilt was slowly killing her. She had to tell someone— someone who wouldn't view it from a purely tactical standpoint like Tristam or Malikel. "I was the one who gave James run of the Palace. I unlocked the armory so the Guild could steal armor for the barbarians. I copied the trade and guard schedules that the Demon Riders used to time their raids. The barbarian attacks—they were successful because of me."

Her voice wavered and she stopped. Flick shook his head, blinking in confusion. "What do you mean? You got supplies for the Demon Riders? Helped them? Did you know?"

"No. I mean"—Kyra stumbled over her words—"I didn't know why I was doing the jobs. There were some hints, but James said I was imagining things, and I wasn't sure—"

"There were some hints?" Flick raised his voice, incredulous. "You thought you might be helping the Demon Riders, but you just kept going?"

"It wasn't that simple, I—"

"You did what, Kyra?" He was angry now, grief and shock lending a terrible force to his words. "You just ignored the signs? That was always your problem. You fix your eyes on whatever new challenge you fancy, and it doesn't matter what I say, what other folk say, or even what you see with your own eyes. You just keep going, and it doesn't matter what gets destroyed along the way."

His accusations rang true, and Kyra cowered under the

brunt of his tirade. "I'm sorry," she whispered, eyes burning. "I was wrong."

"Tell that to Bella." His voice was raw from tears and smoke. Without looking at her, he stood and walked toward the door.

"Flick, don't go."

He didn't, but he didn't turn around either. Kyra watched him from where she huddled, taking in the curve of his shoulders, his hands as they clenched into fists and unclenched again. She had never seen him so angry.

Kyra retreated into her misery, turning both Flick's accusations and her own self-recriminations over in her head. She couldn't lose both him and Bella in one night. For a long time, the only sound in the room was Flick's breathing.

Finally, he straightened and shook his head. "I'm sorry, Kyra." He didn't look at her as he turned toward the door. "It's just too much to take right now."

She didn't call after him to stay.

TWENTY-SEVEN

Kyra stared at the map in front of her, seeing nothing but refusing to look up. Beside her, Malikel, Tristam, and Martin bent over the parchment, eyes focused on Flick as he recounted the fire for them. Kyra, for her part, avoided looking at Flick as carefully as he avoided looking at her, though she snuck some glances when he wasn't paying attention. Her jovial friend had aged in the past few days. His face was gaunt, and there were deep circles under his eyes.

"The fires started around midnight," said Flick. "We smelled smoke and saw the kitchen burning. At first, we thought it was just The Drunken Dog, but then the fire got out of hand and we ran outside. The entire street was in flames."

"Any idea who started the fires?" asked Malikel. He'd rushed back to Forge upon receiving news of the attack and was now beginning his investigation in earnest.

Flick shot him a disgusted look. "That's your job to know, in't it?"

"You'll address the Minister of Defense with respect," snapped Tristam.

Martin half successfully hid a long-suffering sigh behind his hands. He caught Kyra looking and grinned. Kyra managed a small smile back, wishing she could laugh about the constant friction between Flick and Tristam as easily as Martin did. Instead, it just wore her down.

"We're working toward the same goals, Faxon," said Malikel. "The quicker we can piece together what happened, the quicker we can punish those responsible."

"My name is Flick." No one responded. "I didn't see anyone, but some folks at the market saw masked men with torches."

"That fits with the Guild," said Tristam.

Who had started the fire? Alex? Shea? Bacchus? Kyra imagined Rand dressed in black and gripping a torch, a carrot-colored curl peeking out from under his mask. She saw Bella's pale, ashen face.

"When did the Demon Riders come in?"

"I don't know. A couple hours after the fire started? Everyone was distracted."

"Did you see any Riders?" interjected Malikel. "Or just cats?"

"Just cats," said Flick.

"As did I," added Tristam. "When Kyra and I arrived."

"Where were the Riders?" asked Malikel. "Kyra, you saw them heading to the city from the forest. Kyra, are you paying attention?"

Kyra snapped out of her reflections, flinching at Malikel's tone. "Mostly Riders going toward Forge," she said. "There were a few cats, but just a handful."

There was a pause as everyone thought this over. "We

still don't know nearly enough about the Demon Riders," said Malikel.

"Kyra might be able to learn more if we go back into the forest," said Tristam.

"Yes," said Malikel. "Continue those trips. But we need to strike at the Assassins Guild as well. We can't afford merely to observe them anymore. Another attack like this would destroy the city."

The map blurred before her, and Kyra rubbed her eyes. Perhaps James had started the fire, put a torch to The Drunken Dog himself.

"A full attack on the Guildhouse, then?" Tristam was saying.

"Let's think about this," Malikel said. "We want to capture members for questioning and search the place for clues about their relationship with the Demon Riders. Kyra, we need your help to plan this."

"It won't work," she said.

The table fell silent. "Do you care to elaborate?" said Tristam.

"I've seen these men work," said Kyra. "They're dangerous. As well trained or better than any of your knights, and they don't bother with honor or chivalry. You'd need to outnumber them to pull it off, but you send that many soldiers, they'll see you coming. At best, they'll be gone before you step foot on the grounds; at worst, you'll walk into a trap."

"A smaller strike party, then," said Tristam. "We capture who and what we can and retreat."

"You'd be sending them to die."

Tristam glared at her, his patience also wearing thin in the exhausting days since the fire. "Will you just shoot down suggestions? We could use some ideas."

Kyra opened her mouth to speak, but found that she couldn't. Bella's face swam in front of her. "I'm sorry," she said. "I . . . I can't do this."

She bolted before anyone could stop her, running up stairs and around corners before finally collapsing in a dead end. It was all too much. Bella was not cold in her grave, yet they expected her to put it all aside and go after the Guild.

Footsteps sounded. Flick's familiar form rounded the corner.

"I must be a bad thief if you found me so easy," she said.

"You always run upward when you're upset." He sat down beside her. "And you favor right turns. You're lucky they didn't sound the alarm."

She'd forgotten about that. "I still have one more dose of antidote. I can't run."

Flick looked like he was mulling over his words. "I suppose we have enough troubles already that we don't need to be tossing blame at each other," he said.

A weight lifted off of her at those words. Kyra looked at him, and the forgiveness in his eyes made her want to burst into tears again. "No, you were right. I should've listened to you. I'm . . . sorry." The words felt woefully inadequate. "I was stupid. It was just maps and trade schedules at first, and I wanted to prove myself. It's no excuse."

Again, they sat in silence. Through the window, Kyra could hear the murmurs of refugees in the Palace courtyard.

Finally, Flick spoke again. "How much do you remember from your gutter-rat days?"

"Not much," she said dully.

"Do you remember back before you were climbing buildings? You weren't that great at it when we met."

"No." She was in no mood to reminisce. "I guess I didn't have any reason to be."

"But once you started, you loved it. Every time I saw you, you'd scamper up something higher and more dangerous. I was plumb sure you'd be dead within the year. You did have your falls. There's probably still some merchants who've not forgiven you for destroying their stalls with your antics."

Kyra smiled despite herself. Flick put his arm over her shoulders, and she let him pull her close, leaning her head on his shoulder as she had when they'd kept warm together as children. "It's strange," Flick continued. "It's not like you're the only lass to make mistakes. We all did. You just manage to do it in a grander fashion. Maybe it's because you climb so much higher than the rest of us."

Kyra chuckled bitterly. "So I'm more gifted than your usual gutter rat—I ruin other people's lives, not just my own. James told me to let go of my delusions of moral superiority. Maybe he's right."

"Do you really believe that, Kyra?"

"I don't know."

Flick sighed. "Kyra, think about it. If James really believed you were like him, would he have gone to the trouble of threatening you or hiring someone to kill you? He's scared of you, Kyra. He might have tricked you into helping him once, but you're a danger to him. He knows you're not his puppet anymore."

244

Kyra felt a rush of blood to her face as she considered Flick's words. James had lied to her and tried to turn her into something she wasn't. And now he'd taken Bella. Even if she didn't know anything else about herself, Kyra knew that Flick was right. She wasn't James's puppet anymore.

She jumped to her feet. "Let's go back."

Martin was in the corridor when Kyra and Flick came back downstairs. "Are they still in there?" Kyra asked.

"They're still planning. Sir Malikel's not happy though. I'd apologize real quick. And sincerely too."

Tristam and Malikel were deep in conversation when she returned, and it took a moment for them to acknowledge her entrance.

"I'm sorry," she said before either of them could react. "That won't happen again."

Malikel gave her a long, measured look. "Make sure it doesn't."

"I have an idea," she said. "For attacking the Guild."

The councilman waited for her to continue.

"Don't send an invasion," said Kyra. "Just send one person. Me."

From the corner of her eye, she saw Flick turn his head and stare at her.

Tristam raised an eyebrow. "An army won't work, and a strike party won't work, so you intend to single-handedly invade their building and bring back prisoners?"

"Everything the Assassins Guild does hangs on James," she said, ignoring Tristam's sarcasm and avoiding Flick's eyes. "He's got a good crew, but he's the core. He makes all the plans, and it's his determination that holds it all together. If we kill James—if *I* kill James—there's no clear person to take his place. It would cripple the Guild."

"Kyra." Flick's voice was tinged with panic. "This wasn't what I had in mind." She ignored him.

"You may be right about James," said Malikel. "The Assassins Guild fell out of power a century ago, and it wasn't until recently that it reemerged, perhaps because of James's leadership. But how do you propose to kill him, Kyra? Can you outfight him?"

"No," said Kyra, remembering her humiliating practice match with James. "But there's other ways. James wanted me to poison you. Why not do the same to him?"

"The Palace doesn't keep clearberry juice," said Malikel. "We can offer you other poisons, though they aren't ideal."

"Just give me what you have," said Kyra. "I might also use the Guild's stores. James keeps his poison in a chest in his study."

"It's especially dangerous for you to go in there, Kyra," said Tristam. "After the fire, they probably know you're alive. And they know your tactics better than anyone."

"Just as I know the Guild better than any of your men," said Kyra. The more she thought about it, the more determined she became. "I'm the only one with any chance of cracking the Guildhouse. No one else here can do this."

"Do what?" said Flick. "Any one of us is perfectly capable of getting killed by the Assassins Guild."

Kyra sighed and looked at Flick, hardening herself to the worry in his eyes. "What else would I do, Flick? Wait around for them to kill me? I in't doing this out of some misplaced sense of guilt. I'm doing this because it's the only thing that will work."

Tristam cleared his throat. "I think she's right, Flick," he said reluctantly. "Tactically speaking, Kyra's our best hope for infiltrating the Guild." Tristam ignored Flick's glare and looked at Kyra. "It will be dangerous though."

"We could watch the perimeter," said Martin. "Keep soldiers and dogs." Kyra shot him a grateful look.

"You have my permission, if you're willing, Kyra," said Malikel. "If you're successful, it could be enough to earn you a pardon from the Council. What do you need from us to do this?"

"I want my last dose of antidote. If I do this, it's my choice and you'll trust me to come back without your leash."

"Yes, Willem filled me in on his . . . arrangement with your antidote while I was away." There was an edge to Malikel's voice that Kyra had never heard before, and she glanced at him. The official was not looking at her, but instead he seemed lost in his own thoughts. "You'll receive your antidote." He looked at her and regained his usual steady demeanor. "What else do you need? Do you have a concrete strategy?"

Kyra bit her lip. "I have a plan, but I'll need help."

The title of "Best Tavern" was a point of much debate amongst the thirstier members of Forge's population. The Drunken Dog had been one of the top contenders before the fire. A few other names also popped up regularly, including the Scorned Maiden, a raucous establishment in the northeast quarter. Kyra had visited a few times and found the patrons too rowdy for her taste. But others refused to get their ale anywhere else. One such devotee was Bacchus.

He was there tonight. If he followed his usual routine, he would come out sometime around midnight, hopefully drunk. As Kyra waited from a nearby rooftop, she once again rehearsed the plan in her mind. The neighborhood was quiet, with gently sloping rooftops all at the same height. It would be easy to trail him from above until he was alone. Periodically, Kyra reached into her belt pouch and fingered a damp cloth inside.

It was a slow evening at the tavern, and people started leaving soon after the dinner hour. They came out in small groups, clutching their cloaks against the wind and bidding each other good-bye in loud voices before walking or lurching home.

Finally, Bacchus emerged. He had one arm around a serving girl, who giggled as he planted a wet kiss on her lips. She playfully slapped him away before retreating into the dining room. Bacchus stood for a moment, as if deciding whether or not to follow her. He must have elected against it, because he fastened his cloak and started down the street. Kyra had expected him to be more on his guard, but he walked alone and his stride was slightly unsteady. Perhaps this meant the Guild didn't think she was alive. Or perhaps Bacchus's opinion of her was so low that he couldn't be bothered to be careful.

She trailed above and behind him, keeping her footfalls soft on the wooden shingles. As he turned into more secluded alleyways, she ran ahead, silently lowering herself down to a ledge just above his height. As he came closer, she reached into her pouch, took out the cloth, and held it tightly in her fist.

Focus.

Kyra jumped the moment he passed underneath. She landed on his back. The impact knocked the breath out of her, and she scrambled to wrap her arms around his neck. Bacchus grunted and collapsed, first to his knees, and then—with a little help from Kyra—flat on his face.

Even drunk and taken by surprise, Bacchus had good reflexes. He lay stunned for a split second, and then reached for his knife. Kyra straddled the assassin and pinned his arms with her knees. She pulled his head back and flung the damp cloth over his face, drawing it tight. He rolled over and she rolled with him, clamping her legs around his waist and keeping a hold on the cloth as her back hit the pavement. As Ilona had promised, the herb mixture worked quickly. Kyra hung on for a precarious few moments, then the assassin went limp. She kept the cloth over his nose and mouth for thirty more breaths before she crawled out from under him.

A shadow moved at the entry to the alleyway, and she jumped, only to breathe a sigh of relief when she recognized Flick's head of thick curls.

"Looks like you didn't need reinforcements," he said.

"He was drunk. Help me move him."

Flick took one arm and they dragged Bacchus's limp body out of view.

Kyra rifled through his pockets. "This one," she said, holding up one key, "and this one."

Flick handed her a thin piece of metal and a file. "You take one, and I'll do the other."

Kyra laid the key on the ground next to the blank Flick had

given her. After comparing the two, she picked up her file. The first stroke of metal on metal shrieked through the quiet alley, and she cringed.

"It's all right," said Flick. "It's not as loud as you think."

She just hoped the people on the other side of the walls were asleep.

The two of them worked without talking, shaping the pieces as quickly as they could. She was almost done when she noticed that Flick had already finished. He had always been good with keys. A few minutes later, Kyra handed hers to Flick for inspection. He held it up against the original, turning it in all directions. One edge caught his attention and he stroked it with his finger, frowning in concentration as he reached a hand to Kyra. She handed him a file, and he made a few finishing touches before handing it back to her.

"This should work," he said. "I can put the real ones back on Bacchus."

Kyra nodded. "Take his coin." According to Ilona, Bacchus would have no memory of the moments leading to the attack. Hopefully, he would blame it on common thieves.

"You'll try to get in tonight?" Flick asked, though he knew the plan as well as she did.

"Best to do it tonight, if I can. We don't know what Bacchus will think when he wakes up. Don't want him getting suspicious and warning James."

Flick squeezed her shoulder, eyes dark with worry. "Be careful."

TWENTY-EIGHT

There was a leather merchant across the road from the Guild-house, owned by a man who hadn't invested in good locks. He slept upstairs at night, and it was trivial for Kyra to slip inside and use his store as a lookout post. She settled herself by the window and kept a mental tag on the snoring from upstairs. The rhythmic sound and the smell of leather were calming, and she latched on to them to still her nerves. Kyra had feigned confidence to reassure Flick, but now she had nothing to distract her from the task that lay before her.

The Guildhouse's layout was deceptively simple. It masqueraded as a large storehouse for trade caravans and was set back from the road to make room for horses and wagons. All that open space also made it easy for those inside to see anyone approaching. And once Kyra got in, the building's close quarters and thin walls would make it hard to stay hidden.

There were dim lights in the windows despite the late hour, and Kyra settled herself for a long wait. Just as her feet started to fall asleep, a handful of men left the building. Kyra weighed her options. She doubted the Guildhouse would ever empty completely, so this was as good a chance as any.

She felt like a bright red target as she dashed across the street. There was no way to stay completely hidden—she just had to trust the shadows and her ability to blend in. Kyra skirted the perimeter, past watering troughs and a post for tying horses, staying a good distance away from a door guard who peered off in the opposite direction. Once out of his line of sight, she crept closer and pushed on a darkened window. The glass didn't budge. She climbed and tried an upper window. That one was locked as well.

Which left the rooftop. Kyra pulled herself onto the shingles and crossed toward the back, where she could look down on the courtyard. She recognized the water basin where she had washed her hands. If she leaned over the edge of the roof, she could see the guard stationed at the back door. Kyra reached into her pouch and took out a pebble, aiming for the fence at the opposite end of the courtyard. Her first pebble fell short, but the second one bounced off the fence with a hollow thud. The guard straightened and looked around. Kyra threw two more stones in quick succession. He drew his knife. As he approached the fence, Kyra lowered herself to the ground. There was a click as she turned the key, but the guard didn't look back. Once inside, Kyra ducked into a storage room. There she waited, breathing through her tunic to avoid sneezing at the dust, and listened until she was sure there was no one nearby.

Kyra cracked the door open and peered into the hallway. It was dark, with a flickering light coming from around the corner. She could hear distant voices. The cadence and tone of one was clearly recognizable—James. He was meeting with someone in a room up front, which meant his study was probably empty. Kyra drew a shaky breath. She needed to think of James as just another person in the building. Thinking of him in any other way would get her killed.

As Kyra crept down the hallway, the other voices came into focus, and she paused. James was talking to a woman. Since when had there been another woman in the Guild? Kyra paused for a split second in front of James's study, hand on the doorknob, and then continued down the hallway toward the voices.

"Our interest is in the livestock and supplies," a lightly accented woman's voice said as Kyra stopped a few steps from the door. "The city raids are an unnecessary risk."

"I understand," said James. "But mayhap I can convince your people to join us on one last raid of the city."

"We have armor and medicine, enough to last a while. What more could you offer us?" said another man.

"Supplies for the winter, for one. Ranged weapons for another. There's no reason for you to rely solely on your cats' claws."

"And why are you so eager to have us attack the city?" asked the woman.

"Our city is flawed. It's a place where the wealthy live their lives and the poor exist to serve them. I would change that."

"You use interesting methods to accomplish your ends." There was a hint of amusement in the woman's voice. "Burning the city to make it better."

"You can't change a river's course with a shovel. You need an earthquake, and earthquakes have a cost. The last attack weakened their defenses. The north gate is destroyed, and the Red Shields will be busy for weeks with repairs. If we strike before they have a chance to recover, we could breach the Palace."

"The Palace? That's your goal?"

"The compound and the Council members who live within."

"That will be dangerous."

"I can make it worth your risk. The spoils from the raid should outfit you for years. Shall we say, another raid in a month?"

It took all Kyra's strength to stay outwardly calm, keep her breathing steady so she wouldn't give herself away. It was one thing to know that James was helping the barbarians, something else altogether to hear him negotiating with them, brushing aside the death of innocents as if they were mere inconveniences. She wanted to run into the room and tear him apart. Instead, she hugged her shoulders to suppress her sudden trembling and gathered herself to turn back. If she did what she came to do, James would cease to be a problem.

The voices faded behind her as she slipped into the study and closed the door. Kyra leaned against it for a few breaths, willing her heartbeat to steady. She could do this.

She checked her pouch for Malikel's poisons. They would work if she had nothing better, but clearberry juice was quick and deadly, her best option for catching James by surprise. James's poison chest was below his desk. The padlock gave way with some work. Inside, there were dozens of small vials. Kyra picked each up one by one, holding the labels to the moonlight. Vial after vial was labeled with the same blue symbol.

Blueflower extract. It was a slow-acting poison, usually left on clothing. In constant contact with the victims, it would leach into their bloodstreams, weakening them until they succumbed to illness or infection. It was too slow to be of use to her. James would no doubt recognize the poison's effect before it became life-threatening. But what was he doing with so many flasks of this? She counted ten vials, enough for over a hundred victims. Was he trying to poison the Council?

At the bottom of the box, she found a bottle of lizard-skin venom—too unstable to leave in food. And finally, a vial of clearberry. Kyra palmed it and set about looking for some way to use it, something that only James would touch. Her eyes fell onto a cup on his desk. She added three drops of poison to the water inside. Then, she poured some onto a parchment and used it to spread the juice around the cup's edges. That would do.

A voice from the corridor made her jump. As footsteps sounded, Kyra snapped the box shut and ran to the window. It refused to budge. The steps drew closer, slowing and stopping on the other side of the door. Kyra abandoned her attempts to escape and vaulted back over the desk, ducking behind as the doorknob turned. Candlelight spilled under the desk, and she shrank back. Someone stepped inside and closed the door behind him. The silence that followed was long and thick.

"That was stupid, Kyra." There was no mistaking the voice, dispassionate, with a cold, hard edge.

Kyra swallowed, steeled herself, and rose. James stood just inside the door. The flickering lamp cast his face in moving shadows. As Kyra stood frozen, he placed the lamp on a stand and stepped closer, reaching casually for his knife.

"It didn't take long for you to switch your allegiance, did it?"

Cold rage, or fear, lodged in her chest. "I owe you no allegiance."

"That so? After all I've taught you?"

He stepped forward. She took another step back. "What are you doing with the Demon Riders?"

"If my suspicions are right, you already heard the answer."

So she'd made noise in the corridor. It was a bad time to make a mistake. "You're not who I thought you were," she said.

"No. I am who I've always been. It's you who continues to be naïve. You think we can keep on with our raids, give hand-outs for the rest of our lives. But that wouldn't change a thing."

"Have you seen the fire?" she asked. "Have you counted the bodies?"

"Did the fire take more than what the Palace would have taken eventually? Lives lost when folk can't buy medicine and food. Homes lost because the fatpurses forever grab for more." He narrowed his eyes. "But you're not here on behalf of the city. You're here because the fire started at The Drunken Dog. Because you want revenge."

Just the mention of the fire brought a wave of images—images she needed to ignore if she wanted to stay alive. She should change the topic or refuse to say anything, but she wanted—needed—to know more. "Why did you do it?" she asked.

"You almost had me fooled," said James. "It was just a few things. . . . A switch in the guard schedules, something not quite right in the way they announced your death. I wasn't sure, so I had to flush you out. I needed a fire, and this helped me choose the starting point." He paused. "I didn't expect it to work quite so well, so soon."

She knew she shouldn't have asked, but it was too late. Rage swept through her. "You killed Bella just to check if I was alive?"

"I gave you a task, and I made you a promise." James's face was hard as he took another step closer. "You failed at your task, and I kept my promise. You shouldn't be surprised. Did you think I would do nothing while you led the Palace to us? Or did you think you could protect your friends by moving them to the other side of the wall? All it takes is a word from me and you'll return tomorrow morning to find your girls dead. Killed in their sleep, if they're lucky."

Kyra's knife was in her hand and out of its sheath before he finished talking. With a ragged cry, she launched herself at James, slashing wildly. There was a brief flicker of triumph on James's face as he stepped aside, wrenching her knife arm behind her and twisting her down. She landed face-first on the ground. Two sharp kicks to the ribs knocked any remaining breath out of her. She curled onto her side, and James closed in, kicking her useless limbs out of the way as he plunged his dagger into her stomach.

She screamed, only to cut off as she choked on her own blood. The pain was unbearable, growing unimaginably worse when he twisted his knife. As she convulsed around the blade, James took her head in his arms, cradling her like a child.

"You could have gone far," he whispered. Was that a tinge of regret in his eyes? She couldn't see through the fog.

Suddenly, James tensed, laid her head down, and walked away, leaving Kyra gasping on the floor. She heard footsteps.

"I'm sorry for this," James said. "This was Guild business, one of ours who betrayed us. I've dealt with it."

"We would like to take her with us," a man said.

"I can't allow that. Even if you were able to save her, she's a danger to us."

"You misunderstand," a woman's voice interrupted. "We want the fresh body for our cats."

There was some more discussion. Then new hands were lifting her and she cried out in pain and confusion. A pair of amber eyes looked down at her and murmured something in a strange language. All the fight left her, and Kyra lay still as the strangers carried her out of the room.

۞ ۞ ۞

Tristam rubbed his arms, both to stay warm and to rein in his nerves as he kept his post on the roof. He had a decent vantage point from here, though no direct view of the Guildhouse.

He heard a scuffling sound and turned to see Flick climbing up the ladder.

"She's got the keys," said Flick. "Should be there now."

Tristam nodded, though he kept his eye on the road. "We really should be closer to the Guild." Kyra had been adamant that everyone stay away.

Flick snorted. "Might as well bring in trumpets to announce our presence."

Tristam let the insult go unanswered. Kyra's friend had been trying his patience all evening, but he had more pressing things to do than take his bait. He hunched his shoulders against the breeze and listened for signs of anything amiss.

"You likely won't see her coming unless she wants you to," said Flick after a while.

"Sounds like you're speaking from experience."

"I've waited on her plenty, back before she was the Palace's errand girl."

Tristam shot him an annoyed look. "It was her choice to do this."

"It was a false choice. You had her by the throat."

Flick was wrong about that. Kyra *had* been forced to go into the forest—and Tristam still felt guilty when he thought of the way he'd coerced her—but this job was personal for her. Flick would have seen it too, if he hadn't been so eager to hate the Palace. Tristam didn't know whether Kyra wanted revenge or redemption, but she'd wanted it.

"You might not believe me," said Tristam, "but I really don't wish her harm. I like her."

"Do you?" If Tristam had meant to win Flick's trust by that comment, the warning in Flick's voice signaled clearly that the effort had backfired.

"I mean that I respect her abilities. What she's accomplished," said Tristam.

Flick shot him a sideways glance. "Better be what you meant."

Tristam gritted his teeth. "Of course it is. What do you think I am?"

"A wallhugger. Who's used to taking what he wants and leaving others to pick up the pieces."

"I've had enough of this," said Tristam, and walked away.

But he couldn't quite leave Flick's words behind. How did he really feel about Kyra? She was like no one he'd ever met before, and he couldn't deny that she was beautiful when she worked. Tristam once again saw her playful smile when she'd teased him about being fat. He still wasn't quite sure what had happened, only that they'd both realized what shaky footing they were on. When Kyra had moved to distance herself from him, he'd let her. He was her jailer, and she was his prisoner. For the hundredth time, he told himself to remember that.

A runner appeared in the distance. Both Tristam and Flick snapped to attention, but Flick shook his head. "It's not her. Too heavy on his feet."

It was one of Tristam's soldiers, running as fast as he could. Tristam climbed down the ladder to meet him, with Flick just behind.

The man was breathing heavily. "The Demon Riders took her."

"What? How—"

Next to Tristam, Flick started to swear.

"One of our scouts saw Demon Riders carry her away. She was alive, but there was a lot of blood."

Dread filled his chest at those last words. "Where did you see her?"

The messenger pointed, and Tristam sprinted off in that direction. He heard Flick's footsteps pounding behind him and sped up even faster, as if he could outrun the voice of guilt. He thought he'd been prepared for anything—but Demon Riders?

A cluster of shieldmen was waiting for him farther down.

Martin was amongst them, pacing back and forth as a crowd of distraught beagles swarmed around him.

"We saw them leaving," Martin said, shaking his head helplessly. "They lost us in the alleys. The dogs just refused to follow."

There was a scatter of gravel behind him as Flick caught up. "What's going on?"

Tristam started to answer, but couldn't. In his mind, he saw Jack torn open from shoulder to hip and refused to imagine Kyra in his place. He tore his gaze from Flick and addressed Martin instead.

"They most likely headed toward the forest," he said, paying no heed to Flick's expletives. "They couldn't lose her. "Search the entire area. We don't rest tonight until she's back safe."

TWENTY-NINE

They carried her through the streets, heading quickly toward the outskirts. She made a few halfhearted attempts to struggle, but each effort sent such pain through her body that she had to stop. After a while, Kyra just lay limply, resigned to her fate. She should have been more afraid, but Kyra found she no longer cared. She was dying. She could feel it, and it didn't matter at this point how it would finally happen. She just hoped it wouldn't hurt any worse.

The man who carried her was tall, with long black hair, sharp cheekbones, and a strong nose. He wore the leather tunic she had seen on the other Demon Riders. Besides the occasional flash of leather and dark blond hair, she couldn't get a good look at the woman beside him.

The sound of rustling leaves grew louder until it surrounded her on all sides. Branches passed perilously close to her face. They didn't go very far into the forest before the woman asked a question in that strange language. The man stopped and laid Kyra carefully on the dirt.

Were the demon cats somewhere around here? She didn't

see or hear anything besides the man and woman. They were talking again, and the woman moved back a few paces. In a few graceful movements, she stepped out of her trousers and untied her tunic, letting it fall behind her.

Kyra blinked. Her eyes were failing; she couldn't make out the woman's features anymore. Then she realized it wasn't her vision. The woman's entire shape was blurring and expanding. Her torso lengthened and the skin of her body became soft with thick yellow hairs. Her face changed as well. The nose became broad and flat, eyes larger and more angular, and her teeth grew and sharpened into fangs. Soon, the woman had disappeared, and in her place stood a giant yellow wildcat. The beast shook itself and advanced toward her.

Kyra screamed and once again tried to move. This time, the sight of the creature gave her strength, and she lifted herself onto one elbow despite the searing pain in her abdomen.

"Don't move," the man shouted, and jumped down, pinning her shoulders with his forearm. She squirmed. A soft weight pressed on her hip—the demon cat's paw, she realized with growing panic. She kicked vainly into the air before her strength left her and she lay, exhausted, watching with muted horror as the cat bared its teeth and lowered its head to her abdomen.

There was the sound of ripping cloth, and more pain. She shuddered, but the man's weight on her shoulders and the cat's on her hip held her firmly. Her stomach felt warm and wet. Was she bleeding again?

The moment of clarity faded, and her thoughts once again clouded from pain and blood loss. She was glad though, because there was no way she could survive this for much longer. It would be over before long, she told herself, and sure enough, everything soon faded.

Kyra floated in and out of nightmares. Sometimes the cat people carried her through the forest. Other times, they chased her, held her down, and fed on her entrails. At one point, someone forced her mouth open. Kyra gagged at the taste of blood and spat out what they fed her. The next time, they held broth to her lips. It scorched her tongue, but she kept it down.

Slowly, the world reassembled itself. She wasn't dead. She hurt too much for that. And eventually her eyes stayed open. She lay in a makeshift shelter, a cloth strung between two trees. She felt cloth beneath her too, but it wasn't thick enough to keep roots and stones from digging into her back.

Memories of the Guild came rushing back. James was planning a new raid. She needed to warn the Palace. Kyra shifted, and pain once again shot through her abdomen. She looked down to see her entire midsection wrapped in bandages. She moaned. There was a flicker of movement to her right, and a woman's face appeared above her.

It was the same woman who had transformed into a beast. Or had Kyra just dreamed it? Kyra lay still and watched her warily. If the woman wished her harm, Kyra would not have the strength to resist.

The stranger spoke, but the words didn't make sense. Only when she repeated herself did Kyra realize the woman was speaking the common tongue, just with a heavy accent.

"Which clan sired you?" she was asking.

"What?"

"What clan sired you?"

"What are you talking about?"

The woman stared at her. "You really don't know? We assumed you were confused from your blood loss." Kyra didn't have a chance to ponder the woman's words before she spoke again. "We can talk, but after I tend your wounds."

Kyra couldn't hold back a groan as the Demon Rider lifted Kyra's torso and propped up her head and shoulders. She unraveled Kyra's bandages with an expert touch. When the soiled cloths were piled to the side, the woman fixed her with a stern gaze.

"You'll stay down this time? There's no one to hold you for me."

With one last glance at Kyra, she stepped back and untied her belt. She wore a strange tunic that wrapped around in front. The woman opened the tunic and shrugged her arms out of the sleeves. Before her clothes hit the ground, she was blurring again in the same way Kyra remembered. The woman's body seemed to lose form like a candle in the heat before remolding itself into a new shape. A few heartbeats later, Kyra knew for certain that her nightmares had been real.

Up close, the creature was fearsome, with long, sinewy muscles that moved under dense yellow fur. Its long tail swished languidly behind it. Kyra held back a scream as the demon cat advanced. If it wanted to eat her, it would have done so already. Still, it was all she could do to stay still as one paw once again pressed down on her hip. The cat ran its tongue firmly but gently over her midsection. Kyra flinched at the sandpaper touch and the sting of saliva on her cuts.

The cat wasn't eating her. It was cleaning her wounds.

The realization knocked any last bit of energy from Kyra. She let her head fall back and concentrated on not passing out. The beast's tongue was forceful and rocked Kyra's body back and forth with each stroke. Eventually, the demon cat stepped back and blurred into human form.

So the rumors about the Demon Riders were wrong. They didn't find cats and raise them as their children, as people had whispered at The Drunken Dog. They *were* the cats. The Demon Riders were shape-shifters, Brendel's felbeasts come to life. The stories had some truth to them after all.

Kyra's mind raced as pieces fell into place. She thought back to the marketplace raid, at how intelligently the demon cats had behaved. Then there was her trip to the forest. Before the fire, she'd spied a line of Demon Riders walking to the city, but once Kyra and Tristam arrived at Forge, they'd only found cats. And Tristam had never been able to find humans camping in these forests. . . .

"What are you?" Kyra whispered.

Beside her, the cat woman retied her tunic. "Answer me first. Where are you from? Who sired you?"

"Who sired me?" Kyra said, shrinking away. "I'm an orphan."

"You were raised by humans, then."

"What?"

The cat woman stepped back again, shaking her head in disbelief. She raised her hand to her mouth and sank her teeth into her own palm. Kyra gasped. When the woman held out her hand again, it was dotted with specks of blood.

"Smell it."

Kyra flinched away, but the woman kept her hand in front of Kyra's face. It smelled like blood. Too much like the stuff of her nightmares for comfort. Obviously frustrated by Kyra's blank expression, the woman scooped up Kyra's bloody bandages and thrust them under her nose.

"Can you not tell? Even in your skin, you can smell our blood."

Kyra noticed it then. There was a common element, a musky smell that made her think of long hunts through the forest.

No, that was just her imagination running wild. For all she knew, everybody's blood smelled like that.

Seeing Kyra's expression, the woman pulled back. "Our blood runs through your veins. What is your name?"

"Kyra." The word came out through numb lips.

The woman knelt down and took Kyra's hands. "Kyra. My name is Pashla," she said. "I, like you, am a daughter of the Makvani."

THIRTY

Kyra pulled her hand back, lightly at first, then with increasing insistence until she wrenched her hand away.

"No, you're wrong."

Once again, Kyra saw the demon cats chasing down their victims. She heard the wounded moaning in the street.

Pashla reached for her again, but Kyra pushed the woman away. "Stay away from me." Kyra struggled to sit up, barely aware of Pashla's protests and the pain arcing down her torso. Who were these monsters? Kyra gritted her teeth and tried again. She needed to leave.

A slap across her face stopped her short. Kyra slumped back, peering at Pashla through watery eyes, terrified that the woman would change shape again.

"Your wounds are fresh. If you struggle, you will die. If you can't understand that, I will tie you down."

Kyra stared at the woman. "You've made a mistake."

"You've noticed that you're different, have you not? You can see better, do things the humans can't."

"There are others who can move like me," Kyra said. *Like*

her, but not exactly, a small voice insisted. No one else from the Guild could have broken into the Palace like she had.

"And you smelled our blood in your own. You can't deny it."

"I don't know what you're talking about."

"Very well, tell me this. How do other animals treat you? Do they fear your scent?"

"I'm a dog talker," Kyra said. "But there are plenty of dog talkers in Forge."

For the first time, Pashla looked confused. "What do you mean?"

"We call them beast talkers. Animals are drawn to them and do their bidding..." Kyra trailed off upon hearing her own words. The truth was, she'd never been a proper beast talker. Amongst the street children, there had once been a bird talker. Birds had flocked to him and sung him songs, perched on his arms. They'd adored him. Animals had never responded to Kyra like that.

"They fear you, don't they?" said Pashla. "They cower or run away or panic. If our blood was weaker in someone, diluted by generations, perhaps animals would be drawn to him. But with you, they would flee."

Pashla gathered Kyra's soiled bandages. Kyra watched the way Pashla walked, the grace with which she negotiated the uneven floor. She felt an involuntary tightening in her own limbs as part of her recognized the woman's movements as her own.

When Pashla returned, she made no further effort to convince Kyra, but settled in front of her and waited.

"There must be some mistake. I never even knew you

existed. And I can't—" Kyra waved her hand vaguely toward the corner of the tent where the woman had changed shape. "If I were one of you, I'd know."

The woman nodded. "Your blood is mixed, and the ability to change shape doesn't always pass on to those with human blood. But you're right. Even if you couldn't change, you would know. It would show through in dreams and the way you move, see, and smell, the speed with which you heal, or a preference for the darkness...."

The woman continued, but Kyra stopped listening. She was suddenly inundated with memories of countless nights roaming the city. Kyra had always thought she was nocturnal because her job demanded it, but if she was honest with herself, that wasn't the whole story. Kyra had chosen that life *because* she loved the darkness. It had felt natural, safe somehow. Even now, she found herself longing for a shadow to hide in. Unbidden, the puzzling memory of someone carrying her through the forest came into her mind. And what about her childhood nightmares, the ones with the bright heat and sharp fangs?

"Have you killed?" asked Pashla.

Kyra went still. Did they know?

"If you've hunted or taken a life, our blood would call to you."

Bile rose in her stomach. "What do you want from me?"

"Tell me about yourself first. What do you do for James?"

The question grounded her and reminded her to be careful. They didn't know she had left the Guild. That meant they didn't know that she had been working with the Palace against them.

"He hired me to sneak into the Palace. As you said, I can do things they can't."

"And why did James want to kill you?"

Kyra hesitated for as long as she dared. "I went against his orders. He wanted me to kill the Minister of Defense," she finally said.

"Why didn't you?"

"It wasn't part of our original agreement. He hired me as a thief, not an assassin."

"And he tried to kill you when you refused him?"

"Aye."

Pashla seemed to accept her answers. "A few months ago, we raided a marketplace in the city; do you remember that, Kyra?"

"I do." How could she not?

"I was the one who chased you onto the rooftop."

For a split second, Kyra relived that moment, watching the creature delicately sniff, then taste, her blood. She had thought that the cat had retreated because of the arriving soldiers.

"That's why you spared me."

Pashla nodded, eyes distant. "We've known about you since the attack. Afterward, I told Leyus about you, but we never saw you again. It was only when we heard you scream at the Guildhouse. The smell of your blood was so thick in the room. It was unmistakable."

"Who's Leyus?"

"Our leader. We'll talk to him tomorrow, now that you're awake. He will decide your fate."

THIRTY-ONE

Tristam dug his hands into his knees so hard as to leave bruises. If he wasn't careful, he would say something to Councilman Willem that he'd regret.

"Your Grace," he tried again, struggling to keep the anger out of his voice, "I'm willing to put in extra shifts, as are some of my shieldmen. It needn't interfere with our normal duties."

"I believe I've made my feelings clear as well, Willem," said Malikel, seated beside him. "It seems shortsighted to me not to pursue a rescue."

"I don't take your counsel lightly, Malikel, and Tristam's dedication is admirable, but I'm afraid it's just too dangerous. Your prisoner is most likely already dead at the barbarians' hands."

Dead. The word conjured up images of Kyra, limp and bloody in the barbarians' arms. Kyra torn limb from limb as demon cats fought over her body. Tristam refused to believe it. "Your Grace, we can't be certain of this. Our scouts report that she was carried off alive. They could be holding her prisoner."

Willem's gaze lingered on Tristam. "You're still young,

Tristam, and unfamiliar with the demands of governing a city. Our coffers are strained due to the barbarian attacks. We simply cannot afford to spread our men any thinner."

Tristam couldn't help eyeing the luxurious tapestries hanging around Willem's study, the gold and silver sculptures on the shelves, and wondering whether they had anything to do with the strain on the city's coffers. "But, Your Grace, she could be—"

"Do you remember the circumstances under which we met?" Willem asked.

"Sir?"

"How your friend Jack was killed?"

Tristam faltered. What did Jack have to do with this? "He was mauled to death by a demon cat."

"That's only half the reason. The other half was because he acted foolishly in his haste to rescue a farmhand. Because of his rash judgment we lost a good knight, and the city will suffer for it. Do you understand my point, Tristam?"

Tristam nodded slowly. "Yes, Your Grace."

"Very well, then." Willem looked over Tristam's shoulder toward the door. "Thank you for your service to the city." It was his cue to leave.

As the door closed behind Tristam and Malikel, the older knight put his hand on Tristam's shoulder. "I'm sorry, Tristam. I know that was not the decision you were hoping for."

Tristam's frustration boiled over at the sheer stupidity of it all. "Sir, she could still be alive."

"The chairman has made his decision."

"You could have said something. Willem would have listened to you if you'd pushed harder." Tristam realized he was raising his voice far beyond what was appropriate for addressing his superior, but he didn't care.

"Tristam." Malikel hadn't spoken any louder, but the look in his eyes brooked no argument. "You're a knight of Forge. Don't ever forget that, and the vows that you made to obey the Council. That is your duty, above all."

And here Tristam had thought that his vows were to protect and serve Forge's people.

Malikel sighed, and his face softened. "I don't like Willem's decision either, but we choose our battles. This one is not worth it."

Not worth it? So Kyra's life was now just a point of compromise. It was hard enough to hear it from Willem, but to hear the same thing from Malikel... Tristam stared at Malikel's back as his commander strode away. The Council was wrong. Kyra had taken a risk for the city, and now they were abandoning her to the barbarians. She didn't deserve that, no matter what her crimes.

As he crossed the courtyard, he saw Flick walking toward him. Kyra's friend had known Tristam was going to appeal to Willem, and the hopeful look in his eyes made Tristam feel ill.

"Flick." He just wanted to get the bad news out as quickly as possible. "I'm sorry. The Council won't reconsider its decision."

Confusion flashed across Flick's face. "Why not?"

"They think it's too dangerous."

Tristam watched Flick's jaw work as the news sank in and he went through the same range of emotions that Tristam had just experienced.

"They can't—" Flick began.

"I'm sorry," Tristam said roughly. He was already angry at Willem's decision, and hearing Flick's complaints wasn't helping. "The Council's decided. There's nothing more I can do."

He had been looking away from Flick and didn't see him raise his fist. As it was, Tristam was a hair too late to duck out of the way. Lights exploded in front of his eyes, and he stumbled back. "What by the Three Cities do you think you're doing?"

"So this is your knights' idea of honor? Use a lass for your own devices and throw her to the barbarians when you're done?"

Shouts of alarm echoed through the courtyard and soldiers came running. As Tristam caught his breath, Red Shields surrounded Flick, knocking him to the ground before dragging him back onto his feet. Tristam put a hand to his still throbbing temple, his own temper flaring. "I've no more patience for you, Flick. I've broken rules, gone before the Council on your behalf to get Palace protection for you and your wards, and all I've gotten from you is—"

"Of course. I'm supposed to be grateful." Flick strained against the Red Shields holding him. "Kiss your shoes because you used us as bargaining chips with Kyra. Thank you, generous sirs."

"That's enough." Tristam curled his hands into fists and closed the distance between them.

Flick glared at him, unflinching. "You go on about honor and service, but you care more for your own skin."

Tristam stopped short at Flick's words. For a long moment, he stood, breathing heavily, fists clenched at his sides. "Take him to his room," he finally said, his voice cold. "And make sure he stays there."

Flick shot Tristam a look of pure loathing as he was led away. One by one, the crowd wandered off. Tristam gingerly probed the side of his face with his fingers. If he'd won that fight, why did he feel so disgusted with himself?

"That was some restraint you showed there. I might've clocked him myself."

Tristam looked up to see Martin. "You were part of that crowd?"

"The shouting was hard to miss."

Tristam shook his head, only to stop when it made his headache worse. "He didn't say anything that I didn't want to say to Willem myself." He sat down on the courtyard grass. It was awkward in his court finery, and he ignored puzzled glances from servants. Martin shrugged and sat down beside him.

"I do feel bad that we lost her," said Martin. "I like her, for all she's a criminal."

"You don't seem that surprised at Willem's decision."

"Guess I expected it, coming from a family of Red Shields. If we get in trouble, they don't usually come rescue us either."

Tristam nodded, absentmindedly fingering the insignia on his tunic that marked him as a knight. "When I took my vows, I pledged to obey the Council and protect Forge's citizens. I never thought those two vows would clash."

"So what do we do now?" asked Martin.

Tristam squinted in the direction of the forest. "I don't know."

THIRTY-TWO

Kyra fidgeted in her chair as Brendel strummed his lute. He hummed a short melody, then stopped to jot down some notes.

She finally gathered the courage to speak. "Why end it this way? Why not stop at the point when they fall in love?"

Brendel tapped his jaw with the end of his pen. "You don't change legends to suit your fancy, Kyra. Ballads tell a truth about the way of things. It means something that Lady Evelyne fell in love with the felbeast in human form. And it means something that she realized he would never turn from his bloodthirsty ways."

"But the story's just so . . . hopeless. Why can't he change? Why can't he learn?"

"The story is a warning for those who would be Evelyne. There was a time when you heard the tale and understood it. Remember when James betrayed you?"

Kyra stopped, clenching her fists in frustration. It was true that she'd agreed with the legend back then. "But I don't like it anymore," she said.

"Why not?"

She knew the answer, and so did Brendel, from the look in his eyes. But she couldn't say it.

Brendel smiled sadly. "You've realized that you are not Lady Evelyne, haven't you?"

A new voice joined the conversation, this one achingly familiar. "Don't listen to him, Kyra." Bella stood next to her, smelling of flour, stew, and spices. She sat down beside Kyra and stroked her hair. "Evelyne's not the only legend. Other tales end differently. You'll find your way."

Bella stood and offered Kyra a hand. Kyra let the cook pull her to her feet, but Bella winced. "Careful, lass. Not too hard."

Kyra looked down at her own hands. Where her fingernails should have been, she instead had five sharp claws. . . .

Kyra woke up feeling deeply and acutely alone. It was dark outside, and the wind had a frigid bite. She clutched her blanket tighter and blinked back tears.

"I'm sorry, Bella," she whispered. No one replied.

It was funny, the way life turned out. She looked at her hands, half expecting claws. But what did it matter? Her dagger was just as deadly. Her demon cat kin had spoken of murder as if it were simply a rite of passage.

There was a rustling in the trees. Kyra wiped a quick hand over her eyes as Pashla came into view carrying a large bowl. At first, Kyra couldn't make out what it contained, but then the smell of raw meat wafted over to her side of the shelter.

"Now that you're awake, you'll eat raw like the rest of us. We already risked too much building a fire for you."

Pashla held the meat out to her, and Kyra thought again

of Bella, of gentle hands holding a bowl of lamb stew. Kyra's breath caught and, to distract herself, she grabbed a piece of Pashla's meat. It was cold to the touch, dark red and marbled with fat. Kyra dropped it into her mouth, suppressing a shudder as the juices ran over her tongue. She couldn't bring herself to chew, so she swallowed it whole. It slid down her throat in one lump.

"You do well," said Pashla. "Even some who grow up with us refuse to eat raw flesh when they're in human form. The taste is more appealing to a cat's palate."

If only the woman would stop praising her for being like them. "Do you always eat like this?" Kyra asked.

"We've roamed for many years," said Pashla. "And we live less comfortably when we roam. This country is fertile with plants and fat prey, but the humans here are better armed. So we stay hidden. No fires, no shelters, sleeping in trees. We stay in our fur unless we need to talk."

"You can't talk when you're cats?"

"We can talk in the way of animals, sharing simple desires or commands. But we can't speak as we do now."

Kyra studied Pashla's profile in the dim moonlight. If these people aged like humans, the woman was probably about ten years older than Kyra. It would have been easier to hate her if she'd matched Kyra's expectations of barbarians. But she was gentle when she spoke. Her hands were as soft and deft as any Palace healer's, and she confided in Kyra as an ally.

A distant roar echoed through the trees, momentarily silencing the chorus of insects around them. Kyra instinctively lifted her head toward the sound.

"Come," said Pashla. "The clan is gathering. Don't worry. Leyus is a fair leader."

The Demon Rider helped Kyra up and wrapped her in animal hides. She let Kyra lean on her shoulder as they ducked out from underneath the makeshift tent. The sky was beginning to lighten, and a hint of red stained the eastern side of the trees. Around her, the forest was surprisingly empty. She hadn't exactly expected to step into a camp of Demon Riders, but the forest looked completely wild. The only sign of human habitation was her own shelter.

Kyra shivered despite her wrappings as they wound their way through the trees, growing warier as other figures converged on their path. At first, the majority of them were in cat form, with leather pouches around their necks. But as they traveled, more and more of the beasts stepped off to the side and changed shape, dressing themselves in tunics they'd carried in their pouches. Most of the Makvani were tall and long-limbed in their human skin, certainly taller than the average citizen of Forge. If Kyra was indeed related to them, she must have gotten her height from her human side. But the way they moved was unmistakable. It was the same inhuman and uncomfortably familiar grace she had seen in Pashla. Kyra stared at them, unable to help herself, and the Demon Riders made no effort to hide their glances back—some friendly, some disdainful.

Pashla's arm was firm around her waist, gently supporting and steering her through this forest of trees and faces. Finally, they reached a small clearing where a group of Demon Riders was already gathered in a loose circle. The clear focus of the crowd was one figure—a man, half a head taller than the others, who held himself with a strength that signaled authority. He looked older than Pashla but was still in his physical prime.

"This is Leyus," said Pashla, slowing Kyra to a stop in front of him.

What was she supposed to do? Bow? Curtsy? Beg for mercy?

Leyus looked her over with a careful eye, and Kyra immediately felt her guard go up. Something in his manner reminded her of James. He had the same air of power, the look of someone who was used to being obeyed. "You call yourself Kyra? Pashla says you know nothing of us."

"I grew up amongst humans." It felt strange, talking of humans as if they were a separate group.

"What did James want with you?"

Kyra repeated what she had told Pashla earlier, hoping that any quaver in her voice would be interpreted as nervousness instead of deception. She stuck to the truth up to the point where James commanded her to kill Malikel. Then she told the story as if the disagreement had happened right before James tried to kill her.

Pashla stepped in front of Kyra. "Our blood runs strong in her. You can't see it because she's injured, but you can smell it clearly in her blood."

"Let me see." Leyus held out his hand.

Pashla nudged her toward him. "Let him smell your blood."

"What?"

Pashla motioned with her hand toward her mouth. "Draw blood, like I did to show you."

Kyra stared dumbly at her palm. Choking down raw meat

was one thing, but this . . . Her hand refused to move any closer to her mouth.

Pashla exhaled in frustration and grabbed Kyra's arm, clamping her teeth down before Kyra had a chance to react. Kyra flinched, but she felt only a pinch. When Pashla released her arm, a small patch of skin was broken and a drop of blood pooled on top. With one last exasperated look, Pashla offered Kyra's arm to Leyus. He pulled her closer and held her arm beneath his nose the way a nobleman might sample fine wine.

"Half human," he finally said. "Can you change?"

"I've never done so."

"We can try after her injuries heal," said Pashla.

Leyus regarded her closely. "It's unusual to find a halfblood so far from any clan. Are you sure you remember nothing of where you came from?"

She wished people would stop asking her that. "I've always been in the city, amongst humans."

"Her injuries are severe," said Pashla. "She must stay at least until she heals enough to travel."

"In these times, it may not be wise to harbor a halfblood," said Leyus.

A chill went up Kyra's spine as she looked from Leyus, to Pashla, and back to Leyus. If it wasn't wise to harbor a halfblood, what was the alternative? She doubted it involved sending her off with a basket of food and well-wishes.

"She's under our care now," Pashla said. "I found her and brought her here on your orders."

Pashla switched to their own language as Kyra studied their faces, trying desperately to read their conversation. It was madness to escape death just to be executed here, but she was too weak to run. After a few more exchanges, Leyus put up a hand.

"You've made your case. We will keep her with us until her injuries heal," he said.

"This is madness!" shouted a man from the crowd. Everyone turned to find the new speaker.

"You speak out of turn, Brona," said Leyus.

The challenger, a young man with a striking mane of silver hair, pushed his way forward to the center of the circle. He threw Kyra a look so hostile she had to fight the urge to back away. "I speak because it's important," he said. "The girl's human blood makes her untrustworthy, especially since she was raised amongst them. She'll betray us first chance she gets."

Leyus, Brona, and Pashla stared at one another over Kyra's head, completely ignoring her presence as they discussed her fate. "She's too injured even to leave the camp," said Leyus. "She's unlikely to betray us in this condition."

"We only have the halfblood's word for that," said Brona. "And Pashla's."

"And that's just as worthless," said Brona. "We all know her past. Pashla pretends to be a member of the clan, but she's still a stray at heart. She thinks nothing of the clan's welfare."

A murmur ran through the crowd, which Brona seemed to acknowledge with satisfaction. Kyra took a half step back.

"Those are strong words, Brona," said Leyus.

"I stand by them," he said. "For the good of the clan."

Leyus turned slowly to Pashla. "Do you have anything to say?"

Pashla's jaw was clenched in anger and she stared Brona down as she spoke. "I serve the clan."

"Your lies convince no one, foundling," spat Brona.

"Enough!" said Leyus. "I don't believe the halfblood is a threat to us right now."

"I disagree," said Brona, "and if you won't do anything about this, I claim my right to Challenge Pashla on this question."

Leyus narrowed his eyes. "Are you doing this for the clan, Brona, or for your personal grievances?"

"My loyalty is to the clan. Always."

Leyus looked at him long and hard. Finally, he gave a curt nod. "You may Challenge. Pashla, do you accept?"

"This is not the best time," said Pashla.

"I will decide what time is right," said Leyus. "Do you accept?"

Pashla's eyes snapped with fury. "If I must."

She untied her belt in a routine quickly becoming familiar to Kyra. Again, her body was shifting, changing. Brona moved to the other side of the circle, slowly assuming the shape of a silver cat. The crowd stepped back, widening the ring as Kyra struggled to make sense of what had just happened. Kyra gasped as firm arms gripped her from behind and pulled her backward, wrenching her wounded middle. A Demon Rider she didn't recognize stared down at her. She pulled away, but his grip stayed tight.

"Watch her until this is settled," Leyus said to him.

Her guard was already leaving bruises on her arms. A Challenge, Brona had called it. Did this mean they would decide her fate based on who won? Kyra gritted her teeth and twisted, fighting her guard's hold, but she might as well have wrestled a tree.

She cast about for a way to escape, but the scene before her soon drew her attention. A few times at Forge she'd seen gamblers stage dogfights for sport. She sensed the same blood-lust now, the raw aggression between the combatants and the crowd's expectation for a good show. The air was tense with excitement as the two cats circled each other, punctuating their movements with low snarls and growls. Unlike the dogfights, however, the demon cats gave a clear impression of intelligence and restraint. There would be no rush to destruction here.

There was a collective gasp as Brona made the first swipe. Pashla reared up on her hind legs to avoid his claws. The fight began in earnest, a confusion of limbs, fur, and snapping teeth. Brona was larger, but Pashla was faster, and neither had the clear advantage.

Suddenly, Pashla charged. Brona roared as Pashla's teeth sank into his shoulder and both cats went rolling backward, colliding hard with a tree. A murmur went up as the two cats staggered apart. A new energy ran through the crowd. The circle seemed to press in closer to the two fighters, though Kyra didn't see anyone move.

"First blood," someone whispered.

And Kyra smelled it too. The musky fragrance teased at her nostrils, awakening an ominously familiar hunger in her that cut through her fear. With a start, she recognized it as the same bloodlust from her dreams—the dreams that had started after her first kill.

The crowd's energy roused her from her shock. Pashla

moved aside to reveal a deep gash in Brona's shoulder. When the silver cat turned to face her, he moved with a pronounced limp. Pashla shook herself and lunged again, attacking with renewed fury. Brona fought back, hissing and blocking, opening his own gashes in Pashla's paws and flank, but he was weaker now. Pashla seemed to feed off the crowd's excitement, advancing with unrelenting focus. It was over in a few moments. Pashla sank her teeth into Brona's neck and held on until he stopped convulsing and lay still.

A bloodcurdling scream split the air and a woman hurtled into the circle, pushing Pashla aside and throwing her arms around Brona's neck. She was followed by several others. Kyra stared, transfixed by their grief, until she realized that everyone else was ignoring them. A Demon Rider woman picked up Pashla's tunic and ran to her, holding it out as Pashla shifted back. Pashla's blood-smeared arms shook as she retied her belt, and her face was lined with exhaustion as she met Leyus's eye. The clan leader inclined his head and grasped her hand.

"Well fought, Pashla," he said. "The clan will abide by this decision. The halfblood stays with us until she heals."

THIRTY-THREE

As tension from the fight faded away, pain from Kyra's wounds came rushing back. Demon Riders surrounded Pashla, completely blocking the clanswoman from view. Kyra watched them, swaying side to side as her balance left her, wondering if the Makvani had forgotten her in the excitement. From Leyus's pronouncement, she gathered that she was safe, but beyond that, she was lost. Another clanswoman took Kyra's arm and she stifled a scream.

"Come," said the clanswoman. "I will take you back."

"But Pashla—"

"She will see you when she's ready."

Kyra was too exhausted to resist. The clanswoman escorted her back, and Kyra spent the rest of the day drifting in and out of sleep. The forest was quiet during the afternoon, but as it grew dark, Kyra couldn't shake the feeling that she was being watched. Occasionally, between layers of cricket chirps and cicada calls, she thought she heard footsteps. When she closed her eyes, she saw snapping teeth and flying fur.

Halfway through the night, Kyra awoke to a racket she

couldn't ignore. Something was crashing through the underbrush. She scrambled unsteadily to her feet, gasping at a jolt of pain through her middle as a doe lurched into view, falling to its knees a stone's throw from Kyra's shelter. Before Kyra could react, a demon cat burst through the trees, knocking the deer over with a massive paw and closing its jaws around its throat. The doe kicked at the air and fell lifeless.

Kyra edged out of her shelter, shocked by the brutal kill, yet drawn to the raw display of strength. The demon cat paid her no heed as it tore into the deer's flank, ripping away chunks of flesh. There were more crashing sounds, both from the ground and the trees above her, as other demon cats arrived. The other cats watched from a distance, amber eyes reflecting the moonlight, tails swishing in anticipation. Finally, the first cat raised its head, shook itself, and loped away. One by one, the others took their turn, each tearing off a chunk of meat or limb. As in the Challenge, Kyra was once again struck by the strange coexistence of brutality and intelligence. The cats followed some sequence that Kyra could not understand. Once or twice, a cat approached the kill only to be chased away with a warning growl. It was frightening. Horrifying. Yet she found herself moving closer.

Another growl stopped her—not the short growl to warn others away from the kill, but a deep-throated snarl that froze Kyra in her tracks. A light-colored cat with brown stripes across its legs turned from the deer and advanced on Kyra. A few other demon cats jumped between the two of them, only to move away when the striped cat bared its teeth. Kyra stumbled back, mind spinning. Hadn't Leyus ruled that she was to be spared? But the cat came closer, its eyes narrowed in rage.

An arm reached out from behind her and thrust her aside. Pashla—in human form—pushed herself in front of Kyra.

"Leave her be. You'll honor the Challenge."

The striped cat bared its fangs and moved to step around the clanswoman. Pashla narrowed her eyes and hissed—as if she were still in her fur. The beast was twice her size and could have gutted her with a swipe of its paw, but Pashla exuded an authority that somehow evened the scales. Other demon cats moved in, forming a protective wall between the two of them. For a long, tense moment, nobody moved. Kyra held her breath, not daring to do anything lest she push the fragile standoff in the wrong direction. Finally, the striped cat turned and disappeared into the trees. Pashla's shoulders relaxed, and the other cats directed their attention to what was left of the deer carcass. The clanswoman put an arm around Kyra and guided her back to the shelter.

"That was Brona's widow," Pashla said. "She blames you for his death." The clanswoman might as well have been telling her that it would be a warm day. Kyra found that she was shaking.

"You'd be wise to stay away from the others when they are in cat form," said Pashla as Kyra lowered herself to the ground. "At least until those who mourn Brona have a chance to get over their grief."

"Only when they're in cat form?"

"Leyus wants you alive, and the clan will obey. But it's hard to control our impulses when we're in our fur. Instincts and emotions take over. That's why some of us take human form during the raids, to keep the others from going too far. I don't think Brona's widow, as much as she hates you, would attack you if she were in her skin."

Hard to control our impulses. Just like the felbeasts of legend. This was the blood that ran through Kyra's veins? "Mayhap I'll avoid her completely, just to be safe."

Pashla gave a small smile, and Kyra suddenly noticed the stiffness with which the clanswoman held herself. Fresh scars crisscrossed the Demon Rider's arms and neck, angry lines in the moonlight.

"You've defended me twice now, at risk to yourself." Kyra was unable to keep the question out of her voice.

Pashla waved away her words. "You became my ward when I saved you. I wouldn't nurse you to life just to hand you over to die. And you should not feel responsible for what happened. The question of your fate was important, but it only went to Challenge because Brona wanted to get rid of me."

"What do you mean?"

"The Challenge," said Pashla, "is a right of anyone with Makvani blood. The humans you lived with have a layered society. Those born poor are doomed to subservience. It's different with us. Not all our clan members have equal status, but no matter what rank we hold in the clan, we can always petition the clan leader for our right to Challenge. It's a fight to the death, and the clan honors the outcome."

Pashla paused, fingering one of her new scars. "The Challenge is sacred, but some will bend it to their purposes. Brona and I had long been enemies for...various reasons. The

Challenge was a way to get me out of the way, or at least dishonor me if I refused to fight."

"So you could have refused. You didn't have to risk your life for me."

Pashla shrugged, her face serene in the moonlight. "Dying in Challenge is an honorable death. And Brona had always been overconfident."

Over the next few days, Kyra started noticing patterns. Late morning and early afternoon were quiet, and the clan woke when the sun set. As Kyra became more attuned to signs of their presence, she glimpsed them moving through the trees at night and in the early mornings, though they never came close. She asked Pashla why the others never approached her.

"They watch, but they are wary," she said. "In time, they will come."

One evening, two young clanswomen wandered within view of her shelter. Kyra watched them from where she rested, eyes half closed in the semi-drowsy state that still overtook her waking hours. To her surprise, they didn't disappear back into the trees, but came closer. They looked about her age. One clanswoman was tall with large eyes and wispy brown hair that curled around a slender neck. The other was smaller, with pale, almost white skin that contrasted with her straight black hair. The two approached cautiously but deliberately. Like Pashla, they moved with Makvani grace, although they didn't have Pashla's air of quiet confidence. Kyra finally roused herself and climbed to her feet.

"You are Kyra, the halfblood," said the taller one.

"I am," Kyra said warily.

"I am Mela, and this is Adele."

For a moment, they stood without speaking. "We brought you some berries," Adele finally said. She took a handful out of a pouch around her neck and held them out.

The two of them didn't look hostile, and Kyra opened her hands, letting Adele dump the berries into her palms. She paused, completely at a loss about Makvani etiquette. "Would you like to join me?" she finally asked.

The clanswomen nodded, and they settled down on the floor of Kyra's shelter. Kyra carefully placed a berry into her mouth. It was good—plump, sweet, and a little tart. She let the juices pool under her tongue, hesitant to swallow, but then decided her companions had easier ways to harm her than to give her bad berries.

Mela straightened and looked Kyra in the eye. The sun had almost completely set, but like other Makvani, she seemed unfazed by talking in the dark. "Did you really grow up amongst the humans?" she asked.

The questions both relieved Kyra and put her on her guard. It seemed that these two were simply curious, but Kyra didn't know what was safe to share. "I had no idea I was anything but human," she said.

Mela leaned forward eagerly, her earlier caution falling to the wayside. "What are they like?"

"I—I don't know. I guess I've nothing to compare them to."

"How do humans live so closely packed all the time?" asked Mela. "I would go mad."

Kyra realized that she'd never seen the Makvani gathered

together for long periods of time. They'd come together for the clan gathering and the deer kill, but otherwise, Kyra never saw more than two or three together at once. "Don't the Makvani live in groups?"

"Yes, but not piled on top of each other like humans." Mela shrugged. "It keeps the peace. Though I suppose it's good for us that the humans are so closely packed. It makes for easier hunting."

Kyra felt bile rise in her throat. "Do you...hunt the humans?"

Adele shook her head. "Just their livestock, though it's a different matter if they get in our way. It would be strange, hunting them, since they look so much like us."

"Do you ever trade for their livestock?"

Both clanswomen looked curiously at her. "You have strange ideas, halfblood," Mela said. "Should we bring clover to the bees for their honey?"

Kyra hesitated to respond. Thankfully, Mela seemed more interested in their previous topic, because her eyes lit up mischievously. "Perhaps the humans live in crowded groups because all their females bear children. They multiply too quickly to spread out."

Adele gave Mela a long-suffering look. "That is not the reason. They only have one child at a time, whereas our mothers have many."

Kyra got the impression that the fair-skinned girl often talked her friend out of fanciful ideas. She wondered what it would have been like to grow up with these two as sisters. They reminded her of serving girls, in the way they spoke and acted.

"What do you mean by 'all their females bear children'?" asked Kyra.

Mela raised her eyebrows. "Do they not? If they choose to?"

"I suppose so, but—"

"Not all our women take mates," Mela interrupted. "Leyus chooses the ones who can be mothers. The rest of us help with their children, but do not have any of our own."

"You're forbidden from taking mates unless Leyus approves?"

Mela shrugged. "The clan can only support so many."

It was a strange concept, but on the other hand, it didn't seem worse than the noble men and women in Forge whose marriages were dictated by politics.

"Pashla will be chosen this time," said Adele quietly. "Especially since she fought so well in the Challenge."

Mela tossed her head, making her curls bounce lightly on her shoulders. "I'm glad. Brona got what he deserved."

"Wait." Kyra pounced on the topic. "What do Brona and the Challenge have to do with it?"

"Brona was a—" Mela stopped at Adele's warning glance. "Brona and Pashla never liked each other. They disagreed about many things, from where we should travel to our dealings with James. When it became clear that Leyus would allow a new clanswoman to take a mate, we knew Brona would try something. He wanted his sister to be chosen, but Leyus favored Pashla. It wasn't right for him to abuse the Challenge though." Mela looked indignantly at Adele. "I can say that. It's true."

Adele sighed. "I do think Pashla would make a better mother than Naleh. She sees things differently sometimes, but she's good with the young ones, and patient. I'll wager she's patient with you too, Kyra."

A roar echoed through the forest, similar to the one Kyra had heard the morning of the clan gathering. Treetops rustled in the distance, as if demon cats were traveling. Both Makvani girls turned toward the sound.

"Leyus calls," said Mela. The two of them licked the berry juice off their fingers and stood.

"Should I—" Kyra paused.

Mela and Adele exchanged a look. "This gathering is not for you, halfblood," said Adele. She gave Kyra an apologetic look before taking Mela's hand and pulling her away.

Kyra stared after them, puzzled by Adele's last statement. Granted, she wasn't surprised to be left out of their gatherings, but something about the way Adele had spoken made it seem like something more. She pressed a hand on her bandaged middle, probing her wound and trying to remember how far the clearing had been. It was a good distance, but she was stronger than she had been last time. If she walked slowly, she could probably make it there by herself.

Kyra had a vague recollection of the way, and there were faint hints of movement to lead her. After a long, unsteady walk, she saw the clearing ahead. The clan was gathered there, this time in a tighter circle. Kyra edged in as close as she dared, straining her ears. The Demon Riders looked to be passing around a sheet of parchment. Leyus was speaking, and Kyra leaned in closer. She stifled a gasp at the word *raid*, and strained to hear more.

A rustle made her jump, and she spun around to see a Makvani man behind her.

"You are not permitted to join the circle," he said. "Go back to your shelter." He planted himself between her and the others, arms folded across his chest.

Kyra backed away. "Sorry, I didn't know." She was painfully aware of the voices fading behind her with each step, but she didn't dare stop. She glanced back after a short distance, but he was still there, watching.

She was almost at her tent when she glimpsed two other demon cats—a yellow one and a gray one running amongst the trees. At first Kyra froze, wondering if she'd broken some other rule, but these cats seemed to pay her no attention. Curious, Kyra came closer. These demon cats were smaller than the others, coming up only to her thigh. Also, their features were softer and their heads bigger in proportion to their bodies. Kyra watched as the gray cat stopped to stare at something on the ground. The yellow cat stalked up behind him and pounced on Gray's tail, causing him to yelp.

Kyra laughed despite herself. It was unmistakable. These were demon kittens.

The two kittens startled at the sound and froze, staring at Kyra with wide eyes. Yellow led the way, cautiously approaching step-by-step while Gray followed behind. They stopped five paces away and blurred, changing into two naked children. Yellow was a girl about Lettie's age. She said something to Kyra in the Makvani language that sounded like a question. Gray, a toddler boy, watched expectantly.

Kyra shrugged an apology. "Sorry, I don't understand you."

They stared at each other for a few more moments. The children blurred back into their cat shapes, although they continued to circle and sniff at her from arm's length. Kyra picked a long stick off the ground and trailed the end in the dirt. Yellow pounced and attempted to trap the stick with her paws. Kyra pulled the stick away and wiggled it enticingly. Gray joined in the chase. If these had been ordinary kittens, Kyra might have held her own, but she was no match for these half-grown demon cats, and Yellow soon paraded in a circle with one end of the stick in her mouth, tail held high in triumph. This proved too much for Gray, and he attacked the stick again. Soon both kittens were rolling in the dirt.

"I see you've discovered Libena and Ziben."

Kyra whipped around to see Pashla standing a few paces away. The two kittens stopped wrestling.

The woman smiled and knelt in front of the little ones. She spoke to them at length, looking back at Kyra from time to time as if she were talking about her. Pashla ran her hand affectionately down their backs before sending them off to play.

"You have something in common with them," Pashla told Kyra. "They spent their early years without a clan, as did I."

"They did?"

"Our people lead a warlike existence. It is not uncommon for cubs to be left without a family. Most of the time, other clan members take them in. But sometimes they end up alone."

"Who raised them? Humans?"

Pashla shook her head. "No, they're pureblood. While you spent your early years as a human. Libena, Ziben, and I spent ours as cats."

On one hand, the idea of growing up as a cat stretched the limits of Kyra's imagination. On the other, the story felt familiar. The two kittens were playing a game now, something requiring the involuntary participation of an unlucky insect. They might have fur and sharp claws, but their play wasn't that much different from the orphans back at Forge. She wondered if Idalee and Lettie had recovered from the fire, and how they were getting along with both her and Bella gone.

"Do you remember what it was like?" she asked Pashla.

Pashla exhaled slowly. "It was a long time ago, but I do have some memories. I remember my mother. I remember being carried around by the scruff of my neck, huddling under her belly with my littermates. It's not uncommon for mothers to stay in cat form with their children when they're younger. The mothering instincts, like all other instincts, come stronger in our fur."

Kyra felt a touch of envy. She had nothing like those memories. "And then what happened?"

"I don't know." Pashla's voice was suddenly sad, although it must have been decades since those early years. "She sometimes left us, I assume to go hunting. If she was with a clan, we never saw the others. One day she didn't come back. By then, my littermates and I had grown enough to fend for ourselves, although we didn't know enough to stay together. We drifted apart. I hunted small animals and kept myself from starving. When you don't have language or reason, you think differently. When I was hungry, I knew to hunt, and when I was tired, I slept. Sometimes I was scared, or lonely, or angry, but I didn't know what it meant. I made no plans. I just existed. In the same way, my memories are different. I have images and impressions, but nothing like the memories I have of later."

Struggling for survival amid a confusion of emotions. Fighting to fulfill basic needs. It was eerily familiar. "And then what happened?"

"I met another cat. There was a wounded deer, and we found it at the same time. I was ten years old, not yet fully grown, but still ready to fight the other cat for the carcass. She stepped back and let me eat first. After that, she brought me food. That was enough to win me over." Pashla smiled wryly. "It really did not take much. Back then, I had no concept of language, rules, or loyalty. All I understood was my next meal."

Kyra scrutinized Pashla's face, trying unsuccessfully to imagine this graceful, self-possessed clanswoman as the wild thing she had described, tamed finally by food and kindness. Flick had won Kyra over with food as well. She lowered her head to hide a sudden pang of loneliness.

Pashla continued. "I remember the first time I saw her change. It took me completely off guard, seeing her in her skin. I almost attacked her. She must have known the risk, but she was determined to show me what I was. And she did win me over.

"A while later, I changed for the first time. I was sated after my meal. She had brought others from the clan to see me, and when they changed, my body followed suit. It was frightening. Suddenly, I was naked, cold, vulnerable. My mind was clearer, but my senses were dulled. They made noises at me that I didn't understand. That time, I did attack. You can draw blood with fingernails, if you're vicious enough. It took weeks to tame me.

Months to teach me language, and years to bring me into the clan. But the woman—Dala was her name—was very patient, and Leyus was good to me. Other leaders would have killed me for my rebelliousness, but he liked my spirit. I'm indebted to both of them. It is good to be in a clan."

Pashla looked at Kyra as she said those last words, and Kyra got the distinct impression that Pashla wanted her to experience this for herself. And there was such concern, such compassion in the clanswoman's eyes, that Kyra suddenly found herself telling her own story. She told Pashla about her own fragmented early memories, of scavenging in the city's trash piles and balancing on the edge of survival. She talked of things that she hadn't even told Bella or Flick, not because they wouldn't have cared or because she feared their judgment, but simply because they wouldn't have understood. Pashla knew about desperation, about being utterly alone those early years. After Flick and Bella had taken Kyra in, she'd felt loved, but she'd never felt like she truly belonged. Nighttime was her element. As she'd grown in confidence and skill, Kyra had struck out more and more on her own, and though Flick and Bella would have been willing to follow her, they simply could not keep up.

Pashla listened without interrupting, rubbing Kyra gently on the back as the words spilled out. When Kyra ran out of things to say, Pashla finally spoke. "Now you've found your people."

But even as Kyra gripped Pashla's hand in gratitude, she remembered her dream. How Bella had pulled her to her feet, and how Kyra's claws had pierced her skin and brought forth five drops of blood.

THIRTY-FOUR

Kyra healed more quickly than any human, yet it still felt agonizingly slow. Every day was one day closer to the coming raid, and she desperately needed to get word to the Palace. At the Guildhouse, James had proposed a raid in one month. If that were true, Kyra guessed she had two more weeks. But who knew what might have changed since then?

"Are you well enough for a longer walk tonight?" Pashla asked her one evening.

"I think so, if we go slowly." In truth, the shelter had started to feel restrictive. It was time to start building her strength.

"Good. I had an idea. We can take the kittens."

Curious, Kyra followed Pashla out into the forest. They found Libena and Ziben tumbling at the foot of a nearby boulder. Pashla barked a command, and the kittens fell into step with them. It was a cool night—autumn was starting in earnest. Kyra shivered and wrapped her animal skin tighter around her. They walked in silence for a while. Then Pashla finally spoke.

"Changing comes naturally to us," she said. "It is hard for me to teach you how. It would be like trying to tell you how to breathe or lift your arm. But we will try. You'll have to hunt with me."

"Hunt?" In her mind's eye, Kyra saw the wounded deer crashing through the forest.

The woman nodded. "Four legs feels the most natural when we're hunting. That's when it makes the most sense to be in our fur. Our senses are sharper then, our instincts stronger. Some of our younger ones have trouble changing back into their skin after a satisfying hunt."

Following Pashla was like following a ghost. She made no sound and left the ground undisturbed as she glided through the forest. Kyra felt a twinge of jealousy. All her life, she had been the graceful one, and now there was an entire race of people who could do this better than she.

Pashla stopped and raised one finger. "Deer upwind," she said softly. "You can smell them."

Kyra might have smelled something, or she might have just imagined it. Either way, she nodded and followed.

A few steps later, Libena's stance changed. The kitten arched her back and moved forward with high, mincing steps. Pashla held Kyra back with a light touch as Libena focused on an invisible prey. Suddenly, she pounced in a rustle of leaves. There was a scuffle, and Kyra thought she saw a small shadow scurry off. Libena's head drooped, and Pashla said something to her in an encouraging tone.

Pashla led them around like this, stopping to point out sights and smells. It was fascinating. Kyra had always taken pleasure in finding things in the dark, and now Pashla pushed her to her limits, showing her faint footprints, shadows that were no more than a flicker or a feeling. They had continued a while when Pashla stopped and brushed Kyra's elbow. The woman didn't look worried, but Kyra followed her gaze to a telltale rustle in a nearby tree. There was a crash of branches as a shadow dropped to the ground. Silence; then a two-legged shape walked out of the trees.

"Leyus." Pashla brushed three fingers down the front of her neck as she dipped in a slight bow.

The clan leader was just as Kyra remembered from the gathering, with the same air of authority even when walking alone. He acknowledged Pashla with a nod. "Pashla. You are healing well?"

"Yes, as is Kyra."

"I would speak with Kyra," he said to Pashla. "I will return her to her shelter after we finish."

"Of course." Pashla touched Kyra's wrist. "We will continue tomorrow."

Kyra watched helplessly as Pashla gathered the kittens and disappeared into the trees. The clanswoman was sometimes strange and not completely predictable, but at least Kyra knew Pashla wouldn't harm her. Leyus was a different matter.

"Let us walk," said Leyus. Kyra obeyed, muscles tense. Somehow, this didn't seem like a social visit.

They continued through the trees. Kyra once again noticed the Makvani's grace of movement, though Leyus didn't take as much care to leave the forest undisturbed. It was as if Pashla wanted to blend into the forest, while Leyus saw no reason to. Finally, he spoke.

"Tell me again what happened with James."

303

His tone was casual, but Kyra didn't miss the suspicion behind his question.

"We disagreed about my job," she said. "James wanted more than I was prepared to give."

"And when he tried to kill you, what happened?"

"We had an argument, and it turned into a fight."

"I see," said Leyus. "What puzzles me, Kyra, is why this happened at that hour, halfway through the meeting with Pashla and Czern. And Pashla says James called you a traitor."

Kyra struggled to keep a tremor out of her voice. "James stretches his stories sometimes."

Leyus turned to face her. "And if I talk to James myself, will he give me a similar account of what happened?"

She didn't answer. Leyus held her gaze, daring her to look away.

"The truth is, Kyra, I don't care about your relationship with James. Our alliance with him will only last as long as it is useful. Neither do I hold you accountable for your actions before you learned what you were."

There was an edge in his voice as he continued. "What I do care about is your loyalty to the clan. Pashla is a strong clanswoman, and capable, but her past affects her judgment. It is important to her that those with our blood have an opportunity to be in the clan, and I honor her wishes because she won the Challenge. We spared your life, and we will even teach you our ways if you desire. But make one step that harms the clan, and we will deal with you like any other human. Are we understood?"

Kyra forced herself to meet his eyes. "Aye."

He studied her face, as if mining for answers. A brisk wind blew around both of them, swirling dust and leaves about Kyra's ankles.

"Good. Do not forget our conversation."

The conversation with Leyus brought things into sharp focus. Pashla's kindness and Kyra's own curiosity had taken the edge off her urgency, but she saw that she needed to leave, and leave soon. Kyra heard another roar the next evening, a summons to yet another meeting she couldn't attend. This was her chance. Everybody else would be at the gathering, possibly for several hours. And she was well enough to travel.

The thought of escape set her heart beating and her mind racing. If she wanted to take advantage of this chance, she had to act quickly. There wasn't much she could take with her. A few pieces of leftover fruit, the clothes she wore, and a blanket. The fruit would only last her half a day, but she couldn't be more than a day or two from the city, and she'd been hungry for longer periods of time than that. Perhaps she could use what she'd learned from Pashla to forage along the way. The thought of Pashla was the only thing that nagged at her. It felt wrong to leave without a word, but she saw little other choice.

Kyra didn't know exactly where she was, but the city was roughly to the west, and hopefully she would be able to find a road along the way. She pointed herself away from the morning sun. The forest was changing for winter. She was surrounded by yellow-orange leaves, and some trees already sported naked branches. Her nerves carried her the first quarter hour, but then doubts began to surface. The Makvani, however dangerous they were, were the only link to her past. She still had so many questions and so much to learn. Would she ever get another chance? And once she got to Forge, what would she tell them about her time in the forest? Could she betray the Makvani, betray Pashla, after they had saved her life?

"Kyra, what are you doing?" Kyra jumped as Pashla stepped out through the trees. Had the clanswoman been at the gathering? Perhaps the Makvani were watching her more closely than she'd thought. Kyra forced herself to relax and smile, even as she took a frantic inventory of how she looked. She only had a little fruit on her, an amount that was more suitable for a short walk than for a multiple-day journey to the city. The blanket was more suspect, but she had it thrown around her shoulders like a cloak.

"I was feeling strong and decided to go for a walk, although I might have been too optimistic." She put a hand to her bandaged middle.

Pashla's face instantly clouded over with concern. "Are you unwell? I can help you back."

"That would be good." And it wasn't even a lie. Her wound was throbbing and her limbs were weak. Even with Pashla's help, she was exhausted by the time she made it back to the shelter. She'd been a fool to think she could make it all the way back by herself. She would give herself another week to heal. It *should* still be enough time, she hoped.

Yet as Kyra collapsed and drifted off into sleep, reflecting over her failure to escape, she had to admit that part of her felt relieved.

It wasn't that Kyra's senses got sharper. It was more that she finally learned to use them. Pashla taught her to be aware of every detail—the faint scent of a crushed leaf, a telltale snap of a twig, the scratch of tiny claws. But it was more than just paying attention. As a thief, Kyra was used to being alert, ready to hide at the smallest sign of a guard. Now she learned to approach the world as predator, not prey. Rather than reacting, she searched, and the world came to her in more vivid detail than she'd ever thought possible.

She looked forward to her walks with Pashla and the kittens. Every day was a new challenge and a chance to learn. Kyra stopped Pashla during one early morning walk, raising her finger in warning as she sampled the wind. The scent was familiar; Pashla had pointed it out to her just a couple of days ago.

"Geese somewhere close," she told Pashla. "Probably flying through for the winter."

"Very good," Pashla said.

Kyra allowed herself a small smile as she shifted her attention to the ground before her. Leaves covered the dirt, decorating the forest floor with red-and-yellow piles that shifted in the wind. It all looked normal—except for one mound of leaves that moved too much. Kyra froze in her steps and pointed. Pashla nodded slightly and gestured to Libena, who was also staring at the pile. At Pashla's signal, Libena approached and waited, one paw off the ground. Kyra saw the rabbit dart out just as Libena attacked. The kitten's teeth closed around the rabbit's neck.

Pashla said something in their language, which Kyra understood to be praise and a suggestion that they take a break. They settled on the ground, and Pashla handed Kyra a plum. It was a welcome change from the steady diet of raw meat, and Kyra ate slowly, savoring the sweet juices as she watched the kittens tear into their catch.

"Tell me," Pashla asked Kyra, "do the humans really not suspect our shape-shifting?"

Talk of humans made her uneasy, reminding her that she was running out of time. "There are stories. Rumors of shape-shifters beyond the Aerins that some people believe, but no one has suspected it of you yet. At least, I haven't heard anything."

Pashla nodded thoughtfully. "We are most vulnerable when we change, so we don't do it in front of our enemies. The humans always find out eventually, but it is easier when they think the cats are mere beasts."

"Does James know?"

"James is an interesting one. If he fears us, he doesn't show it, but I don't think he has guessed yet. He approached us soon after we came to these forests. Back then, we were raiding farms in the countryside and the occasional trade caravan, but he wanted us to come closer to the city. He offered us supplies and access to trade schedules if we'd help him. It works to our advantage. The armor he traded us has been very helpful."

The detachment with which Pashla spoke about the city raids was unsettling. "Why do you fight the humans?"

Pashla gave her a curious look. "You think like them."

It was the same response she had gotten from Adele and Mela—not flat-out disagreement, but puzzlement, as if the idea were so bizarre that it didn't even brook consideration. Kyra waited for Pashla to explain, but she didn't.

"Pashla," Kyra finally said, "you never told me why the clan came here in the first place. Why are you wandering?"

"It's a long story, going back to when I was very young. Our people lived on the western side of the Aerin Mountains, in lush forests with good hunting. About twenty years ago, there was a war with a human clan. They poisoned our land and forced us to leave. At first, we stayed on the western side of the Aerins, in the unsullied parts, but there was not enough space. Our own clans started fighting each other. Leyus was young compared to the other clan leaders, so he led us across the mountains in search of better forests."

"What you mean, 'poisoned the land'?"

"That is a story better told by others, after you become more settled with the clan."

Another question nagged at Kyra. "If all the Makvani are from across the mountains, how did I get here?"

Pashla chewed her fruit thoughtfully. "It's a mystery. You must have come from the west somehow. None of the Makvani tribes came here before us, and we have not been here two years."

"But all I remember is Forge. How could I have traveled so far if I was too young to remember?"

"The only humans who travel such long distances are the Far Rangers. Perhaps you could find them after you heal. Traders have long memories."

"Do you know the traders?"

Pashla shook her head. "No. We do not deal with them. Though before we started roaming, we traded in humans."

"Traded in humans?"

Pashla gave Kyra a sidelong glance. "Humans are funny creatures. They think nothing of raising and keeping horses or dogs, but they complain when others do the same to them."

The plum juice suddenly tasted sour in Kyra's mouth. "You were slavers," she said.

"As were the humans who bought our goods. Does this bother you?"

Kyra gripped the leftover plum pit. The edge dug into her palm. "Slavery is a harsh fate."

"The world is not an easy place, Kyra. We all do what we must. If you have any doubts, do not speak of them to the others. It would not reflect well on you." Pashla stood, dusting herself off. "How are your injuries? If I hunt, can you keep up with me?"

It was a purposeful change of subject. "I can't sprint," said Kyra, "but I can follow you."

"Are the geese still there?" Pashla asked.

"Aye," Kyra said after a pause.

"Well done. I'll go after one now. Try to keep up."

Pashla handed Kyra her clothes and her pouch before changing shape. Once in cat form, she started upwind toward the geese. Kyra tucked Pashla's things under her arm and gathered the kittens to follow, but then Pashla stopped and turned around, running back toward Kyra and then past her, speeding up as she went. Despite Kyra's best efforts to keep up, Pashla disappeared into the forest, only to reappear a few moments later as she scaled a particularly tall tree. In a flash, she jumped from that tree to another, then another, before she dove toward the ground.

Kyra heard a scream—a man's scream—and sped up, weaving through the trees as quickly as her healing body would allow. She heard a scuffle, growling, and more screams. Kyra burst through the foliage to see Pashla, still in cat form, dragging a man by the arm through the dirt. Next to them, another man lay on the ground, bleeding from a head wound. She couldn't see his face, but he looked to be a guard from the Palace. Kyra stood there, frozen in indecision, until another movement distracted her. The first man, the one whose arm was still between Pashla's teeth, raised his head and looked directly at her.

It was Tristam.

THIRTY-FIVE

Kyra! For a moment, the elation of recognition cleared Tristam's head of pain. But then, they locked eyes. Horror flashed across her face, and then panic. It was unmistakably her. But why was she healthy? And free?

The demon cat tightened its jaws, and once again Tristam couldn't think about anything except the pain. He heard Kyra shouting in the background. The forest was overrun by a chorus of snarls and snapping branches. Another demon cat landed in a shower of leaves. Martin moaned.

No, not Martin. Tristam gritted his teeth and twisted his head. His companion was covered in blood. More demon cats arrived, followed by their Riders. Suddenly, the cat released his arm, and Tristam fell face-first onto the dirt. There was a shadow as the cat stepped over him and walked into the trees.

"Did you see this?" a man asked.

Tristam spat sand out of his mouth.

"No." Kyra was speaking to them as peers, not as a prisoner. "I only caught up to Pashla after it happened."

Another woman spoke. "They were sneaking around. I took them by surprise." Tristam raised his head. It was the Demon Rider woman who'd killed Jack. Raw hatred ran through him.

"Was there anyone else with them?" asked the man.

"I don't think so, Leyus," the woman answered. "But James is after this one." The woman jerked her thumb toward Tristam. "He's the same knight I caught spying last time. You will recognize him from James's portraits."

"You're right," said Leyus. "Kyra, did James ever speak of him?" Leyus asked.

"James never told us much of anything,"

What now? Was Kyra still working for James? He struggled to think of another explanation, any explanation, of what he was hearing.

The one called Leyus turned his attention to Tristam.

"What were you doing in the forest?"

Tristam raised himself onto one elbow and lifted his face toward the Demon Riders. "Regular patrols." Dust from the ground coated his throat and made his voice hoarse.

"You are not in a position to lie to me, knight."

A cat swiped at Tristam with its paw, knocking him sideways and ripping a trail in his tunic. The blow knocked the breath out of him, and he couldn't have answered even if he wanted to.

"How is the other one?" asked Leyus.

Tristam saw some movement from Martin's direction. He clenched his fists as Martin first groaned and then screamed.

"Useless." Leyus's voice dripped with disgust. "Are there others out there?"

Tristam stared stone-faced at the ground and steeled himself for another blow. None came.

"So James is looking for the knight?" said Leyus. "What about the Red Shield?"

"We have no use for him," said Pashla.

"What are you going to do with them?" Kyra asked. Her voice was high-pitched, bordering on hysteria.

"That is not your concern. Leave us," the man said. Tristam looked up to see someone pull Kyra out of sight.

"Deal with the Red Shield."

Almost before Leyus finished speaking, a cat grabbed Martin by the arm and dragged him toward the trees. Tristam felt the blood drain from his face as Martin's screams grew worse. The cries echoed through Tristam's head, and he squeezed his eyes shut. It was a horrible relief when Martin finally quieted.

"Take the knight and watch him," said Leyus, looking this time at Tristam. "We will hand him over to James when he comes."

⊗ ⊗ ⊗

Martin's screams were impossible to ignore. Kyra longed to clamp her hands over her ears, but Pashla gripped her arm in an unforgiving hold. Then his screams stopped, and Kyra went limp, unable to face what had happened.

"Will you kill Tristam, too?"

"That is Leyus's decision," said Pashla. She pulled Kyra farther away from the crowd.

"You can't," Kyra said.

"Why? What is he to you?"

Kyra wrested her arm away and pivoted to run. She made it five steps before Pashla tackled her to the ground. Kyra kicked and struggled, yelling incoherent insults, but the clanswoman was more than her match.

"Kyra, listen to me."

Kyra made a few more halfhearted attempts before she succumbed to exhaustion.

"I know this is hard, Kyra. You grew up with humans," said Pashla, "but you have to let it go. Sometimes, a few humans have to be sacrificed for the good of the clan."

Kyra choked and spit. "How can you just say that?"

"Think about it, Kyra. There is always some sacrifice. What about the meat we eat every day? The animals had to sacrifice their lives. This is no different."

"You keep talking about humans as if they were something else," said Kyra. "But I'm half human. Have you forgotten that?"

There was a long pause.

"Yes, I have," Pashla said quietly. "And you need to as well. For better or worse, you are with the clan now, Kyra, and you must live under its laws. Consider your human self dead by James's hand. If you want a second chance at life, you have to take it as a daughter of the Makvani."

THIRTY-SIX

Tristam struggled to swallow the lump in his throat. *Don't think about Martin. You're a knight, Tristam. Act like one.*

They searched him for weapons and confiscated the knife in his boot. Leyus dragged him up by his collar and grabbed him by the shoulders.

"Look at me." The Demon Rider shook Tristam until he raised his head. "James wants you alive. This will be easier for both of us if you do not struggle."

A Demon Rider tore off Tristam's tunic. They bandaged his shoulder wound, bound Tristam's hands in front of him, and pushed him against a tree. Rough bark dug into his back as Leyus tied him to the trunk, then walked in a slow circle to inspect his knots. A few times, he pulled the bindings tighter, and Tristam gritted his teeth as the ropes dug into his arms.

"Rest well, knight," Leyus said.

Leaving one cat to guard him, the Demon Riders retreated into the forest. Tristam waited until he was sure they were gone. Then he slumped against his ropes, closing his eyes as a wave of grief washed over him. For a long time, he stood there, fighting despair. Martin was dead, and he was captured—all for a girl, who for all appearances didn't need rescuing. The image of her, uninjured and unbound amongst the Demon Riders, flashed again through his mind. What an idiot he'd been.

Around him, the forest was empty, with no sign of the Demon Riders except for the one cat that guarded him. There was something about the beast that made Tristam's hair stand on end. The cat watched him through intelligent eyes, and when it circled Tristam, he swore it was examining the rope for weaknesses. It was more than a well-trained pet.

Midway through the night, a Demon Rider brought him raw meat and allowed him to relieve himself before tying him up again. Tristam only managed to choke down a single piece of meat, but it didn't take him long to realize he should have forced himself to eat more. By morning, his throat was parched and his stomach ached with hunger. He pulled against his ropes in the vain hope that they had loosened during the night, but they didn't budge. All the while, his feline guard watched his efforts through half-closed eyes.

The sun climbed overhead, passing the halfway mark and sucking any remaining moisture from his skin. Some time in midafternoon, his guard suddenly sprang to its feet, staring into the forest at a shape that took Tristam longer to make out.

It was Kyra.

She approached slowly, with a bag in one hand and a flask in the other. She was dressed in the same leather tunic the other Demon Riders had worn. Her cheeks were flushed from the crisp breeze, and she maintained an aura of forced calm. The cat growled in warning and blocked her way.

"I'm bringing water and food. Leyus wants me to talk to him," she said, addressing the cat as if it were a man. It didn't budge.

"I won't untie him."

The cat moved aside, still watching her movements carefully. It made Tristam uneasy, how human these cats were.

"Are you thirsty?" Kyra asked.

He nodded, mouth too dry to speak.

She lifted the flask halfway. "I'm going to have to feed you."

Her obvious discomfort wasn't a good sign. If she had been scared or defeated, he might have held out some hope of a misunderstanding. But instead, she looked ashamed.

She lifted the flask to his lips and slowly let it pour into his mouth. It was easily the most refreshing drink he'd had in his life. For a moment, he was grateful despite her betrayal. When he'd had enough, Kyra put the flask down.

"The meat's hard to get used to," she said quietly. "I brought some berries."

"You're in better shape than I expected." He made no effort to mask the bitterness in his voice.

Her eyes flickered briefly to his before she busied herself with sorting the berries. "A lot has happened," she said.

"Is that all you're going to tell me?" He struggled to control his anger. "The last I heard, you were being carried into the forest by Demon Riders."

"Why did you come this far in?" she asked.

"To rescue you. Martin and I have been coming out here against Palace orders."

That got through to her. Her face twisted briefly before

she schooled her features again. "I'm sorry," she said. "About Martin."

Tristam gave up any attempt at self-control. He strained against the ropes, hardly noticing the resulting pain through his injured arm. "You owe me more than that. Were you working for James this entire time? Gaining my sympathy for Palace secrets? You played me for a fool." Kyra held some berries to his lips and he turned his head. "How do I know these aren't poisoned?"

"Don't be stupid," she snapped. "Starving yourself won't help anyone."

Tristam accepted the berries. He was so hungry he couldn't have held out long anyway.

"I in't working for James," she said finally.

"Then what are you doing here?"

She looked away. "It's complicated."

"Of course it is."

She flinched at his caustic tone.

"At least tell me what they're going to do with me," said Tristam.

Kyra glanced briefly behind her, meeting the cat's eye, then nodded. "James has been trying to get rid of you and Malikel for a while now. He's meeting with the Riders soon. They'll turn you over, in exchange for some favors from the Guild."

He crumpled against his ropes. "How long do I have?"

"One day, maybe two. I'm talking to Leyus, trying to change his mind."

"I appreciate your efforts on my behalf."

She ignored his sarcasm and dug into the pouch again. "I

may not be able to come back for a while. Here are some berries for later." He felt her press something into his hands.

She turned and left, walking quickly past the demon cat without looking back. Instead of helping him, she had left him with more questions, and a handful of berries that he couldn't even lift to his mouth. He looked at them, entertaining some vague hope that Kyra had slipped him something to help him escape. But no, they were just regular bush berries, some already bleeding black juice into his palm.

His guard padded over, eyeing the gift suspiciously.

"It's just berries," he said, holding them out as best he could. The cat growled and came closer, tail swishing as it stuck its nose into Tristam's hand. Tristam held very still. There was a movement in the corner of his eye, but instinctively he knew not to look. A moment later, he heard a loud crack. The cat staggered back to reveal Kyra brandishing a rock. She followed her first blow with another to the beast's head. For a moment, the cat looked dazed. Then it launched itself at Kyra. The girl barely had time to dart away—right into Tristam. Pain streaked through his shoulder. He felt something heavy drop into his palm. Kyra wobbled and looked into his eyes as she steadied herself. Then she ran, the demon cat close on her heels.

Tristam closed his fingers over the new object. It was a knife—Kyra had found his knife. His guard, as far as he could tell, was still chasing Kyra and hadn't noticed. Tristam took a slow breath. His arms were completely bound, and he could only move his wrists and fingers. If he dropped the dagger... well, he wouldn't. Slowly, he eased off the leather sheath and let it fall. If he twisted his wrist, he could just graze the ropes with the blade.

The cat chased Kyra up a tree and into the higher branches. Tristam kept an eye on them as he worked. As strand by strand gave way, the ropes loosened, and he sawed more quickly. Finally, his arms came free and Tristam pulled at the rest until they lay in a pile on the ground. He took a step and grabbed the tree for support as a million invisible needles attacked his limbs.

There was a loud crack, followed by a crash. Tristam looked up to find Kyra crumpled on the ground, surrounded by leaves and twigs. A few paces away, the demon cat crouched, also disoriented. Then it stood up, shook itself, and limped toward Kyra. The girl lifted her head, making no move to defend herself.

Tristam lurched toward the cat with the knife, aiming for the tender flesh under its neck. The beast whipped around, and Tristam brought the knife down, angling the blade so it slipped between strands of fur. The dagger lodged in the demon cat's shoulder. The animal roared in fury. Desperately scrambling for another weapon, Tristam grabbed a large branch and put all his remaining strength behind his attack, pummeling the creature as hard as he could. One hit connected with the base of the demon cat's skull, and the beast sank to the ground.

Kyra groaned, and Tristam turned to see her slowly push herself to her feet.

"That was a bad idea," she said.

"Was our earlier conversation all an act?"

"Some of it," she said, rubbing her backside. She grimaced

and staggered over to the cat, placing her hand in front of its muzzle to check its breathing. "He's still alive."

"Not for long." Tristam wrenched the knife out of the cat's shoulder and pried its mouth open.

"No!" Kyra's eyes were wide, horrified.

"Give me one good reason not to," he snarled. First Jack, then Martin, and the countless in the fire. He would kill one of these creatures before he died.

"Please..."

He looked at her incredulously and stepped toward her, only to grab a tree for support as a wave of nausea hit him. She reached out to steady him, but shrank back when he glared at her. Was he that frightening to behold?

He doubled over, his strength draining as his anger lost momentum. "Who *are* you?" he asked.

Kyra looked frantically between him and the prone demon cat. She started to talk, but then she stopped, her eyes widened, and she cast around the forest.

"They're coming after us," she said. "We need to go."

THIRTY-SEVEN

The moment they started running, Kyra knew they were in trouble. Tristam's ordeal had taken its toll. His balance was off, and strain showed on his face with each step. Still, they had no choice but to run.

They needed a river to wash out their scent and hide their tracks. Even then, Kyra wasn't sure the Makvani wouldn't be able to pick their scent out of the air. Running alongside Tristam, her own recently trained nose caught the fresh blood of his wounds, and more disturbingly, another layer of fever and sickness underneath. More than once, she saw him stumble.

"We're almost there," she said, squeezing the words out between gasps. "There's a river up ahead."

Already, the ground was sloping down. They slowed, stepping carefully over roots and rocks toward the rushing water. She broke through the trees on the riverbank and stopped at the edge. It was a small river and looked to be waist deep. Icy water swirled around her ankles as she waded in.

"How are you doing?" A rock tipped as she put her weight on it and she barely avoided twisting her ankle.

"I'll live," said Tristam through gritted teeth.

They followed the river until Kyra had no feeling left in her submerged feet.

"Do you think we can cross?" she asked.

Tristam nodded and they turned into the deeper water toward the opposite bank. The current took her breath away and she clenched her teeth to keep them from chattering. Behind her, Tristam stumbled and she rushed to his side, bracing against the slippery stones as he steadied himself. Kyra ducked under his shoulder. His weight made her knees buckle. They fought through, resisting the flow, until they finally clambered up the opposite bank. At the top of the slope, Kyra collapsed onto the dirt, only to jump up again as the smell of demon cats filled her nostrils. Kyra turned her face into the wind. There were definitely cats in that direction, and they were close.

"We need to—" She stopped when she saw Tristam's face. He was scrutinizing her, eyes wary.

"You're different. . . ."

She ignored him. "The demon cats are everywhere. We can't stay." But then she stopped. They couldn't run either. Tristam could hardly walk at this point, and just helping him across the river had exhausted her. Tristam's grim expression told her that he had reached the same conclusion.

"There was a small alcove by the riverbank a little upstream," he said. "Maybe we can wait out the search there."

It was a painful scramble back down the riverbank to retrace their steps, but they found it. On one side of the bank, the water had worn a depression in the river wall and then receded away, leaving a small cave. Some grass grew at the opening to provide cover. It wasn't great, but it would have to do. They climbed into the cramped space and sat there, leaning their heads against the packed dirt as they struggled to catch their breath.

"So what happened?" Tristam finally asked.

Kyra sighed and closed her eyes. "James caught me at the Guildhouse. We fought. He won. I thought I was going to die, but the Demon Riders rescued me."

"Do you know why they helped you?"

Kyra paused. "The Demon Riders thought I was one of them."

"That's very strange."

She pulled her knees closer and hunched over, aware of his eyes on her and unable to face him. It had taken him long enough to trust her when he'd thought her simply a criminal. What would he think now, if he knew she was kin to the creatures who'd now killed two of his comrades?

"I don't want to talk about it," she said.

To her surprise, he didn't press her. "I guess this means you're not one of them? Are you coming back to Forge?"

Kyra chuckled bitterly, wondering if Tristam had any idea what the question meant. She didn't regret her decision to run. There was no way she could have stood by as they killed Tristam. But at the same time, there was still so much she didn't know about the Makvani. Would she ever go hunting again? Was that side of her lost forever? "I need to speak with Malikel," she said. "James is planning another raid. I found ten vials of blueflower extract in his study."

"Blueflower extract?" Tristam's half-closed eyes fluttered open. "That's strange. Who do you think he's after?"

"I don't know. The Council perhaps?"

"The Council only has twenty members. He could poison five times that number with ten vials."

"The Palace guards, then?"

"Not enough for that. We have a regular force of two hundred." Tristam closed his eyes. "You're right. We do have to tell Malikel."

Minutes ticked into hours, and Kyra lost track of time. Their hiding place was damp. The dirt was moist, and occasional sprays from the river carried the promise of a chilly night. The sound of Tristam's breathing next to her became labored and shallow. She took his hands and tried to rub heat into his icy fingers. He acknowledged her efforts with a glance, but otherwise lay back against the dirt wall, unmoving.

She climbed to her feet. "I'm going to look around."

Kyra didn't smell the cats as she made her way up the bank. Perhaps the search had moved on. But the scent hit her again as soon as she topped the slope. Kyra bit her lip and climbed back down. She needed some way to make them leave.

"Do you have bandages under your tunic?" she asked Tristam.

"Yes, why?"

"Let me look at them."

Tristam looked confused, but peeled off his tunic, grimacing when he had to move his injured arm. Spots of blood seeped through the top layer of his bandages.

Kyra scooted closer and unwrapped them, careful to keep

the cleaner layers free of dirt. She had to look away briefly when she unraveled the rest. The muscles of his shoulder bore deep, ragged wounds, and she definitely smelled infection.

Noticing her reaction, Tristam gave a wan smile. "I'd hoped you'd be more impressed at my battle-hardened brawn."

It would have been funnier if his voice hadn't been quite so weak. Kyra squeezed his arm. "Once we get you sewn up, you'll be plenty impressive."

She briefly wondered if her saliva had any healing properties, but her stomach flipped and she dismissed the idea. The Makvani only cleaned wounds in cat form anyway. Her best bet was to get Tristam back to Forge.

The inner bandages were soaked through with blood, and she tore that part off, rewrapping the rest as best she could. It bothered her how passive Tristam was acting. He was more lethargic than he'd been even half an hour before, and he was shivering, even though he was clearly trying to hide it. She took his arm to thread it back into his tunic. His skin was hot to the touch and damp with sweat.

"Tristam." She spoke slowly and clearly. "I'm going to take your bandages outside and away from here. Maybe the scent will lead the search somewhere else. We need that blind to escape."

He shifted and looked at her. "You're going to try to lead them away?"

"Aye, you stay here. I'll come back."

"It's not worth the risk. Just try to get to Forge and send help."

"You won't last that long, not with all of them looking for you. Just stay put."

She grabbed the bandage and crawled out before he could argue. At the top of the bank, she looked around again. Where could she go? After a moment's hesitation, she picked a direction and ran. She jumped over roots and ducked under branches, thinking just to get away from the river.

After a while, brown fur flashed behind her and to the right. Someone had found her. She cut to the left and down a hill. The hard dirt pounded against her feet as she barreled down. A quick glance behind showed that her pursuer still trailed her, and if anything, was gaining.

Desperate, she dove into a cluster of bushes and scrambled through, only to stop at a glimpse of white fur through the trees ahead of her. She turned again, willing herself to run faster. She could hear the cats behind her now, their footsteps heavy as they abandoned silence for speed. There was a rustle of branches in front of her, and a third demon cat dropped straight in her path, blocking her way. Kyra skidded to a stop as the two others closed in from behind. For a few long moments, they stayed there, the three cats ready to block any move she made. Then, a familiar yellow cat ran in, looked around, and slowly changed shape.

Pashla hadn't finished settling into her human form before she crossed over to Kyra and struck her across the face.

THIRTY-EIGHT

The blow knocked her to the ground. Kyra fought back a cry as her elbow skidded across the dirt.

"This is how you repay me."

Kyra looked down, unable to meet Pashla's eyes. It was true. Pashla had saved her life, fought for her, and taught her the ways of the clan. And Kyra had betrayed her.

Pashla dragged Kyra to her feet and spun her to face the other three demon cats. "Back to Leyus."

They didn't tie her up, but instead herded her back, one demon cat flanking Kyra on each side. When Kyra slowed, the cat behind her snapped at her heels. Kyra desperately scanned the trees ahead and behind her as they traveled. The cats were watching the path, not her. If she could break away for long enough to get to a hiding place . . . One cat turned its head and gazed at Kyra out of the corner of its eye, as if to assure her that they were indeed watching.

Demon Riders were already gathered at the clearing when Kyra arrived. Had they assembled at her escape? No, most didn't even look at her as she was brought in. They clustered in groups, deep in discussion. As her captors pulled a rope tight around her wrists, Kyra glimpsed Tristam, also captive, slumped against a tree. He raised his eyes to hers and then looked down again, as if he were too tired to meet her gaze.

Pashla fixed Kyra with a burning stare. "Why did you do it?"

Why? Because they were slavers. Because Kyra couldn't stand by and watch them murder Tristam. Because all she wanted to do was go home and cry on Bella's shoulder, but she couldn't, because they'd killed Bella too.

"I couldn't let him die," was all she said.

"You failed. He will still die tomorrow, and now you will too." Pashla's tone was sharp with bitterness and regret. It looked like she would say more, but she turned and wove into the crowd of Demon Riders. Kyra let herself slump when Pashla left, but her respite was short-lived. When Pashla returned, Leyus came with her.

The head Demon Rider fixed his gaze on Kyra and Tristam, and Kyra suddenly felt deeply ashamed. The two of them, filthy and exhausted, must have looked pathetic. "Keep them apart. I will speak to them separately," he commanded.

Tristam threw one last glance back as two Demon Riders dragged him away. Others shoved Kyra against a tree, binding her tightly. At a nod from Leyus, everyone left except for two cats who watched from a distance. Kyra closed her eyes, digging for the resolve to face his questions.

The Demon Rider spoke calmly. "You have betrayed the clan and thrown Pashla's trust in her face. What do you have to say for yourself?"

"What will you do with me?" she asked.

"I warned you. If you betray us, we will treat you like any other human. Even dying by our hands is more dignity than you deserve. Tomorrow, we return you to James to deal with as he wishes."

James. He was the reason for all of this. "You're fools to deal with him. He'll betray you as readily as he betrayed me."

"That's enough." Now Leyus was also angry. "Bold talk for someone who herself lied so readily. Or do you still expect us to believe that the knight is a stranger to you? That you have no ties to the Palace?"

Kyra looked down, unable to answer, but then her eyes fell on Leyus's hand. He was holding a parchment—a strikingly familiar one. "The map," she blurted. "You have my map of the Fastkeep."

Leyus glanced at the parchment. "So you were the cartographer," he said. "The map was well drawn."

Kyra stared at him with dread. "When is the raid?"

"You worry too much about things that no longer concern you, halfblood."

He left before she could answer.

Dawn was cutting through the mists when Kyra woke to the footsteps of unfamiliar Demon Riders. It was a cold morning, and moisture from the fog had settled on her skin while she slept. The Demon Riders didn't speak as they led her back to the clearing, where the clan had gathered in its usual circle. Tristam was in the center, bruised and leaning on one of his guards for support. Next to him stood Leyus. Kyra steeled herself to join them, but to her surprise, her guards kept her at the edge of the circle.

The crowd shifted at the sound of approaching hoofbeats, and three riders came into view. Even from his outline amidst the haze, Kyra recognized James. The scar on her stomach throbbed, and she suddenly found it hard to breathe. If they untied her, she didn't know if she'd go for his throat or flee.

The circle opened into a horseshoe to let in the newcomers, and Kyra's guards pulled her behind the other Demon Riders, hiding her from view. Kyra recognized Alex's black locks and Shea's quick stride. They stayed back while James dismounted to greet Leyus, and Kyra strained to hear the conversation. Everyone else must have been doing the same, because the two men's voices echoed unchallenged through the forest.

"How did you find him?" James asked.

"He was prying around the forest. We killed his companion but kept him alive."

"I am grateful," said James as Shea and Alex unloaded several saddlebags. "Here are fifty sets of winter garments, made from Forge's best imported silk. The cloth wicks sweat away from your skin, keeps you dry in the cold."

Leyus opened the case and nodded approval. At his signal, Tristam's handlers pulled him toward James. The knight stumbled, then shook off his guards to take the last few steps to James himself.

James bowed. "Sir Tristam of Brancel. I don't believe we've met." Even from that distance, she caught the mockery in his voice. The assassin turned to Leyus. "It's a pleasure doing business with you, as always. You'll get the other half of the payment after the next raid."

"We've studied your maps," said Leyus. "It won't be a problem if you provide the diversion you promised."

Kyra's entire body clenched, and she leaned closer. Diversion? Was that what the blueflower extract was for?

"It's taken care of," said James. "Just be careful inside the compound. I need enough left alive to keep Forge running. A city in anarchy is of no use to me."

"I will send my most experienced cats in there. They won't lose control."

"Then we'll meet again soon," said James. "Do try the garments and let me know if they're to your liking."

As he turned away, Leyus spoke again. "There is one more prisoner you might be interested in."

Kyra's guards dragged her forward. James's eyes widened and he wheeled on Leyus, furious.

"Why is she still alive? Your people told me they'd feed her to your cats."

"We had need of her." Leyus's tone held no hint of an apology. "But now we're through. She is yours to deal with as you please."

"It's not like you to treat our agreements so loosely."

"This was a special case. I assure you it will not happen again."

For a moment, James glared at Leyus. But he was outnumbered, and judging from the frustration in his eyes, he was all too aware of it. Kyra only had a moment to savor this small victory before he turned to her.

"She's too good at staying alive," James murmured. He reached for Kyra. She tried again to break free, but her guards still held her with a bruising grip. Gathering what moisture was left in her mouth, Kyra spat in his face. It was a pathetic attempt, but James's jaw tightened.

"This time I'll make sure you're dead." James unsheathed his dagger and stepped close to her. "You say she's mine to deal with, Leyus?"

"Do as you wish."

Kyra felt the entire clan watching as James raised the blade. In the corner of her eye, she saw Tristam straining against the assassins holding him. She squeezed her eyes shut, hearing nothing but the sound of her own harsh breathing. She felt her guards behind her, muscles taut in preparation for any final escape attempt. So this was it. She'd die here, and the clan would attack the Palace, killing all of Malikel's people in exchange for a hundred winter garments.

A hundred winter garments, to be worn close to the skin.

Ten vials of blueflower extract.

"Poison!" she shouted.

James's blade halted.

"James has betrayed you, Leyus." Kyra spoke in a jumble, desperate to get the words out before James slit her throat. "The garments are poisoned."

Strong arms jerked Kyra back and a Demon Rider pushed himself between her and James.

The assassin's eyes narrowed. "You said you wouldn't interfere, Leyus."

"I will hear her out," Leyus said. He came to stand in front of Kyra. "What do you mean?"

Kyra heard a hiss from Tristam's direction. The knight was looking at her, eyes wide with realization, and she knew he'd come to the same conclusion. Kyra ran her tongue over dry lips, willing her heartbeat to slow. "The night Pashla found me, I raided James's study. He had ten vials of blueflower extract in his poison chest. I believe he's used it to taint the garments he just gave you."

"The girl grasps for anything to delay her death," said James. "Why would I poison you on the eve of our biggest raid?"

"Because it's a slow poison," said Kyra. "You'd be fine for the raid, even for several weeks afterward. But once the winter's over and you've outlived your usefulness, you'll sicken and die."

Leyus looked slowly from Kyra to James and back. "Do you have proof?"

"Ten vials is enough to poison a hundred garments. And James has just delivered fifty garments to you, with the promise of fifty more. . . ." Kyra trailed off as she realized how flimsy her logic was. It was a stretch, she realized. But there was something about her suspicion that felt right. This was something James would do. He needed the Demon Riders in order to weaken the Place, but he wasn't a fool. James knew that his alliance with the Makvani was tenuous at best. They bore no loyalty toward him, and he'd always been careful to eliminate threats preemptively, before they had a chance to strike.

Leyus's expression changed from concern to disdain. "You disappoint me, Kyra, grasping at stories to add a few more moments to your life. You disgrace your blood heritage."

Blood heritage. Kyra clung to those words as her last hope. "If you really acknowledge my blood, grant me my right of Challenge."

A shocked silence followed her statement. Then, a murmur ran through the crowd.

"Explain yourself," said Leyus.

James eyed her suspiciously, but Kyra ignored him and plunged forward. "Let me face the one who would kill me, in combat."

"You make a mockery of the Challenge," said Leyus. "It is a right of someone who has something to lose, not a last-ditch option for a prisoner about to die."

"I don't want to Challenge for my life. You can kill me either way."

Leyus came closer. "What do you mean?"

"Let me fight for the right to prove myself," said Kyra. "If I lose the Challenge, so be it. But if I win, let me take the garments to a healer who can test them for poison. If I'm wrong, you can kill me then."

Around her, the murmurs died down, and all eyes turned to Leyus.

James spat on the ground. "My patience is wearing thin, Leyus. How long will you humor the girl's attempts to delay the inevitable?"

Leyus examined Kyra's face, deep in thought. "Very well. I grant your request." He turned to James. "You heard her. Will you take the Challenge? If you do not wish to fight her, we can guard her until we test the garments."

"I refuse to play your games," said James. "When you start honoring our agreements again, we can do business. But until then, we part ways." He spun back toward his horse. Alex and Shea picked up the bags of clothes.

"Where are you taking the garments?" asked Leyus.

"If your people can go back on a deal, so can I. Keep Tristam. Come find me when you'll trade honestly," said James.

"Is that the real reason, James?" Kyra asked loudly. "Or are you taking them back so they can't be tested for poison?"

James rounded on her and slapped her across the face. "I won't have you here corrupting their minds against me," he hissed. Kyra blinked the tears from her eyes, holding her breath until the blow's sting faded. She had never seen James lose his composure like this, and it both frightened her and convinced her that she was right.

The assassin turned to Leyus. "I've changed my mind. I'll accept the terms of your Challenge. Untie and arm her if you must, but she's caused me too much trouble to leave her here alive."

"So you'll fight her?" asked Leyus.

"Aye."

Suddenly, a Demon Rider was cutting the bindings around Kyra's wrist. Blood rushed into her hands, followed by tiny needles that stabbed her fingers. She stumbled forward, reeling at the turn of events. Leyus handed her a knife. "You fight now, as you are."

The circle had already begun to expand, its members

337

making as much room as they could for the combatants. James shed his cloak and stretched his arms and legs, watching Kyra from a distance. She could feel him making note of everything she did, every stumble. Kyra was all too aware of her weak legs as she tried to walk some life into them. The last two times she'd fought James, he'd beaten her easily. How could she hope to face him after a night's imprisonment? She shook out her limbs again. No matter. Better to go down fighting.

James regarded Leyus warily. "Your word, then. No interference."

"My people will stay out of this, as will yours."

Kyra saw a few Demon Riders move closer to the other two assassins. Then Leyus nodded and backed out of the circle. It was a clear signal to begin. Kyra gripped her blade tight.

James focused his eyes on Kyra and advanced slowly. "What's your secret, Kyra? Why can't I get rid of you?"

Kyra backed away, staying out of his reach. "Lucky, I guess."

"I think it's more than that. It really is a pity. You could have become one of our best."

She knew he was trying to distract her, to provoke a reaction so she'd drop her guard. Still, his words were oddly hypnotic.

"From the first time I saw you work," said James, "I knew you were different. You're the closest I've ever seen to a natural assassin."

James attacked before he finished the sentence. Kyra jumped aside but lost her balance and tripped. She scrambled up and out of his reach, curving her path to avoid running into the Makvani. Kyra had a feeling they'd throw her back in if she came too close.

"You're beautiful to watch, you know," James continued, as if they'd been talking all along. "Your grace—it's impossible to ignore. Even now, when we're at each other's throats...Did you notice the way my men looked at you? Especially after watching you break into the armory. And it wasn't just them." He paused. "Maybe that was the problem. As an assassin, I valued your skill. But though I knew better, my admiration grew beyond just business."

A shudder ran through Kyra's body, and she was grateful she couldn't see Tristam's reaction. A couple of months ago, such an admission from James would have enthralled her. But that was before she had killed for him. Before he'd murdered Bella.

James lunged again, and this time she ducked aside without falling. He was slower than she remembered. Last time they'd fought, he'd been impossibly fast. Was he teasing her now?

"Remember the afternoon we spent planning the raid?" James asked.

She did. And she remembered what happened afterward. She pushed the memory away and feinted to the left. James stepped aside, but again, not as quickly as she'd expected. Kyra searched his face for any sign that something might be wrong, but as always, James was a master at hiding his feelings.

"We really do have a lot in common," said James. "We think the same way. We both enjoy the thrill of the chase, of outsmarting our enemies. Tell me you didn't get a thrill from bringing the wallhuggers down a notch. You loved that power. I dare you to deny it."

She wanted him to be wrong. She needed him to be.

"So you don't deny it," said James.

The rock Kyra stepped on tipped over and she stumbled. In a heartbeat, he was on her, blade coming down at her face. She recoiled and gasped as it glanced off her collarbone. Kyra drove her own knife up and jumped to her feet as James skipped back unscathed. Kyra kept her dagger between them, breath coming in quick gasps as she probed her collarbone with her free hand. Her fingers came away sticky, but at least she could move.

The pain snapped her out of his spell. Kyra gripped her blade, shifting her weight back and forth. If James wanted her dead, he'd have to work for it. She had no intention of being an easy kill. James must have noticed her change of focus, because he stopped speaking. They circled each other, no sound between them but their breathing and the crunch of autumn leaves.

A few more feints and parries, and she realized why James seemed slow. He hadn't changed. But after weeks of hunting with Pashla, Kyra had. Her senses were sharper, her reflexes smoother. Kyra saw her opponent now with new eyes. What if he were not James, the assassin she feared? What if he were her prey?

The next time he attacked, Kyra was ready. She danced aside and slashed at his knife arm. Her blade cut deep, and James's weapon fell on the rocks with a satisfying clang. Kyra grabbed his tunic and pulled him close, pressing the point of her blade to his throat.

For an instant, they were frozen there, eyes locked, so close she could feel his lungs expand with each shallow breath. Kyra felt his body tense. She could kill him. She had every right.

Around her, she sensed the energy from the crowd leaning in for the kill. She willed her wrist to deliver the final stroke.

A sudden blow to her midsection knocked the breath out of her. Kyra thrust her knife forward with all her strength, but James had already moved out of the way. He clamped his hand around her wrist and twisted. Pain shot up her arm and drove her to the ground. His knee dug into her back, forcing it into an unnatural arch.

And then the world imploded.

A fog covered her vision. Heat rushed through her, melting her insides and forcing its way out through her skin in the form of tiny hairs. Her clothes stretched tight, then ripped and fell away completely. Her bones elongated. Her muscles lengthened to match. A murmur ran through the crowd, and she realized what was happening. Finally, her vision cleared and the world came back, cleaner and crisper. In front of her, James stood, staring at her with disbelief and horror.

For a moment, Kyra stood dumbfounded, unsure in her new body. She tried to step forward but didn't know which legs moved together. Behind her, she felt what must have been her tail, snaking back and forth as she shifted her weight.

Then James turned to run, and her instincts flared. She overtook him in two bounds and coiled around. Her claws opened three slashes across his chest and one across his face. It was so easy to push him over and pin him to the ground. As she held him there, she saw her forelimb for the first time. Dark brown, the same color as her hair, with wiry muscles underneath the fur.

James's face, crisp in her strange new vision, held an expression she had never seen on him before—eyes rolled to the side, edges of his mouth pulled back in a grimace. He was scared. She could smell his fear, mingled with the blood that seeped through his cuts. She breathed in deeply, relishing the scent. A mere swipe from her and he would fall lifeless. Around her, she sensed the clan watching. She itched to tear him open, dig into his throat, but would the others interfere? Would they protect him? Instinctively, she knew that they wouldn't. It was her kill, and they wouldn't intrude. Kyra unsheathed her claws.

The circle, the victim, the smell of fear and blood . . .

She'd been here before. There was something she needed to remember. It was hard to make sense of these memories with this bloodlust urging her toward her victim. Kyra raised her claws to strike.

Then she remembered. The dream. The raid. Once again, she felt the manservant sink to the ground as the life drained out of him. Kyra saw herself in the courtyard of the Assassins Guild, shaking with horror as she scrubbed an innocent man's blood off her hands.

Kyra sheathed her claws just before her blow connected. James's head smashed against a rock, and he went limp.

THIRTY-NINE

Kyra staggered back, tripping over her own legs. Already, her body was melting into itself. Her fur smoothed out into skin. A chill wind brushed her, and Kyra realized she was naked. Demon Riders surrounded her and guided her limp arms into a tunic.

She was drowning in images—like the pictures from her nightmares, but so much stronger. She tried to distinguish dream from reality, cat instincts from human, but everything slipped away.

"Take care of the other two," she heard Leyus say.

Kyra looked up to see Shea and Alex scramble onto their horses and flee into the trees. Five demon cats streaked after them. Something stirred within her. She longed to join the chase, bring the riders down and tear them to pieces. A growl stirred at the base of her throat.

"Kyra!" Pashla was shaking her, hard. "It is done. Stay with me."

The head Demon Rider drew near, looking Kyra over carefully. "Our blood runs stronger in you than we thought," said

Leyus. Was he pleased? Angry? She turned again to follow the chase.

"You have defeated James in Challenge," Leyus was speaking again. "We will honor your request to test the garments."

Garments... Slowly it came back to her. She had wanted to test the garments for poison. "We need someone who knows poisons," she said, her words and the thoughts behind them thick and unfamiliar.

They were interrupted by the sound of Tristam coughing, a dry, rasping sound. The knight was curled in on himself, spasming with each cough. He looked so weak. Puny, even.

"You don't need a healer," Tristam said, raising his face to Leyus. "Just check his hands."

Leyus snapped an order and Tristam's guards dragged him over. The young knight was staring openly at Kyra. She stared back, blinking in confusion. Was that fear in his eyes? Part of her relished it, but another rapidly returning part of her was ashamed.

"What did you say, knight?" Leyus said.

"Check his hands," said Tristam, tearing his eyes away from Kyra. "See if they're coated with anything."

At Leyus's orders, a Demon Rider inspected James's limp hands. "They are covered with something like wax," he said. "I can scrape it off with my fingernail."

Tristam nodded. "The coating protects his skin from poison. James betrayed you today."

Kyra slumped forward, exhausted, as her demon cat instincts slowly seeped away. She watched as Leyus knelt next to James, inspecting the assassin's hands himself. He went to the basket of garments and bent down to smell them.

"You're right." Leyus turned to Kyra. "The clan owes you its gratitude. We do not take debts of blood lightly."

He paused. Around them, the clan seemed to hold its breath. Kyra stayed still, unsure of what this meant.

"You are free to go, as is the knight."

Kyra bowed her head, mind reeling. Was that it? Would they forgive her betrayal just like that? "Thank you," she managed to say.

Leyus smiled thinly. "Don't be too grateful. This pays our debt in full. If we meet again, we will start anew."

The crowd dissipated, transforming one by one into cat shape and melting into the forest. They made no attempt to hide their shape-shifting from Tristam. Would they just let the knight go, knowing their secret? Tristam watched the Makvani with fascination and confusion. When he noticed her gaze, he turned toward her. Kyra turned away, remembering the fear she'd seen before and unable to face it again.

"Kyra." It was Pashla again. "You and the knight will come with me. We will put you in the shelter tonight and escort you back tomorrow."

Tristam dragged himself to his feet, suppressing a cough, and Kyra followed suit.

"Pashla," said Kyra. "Your shape-shifting. Will it be all right now that..."

"Now that the human knows?" asked Pashla. Kyra winced

at Pashla's use of the term. "It's fine. They always find out eventually. It is a hard secret to keep. If Leyus has ruled to spare his life, you need not worry about him."

Pashla's voice was calm, without any hint of anger. But her face was more closed to Kyra than she had ever seen. It hurt, but Kyra was too exhausted to do anything except acknowledge it. They walked the rest of the way in silence. At the shelter, Pashla tended both their wounds, although she told Tristam that her saliva wouldn't be as effective for him. Another clanswoman came with some food, then both Makvani left, leaving Kyra and Tristam alone.

Kyra studied the ground, the trees, anything to avoid looking at him. A strong wind blew through the tent, bringing down a shower of leaves around them.

"Are you really going to make me ask for an explanation, Kyra?"

She didn't want to talk about it, *couldn't* talk about it without the threat of memories she wasn't ready to relive. But she also couldn't avoid facing him forever.

"I didn't know," she said miserably.

"Know what?"

"Anything." Her voice cracked, and she cleared her throat. "When the Demon Riders found me at the Guildhouse, they told me I was part Makvani."

He was quiet, eyes cast toward the ground but focused beyond it. "And they taught you how to change into a cat."

"Pashla thought it worth trying. But it never happened until..." She trailed off.

"Until you faced James?" he asked. He raised his eyes to

her face now, and she couldn't tell if it was dread or wonder in his eyes.

"I had no idea. I wasn't even trying," she said. "You don't have to believe me."

He paused. "I believe you. I don't think you'd be shaking so much if you were lying."

Kyra wrapped her arms around her knees and tried to squeeze herself still. "You fear me," she said.

"I'd be a fool not to," he said.

It was one thing to know it, but another altogether to hear him say it so plainly. Kyra rounded on him in fury. "I saved your life back there. You of all people—"

Tristam laid a hand on her wrist, gentle but firm. "I'm sorry, Kyra. That came out wrong. I only meant that any creature capable of what you did deserves respect. But what I saw doesn't change the fact that you saved my life, or that you disobeyed your...people...to protect me." He let out a long breath. "I've harbored doubts about you before, Kyra. First because you were in the Guild, and then when I thought you'd betrayed me to the Demon Riders. And each time, I was wrong. I'm not making the same mistake again." He paused. "Though there might be problems ahead."

"What do you mean?"

"I'm thinking about the Council. You're still under a death sentence that we need to clear. It'll be hard to prove you aren't a threat to Forge if you're one of them."

Kyra closed her eyes. "What do I do?"

"I don't know. Maybe we can keep this hidden."

"James will rat me out as soon as we turn him over."

"He might, but who would believe him?"

"Mayhap for a while, but people would start to wonder. And notice things."

Neither of them mentioned the next logical step—that this problem would disappear if James did as well. But Kyra only contemplated it a moment before thrusting the thought aside. She'd had that opportunity already. Plus, James still had too many secrets—about the Guild, the Palace, and even the Makvani. She owed it to Bella, to the others who'd suffered in the fire, to get those secrets out of him.

Tristam exhaled. "I can send for Malikel once we're closer to the city. He's a skilled negotiator. If we can win him over, perhaps he can convince the Council to put you on probation."

Probation? A prisoner again, after all she had gone through? Instead of James's lackey, she would be the Palace's. What other uses would Willem find for her?

"Or . . ." Tristam's voice was hesitant. "You could run."

Kyra gave him a questioning glance. Tristam looked around and lowered his voice, as if worried that Palace officials might hear him. "The Council already doesn't trust you. If they find out what you are, I don't know what they'll do. I could tell them I never found you. You could flee to Parna. Start over." There was an urgency in his words, though he spoke softly.

"You'd lie to them?" Kyra knew Tristam well enough by now to know how much this would cost him.

There was the slightest of pauses as Tristam's eyes grew distant again. "I won't pretend I like the idea. But I would do it."

The idea of leaving Forge had never occurred to her, but

it was certainly possible. Every city had rich houses with bad locks. But she'd be alone. A petty thief in a strange city.

"I can't. . . ."

"The Council might kill you, Kyra, if they knew the truth." There was real fear in his eyes, enough to scare her into reconsidering. But she was tired of reacting, of running from every new threat. If she really could do so much, if so many people wanted her skills, why was she at everyone's mercy?

"Tell me," she asked. "How much is James worth to the Council?"

"What do you mean?"

"What if I don't give them James until they've agreed to my pardon?"

He turned a wary eye to her. "That's a dangerous plan."

"So is fleeing the city, or meekly turning myself in. I'll get my pardon, and then I'll lay low in the city. Wait and see how things play out with James." She gave a resigned smile. "And if they really decide to come after me, I in't exactly defenseless."

Tristam shook his head, again looking at her with an expression she couldn't quite read. "I still can't believe that you're . . ." He trailed off.

Kyra didn't answer. She glimpsed shapes moving through the trees, moving on padded paws. Amber eyes blinked in and out of the darkness. And though she could see them clearly and even found them distracting, Kyra could tell from the way Tristam stared into the darkness that he saw nothing. She thought again of how it'd felt to melt into that shape, to dissolve into lean muscle and sleek fur. Kyra felt the rush of raw instinct and bloodlust, so strong that she cried out and jerked away from Tristam, convinced that it was happening again. But moments went by and she stayed in her skin. Slowly, slowly, her heartbeat slowed to normal.

"Kyra?" One of Tristam's hands was raised hesitantly toward her.

Kyra collapsed into herself and dug the heels of her palms into her eyes. "It's so strong," she whispered.

"It's all right, Kyra." Slowly, Tristam peeled Kyra's hands from her face and held them between his own. "It's all right."

She let him hold her like that, taking comfort in the solidity of his touch. They sat there, heads bowed and not speaking, until the sun set.

Pashla met them the next morning, accompanied by three Demon Riders who would escort them to the city. Kyra had never seen Makvani shift for travel before, and she watched as closely as she could without staring. In the forest, the Makvani left their clothes where they shifted to retrieve later, or carried them in their mouths. This time, though, the Demon Riders folded their clothing carefully and tucked it into pouches with long straps. After they changed form, they threw the pouches over their necks with a flick of a paw and a well-practiced duck. Meanwhile, Kyra and Tristam readied James's horse. The other two horses, and presumably their riders, had been killed.

"The knight will ride the horse," said Pashla. "I will carry you, and the prisoner will walk. He is yours to deal with as you choose, since you defeated him." Pashla indicated James with a flick of her head. The assassin was conscious now, bound and under guard by another Demon Rider. He shot Kyra a look of pure hatred. She turned away.

"You'll carry me?" she asked Pashla.

Pashla nodded. "It's unwise for you to change your shape with prey nearby. It takes time to learn control, to keep your cat instincts from overwhelming you. Dealing with the shift takes weeks of practice and guidance."

"Guidance? Where would I get that?"

"The clan is closed to you now. We cannot help you."

Again, spoken so unfeelingly. And again, it hurt. Kyra turned away. In the corner of her eye, she saw Pashla remove her clothes and transform. The tawny cat knelt in front of her. Kyra grabbed the loose skin at Pashla's neck and pulled herself onto her back. Stiff fur dug into her palms.

Pashla moved differently than a horse. Her gait was smoother, for which Kyra was grateful. As they traveled, a profound sense of loss filled her. She'd made her choice. Kyra couldn't give up her humanity to be part of the clan, but still, she wished her departure didn't have to be so complete. Eventually, the trees thinned, and Kyra recognized the guardhouse by the road where she and Tristam had stopped on their first trip into the forest. With a soft roar, Pashla signaled them to stop and shifted into human form.

"We part ways here." She gestured toward one of their Demon Rider escorts. "Czern will stay and help you watch the prisoner until you can put him under proper guard. Don't underestimate this one."

Tristam eyed James grimly. "We won't," he said.

Pashla nodded and then looked straight into Tristam's eyes.

"The things I have done, I did in service of the clan. I have my loyalties, as do you."

Kyra didn't know what she meant, but Tristam's jaw clenched and a myriad of emotions flashed across his face. "I understand," he said, though his tone belied his words. Kyra wondered if the two of them had a history she didn't know.

The clanswoman turned to Kyra. Kyra swallowed, suddenly feeling a lump in her throat.

"Thank you," she said. "For saving my life. And for teaching me to—" She fumbled for words. Between the Guild, the Palace, and the Makvani, Pashla had been the only person who hadn't wanted to use her. The clanswoman had risked her own life for Kyra and asked nothing in return except that Kyra find a home amongst the clan. Yet this was a home in which Kyra could never belong. "I'm sorry I let you down."

Pashla looked at her long and hard, and Kyra finally saw it—the hurt and betrayal in the woman's eyes. The emotions she had hidden behind a mask of calm. "You've made your choice, then. You prefer the humans."

"I grew up with them. It's all I've known." She wanted to continue, but stopped at the expression on Pashla's face. She might as well have tried to explain to Pashla that she wanted to live with chickens.

The clanswoman stepped away, pulling at the belt of her tunic to change back. Kyra felt a wrenching in her chest.

"Wait," she said. "At least give my love to the kittens. I didn't get a chance to say good-bye."

Pashla stopped and sighed, eyes finally softening. "That I

will do. You have my word." The clanswoman clasped Kyra's hands. "We will meet again. I'm sure of it."

Yes, and I hope it will be on better terms, Kyra thought.

She watched as Pashla transformed and rejoined the others. The three cats disappeared into the forest.

FORTY

Tristam was the first to break the silence. "Come. We'll camp tonight away from the road and approach the Palace tomorrow."

Setting up camp was an uncomfortable process. Czern, the Demon Rider who'd stayed to guard James, was aloof and taciturn. He barely spoke, and he changed into cat shape after securing James to a tree, clearly uninterested in helping Kyra or Tristam with their preparations. Kyra helped Tristam gather sticks for a fire, all the while aware of James's eyes on her. Czern wandered off briefly and returned with two rabbits, which they cooked for supper.

As the sky darkened, Kyra slipped away from the fire into the surrounding shadows. The stars were more visible here than in the city, and she leaned against a tree, staring up at them through holes left by fallen leaves. Was she making a mistake? This plan could end with her back in the dungeons, but she had to try.

She heard footsteps behind her. And though she'd come out here hoping for solitude, her mood lifted when she saw it was

Tristam. He still walked as if it pained him, but he'd regained some color and his eyes were clear.

"Sneaking off?" he asked.

"I needed to clear my head."

"I thought the open forest made you uncomfortable."

"It's better at night."

He was quiet, and she could imagine the thoughts turning around in his head. He spoke hesitantly. "Is that because—"

"Probably." She wondered if this was how it would be from now on. Every time she displayed some new character quirk, she would wonder if it came from her Makvani blood.

He took a place next to her, and for a while, they watched the stars together. There was something comforting about his silent presence next to her. Behind them, the fire crackled and popped, casting shadows on the ground.

"Tristam, did you really come here against orders?"

There was the slightest hesitation before he responded. "I did."

"Will they give you trouble when we get back?"

Again, a pause. "The consequences I face will be nothing compared to Martin's fate. I'll be fine."

He'd avoided giving her a straight answer. "I'm sorry," she said.

"Don't be. I came of my own choice, as did Martin." There was a haunted quality to his voice. His face was drawn, and he was staring intently into the forest, though Kyra was sure he couldn't see anything. "Yet I can't help but wonder if I should have stopped him. As much as I chafe against Councilman

Willem's leadership, I can't deny that I led Martin to his death."

Kyra thought again of the young Red Shield, with his infectious smile. Then she remembered his dying screams, and her insides twisted.

"Why do you think Martin came with you?" she asked.

"He looked up to me, and trusted me."

"But he wouldn't risk his life simply for that."

For a moment, it looked as if Tristam was going to argue. But then he nodded. "You're right. He disagreed with Councilman Willem. If a knight had been lost, we would have tried to rescue him. The knight's kin would have forced Willem to do something. But for a common soldier, or a criminal like you with no one to vouch for them . . . Willem saw you as a disposable chess piece. I couldn't condone that, and Martin agreed."

"You don't like Willem," she said.

He shook his head. "I don't know anymore. I've always believed in the knights of Forge, in the Council, in their mission. And to some degree, I still do. My father and brothers serve well in the road patrols. The citizens they guard are genuinely grateful for their protection. But in the city, things are less clear. Maybe there are just too many people. It gets too loud, with everyone shouting to be heard, and some people get drowned out."

"Do you think it has to be like that?" asked Kyra.

"You mean, do I think things could change?" Tristam tipped his head up again and looked at the trees. "Malikel does things differently, and sometimes others follow his lead. But there are many in the Council who think like Willem."

"James thought he could change things," said Kyra. She thought again of the fires. *You can't change a river's course with a shovel. You need an earthquake,* he'd said. Funny that the assassin, with all his talk of bringing the wallhuggers down, also saw fit to sacrifice the lives of his fellow citizens.

Tristam glanced in the direction of the campfire. "Let's hope, for all of our sakes, that James's way is not the only way." He pushed off from the tree and turned to face her. His eyes were solemn in the firelight. "I don't regret disobeying the Council, and tomorrow brings what it will. But I want to apologize."

He was still able to surprise her. "Apologize? For what?"

"For misjudging you at the beginning. For assuming the worst. I wonder, if we had met under different circumstances..."

Kyra wished he'd stop talking as if they were preparing for their funerals. She forced a smile. "I wasn't exactly on my best behavior either, but there's no reason we can't start anew."

He smiled. A genuine smile that took the exhaustion off his face. "I'm glad you think so."

A lock of hair had fallen across Kyra's forehead, and Tristam brushed it away, though he faltered at the end, as if realizing the intimacy of his gesture. For a moment, neither of them breathed. Then Kyra stepped toward him, and it was with something like relief that Tristam cupped the nape of her neck and coaxed her even closer. Strangely enough, it reminded Kyra of the time she'd shown up poisoned on his doorstep, when he'd tipped her face to the light. But this time she was lucid enough to be acutely aware of his fingers buried in her hair, the newly familiar scent of his skin. And there was something in his eyes that hadn't been there before. Had it only been a few weeks ago when they'd been enemies? But she trusted him now, after all this.

She closed her eyes. His lips, when they touched hers, were soft. Hesitant at first, but growing more confident as she responded. Kyra melted into him, savoring the way his arms tightened around her waist and losing herself in the feel of him. For the moment, at least, she could forget about what would happen tomorrow.

Suddenly, Tristam went still. Confused, Kyra looked up. He was looking past Kyra, and his expression was guarded. Kyra followed his gaze to the campfire behind her. Czern, in cat form, lay by the fire, and James, still tied to a tree, was looking straight in their direction. Kyra turned back to Tristam. Their arms were still interlaced, and she wished she could retrieve the moment. But it was gone.

Tristam took one last look toward the fire and reluctantly backed away, letting out a shaky breath. "I should go make preparations for tomorrow," he said. "Try to get some rest." He touched the backs of his fingers lightly to her cheek, and then disappeared into the forest.

She stayed there a long time, looking in the direction he'd gone and feeling the lingering imprint of his lips. When she started to shiver, Kyra returned to the fire and rubbed warmth back into her limbs. Even facing away from James, she could feel his eyes on her.

"I would have expected better from you," James said.

Kyra didn't answer.

"Some women try to pull themselves up by becoming a rich man's plaything. They soon learn the folly of taking such fickle lovers."

Kyra thought of Flick's mother and immediately hated herself for it. But now that the story had been evoked, she couldn't stop thinking of how the woman had left everything for her noble lover, and lost everything.

"You imagine more than you saw," she told James.

"I saw clearly. And though you might not believe me, remember my words for later. After you've lived in his world, placed your hopes with him, made sacrifices for him. He'll betray you when he's done with you. Toss you aside when you no longer amuse him."

There was a hint of grief to his voice, and for a moment, Kyra was surprised that her betrayal would awaken that strong of an emotion in him. Anger, bitterness, disappointment, perhaps, but not grief. Then she realized the grief wasn't for her.

"You're talking about Thalia, aren't you? Something happened to her, with a nobleman. Rand told me...."

And just like that, James's expression turned to contempt. "Don't think to understand what you don't know. Thalia suffered more at the wallhugger's hands than you'll ever fathom, and she sacrificed more than you'll ever have the nerve to risk. With your abilities, you could have surpassed her, but you don't have the stomach for it. By the time you learn how things really are, it'll be too late."

The night wind tickled the back of her neck, and Kyra wondered about Tristam. Would he use her and toss her aside?

There was something about James. Even captive and bound, he could still speak with authority, weave his words into a poisoned web around her if she let him.

But only if she let him.

Kyra stood and looked James in the eye. "I don't believe that all noblemen are as you say. Mayhap I'm a fool, but that's a risk I will take."

She put the campfire between them, and he didn't bother her the rest of the night.

Tristam didn't return before Kyra went to sleep, though he was sitting at the campfire the next morning. There were circles under his eyes, and Kyra wondered if he had slept at all. He handed her some dried plums for breakfast. Their fingers touched briefly, and Kyra wanted to ask him where he'd been. Would he really be safe returning to the Palace? What had happened between them last night?

"Will you leave soon?" she asked instead.

"Right after breakfast."

Under James's and Czern's watchful eyes, neither of them said any more.

Finally, Tristam stood and dusted off his tunic. "It's time. I'll pass along your message."

Kyra nodded reluctantly. "Do you think they'll come?"

"They will. Give them a day, two at most."

If she were braver, she would have said more, but the words wouldn't come out. Impulsively, she took his hand and gave it a quick squeeze, all the while aware of the others watching. Tristam's eyes widened in surprise, but then he squeezed back.

"We'll speak again soon," he said.

Then he turned for the road.

She followed him at a distance. Two squires tended their steeds at the guardhouse, most likely readying for the morning patrol. They looked up at his approach, and their expressions quickly grew alarmed. The one in back reached for his sword, but then relaxed at something Tristam said. He opened his hands, and the squires searched him for weapons. They were treating him like a criminal. But Tristam looked like he had expected this, and after the squires' search turned up nothing, he let them lead him toward the city.

Kyra trailed them for a while, mostly to assure herself that he wouldn't be harmed. Then she returned to the meeting place they had chosen. They'd found a clearing close by, where it was easy to see approaching horses. She found a decent vantage point in a nearby tree and settled down to wait.

Late in the afternoon, she heard hoofbeats, followed soon by glimpses of red livery between the orange leaves. Willem and Malikel rode in front, followed by a small contingent of shield-men. Kyra wondered if she'd have to flee after all, but then the Councilmen ordered their soldiers to wait on the road. Willem and Malikel entered the clearing alone, as she had requested.

It was hard not to be intimidated by the two Councilmen awaiting her. Even though they wore plain riding cloaks, they carried themselves like men who ran a city. Malikel, though stern, didn't show any overt signs of hostility. Willem, on the other hand, barely even looked at her, as if she were not even deserving of a straight glance. He was the one she would have to be careful of.

"We'd given you up for dead," said Malikel.

"Not yet." She was tempted to ask after Tristam, but it would have made her look weak.

"Well, Kyra," said Malikel. "You have our attention. What do you have to say?"

"James, the Head of the Assassins Guild, is my prisoner. He's under guard in a safe place, and I'm willing to turn him over to the Palace."

Malikel's eyes widened slightly. "That's not what I expected to hear. We will take him."

"I'll hand him over after the Council announces my pardon."

There was a pause as her meaning became clear to them. Then Willem gave a disdainful laugh. "This is what happens when prisoners forget their place, Malikel."

"Malikel already gave me his word that the Council would consider my case if I helped bring James down," said Kyra. "I just want to be reassured of the Palace's promise."

"What happened after you were taken by the Demon Riders?" Malikel countered.

Kyra chose her words carefully. "They held me prisoner, but they released me as a reward for exposing a plan James had against them."

Malikel was studying her again, and Kyra forced herself to return his gaze. Finally, the councilman looked at Willem, and there was a hint of amusement in his eyes. "It seems that councilmen are not the only ones who can play games. I'll leave the final decision to you, Willem, since you're already accustomed to making unilateral decisions with this prisoner." Malikel voice was pointed as he said this, and Kyra saw Willem's eyes flicker

362

toward Malikel. For the briefest moment, rage flashed across Willem's face, so quickly that Kyra almost thought she'd imagined it. The councilmen were not friends, she realized. Far from it.

"How will you deliver James to us?" Willem was focused on her again, as if Malikel had not spoken at all.

"The Council will write the conditions of my pardon. After it's announced in the city square, I'll lead your men to James."

"Forge's laws are not games, Kyra," said Willem. "You step in dangerous territory."

Kyra didn't reply.

"I will grant your request under one condition. We will lift your death sentence. But you will serve the Council for a period of five years. You'll live within the compound and report to the Minister of Defense."

This was unexpected. She needed to be out of the compound and safely hidden in the city in case James exposed her.

"No. Absolutely not," she said.

"Then we have no deal," said Willem.

There was a tense silence, then Malikel spoke. "This could work in your favor, Kyra. Remember that your home is gone, as is your place in the Assassins Guild. You need to eat, and you need a roof over your head. And if I'm guessing correctly, you'd want a stake in our mission. With James as our prisoner, we could track down the rest of the Guild. Bring justice to the victims of the fire."

It was shrewd of Malikel to bring up The Drunken Dog. The memory of its loss was still sharp, and even the thought of Bella awakened a fierce desire for revenge. But on the other hand, did she really want to help the Palace consolidate its power? She thought again of the rent collection, of corrupt Red Shields and nobles. Kyra swallowed and hoped she wouldn't regret what she was about to say.

"I want pay equal to the knights'. I'll live outside the Palace, and I take no vows. If the job is fair, I'll carry it out, but I'll be beholden to no one."

"You ask too much, girl," said Willem. He took a step toward her, and Kyra stepped back, hand curling for her knife.

"Stay back. If you don't like my offer, then find someone else who can do what I do."

Willem's eyes flashed, and for a moment Kyra thought he might attack her. She tensed, ready to run, but the councilman slowly and deliberately relaxed his posture, though his gaze was not friendly.

"Very well," he said. "We will accept your terms."

⛶ ⛶ ⛶

Tristam thought he'd been prepared for his arrest and punishment. He'd suspected that the squires at the guardhouse would have orders to bring him in, and that he'd be confined to his quarters upon his return. In the hours he'd spent before turning himself in, wandering the forest as Kyra slept, Tristam had made peace with what was to come.

But it was one thing to know what was coming, and another to march past the knowing glances of his peers at the Palace— men who'd served with him and under his command. There were whispers just out of earshot, though he heard bits and pieces. *Disgraced . . . Disobedient . . . Promising young knight . . . All the more shocking . . .*

"I won't be able to shield you from the consequences of your actions," was all Malikel had said. And when Tristam revealed that Martin was dead, his commander had just acknowledged it with a sad nod.

Now confined to his room, all Tristam could do was wait. He paced the length of his quarters, futilely wishing that someone would tell him what was happening outside. Guards brought him meals, but they didn't even look him in the eye, much less tell him news of Kyra. He had plenty of time to think over their last conversation, remembering how she'd felt in his arms—firm muscle over a delicate frame—seeing the trust in her eyes. Things had seemed so simple out in the forest.

On the second day of Tristam's imprisonment, Councilman Willem arrived unannounced. He came alone and closed the door behind him.

"Sit down," Willem commanded.

Tristam carefully lowered himself into a chair. The councilman remained standing, staring down at him like a schoolmaster berating a pupil.

"You disobeyed my direct orders to stay out of the forest. And not only that, you led one of your own men in with you." Willem paused. "Your actions led to your soldier's death. Do you have anything to say in your defense?"

"No, sir. I will take my punishment."

"Which the Council is discussing now." Willem turned to face him. "Truth be told, you should be charged with more, but the traitor Kyra is adamant that you had no part in her scheme."

Tristam lifted his head despite himself. He was too eager to hear about her, and the flash in Willem's eyes showed that he'd noted it. "I don't believe her. Few do, but your mentor has argued strongly that we only charge you for the crimes for which we have proof." The councilman's lips curled. "Malikel, despite his foreigner's ways, still commands some influence in the Council."

Tristam began to feel a spark of hope.

"We've agreed to Kyra's terms," said Willem. "Does that please you?"

He didn't answer.

"She's pretty, isn't she?" said Willem.

Tristam stuttered, caught off guard. Again, Willem noted his reaction and gave a knowing nod.

"Mistresses are an unavoidable reality of court life. We're willing to look the other way, provided you're discreet. I'll remind you that disobeying orders and flouting the Council would not be discreet."

Tristam bristled at the implied insult. "Thank you for the warning, Your Grace, but I assure you that I have no plans for taking on a mistress."

"I'm glad to hear that. You come from a fine family, Tristam. By all reports, you're well-bred and well-taught. I trust you will conduct yourself in a manner to preserve your family's reputation. Some restraint on your part would save both of you a good deal of pain and embarrassment."

"Your Grace, I—"

"I don't need your opinion, Tristam. Do you understand me, or not?"

"I understand," he said.

"I hope, for your sake, that you're telling the truth. I will see you at your sentencing."

※ ※ ※

The terms of Kyra's pardon were announced the next morning by the Palace herald, along with the rest of the day's news. Although she didn't dare be there for the announcement itself, she questioned enough people afterward to satisfy herself that the Palace had kept its side of the bargain.

Later that morning, she met Malikel and his knights at the city gate and led them through the forest to where James was kept. By all appearances, the assassin was bound but unguarded. Only Kyra noticed the amber eyes looking down from an adjacent tree.

"This is him," she told Malikel.

James was pale and more gaunt than he'd been before, but otherwise didn't look injured. He said nothing as the Red Shields unbound him. They handled him roughly, and when a soldier struck him for moving too slowly, James held Kyra's eyes as he took the blow. Only when the soldiers were in formation around him, ready to begin the march back, did he finally speak.

"Have you told them what you are?" he asked. His voice carried clearly through the crisp fall air.

Kyra faced straight ahead, though her heart quickened and she looked out of the corner of her eye for escape routes.

"You didn't, did you? The Palace will regret this, bringing their enemy into their midst."

Malikel cast a glance toward Kyra. "What is this?"

She hoped her voice wouldn't give her away. Flick was better at this sort of thing, but he couldn't help her now. "I've told you, sir. This is what he does. He knows what to say and how to make people do what he wants. When you interrogate him, most of your work will be separating the lies from the truth."

She sensed Malikel's eyes on her as they continued walking, and she focused on keeping her face relaxed, her breathing steady. After what seemed an endless stretch, Malikel looked away.

The laugh, harsh and biting, took everyone by surprise. Kyra turned to see James with his head thrown back as if he had just heard the world's funniest tale. When he finally stopped, he looked at Kyra with something akin to respect in his eyes.

"Well done, Kyra. Well done."

EPILOGUE

The antechamber to the Council Room was one of the Palace's finest spaces, built with the intention of intimidating visiting dignitaries. The floor was fine gray stone and the walls all black, inlaid with gold leaf. As Kyra awaited her audience in the antechamber, she had to admit that the architecture was accomplishing its purpose. Surrounded by all this luxury while dressed in her own plain tunic, she found it hard not to feel small.

Two Red Shields escorted her. Though Kyra wasn't bound, she still kept a careful eye on them. Willem had grudgingly allowed her to spend the two weeks before her audience in the city, but he'd insisted that she appear for the audience itself. It was a risk, coming back to the Palace, but she didn't think the Council was so bold as to break promises it had announced to the masses, and she could only jump at shadows for so long.

The antechamber's focal point was a pair of massive oak doors leading to the Council Room, and an attendant pulled them open. "The Council is ready to see you."

She took a deep breath and stepped inside. The Red Shields trailed a step behind her. Kyra had never seen the Council Room before—there had been no need, since no records were kept there, and no important supplies. Facing the door were two semicircular rows of tables, the outer raised above the inner, where the twenty Council members sat. Councilman Willem presided in the center of the outer row. Kyra spotted Malikel in the inner row and once again wondered what the councilman thought of her, and what he made of the accusations James had leveled at her in the forest.

The Red Shields escorted her to a bench and motioned for her to sit. They stood behind her to watch the proceedings.

A herald cleared his throat. "We call Sir Tristam of Brancel to stand before the Council."

Kyra jumped at the name and scanned the room, eager to catch a glimpse of him. He stood by a bench on the opposite side of the room, and he was also flanked by two soldiers. He didn't look hurt, and he held his head high, though his lips were pressed in a grim line.

Councilman Willem cleared his throat. "Sir Tristam of Brancel," said Councilman Willem. "You are guilty of disobeying the Council's orders and attempting to rescue Kyra of Forge, causing the death of a Palace soldier in the process. Do you deny these charges?"

"No, Your Grace, I do not."

"Because of your disobedience, you will be stripped of your knighthood for one year. You will serve as a Red Shield and perform all the duties required of your new station. At the end of the year, the Council will review your behavior and make a decision as to whether to reinstate your rank."

The slightest of shudders passed through his body, but his voice was clear when he responded. "I accept the judgment of the Council."

"You are dismissed. I call Kyra of Forge to stand before the Council."

Kyra threw one last look at Tristam's back as he was led out the door.

"Kyra of Forge," said Willem. "You are guilty of high treason and murder. Do you deny these charges?"

Her crimes were common knowledge by now and denying them would have been useless. Still, it was hard to get the words out. "I do not deny these charges," she said.

"The penalty for these crimes is death. Do you understand this?"

"I understand."

The councilman paused and studied her face, as if he were trying to see if his words scared her. "Your crimes are grievous, but you've performed a great service to the city. By capturing the assassin James, you've removed a grave threat. The Demon Riders still attack the countryside, but without the Guild's encouragement, they stay away from Forge." The councilman glanced at the documents in front of him. "In light of your service, the Council hereby revokes your death sentence."

Kyra hadn't realized how tense she'd been until a wave of relief swept over her. She swayed slightly on her feet. "I accept the judgment of the Council."

"Take care you do not abuse the Council's good faith in this matter." The threat in his eyes belied his formal tone.

Kyra said nothing.

Willem put his documents aside. "You are dismissed."

She let the Red Shields escort her out through the atrium, and then to the compound gates. Nobles and staff hurried about their tasks, and no one paid her any particular heed. The soldiers left her just outside the main gate. Alone in the open air, Kyra finally felt the tightness drain out of her muscles. It was hard to believe that she was actually free. She was turning toward the southwest district when she saw a familiar form waiting by the compound wall. Tristam inclined his head in greeting. His clothing was different, she noticed. He still wore a tunic of Palace red, but it lacked the knight insignia, and her heart fell. Kyra suddenly felt uncertain as she approached him. His expression was calm. Not bitter, but he looked at her as if he didn't know what to expect. And neither did she. It was hard to know what a stolen kiss in the forest meant, after all that had happened.

"It worked," Tristam said quietly. "I almost can't believe it."

She nodded. "For now. Though it will be a long time before I see a Red Shield without getting the urge to run." She stopped. Here she was, celebrating her release, while Tristam had been punished. "I'm sorry. About your sentence."

He gave a slight shake of his head. "One year is nothing. It could have been much worse."

She suspected he was downplaying the repercussions, but there was no point in dwelling on it. It was strange, how much difference one's surroundings could make. When it had just been the two of them in the forest, it was easy to overlook their differences. But here, even in his guard's tunic, Tristam looked like he belonged at the Palace. It was written all over his bearing, his refined speech. She, on the other hand, was from a different world altogether.

"So what will you do now?" he asked.

"I'll lay low for a while. I had some coin that made it through the fire, and Flick's found a place near his quarters where I can live with Lettie and Idalee. Malikel wants my help dealing with the Assassins Guild and the Demon Riders. I'll work with him for now, at least until I learn more about what's going on. He makes me nervous sometimes, but I respect him."

"So does that mean I'll be seeing you around?"

"Most likely." For a moment, neither of them spoke. Kyra looked up at him. "Take care, then. Until next time."

She reached for his hand to give it a squeeze. Tristam squeezed back, and then, without breaking his gaze, raised her hand to his lips. "Until then."

Kyra smiled despite herself, suddenly shy, and took her leave. She could sense Tristam watching her as she walked, and the touch of his lips lingered on her hand well after she turned the corner. She wandered the city without thought, meandering past markets and houses and enjoying the sunlight. Eventually, she found herself in the fire-damaged district. The worst of the wreckage was cleared away by now, and the streets were cleaned of debris. The charred frame of The Drunken Dog, however, still remained. Kyra stood at the threshold for a moment, tempted to go in, but turned away.

She continued to the stone market building where they'd

waited out the Demon Rider attack. In front of the building, people had set up a memorial. Stones, flowers, and parchments with names of the perished were piled by the door. Kyra crouched before the stones and tried to read off the faded parchments. She saw the name of a serving girl at The Drunken Dog, as well as the baker's son. She grabbed a parchment that had faded almost completely away. There were no bits of charcoal nearby, so she contented herself with tracing Bella's name out with her finger.

"I figured you'd be here," said a familiar voice.

Kyra moved aside to make room for Flick. "I wanted to pay my respects, now that I'm free."

"She'd be glad to see you safely back."

"I wish she was still here."

For a while, they stood in silence, contemplating the memorial. Finally, Flick spoke again.

"So, the cat thing," he said. "Have you tried it since?" Flick had taken the news of Kyra's parentage surprisingly in stride. After the initial shock, he'd told Kyra that he wasn't that surprised. Too many years of watching Kyra do the impossible, he supposed.

Kyra shook her head. "It in't safe with people nearby, without the clan to teach me. But even if I did have help, I don't know if I'd want to."

"Why?"

Kyra twisted her tunic in her hands, struggling to put her thoughts into words. "When I worked for the Guild, I was shocked by their violence. I worried they would change me, but I pushed my worries aside because it was easier. And because of that, I'll always have innocent blood on my hands. You weren't there at the man's funeral, Flick. His wife, his children, their lives changed forever because I ignored my doubts."

She drew a shaky breath and continued. "After he—after I killed him, I knew I had to leave the Guild. And when I told James, he told me not to bother. He said I wasn't a talesinger's heroine, that I was a former gutter rat who stole for living. I thought I'd prove him wrong by working with the Palace, but everything kept getting worse. He'd sent me to kill Malikel, but soon, I was the one volunteering to poison *him*. After that, the Makvani found me. The way they killed people in cold blood—it confirmed everything that James had ever thought of me. The feelings that I had when I was a cat, the bloodlust—it wasn't pretty."

"But you didn't give in, did you?" asked Flick. "You captured James—alive. You saved Tristam's life. And you've stopped the demon cat invasions of the city. Aye, your bloodline got you in trouble, but it was also what got you out of this mess in the end. And now that you have one foot in with the Palace, and knowing what you do about the Guild and the Demon Riders, I think you could do a lot of good, if you wanted to."

Kyra grimaced and smoothed out the wrinkles as best she could. She *wanted* to believe him.

"Do you think Bella would have loved you any less if she knew what you were?" asked Flick.

"I suppose not. Bella loved everyone," said Kyra.

"And Idalee and Lettie, if they knew?"

"No, they would trust me even if it wasn't good for them."

"And does Tristam trust you less, knowing your secret?"

"Well, I did risk my life to save him."

"Exactly. And what about me? Do I show any signs of running for the hills?"

Kyra smiled. "I guess I'm blessed with foolish—and forgiving—friends."

"Mayhap we're wiser than you give us credit for."

Flick rooted around in his belt pack. "Here," he said, taking out a scrap of parchment and a piece of charcoal. "Use these."

Kyra accepted them with gratitude. Taking a deep breath, she wrote Bella's name in clear, large letters. She knelt down to place it beside the others, but drew her hand back and looked at Flick. "She said she was proud of me, you know. As she lay—" She couldn't bring herself to say *dying*. "Why would she say that, after I had just ruined everything?"

"She loved you, Kyra."

Kyra lowered her eyes. She supposed that was all she needed to know. "Would you like to place it with me?" she asked.

Flick knelt and took a corner of the parchment. Together, they tucked it between two stones. They stood without speaking for a long time, lost in their own thoughts, before finally turning for home.

ACKNOWLEDGMENTS

Every debut novel has a story behind it, and *Midnight Thief* is no exception. I have many, many people to thank.

Thank you to my parents, Andy and Judy King, for instilling in me a love of stories and language.

Kyra is actually a character from a story I started in high school, and there were three English teachers in particular who had a large influence on my creative writing endeavors: Kate Davis, John Gray, and Stuart Lipkowitz.

Thank you to my husband, Jeff Blackburne, for putting up with endless chatter about demon cats and for hugs through writerly mood swings.

The story would probably never have been completed without my dear friends at Courtyard Critiques, who patiently pointed out all the good and bad as I churned out those awkward early drafts: Amitha Knight, Coral Frazer, Peta Andersen, and Rachal Aronson, who were there from the beginning; and Lara Ehrlich, Jennifer Barnes, and Emily Terry, who offered astute comments on later pages.

A slew of generous beta readers helped me with the completed manuscript: Harold Hsiung, Karen Zee, Karen Ng, Kenli Okada, Bart Cleveland, Stephanie Del Tufo, Todd Thompson, Lisa Choi, Lianne Crawford, April Choi, Joseph Selby, Irene Kim, Amy Shi, Haley Alexander, Rebecca Stoll, Cami Lau, Eric Jacobson, Rachel Winter, Greg Newby, Emily Lo, and Anisha Keshavan.

Love to the ladies of the Fourteenery for laughs and hugs during the rollercoaster debut process.

A huge thank-you to my agent, Jim McCarthy, for believing in Kyra and for his constant support as *Midnight Thief* made its journey into the world.

And of course, thank you to my editors, Abby Ranger and Rotem Moscovich, who took my sapling manuscript and coaxed it into a full-fledged tree. Thank you as well to Laura Schreiber, Julie Moody, and the rest of the Hyperion team. It really is a dream come true.